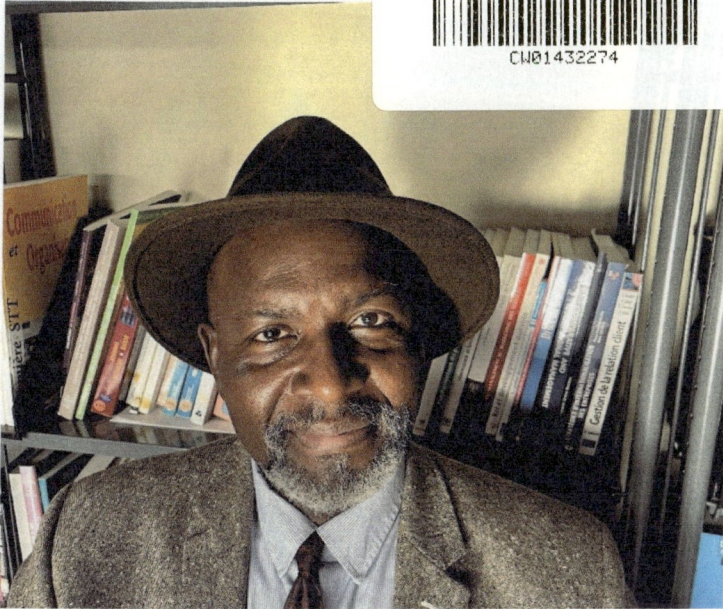

About the Author

Joseph Egwurube is a Nigerian who resides in France. He was born in 1957. He currently teaches in the Faculty of Law, political science and management at the University of La Rochelle but enjoys creative writing, especially poems, which he shares with his university colleagues. Educated in Zaria in Nigeria and Bordeaux in France where he obtained a doctorate degree in political science, he spent several years teaching as a senior lecturer at Ahmadu Bello University, Zaria, in Nigeria before moving to settle in France.

A few of his poems have been published in *Teaching Times*, the France TESOL magazine. He is the author of *Nobody Knows Tomorrow*, a novel published by Olympia Publishers in 2022.

Where Is My Daughter?

Joseph Egwurube

Where Is My Daughter?

Olympia Publishers
London

www.olympiapublishers.com
OLYMPIA PAPERBACK EDITION

A CIP catalogue record for this title is
available from the British Library.

ISBN: 978-1-80439-070-2

This is a work of fiction.
Names, characters, places and incidents originate from the writer's
imagination. Any resemblance to actual persons, living or dead, is
purely coincidental.

First Published in 2023

Olympia Publishers
Tallis House
2 Tallis Street
London
EC4Y 0AB

Printed in Great Britain

Dedication

I dedicate this book to my life companion, Joëlle 'Miss Goodwine' Bonnevin.

Acknowledgements

My sincere thanks to my life companion, Joëlle Bonnevin, who patiently read the original manuscript of this work, made many necessary corrections and offered a huge number of suggestions to improve its intrinsic quality.

Though this work is creative and imaginary, I have consulted some secondary material to better understand some of the questions addressed in the novel, such as sexual assault on women, and the way palm oil refineries function. In addition, the book by Professor Mwamba CABAKULU, *Dictionnaire des Proverbes Africains*, Paris, l'Harmattan-Aciva, 1992, and that by Liliane PREVOST and Barnabe LAYE, *Guide de la sagesse africaine, Proverbes et citations*, Paris et Montreal, L'Harmattan, 1999, provided me with a treasure of African proverbs which many of the characters in the story have used now and then to make their points.

Painting *"The African Lady"* by Bayo Ogundele, Ife, Nigeria, 1989.

1

The gods were visibly no longer quarrelling angrily. The thunderous rainstorm that had hit the village of Agila furiously and continuously over the past ten days, destroying the thatched roofs of many huts and turning the quiet Igbilede stream into a fast-flowing river that uprooted many of the trees along its banks, had, by magic, fallen silent. Today, the sky was cloudless and blue. Several hawks with their wings widely spread could be seen floating lazily in the warm air, above the market square.

It was the long-awaited monthly market day. Many traders had come from surrounding villages, some from as far as Igumale, thirty kilometres away, to sell their wares. Hawkers with large trays filled to the brim with an assortment of objects on their heads, were rushing from one section of the market to another, some armed with whistles which they blew now and then to draw attention to their presence. They then went on to announce very loudly what they were selling. These ranged from things edible such as roast and boiled corns and groundnuts, peeled oranges, bunches of yellow bananas and freshly decorticated coconuts to other necessities such as torchlights, matchboxes and pen knives made by the village blacksmith.

The market was full of colour, loud noise and excitement. Greetings were exchanged between people who had not seen each other for quite some time and news traded about their respective families. Men and women, buyers and sellers could be seen and heard haggling here and there, trying to find the mutually agreed right price for different sorts of wares. Blue smoke rose into the air from some parts of the market, where some women, many with their babies tied securely to their backs, were frying *akara* which they wrapped in old newspapers to clients, many of whom demanded that some *gyara*, or extra *akara* balls be added. The women responded with warm smiles and sometimes open laughter, before going on to diplomatically announce that times were difficult, that the price of one *mudu* of beans had more than tripled since the beginning of the year and telling the buyers, "Make you no vex, I beg."

In one of the sheds at the centre of the market, there was a particularly animated conversation between the seller of textile materials, and one woman dressed in navy blue *kampala* who was visibly interested in making a large purchase. She wanted to buy several yards of colourful Ankara prints in preparation for a marriage ceremony which her family was organising not long afterwards.

"Do you have Nigerian Ankara," the woman asked.

"Nigerian Ankara? Are you serious?" the seller responded with awe and disbelief.

"Which type of question are you asking? Are you telling me you do not understand the language I am using? Do you have local fabric, something made here in Naija country?"

"Aha, now I know you are joking. Something made in naija country, abi? Well, naija country has stopped making Ankara even before the Biafran war started. The Ankara I sell comes directly from Ghana, Côte d'Ivoire, and China. Original quality, I swear. Very colourful designs. And they wash very well because the colours do not fade but remain as bright as they are today after many washes," the seller added.

The woman asked a few other questions before the seller

proceeded to use a long cane to measure the quantity of the textile material required by her.

Close to the textile seller was an open 'boutique' of used clothes, which did not have any prospective buyer. The owner, a young Ibo man, wearing dark glasses and a red bowler hat, was loudly trying to attract customers.

"Come and buy original *okrika* for almost free of charge from my fine boutique, I beg. Original *okrika* directly from London, Paris, and Rome, I swear. These cost many thousands of naira in Lagos but here, the price is low and of course negotiable. Just wash them with starch and they will look brand new. First come first served. An opportunity once lost shall never return, I tell you. Original *okrika* from Oyiboland for almost nothing. No need waiting until tomorrow because I will be gone by then when you will be weeping and gnashing your teeth."

Suddenly, the sound of some women singing could be heard approaching the market. The sound got louder and what the women were singing could now be heard by everyone in the market, who all listened attentively. The women were singing:

The Chief has brought us the light
As the Oga patapata
And strongman in government
His village and people he has never abandoned
He is our eyes and ears in Abuja
When he speaks there, everybody listens
And stands at attention
He never raises his voice
Before government does what he wishes
Long live the honourable Chief
Honourable Speaker of a very honourable federal parliament

We must say yes once more to him
So that his good work in Abuja he can continue
For all Agila sons and daughters to be proud
That their honourable father, uncle, and benefactor
Can bring wealth and more wealth to our community.
And give us our share of the national cake
In the name of the Lord Jesus
Who has blessed him without question.

The group of singing women could now be seen. They were preceded by another group of young maidens, all dressed similarly. All of them had colourful Akwete clothes that covered their bodies from their breasts to their knees. Around their waists were three layers of enormous orange bead belts. Each wore coral bead hair ornaments and large bead necklaces, bead bracelets and bead anklets in black and white colours. They were dancing in unison, moving their waists from one direction to the other, and stamping their feet in perfect accord, the sound of the beads on their waists and ankles providing an additional note to the songs sung by the women. The singing women were all wearing very expensive white lace dresses and were slowly following, from a respectable distance, Chief Agbo Aje, the very worthy son-of-the soil, who was campaigning to be re-elected to the Federal Senate, where he had spent the last four years as Senate President.

The Chief, preceded by two uniformed police sergeants, was walking side by side with two people, one of the titled village elders who served as his lieutenant, his eyes, and ears in the village, and his one and only son. He was walking very slowly and proudly in front of the singing women. He held a lion-headed sculptured cane in his left hand and a small fan made of colourful bird feathers in his right hand. He was dressed in sky-blue

Agbada and wore an expensive looking hand-woven Borno *fula* in colourful embroidery. As he entered the market, he dipped his hands into the pockets of his *Agbada* and brought out wads of fresh one-hundred-naira banknotes which he threw into the air. There was stampede and pandemonium as many people in the market rushed to grab as many of these as possible, while heaping praises on the one and only Chief, the one and only benefactor of the village, worthy ambassador of the village, and every Idoma man and woman in the capital city of Nigeria and well beyond. This was the message given by the village elder who accompanied him to the market. Did the Agila village, district, and its neighbouring communities not need an experienced man, someone who was on first-name terms with the Nigerian President, to continue representing them in Abuja, the man asked the large crowd of people who now formed a circle around the Chief and his women singers. The response from the crowd was a resounding, "Yes, to a heavy man of timber and calibre." Did the very serious-minded villagers not require someone equally serious, generous, down-to-earth and who resembled them, to be their eyes, mouth, and ears in Abuja, where receiving government attention was not easy and where success depended on who one knew and could influence? he continued. "A big and clear 'yes' to an original juggernaut and heavy weight," the crowd cheered. Did Abuja and all the important federal Ministries have any secrets that the honourable Chief and President of the Senate did not know? Did the honourable Chief, who was the owner of the only palm oil refinery in Idoma land, not provide a constant source of livelihood to the village and its inhabitants by buying the abundant palm fruit produced by the village each year? Did the very intelligent villagers really wish to give the responsibility of representing the village and district

17

to his opponent, Dr Ada Ocheme, whose only credential was the fact that he was a professor of political science at the University of Zaria and that this made him very knowledgeable in how to exercise power and influence its exercise? he pursued. "No, no, no and no, no way to a johnny-just-come. Once a President, always a President," the crowd now roared. Did Dr Ada Ocheme think that governing was child's play, that governing was easy, that governing meant speaking Queen's English? Tuffia! he concluded. This time the crowd joined the women who had begun to sing a new song:

> *It is not long grammar that brings wealth*
> *It is not long grammar that brings kindness*
> *It is not long grammar that brings generosity*
> *Our Chief needs no introduction*
> *Our Chief needs no opposition*
> *Our Chief, Oga patapata*
> *Who understands his people very well*
> *Can sleep without any worry at all*
> *For his landslide victory*
> *Is already a foregone conclusion*
> *As we, his people*
> *Shall speak with one united voice*
> *For him to remain our voice*
> *Our eyes*
> *Our ears*
> *And our body and soul*
> *In Abuja, the heart of government*

Before leaving the village, it was customary for Chief Agbo Aje's delegation to pay a courtesy call on the Village and District Head in his compound. This time, the delegation decided to go in a convoy of many four-wheel drive vehicles. As they were walking towards their vehicles, they passed in front of the palm wine joint, where there was usually on market days such as this, a crowd of people gathered inside and outside talking noisily while gulping down cups of sweet palm wine. The joint was owned by the renowned village palm wine tapper, Obande Ofu, whose fame as an experienced palm wine tapper was district-wide.

Obande's wine was never bottled. It was always stored in large kegs, was unique in its fresh sugary taste and people enjoyed the floating sensation they always had after two or three cups of it. It was to Obande that elders went to reserve kegs so as to offer something to drink to visitors. It was to Obande that those who organised the annual new yam *ujo* festival went to place an order for the many kegs of unadulterated palm wine that would make the dancing, singing, and wrestling matches that accompanied this festival more joyful. The palm wine joint was curiously empty this morning. This was quite strange because never had the joint been closed on a market day.

Chief Aje only fleetingly observed the joint before walking on towards the vehicles parked close to the market. The first vehicle in the convoy was a Police Land Rover, with three policemen, the two who had accompanied him to the market and the driver. This was followed by a bright Toyota Land Cruiser with a Nigerian flag mounted on its bonnet. The Chief sat alone in the rear seat. Following the Land Cruiser were three other Land Cruisers that carried members of the Chief's family and the titled village elder that was his spokesman in the village. One of these Land Cruisers was full of presents the Chief was going to offer the District Head. There were several crates of soft drinks, five cartons of different brands of beer including Gulder, Star and

More, three large bottles of Beefeater Gin, three large bottles of Scotch whisky and five bottles of South African red wine. There were also five bags of imported rice, two dozen yam tubers and three large bags filled with potatoes. Then of course there were several cans of Nakowa Oil, the brand of palm oil produced by the Chief. He had called his brand Nakowa because this meant "everybody" in the Hausa language which was one of the dominant languages in the country.

"Greetings to Ogaba-Idu from a son returning home," the Chief announced.

"Peace be to you, and welcome to my abode, Mister President" the District Head replied in a very low voice.

"May your reign be long," the Chief continued.

"We do not determine the length of our stay in this abode. We know we are only temporary representatives of our ancestors here on earth," the District Head replied.

"This does not stop us from wishing you long life, so that all the good things you have done for us, the peace you have maintained, the prosperity you have invited, the big bountiful harvests you have accompanied will continue for a long time, Ogaba-Idu," Chief Aje added.

"I am not the only one who has done good things for the village and district. Very able sons of the village like you have performed wonders too," the District Head said.

"Do our people not say that it is the stomach that precedes the back and not the contrary? Do our people not rightly say that a piece of meat is only strong if it contains a bone? Do our people not wisely say that all the teeth surround and protect the tongue? What would the village have become without you, Ogaba-Idu, whose wisdom has led to all the village can boast of today. We praise the hunter who has been able to kill an antelope and not the arrow the hunter uses. So, the praise must be to you, Ogaba-Idu," the Chief maintained.

"Talking about the village, when do you think government will tar the road between our village and the district headquarters?" the Village Head enquired.

"The project is under consideration. You know that this is the responsibility of the Benue State government rather than the federal government. The State Governor is not from my political party, so it has not been easy convincing him. But like I said, things are under control," Chief Aje explained.

"It is the very bad state of the road that frightens our sons and daughters who live far away from the village from coming to visit us regularly, as you know," the District Head opined.

"Yes, Ogaba-Idu, I am very much aware of this. Not everyone has a four-wheel drive. Even with a four-wheel drive, the journey remains very tiring. The state of the road in our State is very deplorable. As a matter of fact, I usually use a police helicopter when I come to the State from Abuja. It is much easier and less tiring," the Chief stated.

"Welcome to my abode, Mister President. I am sure you know you do not need to worry for the election. My people know who is who. You do not cut down the tree that saved you when you were being chased by a buffalo. When you eat, you should say thank you to the person who has provided you with the food to eat," the District Head affirmed.

"I have humbly brought you a few things to eat and drink. Please do not be angry that I have not brought you as much as is expected. The hen cannot pick up and swallow something that is larger than its beak. If you do not have the means to build a house, start by building a hut," Chief Aje said.

"You have brought more than enough. The hands go farther

than the legs. Your reputation as someone who is extremely generous has been known for long. Unfortunately, you have to forgive my apparent inhospitality because I do not have what I should normally have to spread on the ground for our ancestors before offering you a cup or two. I have heard no news from Obande Ofu for quite some time, which is very strange. Do you have any news? I know you have been trying to buy his forests of palm trees?"

"No Oga-Idu, I have no news. It is my son who is in charge of our refinery in the district and who has been engaged in discussions with Obande. I am told Obande does not want to sell because the forest is sacred," Chief Aje responded.

"That is quite true. But only part of the forest is. I am sure if you speak to him gently and make him see reason, you should be able to acquire what you hope to," the District Head opined.

"I trust my son will be able to do that," Chief Aje added.

"Mister President, in the absence of good palm wine to offer to our ancestors, I am going to break this red kola nut into three pieces. I am going to break one of the three pieces into smaller pieces and spread them humbly and carefully on the ground to appease our ancestors and implore them to give us all the wisdom we need to lead our lives while thinking of others, to be generous and not to have ill feelings. As it is not necessary to point your fingers while describing an elephant in the midst of other animals, so is it clear that generosity and goodwill will breed more generosity and goodwill. I will give you the second piece to chew and I will myself chew the third while calling on the gods of the village to ensure that your journey back to Abuja be safe. The gods of the village will guide you, Chief."

"Oga-Idu, may your reign be long," Chief Aje ended.

The convoy was driving back to the district headquarters. The Chief asked his son and the village elder to join him in his Land Cruiser. He wanted them to appraise what had happened in the village and to make sure all was in place for his victory.

"Owobi, did you notice that Obande's joint was very quiet today? I know you have been trying to reason with him for some time now," he addressed his son.

"Yes, Papa, I have been trying to convince him to sell his palm forest to us. I have promised him I will pay him extremely well, but he insists that it is out of the question to sell something that has been in his family for many generations. Many of his forebears were buried there and he doesn't want strangers going in to desecrate their bodies and spirits," Owobi explained.

"It is unheard of in the village for such a thing to happen. We are a continuation of our forebears and Obande goes to his forest regularly to make sacrifices and converse with those whose bodies and spirits inhabit there," the village elder added.

"Yes, but this means we are allowing more than thirty hectares of good palm trees to be wasted. I need those palm trees. I have promised my Italian associates who depend on the palm oil we supply them in order to increase the production of the renowned Mouzzilla cream. They would like to challenge the market leader, Nutella, and I have told them that they can count on me and on my village and district for an uninterrupted supply. If I do not keep my promise and provide them with this supply, they may turn their attention exclusively to one of my competitors in Ghana, who is in a position to also provide them with the cocoa they need to make the cream. No, I am someone who always keeps his promise. It is imperative that I obtain that forest. It is a must that will happen. Owobi, did you tell Obande that I might convince the State government to take over the land

23

and declare it government property?" the Chief enquired.

"This is what I told him the last time I spoke to him, which is not long ago. He told me we will accede to his forest and property only over his dead body. I do not know how someone can be as stupid as he is," Owobi said.

"A lion does not give birth to a sheep. Is Obande not the father of that boy who fled the village because he was a shame to his parents? What's his name again? I do not remember," the Chief continued.

"Clement Adole Ogebe. He is now in Lagos we are told," the village elder said.

"Yes, Clement Adole Ogebe. He always preferred playing with girls rather than run and play football with his age mates when he was young and a teenager. Never carried a hoe or a cutlass to follow his father to the farm, but preferred staying at home to help his mother do the cooking, and to plait the hair of his sisters and their friends. He had a very high-pitched voice, come to think of it. So how do you want a man, even if he taps palm wine very well, who is not able to bring up his son in his own image, to be able to see reason?" the Chief asked angrily. "Well, I will have to phone Government House in Makurdi and have the problem solved," he concluded.

Suddenly, the vehicle began to slide on the road after which it bumped violently and almost crashed into a huge tree along the muddy untarred road.

"You will have to drive more carefully," the Chief warned the driver.

"Oga, biko, make you no vex. Na dis road be the wahala. See as potholes full the road. Which kind road be dis, for God's sake?" the driver responded.

"This is why only people with four-wheel or front-wheel

24

vehicles dare travel to the village during the rainy season. The thunderstorm that affected the village recently has only made the road worse," the village elder explained.

"Just try to drive more carefully, will you?" the Chief added. "So, as I was saying, I will contact Government House before I leave for Abuja. Talking about Government House, how are the arrangements for the elections going, Chief? The last time, we had a problem with a Youth Corper who was put in charge of the polling booth in the district by the State Electoral Commission, and who wanted to check and control the identity of every voter in order to ensure that no one person voted more than once," the Chief demanded.

"Yes, he was the one who was always quoting what he said he had learnt from his political science teacher, Dr Ocheme, in Zaria. He was always talking about Nigeria as a corrupt neo-colonial entity in the hands of agents of international capital who were hell-bent on oppressing the Nigerian lumpen proletariat, and that it was the objective of his generation to put an end to such exploitation. He believed that Nigeria needs a political, economic, social and cultural revolution to eliminate those he qualifies as parasites, the rich, who think it is their birth right to rule and accumulate ill-gotten wealth and he thought the best way to start such a revolution was to ensure free and fair elections. Yes, he was a very hot head, but we were able to calm him down at the end, fortunately," added Owobi, the Chief's son.

"I do not really know what students are taught at the university," the village elder mused. "All the Youth Corper was saying was long grammar, *dogon turanchi*, for me. What nonsense and rubbish."

"Anyway," continued Owobi, "if another Youth Corper with similar ideas takes over this time around, there is no cause for alarm. All is already in place to ensure our success and it is not a Youth Corper, someone who does not know our culture and values, who will dictate to us what we think and who we choose. The stranger does not know who dances best in a village."

"I trust you can handle things here at home, Owobi," Chief Aje replied.

"As far as the village is concerned, there is no cause for alarm either," the village elder added.

"Thank you, Chief," Chief Aje replied. "I trust you have been able to handle things very well in the village and district. Ogaba-Idu is also someone very reliable that we can count on. I do not regret having backed him during the contest for the chieftaincy title. Like my Italian associates will say, it was a very good investment with a low risk and very high return."

"Yes, I think we can sleep with our eyes closed. The other candidate for the chieftaincy title, Ebenezer Akpoge, would have been a *wayo-man*, a trickster. He would have said 'yes' to you, taken all your money, then stabbed you in the back by saying 'yes' to Dr Ocheme or some other opponent. Ebenezer Akpoge thinks he's wiser than everyone else on the Village Council of Elders because he obtained a bachelor's degree in one of the science disciplines from Zaria. He usually monopolises the floor during our council meetings, talking long grammar that only a few of us listen to or even understand," the titled elder remarked.

"Ah yes, Chief Ebenezer. I have not seen him for quite some time. He is the one who wanted to open a construction company in the State capital and wanted me to lend him part of his initial working capital. I remember telling him that my name is not 'Money miss road' and that I do not pluck money from the trees. He was visibly surprised that I refused to give him the money he was requesting. Yes, he would have been a real *wayo-man*, not at

26

all trustworthy," Chief Aje declared.

"Many of us think that Chief Ebenezer is among those advising Obande not to sell his forest of palm trees to you. How can someone be so full of hate and venom?" the village elder asked.

"I am already aware of that, Chief. There is hardly anything that happens in the village that I do not know. But do not worry. I will get in contact with Government House in Makurdi and iron things out," Chief Aje mentioned.

Chief Aje had a very big compound at the Government Residential Area (GRA) in the district headquarters. The GRA was the area which was reserved for senior colonial officials during the colonial period. It was secluded from the rest of the town, was less noisy, less dirty and all the streets were lined with rows and rows of mahogany trees. Some of the houses were government-built, while others were built by wealthy individuals who wanted to live in peace, far away from the hustle and bustle of city life with hundreds of taxi cabs and *okadas* blowing their horns in order to attract passengers.

Chief Aje's compound was in a very quiet and additionally secluded quarter in the GRA. The street that led to his compound was lined on either side with large colourful billboards. Each billboard had an enlarged picture of the Chief either at the top or in the middle followed by different types of encouraging and laudatory messages. On one of them could be read "The sons and daughters of Igede wish the Honourable Chief Aje, CFR, Honourable President of the Senate, a Long and Prosperous Life. Go on with your wonderful services to our Nation, State and Community. You can count on us, as usual." Another billboard read "The Ijigbam Community Supports Our Illustrious Son For

27

All He Has Done For Us. We Will Always Stand By Him, in God's Name. Amen." All the billboards seemed to be engaged in a competition about who and which would be more laudatory. Several of them were erected by local industrialists and construction companies who wanted to remain in the good books of government from which most of their contracts came.

Chief Aje was not unaware of the ulterior motives of those behind these billboards, but he was all the same proud to see his face and name lined up to the entrance to his compound. The compound was as big as twenty football fields. It was surrounded by a very high wall on top of which pieces of sharp broken glass and barbed wire were fixed in order to prevent thieves and intruders from scaling the wall and penetrating the compound. There was a very large entrance gate which was closed. Chief Aje's driver horned thrice in rapid succession. The gate was opened by a uniformed gateman who bowed down as Chief Aje's convoy went past him.

The drive to the main house was about two hundred metres long and it was lined with large coconut trees. On each side of the drive was a vast lawn within which several flower beds could be seen. There was a majority of bougainvillea with an assortment of red, purple, and pink flowers as well as some hibiscus. It was customary sometime for Chief Aje to ask one of his three houseboys to cut some hibiscus flowers and prepare some hot reddish tea with them. At the end of the drive was a big roundabout which was tarred. It was here that Chief Aje's helicopter usually landed and took off. Three lanes protruded from this central roundabout. One led straightforward to the main two-storey six-bedroom mansion where the Chief and his wife resided. The Chief and his wife spent their time between their two residences, one in the district headquarters, the other in

Abuja, the federal capital. The second lane from the roundabout went left and led to a four-bedroom bungalow that served as the guest house. The lane leading to this bungalow was lined with hedges and a few paw-paw trees. The third lane from the roundabout went right and continued a good distance towards the tall wall protecting the compound behind the main mansion. It led to three three-bedroom houses where all the house-help and their respective families resided. Close to these houses was a big shed where there was a large blue Kohler SDMO power generator that was on. Apparently, NEPA, the National Electric Power Authority, which many Nigerians nicknamed "Never Expect Power Always" had once again cut power as it was prone to do every day.

The Chief's convoy drove on the lane leading to the main house. One of the houseboys rushed out of the house to open the right-hand back door seat of the Land Cruiser so that the Chief could come out of the car without undue effort, while a second houseboy held the door to the house wide open for the Chief and his guests to enter it.

"Oga, welcome," he said, as the Chief went past him.

"Ah, Edet, how is your body?" he asked.

"Oga, we dey do fine. How was your journey to the village? No palava, I hope," Edet replied.

"No, no palava at all, except the road. Three hours to drive seventy kilometres, can you imagine?" the Chief continued.

"Oga, na so be so. Welcome," Edet added.

Chief Aje went in first. He was followed by members of his family and the village elder. The living room was vast and luxuriously furnished. It was divided into two parts. The first was the sitting room with three large sofas, including one in very expensive-looking white leather that was convertible. There was a large wide coffee table made of oak in the middle and several other smaller coffee tables placed on the sides of each sofa. Two very big television sets were placed close to the wall facing the sofas. One gave programs diffused by the Nigerian network, while the second offered a wider choice of foreign networks, British, American, Aljazeera and others. All the walls, apart from that in front of the sofas where the TV sets were placed, had life-size pictures of the Chief hung on them. In most of these pictures, he was not alone but was with local, national and foreign dignitaries. In one of them, for example, he could be seen laughing his head off with a former military Head of State. In another, he was seen chatting with a member of the British royal family. In yet another, he was seen being awarded a medal by the Chinese Nigerian ambassador. There were also pictures of him with a few African Heads of State.

The second part of the living room, equally vast, was the dining area. There was a large mahogany table in the middle with eight Italian design chairs in exotic wood and faux leather, a chair at each extremity and three chairs at each side. Close to the dining table were two polished and shining imported antic French double body cupboards in walnut wood in Louis XIII style from the seventeenth century. The Chief was very proud of this. This was where many sets of cutleries, some in silver, were stored. There were four ceiling fans in the living room, and all were rotating silently. The two air conditioners in the room had been switched on. Chief Aje told the village elder to make himself at home.

"Elder Ella, what can I offer you? I do not have any palm wine, but I can offer some beer, whisky, or red wine. What do you prefer?" Chief Aje enquired.

"Some wine would be fine. Beer will make me want to

urinate regularly and this might disturb other passengers on my way back to the village. And whisky will make my head to turn."

"Edet, can you please bring one of the chilled South African Vintage wines from the fridge in the kitchen. Put the bottle on a tray with wine glasses," Chief Aje ordered.

While waiting for Edet to bring in the drinks, Chief Aje gave a brown envelope to the village elder.

"Elder Ella, please take this small token. It will pay for your journey back to the village and will also allow you and your family to buy salt and *okporoko* in order to put into your *ogbono* soup and some sugar to put into your tea. My driver will take you to the motor park when you have finished drinking your red wine. Thank you very much for your support in the village. After the elections we will be able to celebrate in a more serious manner," Chief Aje announced.

"Thank you, honourable Chief. What you say is what we will do," the elder replied, while accepting the envelope meekly.

After he left, Chief Aje wanted to have the opinion of Owobi, his son.

"So Owobi, it seems all is in place for me to continue in Abuja, don't you think so?"

"Yes, Papa. Although a few members of the Council of Elders think and speak well of Dr Ocheme, I know your success is already in the bag. The majority are on our side," Owobi replied.

"What is strange is that Obande is resisting. I am told that he is somehow being supported by the entire village who do not want us to pollute the Igbilede river that runs through his forest of palm trees with what will be rejected from our refinery. The river is their only source of drinking water for the moment. I have told Ogaba-Idu that boreholes will be dug soon in the village to

31

provide more potable water for the villagers, but that does not seem to have convinced him and other members of the Council of Chiefs much," Chief Aje added.

"How do you know that, Papa? All the time I have spoken to Obande, he has never made reference to water pollution as the reason behind his resistance," Owobi wondered.

"There are many things I know that you do not, my son. There are so many things Chief Ella Ohe, who has just left, does not know I know that I know. I have never put all my eggs in one basket, you know. The man who wears shoes walks on a thorny path without worry," Chief Aje said.

"Do you think the village elder is reliable? He shows you deference not because he agrees with you and what you do, but because you are in a position of power, don't you think?" Owobi asked.

"The question is not whether he agrees or not with what I do, or whether he likes or dislikes who I am. I do not pay him for him to agree with me. I pay him so that I can have one version of what transpires in the village and what questions are discussed during the meeting of the Council of Elders. And something else I wanted to raise with you. I'm told you are having an affair with Obande's first daughter, the one that is teaching in the All-Girls Unity College in Sokoto? Is this what is preventing you from being more aggressive in your discussions with her father?" the Chief questioned.

"Obande's daughter and I were in the same class at the primary school in the village, were in the same co-educational secondary school here in the district headquarters and were in the same university in Zaria. She specialised in Biology, while I did Business Administration and we have always been on very good terms with one another. She visits me each time she comes home to see her parents, which I think is normal. Who told you we are having an affair, Papa?" Owobi demanded.

"There are things I like to know which I know. In the position I am today, I have to know things, period. The man who lives close to the river must know how to swim," his father replied calmly.

"I cannot declare a daughter with whom I have lots of common values an enemy because her father refuses, for the moment, to listen to you and me," Owobi argued.

"It is not such an attitude that will make you become the man I would like you to become. It is not what made me what I am today. It is not what has enabled me to rise up to where I am today, to have built the houses I have built, to have established the refinery I have entrusted to your care. The constituency I am building will be yours in future. In order to hold this constituency, you should ban being soft-hearted, being too romantic. Foes you will surely have. Friends you will certainly not have. To succeed in life, you must throw your romantic sentiments to the winds, for good," Chief Aje lectured.

"I know, Papa that you have plans for my future. But that does not mean I should think that everyone outside our family is an enemy. He who eats alone strangles alone," Owobi responded.

"You cannot know if the water is cold unless you have touched it. Wisdom usually comes from first-hand experience, you know," Chief Aje added.

"I agree with you, Papa. But please let me have my own proper experience. If one mistakenly takes the wrong path to go to the river, this teaches you afterwards to know the right path to take," Owobi maintained.

Chief Aje now had other things on his mind. It had been a very trying and tiring day and he needed to be able to relax. He decided that he needed to go to the nine-hole golf field he had had constructed about fifteen kilometres away from the district headquarters. It always gave him peace when he was in the region to spend one or two evenings there. The golf course was located in a hilly area, and it occupied a vast area of ten square kilometres. It had a tall green iron fence on which several signboards reading "No Trespassing" were fixed here and there.

Chief Aje needed to go there to calm his nerves. He hoped his son, Owobi, would be up to the task he had given him, but he was now not so sure. One had to do things oneself to obtain the desired results, he mused. One had to be in control, one never had to depend on others, especially when the stakes were high, he reasoned. But then, if one could not trust one's offspring, one's blood, one's inheritors, to contribute to protecting one's heritage, who else could one give this responsibility to? Were there not thousands and thousands of parasites out there, some addressing you very meekly, but waiting for the slightest opportunity to take away all you had spent years and years generating, constructing, making, producing, adding, and multiplying? Could these parasites, many of whom bow down when they meet you, be trusted not to wish to take a large part of the cake you have given them for safe keeping? Was it not because he felt that he was better off when he controlled things and when established rules could hardly be flouted that he had chosen to join the army before he found himself one day in the political arena?

Chief Aje had had no friends when he was young. His mother had died when she was giving birth to him, and he felt his father had never forgiven him for this initial unpardonable sin. His father

34

had been invited into the hut by the village medicine man who had been called when Aje's mother was in labour. He had announced in a very low voice that life and death had unfortunately met by accident in his home and that the joy of welcoming had to be tempered by the sadness of saying goodbye. Aje's father spent most of his time saying goodbye to his first wife. He remained a bachelor for several years afterwards, unable to overcome his grief. He decided to spend most of his time in his farm and asked one of his sisters if she could bring his son up. Aje was thus brought up by an aunt, who lived not too far away from his father. His cousins treated him as if he were poison. They would stop playing when he tried to join them. When they ate together, they would deprive Aje of meat, would indicate to him what quantity of food to eat, would tell him he had had enough spoonfuls of rice. Each time something disappeared in the house, they all complained to their parents that Aje was responsible. Aje could not do anything to change this. Sometimes, he tried to join his father in his farm. He would take one of the many hoes his father took with him to the farm and would prepare rows and rows of large mounds of earth in which yam tubers would be buried for them to grow. His father would glance at him without saying a single word.

Aje began to stammer. He would tremble when he was to speak because he knew he would be unable to. He therefore decided to speak less but do more. He became entrusted with responsibilities. At St Patrick's Primary School, although he was younger than others, he was put in charge of beating the drum that accompanied the morning assembly, when all the pupils had to march in a single line to their respective classrooms. When he went to secondary school, he was named class prefect right from the beginning. It was at secondary school that he was attracted to the military profession. There was an Army Club that had been formed in the school, with a strict stern-faced Sergeant-Major as the 'Commanding Officer'. The Army Club went on drills every Saturday, come rain come sunshine. It went camping twice every school term. Aje liked the strict discipline instilled, the order imposed, and the fact that focus was on the group rather than on individuals.

Aje applied to the Military School in Zaria where he was admitted. He successfully completed his training there and was able to reach the rank of Captain a few years afterwards. He decided to go to the Armed Forces Command and Staff College in Jaji to attend a course reserved for Captains which he completed successfully. He had finally found his community, where order, discipline and obedience were the watch words. He was promoted Major soon after. In 1983, a military coup ousted the civilian regime that was brazenly corrupt, inefficient and a national disaster. He had become a Lieutenant Colonel. He was named the Military Governor of one of the States in the north. It was his duty to bring order and discipline to the State and he was hell-bent on doing this. However, Government House, where he resided, continued to be the beehive it had always been, attracting unsolicited visitors every evening, big businessmen who preferred to come and see him at home rather than in his office. All of these came to sing him songs of praise, to wish him success in his governorship and informed him they were happy a northerner had been chosen this time as their governor. They would inform him of their preparedness to help him in his reconstruction effort, in beautifying the State capital, in building new roundabouts, in tarring the streets, in refurbishing old primary and secondary schools and constructing new ones.

Aje was Military Governor for ten years before another coup

d'état removed his group from power. He was forcefully retired from the army as a Colonel. But he had made millions and millions of money and had already been able to build his house in Abuja and in the district headquarters. This was when he decided to invest in something that would yield him interesting returns. Could he go into cement manufacturing? The Nigerian Portland Cement Company was worth a try, but it was unfortunately not offering any shares for sale. The cement sector was a safe and sound sector because Abuja, the new federal capital territory, was going to grow in leaps and bounds over the forthcoming years. The need for cement and other building materials would thus become more and more pressing. Could he go into the transport sector? Why not look for a few partners and start a new air company, that would focus exclusively on a niche market of business executives? Only a few destinations, Lagos-Abuja-Kano to and fro, Lagos-Benin City-Port Harcourt to and fro would be served initially. This was risky, he thought afterwards. How reliable would his partners be? What would happen if his airplanes crashed? How would such planes be maintained in Nigeria? Had the Nigerian Airways, with all the money that the federal government injected into it every year not collapsed because of the bad states of its planes?

It was one day when he was at the large golf club built by the military in Abuja that the idea of starting his palm oil refinery came to him. The military golf club was an eighteen-hole course at the outskirts of Abuja. It spanned a thirty-hectare hilly area that was initially home to a variety of wildlife including crocodiles, antelopes, monkeys, and snakes. It had several ponds around which some such wildlife could be seen regularly. The club had been built by the military but was open to civilians who could apply to be members. It had four five-star restaurants where local and foreign delicacies were available, private parking, free Wi-fi service, a driving range, a shopping complex, several tennis courts, and a big club house with three bars. It also offered free shuttle services to the Abuja Airport.

One of Aje's mates who had also been retired from the army invited him one day to the club for them to have a game of tennis. It was there that he met a group of foreign visitors including two Italian businessmen, who were spending a few days in Abuja. They were being accompanied by a senior official of the Italian Embassy in Abuja and a retired two-star general who was collaborating with them. Aje agreed to meet with them after his tennis game in the club house. He learnt that the group was trying to diversify its source of palm oil and to depend less on supply from South-East Asia where prices had started skyrocketing. The group had major suppliers from Indonesia, Malaysia and Thailand but wanted to diversify their sources and to have more reliable suppliers and partners from Africa, and especially from Nigeria which was said to be among the first five leading world producers of palm oil. In addition, Nigeria was reputed to have better equipped ports than most other African countries. Aje knew he had hit gold. Was his village and region not overflowing with palm trees? Was it not the palm oil that saved him from hunger when he was young? Was it not the red, sometimes thick liquid that he used to turn to in order to eat his boiled yams and boiled cassavas when his cousins prevented him from enjoying the meaty stew prepared by their mother? Was this liquid now going to become his gold mine?

He therefore set up Nakowa Oils as a subsidiary of the Italian agro-industrial company specialised in the industrial plantation of oil palm and processing industries such as palm oil mills, palm

38

oil refinery and fractionation and soap-making. He was able to acquire large plantations of palm trees and to establish an integrated Palm Oil and Palm Kernel Oil mill at the district headquarters. He bought an initial fleet of twenty lorries to transport the palm bunches from the plantation and nearby villages, where he was able to buy large hectares of palm forests, to his mill. The fleet of lorries increased more than tenfold afterwards. His oil mill occupied five hectares. He built an off-loading bay using a rail system where the fresh palm fruits were loaded into cages before being rolled to machines where they were sterilised, threshed, digested, and pressed. The products were then placed on desanding tanks to separate the raw crude oil which was afterwards screened by vibration to separate the liquid oil from dirt, fibres and other unwanted solid objects. Another part of the mill was reserved for the clarification process. There was an ebullition phase in which the crude oil was pre-heated, after which it went to a clarification settling tank where the oil was separated from water before being stored in large palm oil tanks. A third section of his mill was devoted to the kernel recovery plant with a big kernel crushing plant which produced and filtered palm kernel oil that was stored in large tanks.

Aje's mill was able to produce premium grade red palm oil as well as crude yellow palm kernel oil. The main difficulty that Aje's mills faced was how to stock the waste, the debris, that accompanied such oil extraction. He decided to address this question when his venture would be really profitable. His business grew and he was able to buy additional palm forests and build mills in many other areas in his region as well as in farther down south in Iboland. His foreign partners were extremely reliable. He was made an associate and invited to attend the

Board of Governors meeting held in Rome every year. He tried to help his community as much as he could. He offered employment to many and was always willing to assist those who came to him for financial aid. He was given a chieftaincy title by the Council of Chiefs.

Then the military leadership in the country decided that it was time to hand over power to a civilian government. It decided first to create new States. Then it appointed a Constitution Drafting Committee to prepare a new constitution for the country. Once the new constitution had been drafted, it appointed a Constituent Assembly with representatives from all the States of the federation and key interest groups to examine and ratify this constitution. Chief Aje was nominated a member of this Assembly. It was in the course of his work as a member of this Assembly that he became incorporated into a group of citizens from Northern Nigeria who apparently had already laid down the foundations for the formation of a political party. Plans were made and finalised concerning what political messages to deliver, how to better protect northern interests, what campaign methods to use, which sources of finance to seek and which candidates to support for Federal and State elective offices. Chief Aje, being from the Middle Belt, said he would like to be the Senate President. All the representatives from the State where he had been Military Governor some years back, saw him as a true northerner and were able to convince their colleagues from the other northern States that he was reliable. After his election as Senate President, he remained a member of the Board of Governors of his Italian Consortium but decided to hand over the management of his Nakowa Oil to Owobi, his first son. Now he was wondering if Owobi was up to the task.

Nobody in the village had ever said 'No' to him before. No,

nobody had dared stand on his way. Had people not come begging for his favour? Had he not always given, when he was asked, except once in a while when he did not trust those showering praises on him and thinking he was a "Money-miss-road", someone who had the fortune of having lots of easy money in the bank? Had he not been given the chieftaincy title because of who he was, what he was, what he did for his community? Did an ordinary villager, even if he was revered as the best palm wine tapper that ever existed in the village, think he could be an obstacle to him? Bloody civilian! he thought. Gone were those days when as an active military officer, he would have had him locked up. Well, he was going to get in touch with Government House, with the State Governor. But he still wondered if Owobi had enough authority to make Obande see reason.

Anyway, what he needed now was to go to his golf course and relax a little. He had built the golf course as a smaller version of the military golf club in Abuja, and he always liked to spend some time there each time he was visiting the region. Sometimes, he invited guests who visited him in Abuja to come with him to the hinterlands as he would say to them and have the joy of playing golf. His golf course had two big guest houses, a restaurant and a bar. The restaurant and bar were manned by a single person, an Efik man who was an excellent cook. Chief Aje told his wife that he was going to go to his club and spend the night there. He asked Edet to bring out his green Range Rover HSE Sport.

On his way to the golf course, he stopped near a school where a young lady was waiting for him under a mango tree. She got into the vehicle.

"Welcome back, Daddy. How was the village?" she said all

smiles.

"Very fine. You should have come to dance with the girls, Imelda," Chief Aje said with a laugh.

"You know I do not like dancing in public," the girl continued.

"Is that so? You do not like dancing in private either. Except when you go on summer vacation in Rome where you cannot resist dancing with all those skinny Italian boys. You think I do not know what you do when I send you abroad?" the Chief joked.

"You think I have time to waste with small Italian boys? You think I have time to waste with small boys anywhere in the world, whether here in Nigeria or in Oyiboland? Tuffia! What kind of girl do you take me for, Daddy?" she responded, equally joking.

"Are you telling me that you do not spend time with Okafor and Emeka in my absence?" the Chief continued.

"Who are Okafor and Emeka?" the girl wondered.

"Who are Okafor and Emeka? Are you telling me you do not know who they are? Young athletic boys for whom you play Pretty Woman once I have my back turned? So, tell me, have you now forgotten their names? Chei, wonders will never end. The day I catch them with you, I will show them real pepper, I swear. Bloody civilians!" the Chief added.

"Stop teasing me, Daddy. Do you think I have time to play around with small boys? What kind of girl do you take me for?" she complained, while laughing.

"The kind of girl that should always be gentle with me, no be so?" the Chief added this time with a loud laugh.

"My gentility is natural as you already know. Wait until I prepare what I will prepare for you to eat later at the guest house and your belly will become very big and round, your heart will become full of love, your eyes will start shining like stars and

42

your brain will begin to scatter, I swear!" she added.

"Your gentility! What about me? Am I not gentle too? Do you not enjoy going on summer trips to Europe?" the Chief asked.

"Yes, thanks, Daddy. The next time I go abroad, I would like to visit the Niagara Falls. It would be nice if you came with me, like you did when we visited Paris two years ago," she said.

"Oh yes, Paris. It was very wonderful. No police officer following you. No need paying attention to what you do or say. I enjoyed the week we spent in Paris and our visit to the French Riviera. We should go to the Riviera again," the Chief opined.

"No, was it not there that someone drove a large lorry into people walking along the beach? Can you imagine, you leave Nigeria to go and have peace abroad and not worry about Boko Haram and before you know what is happening, you are run down by a mad man crying "Allah Akbar". No, I would prefer to go to the Niagara Falls. I am told that it is possible to ride through the Niagara rapids on a jetboat and that this is one of the most exciting adventures in the world. I would also like to climb the catwalk and the hurricane deck close to the fall at the Cave of the Winds. One of my friends who went there last summer said it is an unforgettable experience," she maintained.

"OK, we'll see what we can do. So, how are things in the office? Owobi tells me one of the pressing machines broke down recently and that a new one had to be purchased. Why wasn't it repaired?" the Chief asked.

"Repairing it would have taken weeks and weeks, and that would have paralysed activities in the mill," the girl responded.

"I'm told the new machine cost several thousands of naira," the Chief continued.

"Yes, it did. We had the option of buying machines made in Onitsha here in Nigeria or made in China or made in Germany.

Owobi chose to buy the German brand, which is more durable. In addition, we have a ten-year warranty," the girl replied.

The girl had been recruited several years earlier by the Chief as his personal secretary. When they had begun having an affair, the Chief made it clear to her that he did not mind her having another boyfriend. He understood that as a young and beautiful girl, she could not spend her life waiting for him. He made her understand that he would always be there if she needed his support but warned her that he would frown at two things she might be tempted to do. First, get pregnant. He made it clear that it was out of the question for him to accept to be father to her child or children. A sugar Daddy remained a sugar Daddy. The second condition was that she needed to be discrete. She knew he was married. It was out of the question for her to go on parading in the city and region as his fiancée or whatever. If she agreed on these two conditions, he would make her life very easy. He bought her a brand-new Volkswagen Passat car and furnished the three-bedroom house she lived in. He liked being in her company. She made him feel younger. A voice somewhere in his mind said this was another excellent investment, with expectedly high returns.

When they arrived at the golf course, the girl told the Efik chef and barman that she was going to handle the cooking.

"Daddy, have you ever tasted *edika ekong* soup?" she asked, excitedly.

"No, never. What is it made of?" the Chief asked.

"Well, it's a specialty from Calabar. It's a vegetable soup with shrimps and smoked fish. Your belly is going to be full and round when you have tasted it and your heart will be full of love and your brain will begin to scatter like I promised," she explained. "For the meantime, go and play your golf."

2

Mary Oyije Ofu was extremely worried. She had several sources of worry.

The first concerned the Unity Government Girls' Secondary School for which she had been named the Principal a few years ago. The school was in Sokoto, one of the States in northern Nigeria that had opted for the Sharia legal system. She was aware of the fact that her arrival in the city and the school had not been well received by many. She was a woman and to make matters worse, was non-Muslim. To make things additionally worse, not only had she refused to follow the advice of some influential local notables who insisted that she impose the wearing of veils by all the girls in the school, she had started to get on the nerves of a few of them by meddling in how some parents in the region brought up their daughters. Recently, she had had an almost violent clash with a father who wanted his daughter to discontinue her school and get married as the fourth wife to a local dignitary. The girl was a very brilliant student in addition to being a respected class prefect. Mary had invited the father to her office to try to talk to him and make him see reason. The father was visibly angered at being invited to the office and had glared at her with open hostility and contempt when he was ushered into her big office.

"Welcome to our school, Alhaji. Ina kwana? Ina gejiya?" she had greeted, mixing English and Hausa.

"There is no need asking how I am doing when you invite

45

me to give me lessons on how to be a father," the man had retorted.

"No, Alhaji. I have not invited you to give you lessons. I just wanted us to speak openly about Zainab, your daughter, who is the most brilliant girl in her class. I am sure you know she's hoping to be a medical doctor in the future. She came to my office weeping with convulsion for several hours last week, telling me she does not want to get married now, that she is too young to bear and rear children and that she wishes to have a medical degree before starting a family. She was afraid of speaking to you directly and begged me to do the speaking for her. I do not wish to tell you what to do, but don't you think she's too young to get married? At sixteen, one is still a child," Mary had said.

"I am very surprised she has asked you to intervene in a matter that only concerns my family. Anyway, her age is hardly a problem. My mother had me when she was fifteen. Zainab will be well taken care of by her husband, I can assure you. She's crying because she's afraid, but she needn't be. She's going to move into a very respectable family, a family that lives according to and respects the lessons of the prophet Mohammed, peace be upon him," the father had calmy replied.

"I respect what you are saying, and I repeat that I do not wish to tell you how to bring Zainab up. I was just wondering if Zainab's prospective husband is in such a hurry to have a fourth wife," Mary had said.

"The question does not concern Zainab's prospective husband but me. It is what I have decided that counts. Zainab will be a good wife and a good mother," the father had insisted.

"I do not doubt that. What I'm saying is why the hurry. Zainab can prove herself to be something and someone else than being just a wife and mother. Can't you tell her prospective husband to wait a little longer?" Mary had asked.

"It is what I decide that counts, and I have decided that Zainab is going to get married. I know she will be very happy and will thank me afterwards," the father had replied.

"Zainab is extremely gifted. She has the intelligence and skills to study medicine and become the medical doctor she plans to become at the end of her studies. Removing her from school at such a young age is not a good decision," Mary had maintained.

The father had listened to her with contempt and arrogance before telling her to mind her own business. He wanted to know if Mary had children of her own. When Mary replied that she hadn't, the father told her that she would have been better placed to provide him with parental counselling if she were herself a parent.

Mary had ended up losing her self-control. She had adamantly contested the father's choice and had told him in very clear terms that his decision was selfish, cavalier and did not take the long-term interest of his daughter into consideration. How could he maintain that Zainab would be happy as a young wife when she had cried relentlessly for days and days at the thought of such a prospect? Was he as a father not supposed to ensure that his daughter was happy and provide her with the needed support to achieve her objectives in life? She had told the girl's father that he was insensitive and authoritarian. The father had insulted her. He had called her an 'Akpoto', a very derogatory word used to describe harlots, prostitutes.

The matter would have been contained had Zainab not absconded from school and ran away from her home. Her father had accused Mary of being the brain behind his daughter's disappearance. The police had been contacted. Her residence at the senior staff quarters within the school premises had been searched and two policemen ordered to keep a watch over the residence in case Zainab turned up.

News had spread all over the city that girls disappeared from her school and that she was not fit to occupy her position. A number of students, encouraged by their parents, started attending classes with their heads and the upper part of their faces covered in blue veils. Mary decided not to enter into an open conflict with them. Though a few teachers had pressed her to take disciplinary measures against such girls, Mary had not heeded their advice. There was no need going into an open war with the few students who wished to be militants for one cause or the other. Her role as Principal was to ensure that lessons were held, that the safety and security of all were ensured, and that Zainab was found safe and sound as soon as possible.

Her second source of worry was her father in the village. She did not know how long he was going to resist the incessant campaigns waged by Chief Aje's Nakowa Oil Mill to acquire his vast palm forest. Owobi, Chief Aje's son, always said he did not know who was the more stubborn between her father and her. He was used to calling her 'My CO'. This was because he thought that not only was she as stubborn as her father, but that she also had a very directive approach like his own father, a former military officer. So, he started calling her 'My Commanding Officer, my CO', and that stuck. Each time they met, usually when she went down home to the village to visit her parents, he would greet her by standing at attention military-style and jokingly saying "My CO. What are your orders?" She would tell him, equally joking to stand at ease or sometimes she would say "Ajuwire", which was a polluted form of saying "As you were", where soldiers who stood at attention were authorised to go back to the relaxed positions they were before.

Mary got on quite well with Owobi. They had spent most of their school days together. They had attended the same primary school, the same secondary school, and the same university. They shared the same values. Even when he had gone to the USA to study for his MBA, he had maintained very regular contact with her, always phoning her to tell her stories about the USA, to share with her his disbelief about the conditions of life of many black Americans he had come across. He had however told her that he found life in the USA much easier than in Nigeria. Mary had asked him if he wished to remain in the USA and work there after his MBA and he had always said it was out of the question. Though life in the USA was much easier, in his opinion, when compared to Nigeria, he had always said that there was something in Nigeria that made the country the only place he would feel at ease living in. He would miss the long go-slow in Lagos. He would miss the resourcefulness of Nigerian mechanics and their capacity to maintain very old Peugeot 404 taxis roadworthy. He would miss the hustle and bustle of city life, especially in Lagos, with its fleet of yellow overcharged panel-beaten *kabu-kabu* buses blowing their horns to attract additional passengers. He would miss the music shops where one could go and have an album copied or dubbed in broad daylight without any questions asked by whosoever on copyright or intellectual property. Whoever spoke of copyright in Nigeria, he wondered. How would he be able to live in the USA in which no bukateria existed, where he could go and order goat meat or cow leg pepper soup each time he felt the need? No, no way was he going to remain in the USA.

Mary felt at ease in Owobi's presence, and she knew Owobi

had the same feeling concerning her company. She hoped that no conflict would arise between her father and Owobi's. Owobi had informed her recently that his father was planning to consult the State Governor and ask that her father's vast palm forest be declared government property. She knew this would destroy her father, for whom the forest was not only a source of living, but extremely sacred. Why was Owobi's father so hell-bent on pushing her own father out of his property, she wondered. As Senate President, did he not have other problems to solve? She thought fleetingly about what Dr Ocheme, the other contestant for the senatorial elections in her constituency, would say. Bloody capitalist, bloody parasite, bloody neo-colonialist, he would say. She somehow did not trust Dr Ocheme either. Who knew what the noisy and boisterous academic would do if he became elected and tasted the forbidden political fruit? Would he be strong enough not to cave in to be a "ten per centre", in other words, accept to give contracts only to contractors prepared to give back to him ten percenter of the value of the contract? Had many academics not been very vociferous against government only to quieten down when they were nominated Chairmen of Government parastatals or made Ministers? Did Dr Ocheme not know that Chief Aje's election was a forgone conclusion? So, why was he still campaigning and making noise if not to draw attention to his capacity to be a thorn in the skin and flesh of government, for government to notice him and eventually give him a carrot to chew and chop?

Anyway, now she was thinking only of her father. The latest news she had had from home was that he had disappeared. She was for the meantime not alarmed. Her father had on a few occasions in the past preferred to spend several nights in his palm forest. This was usually when he had a difficult problem to solve.

He felt he needed to be close to his ancestors who were all buried in the forest. He felt that spending nights with them would provide him the light to chart possible solutions. So, maybe her father had decided to spend some time with his ancestors in order to determine how to face the looming crisis with Chief Aje. But then, what if her father had gone to tap palm wine in his forest and had fallen down from a palm tree and broken his neck? What if he had been bitten by a poisonous snake? What if in reality Chief Aje had laid a trap for him in his palm forest? She needed to get in touch with her elder brother, Clement.

Her third source of worry was her elder brother, Clement. She suddenly softened and thought very fondly of him. Normally, an elder brother was supposed to protect and take care of his younger sister. In the Obande Ofu family, it was the younger sister who took care and protected her elder brother.

Mary understood him extremely well. He did not need to express himself before she knew what he was thinking, what his reactions were and the pains he felt for not being accepted for who he was. Clement cried very easily, and his father was never patient with him. He did not like going to the farm because he got tired very quickly there, to the dismay and displeasure of his father. One day, the father had run out of patience and started beating Clement because he had allowed himself to be thrown down by a boy five years younger than he was in a wrestling match before a large, excited crowd. His father told him he had brought shame on the Ofu name and family, and that he needed to be made a man by force if he had chosen a different path. Clement had started wailing and this was when Mary had stepped out to cover her brother with her arms. She said to the hearing of many, including the elders who were there enjoying themselves as spectators to the wrestling matches, that men should not test their strength by beating their children, that a good wrestler was not necessarily a good man and that watching other people fight and enjoying this was a very strange custom indeed. Her father had looked at her with awe but had not dared raise his hand to discipline her in public. Had he not named his daughter Oyije, a namesake to his own mother who he proudly remembered as someone courageous and fearless? Did the way Mary now stand with her arms akimbo not resemble the way his beloved late mother stood each time she wanted to very vividly make her opinion known to people around her?

From that day onward, Mary had always taken the side of her brother each time he had a clash with her father. She became the go-between between father and son, speaking to her father on behalf of her brother and counselling her brother on what he needed to do or avoid doing in order to remain in the good books of their father. When as a teenager Clement expressed his desire to become a professional cook to the displeasure of her father, she backed him. Cooking was the domain of women in the village. When marriages were celebrated and dancing part of the program, it was groups of women who were given the task of cooking. It was unheard of for a man, a real man in the words of Mary's father, to wake up in the morning and wish to spend his whole day and life allowing smoke to enter into his eyes and making sure the yam was well pounded for other men to judge the quality of the meals they were served. It was unthinkable for a man to have as his only ambition when and how to go to the market to buy the ingredients needed to prepare *ogbono, egusi* or okra soup. How would such a man feed his family, if he did not go very early in the morning to the farm and spend the whole day planting what he would later harvest to ensure that his wives and children never went hungry, he wondered. How could such a person instil courage, bravery, resilience and strength on his male offspring, he asked himself, perplexed.

One day, Mary saw Clement using some black charcoal to make his eyebrows darker but made no comments. When he decided that he needed to go to Lagos where his cooking career would be easier to establish, she was the only one who had backed him. She was thus not so surprised when Clement had informed her that he preferred the intimate company of boys to that of girls. Had her father somehow known this too? She was worried by two things. First, would Clement be able to face the violence that is characteristic of men in their private lives? Was wife-beating not a favourite pastime of men, even the most educated and supposedly refined? Secondly, how could he protect himself from Aids, which had become a common affliction on the homosexual community?

She was thinking of her brother when there was a knock on her office door. She told the person knocking to come in. It was a Police Inspector leading a group of three people in civilian clothes. The Police Inspector informed Mary that reliable sources, from national intelligence services and the Nigerian Security Organisation represented by the other members of the delegation, all pointed to the fact that Zainab may have been kidnapped by one of the new Islamic militant groups that were growing in the region. Zainab's father had apparently been contacted by an unknown person who demanded that he pay a huge sum of money if he wanted to see his daughter again. The Inspector wanted to know what security arrangements existed in the school. He wanted to know how many gates led into the school, if such gates were open or manned, and if strangers could

53

penetrate the school premises without difficulty. He wanted to know where the dormitories of the girls were located, and if such dormitories were easily accessible by vehicles or not. Did the school have a generator? When the school slept at night, was it dark everywhere or were there parts of the school that were lit with streetlight? Was the girls' dormitory always thrown in darkness whenever the National Electricity Power Authority (NEPA) cut power as it often did at night, or was the school generator used very handily as a standby?

Mary answered these questions as best as she could. The team then asked Mary to accompany them for a tour of the school premises and especially the girls' dormitory. They asked her to be very alert and to inform all members of teaching and non-teaching staff and the students to watch out for strangers who penetrate the school premises. Mary asked if the policemen who had been asked to keep watch over her residence could now be given the mission of patrolling the school premises, especially at night. The Police Inspector refused her demand by saying this was not part of the statutory missions of the police. If every school principal asked for policemen to start patrolling their schools, how many policemen would be left to fight crime, he wondered loudly.

It happened one night. Around one a.m., Mary felt some foreign presence in her bedroom. Before she could shout, someone put his large hands over her mouth and gagged her while another blindfolded her. She was violently removed from her bed. She was then dressed in a black kaftan and bundled into a Toyota pick-up. The vehicle went rapidly to a spot behind the girls' dormitory where several other pick-ups were stationed. Each had many blindfolded and gagged girls, equally dressed in black kaftans, seated in them. Many were shaking convulsively and silently crying. Some tried to struggle. Some of the men, who were all dressed in white kaftans with turbans around their heads, would prod the struggling girls with the butts of their guns. If the girls continued to struggle, a pointed knife would be brought out and the girls informed that if they moved further, they would injure themselves. The struggling girls got the message.

One of the men said loudly, "Yalla! Yalla! Yalla!" Then a second one said excitedly, "Mu tafi nan de nan." All the pick-ups rushed out of the school premises. They drove along the Sokoto-Gusau road for some time before veering right into a narrow, rough untarred road that led into a large forest. Though she was still blindfolded and could see nothing at all, Mary knew they had left the main Gusau road and had taken another road, very bumpy. It was when she felt her head being scratched by branches of trees and some thorns that she guessed they were in a forest.

Only the sounds of the Toyota engines and the soft weeping of some of the girls could be heard. Mary thought they must have driven for less than one hour on the tarred Gusau road before veering off into the bumpy one. Then they must also have driven for less than one hour before she felt the branches of the trees scraping her head. The men in the trucks told the girls to bend down and stay very low inside the trucks if they did not want to be beheaded by tree branches. If any got injured at the head, she would face dire consequences, they were told. Mary obeyed. Her heart was beating violently. Where were the men taking them to? Who were they? What did they want from them?

The convoy of Toyota pick-ups advanced further into the woods. Was this not one of many forest plantations that the federal government was building in the northern part of Nigeria in order to forestall desert encroachment, and to encourage the development of wildlife, she wondered. Maybe this was the forest which covered more than seventy square kilometres in a very hilly area that she had visited with some of her students for them to learn the diversity of flora and fauna within it.

The forest she had visited with her students contained a diversity of trees, many of which were used by surrounding villages for medical purposes. There were rows and rows of bush fig as well as mountain fig. The leaves of the bush fig were used as fodder for the livestock raised by surrounding villages. The roots were equally appreciated because when these were boiled, they were used by villagers to treat problems such as intestinal worms. The mountain figs also had important medical value. Villagers used the root to treat cough and often removed the bark which they boiled and drank to treat diarrhoea. Apart from the figs, Mary could recollect that the forest contained other tree species, each with their respective medicinal qualities. There were for example, large expanses of Sycamore whose leaves were used to make quite spicy soup and whose roots could be used as a purgative. Then there were vast rows of mahogany, whose bark when soaked in water could equally be used to attack intestinal worms. And then there were of course hundreds and hundreds of metres along which stretches of mango and cashew trees could be seen. Mary recollected how her students had been very excited at plucking and eating ripe mangoes and cashew nuts easily.

Now was this same forest going to be their penitentiary? She shivered at the thought. She could hear most of the girls in her pick-up van sobbing quietly. The passengers were occasionally thrown off balance when the pick-up ran into a deep pothole though it was driving slowly, like all the others. The silence was eerie. Apart from the girls sobbing silently and the noise of the pick-up engines, what struck Mary as strange was that no one was speaking. Occasionally, the sound of tree branches scratching the body of the vehicles could be heard but no one was speaking.

Mary started to panic. She had never been in such a situation before. Of course, she had known that boarding schools were being harassed by Islamic sects especially in the north-eastern part of the country, sometimes accompanied by the kidnapping of boys and girls, but she felt that Sokoto, where she was staying, which was where the venerable Sultan, leader of and guide to Nigerian Muslims was residing, would be immune to such Islamic militant actions. Then she started thinking of events that had occurred recently. Had the police and security agencies not visited her school not long ago? Were those who had come to see her and with whom she had made a tour of her school, including the girls' dormitory, in reality what and who they said they were? Come to think of it, only the Inspector had been dressed in a police uniform. The others wore plainclothes. What if they were in reality members of the group that had struck this night, performing a reconnoitering act? She started to shiver uncontrollably. She thought rapidly of her father, of Clement, of Owobi, of Owobi's father and finally of Zainab and her father. She wondered why she had thought of Zainab and her father.

The pick-up had come to a halt. She heard the men speaking.

"Ina shugabban?" one of the men asked.

"Yana cikin bukkarsa," another responded.

"Fada masa mun dawo," the first speaker continued.

"Labari mai dadi, kwarai de gaske," the second responded.

"Ina shugaban mata?" a third man enquired.

"Tana cikin dayan motocin," the first speaker replied.

"Maigidan zai yi farin ciki," the third man announced.

"Shin tana da wahala?" a fourth man wanted to know.

"A`a," answered the first speaker.

"Don Allah, a je a kira maigidan da sauri," the first speaker said.

The second man was absent for about five minutes which seemed to be an eternity for Mary. When he came back, he was apparently with someone else who spoke this time in perfect English. It was the warm spicy fragrance of the perfume he had used that first greeted Mary's nostrils.

"Remove all their blindfolds and equally the gag from the eldest, the principal," he ordered. Mary saw that all the pick-ups had been parked to form a large circle with their dipped headlights all pointing to the centre of the circle in which an immaculately dressed man that exuded authority stood. All the girls automatically converged behind Mary as if they were seeking her protection.

"Don't worry girls. We do not wish you any harm," the man announced in a quiet voice.

"You have kidnapped us from our school very late into the night, I have had my house invaded, we have been blindfolded for the past four or so hours and are in an unknown forest and you are telling us not to worry? By the way, who are you?" Mary asked in a voice she could hardly accept was hers.

"You talk too much. You should talk only when I ask you to," the man replied calmly.

"We are in an unknown forest with unknown men, and you do not want us to ask questions to know what is happening and why? You look like someone very respectable and literate. Asking questions when one is lost is normal for anyone to see, don't you see?" Mary continued.

Without any warning, one of the men lashed out with a *bulala*, a long leather whip. The whip hit its target, Mary's shoulder. The girls who had gathered around her tried to run, but they were held back by the circle of men behind the circle of vehicles with their dim lights.

"You see, I told you to stop asking questions. My men do not accept that a woman be rude to me. You will have some of the answers to some of your questions one of these days," the man announced.

"Is it for money that you are doing this?" Mary pursued.

"You are strong-headed. I have told you to remain civilised and not to ask questions or speak until you are authorised to. You will put your fingers into very hot water if you go on in this way. I don't want your students to see you thrashed. Answers will come when they come," the man responded.

One of the other men who had been standing and silently watching both Mary and their leader moved forward and said to him:

"Bari mu bar gandun daji de sauri."

Another man made a suggestion.

"Bari mu kai su makarantan koran karatun da aka saba."

The leader agreed and said, "Lafiya. Zan dauki shugabban makarantar zuwa wurina."

The girls were divided into five groups. They were told to remove all their wristwatches and to hand these over to one of the men. The few who had cell phones were dispossessed of these. Some of the girls had small-sized purses with some money in them. These were also seized. The leader asked that all the girls be blindfolded once again. He also asked that Mary be gagged once more. He then gave detailed instructions to the head of each group before asking his own group to follow him.

Mary was in the leader's group with five other girls. They were closely guarded by two men armed with Kalashnikovs. Their vehicle was following that of the leader in front of them. They were driving quite slowly and had been warned earlier on to keep their heads down. Mary was hurt around her shoulder where the *bulala* had struck. She had many questions for which no sensible answer could be found. What was the leader of the group actually in search of? He had not seemed too dangerous-looking. He spoke perfect English and so was from all intents and purposes someone well read. Surely someone who had a well-paid government job. Who knows, maybe a teacher like her. So, what had broken the bonds between him and the Nigerian society for him to now invade a school devoted to producing the women leaders of tomorrow?

Suddenly, the vehicles picked up speed. Mary imagined that they had now come out of the forest. She tried to listen attentively. All was quiet apart from the humming of the engines of the two vehicles in the convoy and the noise made by the flapping of dresses in the wind. The vehicles then slowed down a little. Mary thought she heard a cock crowing. The vehicle slowed down once more and came to a halt. Mary thought she heard some other voices greeting the leader who gave them instructions rapidly. The two men who had been standing guard to Mary and the five girls jumped down from the vehicle. Mary and the girls were each led by someone inside a building. It seemed that they went past three doors, before veering right. Then Mary thought they crossed a large open space before passing through another door and then going through a room. Then they walked along what seemed to be a narrow corridor before they were all led into a room with some mattresses placed on mats on the carpeted floor. The girls were informed that they were to remain in the room and sleep until they were woken up later. They were told that they would remain blindfolded and gagged until someone came to see them later. They were warned not to try to communicate anyhow with one another. Failure to respect this rule would be very severely dealt with. Further instructions would be given to them when deemed necessary. The door to their room would be locked from outside and two men would be stationed outside their door. The two men had the authority to discipline anyone who was deemed disobedient and unruly. If they wanted to go to the *bayan gida* or toilet, they were instructed to knock on the door from within and one of the guards would lead them to where the toilets were and keep a close eye on them. Two meals would be provided.

Mary had a restless night. She dozed off at one point in time and dreamt that she was hanging from a cliff that was more than one hundred metres above a fast-flowing river, with many crocodiles waiting patiently for her to lose grip and fall down. She started to sweat and to panic as she felt her grip on the rock loosening and her hands slowly sliding down to the edge of the cliff. She tried desperately to hang on but there was no stopping the slide down to inevitable death. She thought she saw the crocodiles crying. Why were they shedding tears? She was about to abandon herself when she felt someone hold her arms strongly and solidly. She looked up and saw her elder brother, Clement, trying to pull her back from the edge of the cliff. She was so relieved that she fainted. Then she felt someone prodding her in the stomach and slapping her first gently, and then afterwards more violently in the face. Apparently, Clement was trying as hard as possible to wake her up and bring her back to consciousness. He touched her gently first, then tried to shake her harder. She began to feel the pain on her shoulder. Someone was shaking her violently. She tried to scream but her mouth appeared to be muzzled. She woke up but everything was still dark. She smelt cigarette smoke and felt someone beside her. The man removed her blindfold. It was one of the men standing guard to the room she had been pushed into earlier on. The man was telling her it was time to wake up and have a meal.

Mary tried to focus her eyes in order to better know where she was. She was lying on a Dunlopillo mattress on the floor in a relatively big round room. The room had no windows and had only one door which had been left wide open. Mary saw that the door led to a room with mats on the floor. The other girls she had slept with had all already been woken up and were sitting terror-stricken. What struck her immediately was what she saw on the walls of the room where the girls were waiting. The walls contained very beautiful and colourful engravings. She imagined the house. This must be one of those typical Hausa compounds with pinnacles or *zankwaye*. If there were such beautifully coloured engravings inside the house, there were no doubt the same engravings on the exterior walls. The house must thus belong to someone who had relatively high social standing, maybe an *ulama*. She thought she could hear some children reciting verses of the Koran very close by. They must be in the open space she felt they had crossed in the late night or early morning when they had been brought by the kidnappers. The children reciting the verses were surely *Almajiris*. If this was so, then she was certainly in the confines of a Quranic school.

She began to panic. Was this one of the many Quranic schools that were affiliates of Iran and the Hezbollah in northern Nigeria? Was this one of the sects that said "Haram" to western-style education and that wished to finish the jihad Usman Dan

Fodio began in the nineteenth century, the objective being to dip the Quran in the Atlantic Ocean? Now she could hear the children clearly, learning the Quran by rote. Maybe there was a long-bearded wise old man sitting close to them, trying to groom them to become devout believers, while very close by, a door away from them, five girls and one woman were being held captive and their will to pursue their learning so as to make their future lives better wilfully arrested. The man prodded Mary and told her to hurry up. The meal was ready, and it would get cold.

Mary joined the five other girls who were sitting silently on the mat. There were three large, covered bowls, six medium-sized empty-coloured plastic plates and six big plastic cups in front of them. One of the large bowls had a big wooden spoon. The girls were told they could begin to eat. The three large bowls were uncovered. Mary saw that one of them contained some liquid that smelt spicy. One of her students told her this was known as *kunun zaki,* a non-alcoholic beverage that was made with millet and lots of spices such as ginger, cloves and pepper. The girl told Mary that this drink was very good for the health. The second large bowl contained several portions of sticky dough. The girl told Mary this was called *tuwon masara.* She explained that this was made with corn flour which was cooked in boiling water before being kneaded into a stiff dough. According to the girl, *tuwon masara* was usually put into small or medium-sized individual portions in transparent cellophane bags. Mary asked why there were no forks, spoons, or knives. Was it because those who had kidnapped them were afraid that they might kill each other with these? The girl replied that she did not think so because *tuwon masara* was usually eaten with one's fingers. The *tuwo,* however, had to be eaten with some soup or stew. This drew everyone's attention to the contents of the third bowl. It contained some dark sticky sauce. The girl who was explaining things to Mary told her this was the *miyan karkashi,* made from Karkashi leaves. This *miya* was thus dried and ground vegetable soup with smoked and dried catfish as well as meat, usually mutton. The girl warned Mary that the soup might be very spicy since most *miyan karkashi* were flavoured with *kayan yaji,* dried and ground cayenne pepper. Mary thanked her for the warning.

After the meal, the girls were asked to go back to the room they had slept in, the windowless room. Mary asked the men what time it was. They refused to answer her. She wondered if they spoke English. She asked the girl who had described the dishes they ate to ask the same question in Hausa. One of them responded very violently. She told Mary that the man had heard and understood her question and did not want to answer. He had been warned that the eldest of their guests spoke too much *dogon turanchi,* and had been ordered to ignore her questions. He had been told to inform the women that they were guests, but that the hospitality that would be offered to them did not include engaging in social chit-chat. They were to go back to their room. They would no more be blindfolded or gagged. They did not need to express their gratitude to *maigida.* They were warned that if they made any noise or tried to attract the attention of the *Almajiris* who all were absorbed by their Quranic lessons, the *maigida* would be furious at their ingratitude and would have them lapidated to death. They were to remain wise, remain in their room and remain behind closed doors as Allah's messenger, the Prophet Mohammed, may peace be upon him, had taught the Muslim community through the Sunna in the Hadiths.

The girls went back to the room which was still dark. Since they had not been banned from talking to one another, Mary decided that it was necessary to get to know the girls better. She learnt that two of the girls were from well-to-do Hausa families, one was of Yoruba origin, one from the Federal Capital Territory and the last from an Ibo family residing in Sokoto. The father of the Ibo girl was a Major in the Nigerian Army. She told Mary of her dreams to become a civil engineer and participate in the conception and construction of new state-of-the-art infrastructure in Nigeria. What would happen to all six of them, she enquired. Mary told her not to worry. The moment her father became aware that she was missing from her school, he would surely leave no stone unturned to find her. He surely would contact military intelligence, would he not, Mary maintained. The girl who came from the Federal Capital Territory said her father was a top-ranking civil servant in the Building Department of the Federal Capital Development Authority in Abuja. As a matter of fact, she had spoken to him the night they were abducted. He had asked her how she was doing and had promised to send her some pocket money by the end of the month. They had spoken about many things, but the girl could not remember any at the moment. The two Hausa girls included the one who had described the dishes to Mary. She said they were surely in the home of someone who was not short of money, judging by the beautifully coloured engravings on the wall of the room where they had had their meal. She was sure the compound was very large. She said she suspected the room they had eaten in was some sort of guest area. She suspected the courtyard they had gone through blindfolded was very large. They had been led towards the right. She said that if the house resembled that of her parents, there must be a big compound to the left of the courtyard that led to the residence of the *maigida* and his family. In other words, there must be a second courtyard leading to one or two reception rooms or *zaure*

65

in the outer area. This second compound surely had the *taraka*, the head of family's unit with a bedroom and a sitting room, as well as an inner women-restricted area and an open space for the women who were forced into purdah. She also told the girls that she was sure there was a *rumfa*, a sitting room common to all the wives where they could meet and interact. She said no one would know they were in the house because the entire building with its multiple rooms, and compounds was surrounded by a high wall. The house would look from the outside like any other house in the neighbourhood. The Yoruba girl was petrified. She was unable to say anything about herself or her family.

Mary told the girls they would all have to be patient. First, she would have to find out more from and about the *maigida*. Though she was inwardly afraid, she did not allow her fear to be transmitted to the girls. She told them in a quiet voice that all is well that ends well and that the room they were in was better than a prison. Though she maintained a cool outward demeanour, she was, however, alarmed and panic-stricken at not knowing what time it was. The room was dark. Was it dark outside? Was it night or day? Had the kidnapping from the school been discovered? Was the school compound crawling with National Security Officers all looking for clues? Was her picture being shown on NTA, the Nigerian Television Authority? The state of not knowing was very unbearable to her. She was used to having a planned daily and weekly schedule, of organizing events, of identifying tasks and determining how to resolve these within a time frame. She was used to being in control of events as much as possible. Being helpless and dependent on another person for how she lived, worked, and spent her time was a new challenge she knew she would have to overcome in order not to go mad. When left inactive in a dark room, without anything concrete to do, without any schedule to respect, without everyday problems to be resolved, how could one not go mad? How could the transition from a very busy active problem-solving life to a boring uneventful twenty-four-hour-waiting-patiently-in a-room schedule be made without untold damage to one's mental and physical well-being? How could time be made to fly and how could such time be counted? She decided that she had to find a way of knowing at least the number of days/nights spent behind closed doors. Each time she slept and woke up, she would cut a piece of her hair with her fingers and place it under her pillow or put it in her pocket. She would look for a way of counting such pieces of hair from time to time, but she hoped she would not have that many pieces to count before she regained her freedom.

She was perplexed and confused. How could someone who was visibly well-educated, who wore perfumes, and who from all indications was socially well off, decide to keep others in prison in his home? Who knew, maybe one of his neighbours was part of the team now involved in searching for the kidnapped students. Such a team would focus on exploring surrounding forests and would certainly reach a dead-end there. Mary reluctantly acknowledged the man's intelligence. Lead investigators to the wrong track while housing the kidnapped students in various beautiful-looking houses admired by passers-by. Yes, that was very intelligent. But then, there were many things she wanted to know and many questions she was asking for which only the *maigida* could provide the answers. So, she waited with the girls.

The waiting was punctuated by a daily routine. The girls would be woken up, they would be asked to go to the guest room to have their meals, one of them would be asked to sweep the floor of the room in which they slept, they would be allowed to go to the toilet when the need arose alone, with a guard standing close by, they would be asked to go to the bathroom to take their daily shower, with a guard always standing close by, and then they would be locked up in the dark in their room afterwards. Mary spent the time trying to learn as much as possible about the meals she ate. She depended on the descriptions made by the student who had offered to do this on the first day. Once or twice, they ate what the girl named *tuwon shinkafa*. She explained that some rice was soaked overnight while some other rice was boiled. The two are then ground together and served with various types of soup such as *miyan gyeda*, made with groundnut, or *miyan kuka*, made with ground baobab leaves. Another meal they regularly had was called *tuwon dawa*, made with ground guinea corn and cassava and served with *miyan kuka*. Sometimes, they were offered some light porridge made with raw groundnuts and rice. The girl called this *kunun gyeda*, which they took either with *kosai*, beans cake, or with *masa*, rice cake. On a few occasions, they were offered some traditional Hausa snacks. One of these was called *kulikuli*, small fried balls made with the peanut paste. Another was called *chinchin*, some type of fried pastries.

Mary counted eight pieces of her hair the day one of the men opened the door to their room and told her that the *maigida* wanted to speak to her personally. Panic could be read on the faces of the five girls, all of whom had lost some weight since the beginning of their plight. Mary panicked too but tried not to show this to her students. She was given a niqab which covered her entire body, head, and face with a small opening for her eyes. She was worried about two things. If she did not come back, how were the girls going to survive? Who was going to tell them not to worry and convince them that their nightmare was going to end sooner or later? Then she wondered what was in store for her. Was this the end of the road for her? Was she going to be separated from her students? Was she going to meet the *maigida* alone or would he be with others? Was she going to be sexually harassed? She went past the *Almajiris* without paying attention to them. She thought she heard the bleating of sheep from somewhere in the compound. She was led through the large courtyard before being told to wait outside a large, white door. Some music was coming from the room. It was traditional Hausa music, played with the *goje,* a one-string fiddle. Mary's escort knocked quietly at the door before ushering her into a wide room.

"I see you have lost some weight. I hope you have not embarked on a hunger strike," the man said. He was sitting alone in a big comfortable leather armchair. He was fiddling a small transistor radio as if he was searching for an appropriate station. The same perfume that had struck her nostrils more than a week earlier, struck her nostrils again. The perfume was certainly not like the ordinary perfumes sold in the open city market which had a cheap overpowering and suffocating fragrance. The perfume this man was using had a delicate, warm, refreshing, and pleasant fragrance. Was it a Dior, a Yves Saint Laurent or an Armani? Then her eyes were drawn to the man sitting in the armchair. Gone was the head turban he had worn in the forest some days earlier. She saw he was bald. He was clean shaven with a very short beard. Mary guessed he could not be more than forty years old because he had a young face. He was wearing a spotless white kaftan. Two other men were in the room with him. They were both heavily armed, had their heads covered in chequered black and white turbans, and were wearing dark sunglasses. Mary thus could not read what expressions they had on their faces.

"That I have lost weight is very normal. You would have,

you too, if you were in my shoes, held captive for reasons beyond your understanding. What worries me is not the weight I have lost. What worries me is the life that the girls you have placed behind closed doors are losing each day they remain locked up as they are. Why are you doing this?" Mary asked defiantly.

"You seem not to have learnt your lesson. I have asked you to stop asking questions. And when you speak to me, look down on the floor rather than try to look at my face. Though your eyes are hidden, I can see you looking directly at my face. My men here will not tolerate any disrespect from you. So, for your own good, try to respect the rules of the house. You do not ask questions; you do not speak until I tell you to do so. And when you speak, look down at the floor. Surely, these are simple rules to understand for someone like you who has been to the university," the man announced calmly while continuing to fiddle his transistor radio.

"I am in your house. When in Rome, do as the Romans do. So, when can I speak?" Mary enquired.

"Now, if you wish. What do you want to speak about? Be careful about what you say and how you say them," the man warned.

"I have questions to ask," Mary replied.

"Questions to ask? We all have questions to ask, don't we? I will be magnanimous enough to listen to your questions. If I think they are reasonable, I might answer them. If I think they are senseless, I won't answer them. So, go ahead," the man said. He found a station that was airing traditional Hausa music but did not seem satisfied and so he continued fiddling.

"All the questions I have to ask are reasonable and sensible," Mary countered.

"You see, I know you have started getting on the nerves of

my men. I have magnanimously offered you the gift of listening to you and telling you that I'm ready to answer your questions, and what you want is for me to give you a long speech, as if we are in a debating society? This is what happens when girls are allowed to go to the schools left behind by our long-forgotten ungodly imperialistic English colonial masters. This is a perfect example of the moral decay that follows Western education where girls, rather than remain at home and help their mothers, while waiting to get married and give birth to children, think they can think for themselves and for others. My patience might run out. So, if you have questions to ask, this is the time to go ahead," the man said. Something had changed in his voice and posture. He was very visibly less affable.

"Are we going to stay captive here forever?" Mary asked.

"No," the man replied.

"If we fall ill, shall we be treated or taken to the hospital?" she continued.

The man kept silent for what seemed to Mary to be more than a minute. She suddenly became very uneasy and decided to ask another question to break the silence.

"Can we have something like a clock in our room, so that we can better know how time flies or not?" she added.

"No," the man replied.

"Why not?" Mary asked.

"Your question is quite senseless. I do not feel like or want to make long sentences," the man responded angrily.

"Can we have something like the radio you have so that we can listen to the news as well as to some music?" Mary asked.

"This time, I'm going to make an exception. I'm going to take a few minutes to try to explain some things to you in plain English, which is about the only thing useful left by the

71

imperialists, something we can use to communicate between ourselves. The radio, like the television, when used by children, women and infidels to listen to all those English language programs broadcast daily are not good for Muslim communities because they try to infiltrate Muslim minds with Judeo-Christian ideologies. These lead to immorality. These lead to evil behaviour. These lead to the development of such ideas as democracy and equality between men and women. These lead to such unislamic behaviour as drinking liquor, listening to Western or Westernised music. No, no radio will be put in your room because you are all going to leave my home reformed, pure and obedient to Allah and his messenger, the prophet Mohammed, may peace be upon him," the man said.

"Something tells me you think providing education to girls is against Islam," Mary wondered aloud.

"Yes," the man replied. "Education for girls should not be tolerated. Teenage girls should be at home helping their mothers."

"At the risk of getting you angry again, don't you think that an uneducated girl is like a blind girl, who cannot see where she is going and so cannot know how to eventually help others including her mother?" Mary ventured to ask.

The man made a sign to one of his men who put down his gun. He seized Mary and gagged her quickly. Then he took out a long *bulala* from his kaftan and whipped Mary several times. Mary tried to escape and run out from the room, but the entrance door was solidly locked, and the second man was blocking it from inside. She could not scream. She had no other choice than to withstand the beating. The man raised his hands and the beating stopped.

"You are strong-headed. You do not seem to hear what you

are told. Why did you choose to give me a lesson on education?" the man, livid with anger, asked.

"I'm sorry," Mary said when her gag was ordered removed. Her body was trembling uncontrollably.

"Okay. You are forgiven. Fortunately, I am not a crude and brutal being. So, go on with your questions," the man continued.

"Are you going to force us to convert to Islam?" Mary asked.

"No, not force you to, but encourage you to," the man replied.

"Will my students be forced to marry your men?" Mary pursued.

"No, not forced to, but convinced to," the man calmly responded.

"Can I ask you a question that is not a "Yes/No" question, please?" Mary pleaded.

"Uhm, Er, Well, Okay, Yes, just one question," the man accepted.

"Why are you doing this and what do you hope to gain from this?" Mary demanded.

"I told you just one question. There you have asked two. But since I gave you the go ahead and since I'm a man of my words and a man of integrity, I will answer both questions. You see, we are here in the region where our great forefather, Sheikh Uthman Dan Fodio, may Allah bless his memory, began his crusade to purify the region, lay the foundations for the building of a solid umma and build a system of education revolving around Allah. Then comes Western education, which is no other than a tool to Christianise Muslims. Then comes a judicial and legal system which tries to displace our sharia system founded on justice, welfare, and civic responsibility. What is the result of the educational system for which you are a willing agent? Nothing but corruption, total debauchery, and immorality. You teach children to drink liquor, which is haram. You accept the intermingling of men and women, which is haram. You recommend the reading of many licentious books to students whereas they should be brought up to read and understand what is written in the Quran and the Hadith. In places like Kano, Bauchi and Katsina, attempts are being made to contain these problems by giving very wide powers of investigation and control to the *Hisba* for example, groups of policemen which are trying to force general obedience to Islamic mores. But then Kano and the other cities here in the north constitute a very small iceberg in a large ocean of decadence, a decadence that is visible in how the young dress, in how family life is organised and in the personal qualities that are sought today. These qualities are foreign to us because they are of Western origin and are intrinsic parts of Western culture. Take the question of equality between men and women, for example. What crazy and mad idea! Whoever said the man and the woman naturally have the same qualities, the same capacities, the same rights, the same duties?" the man said.

"Are you afraid of women?" Mary asked, spontaneously, immediately regretting having asked the question, because she thought the response would be additional whips of the *bulala*.

"No, of course not," the man replied, calmly, to Mary's relief.

"Do you think women are incapable of doing things, of leading?" Mary continued, emboldened.

"Yes, of course. Tell me where a woman is leading or has led successfully," the man went on.

"The Queen of England," Mary replied.

"She does not lead. And anyway, that is in the West. What

happens in the West should not be the norm elsewhere and certainly not here in Nigeria," the man interjected.

"Indira Ghandhi in India," Mary added.

"Are you talking about the Prime Minister that was shot and killed by her Sikh security guards? The supposed leader whose tenure saw the rise of separatist movements in many parts of India, including the Kashmir? Is that what you call leadership?" the man questioned, incredulous.

"What about Queen Amina of Zazzau. She was a very famous Hausa Habe ruler long before your forefather Uthman Dan Fodio established the Sokoto Caliphate in the nineteenth century," Mary countered.

"Ah, Queen Amina of Zazzau. So, what about her?" the man enquired.

"Well, she was known as the queen warrior, wasn't she? She was able to expand the territory of her State and to be more powerful than neighbouring States, wasn't she? Under her, Zaria became a very famous centre for trans Saharan trade, didn't it? There is consensus that Queen Amina was much better at ruling Zazzau than most of her male predecessors including her brother Karama who she succeeded, isn't there?" Mary argued.

"Okay, you have made your point. But how many other Queen Aminas can you name today?" Mary could not so she kept quiet.

"Can I ask you two last questions, please," Mary pleaded once again.

"Go ahead," was the reply.

"You said you would encourage us to convert to the Islamic faith rather than force us to. What do you mean by this exactly, please?" Mary asked.

"Well, the thing is very simple. I know that four of you are infidels, but I have been magnanimous enough to cater for your welfare for several days now. Normally, I abhor infidels. But then I have plans for all of you and for the others. Specifically, the four of you staying in my house who are infidels will have to change your names. You will all be given an Islamic name. I have decided that henceforth, you will be named Aisha. The name means being alive and well. You are alive. You are well. I also like the name because it is the name of the third and youngest wife to the Prophet Mohammed, peace be upon his name," the man announced.

Mary held her breath. If the man was hell-bent on making her become a Muslim, surely, he must have other plans for her and her girls. Forced marriage perhaps.

"I can read your mind. You are surely thinking that you will have to become the wife to one of my devout followers, aren't you?" the man demanded.

Mary was silent. She saw the man raise his right hand with four of his fingers pointing upwards. Apparently, it was a signal to the guard that had whipped her earlier, but this time the signal was to prevent any additional whipping.

"I told you to show me respect. My men are already angry at your tendency to speak continuously. Now you refuse to answer me when I ask you a question. So, I'm going to ask you the question once more. Were you thinking that I might hand you over as wife to one of my men?" the man demanded.

"Yes, I was," Mary answered, meekly, cowered.

"Well, that is not the initial plan. In the first plan, let's see how much value you and your girls have in the eyes of the corrupt non-Islamic government that you are serving diligently. I have tried to get in contact with them but for the meantime, such contact has not been fruitful at all. If the contact is fruitful and satisfactory, who knows, you may not have the joy of taking care of the home of someone who lives according to the lessons handed down to us by the Prophet Mohammed, peace be upon his name," the man concluded.

"Can I make a comment, please?" Mary requested.

"You are strong-headed. This is very annoying. But then go ahead. And again be careful what you say because my men here are already fed up with your childishness and impetuosity," the man warned.

"Okay. I know I'm standing in front of someone who is highly educated and cultivated. The question I have been asking myself over the past days has been "Why?" I seem to have obtained some answers to this question. You say you are a man of integrity. You surely want me to believe you, but I cannot, no matter how much I try. Holding another one captive does not show integrity. I am at a loss at how kidnapping innocent school children, innocent young girls who have their dreams of selfhood and self-fulfilment, at how their capture will erase the problems you think Western civilisation has inflicted on Nigeria. How can my change of name to Aisha change who I am? How can the disruption of activities in my school stop girls and boys elsewhere from reading what you call licentious books, from intermingling, from learning, from believing or not believing things or ideas, from dreaming, from craving for liberty and the freedom to be or not to be, to do or not to do, to choose or not to choose, in other words to live?" Mary digressed.

"*Dogon turanchi*, nothing but *dogon turanchi*. You are lucky I'm in a good mood. You have shown me disrespect again with your long exposé. I will decide on an appropriate sanction later. For the meantime, you will be gagged before being led back to your room. Try to eat what is offered to you because you are losing weight and this not good for your health," the man concluded.

Mary was led away back to where she was sleeping with her girls by the man who had brought her in and who had stood waiting outside the door. She felt some sweat dripping down from her hair down her face but could not wipe this off, since she was still dressed in the niqab. However, she tried to have a more detailed picture of her surroundings as she followed the man inside the compound. She saw that the big courtyard they were crossing had a path that led outside the building. She saw that there were high pinnacles protruding from the roof angles. She was sure that the exterior walls were all covered by beautifully coloured motifs. She saw that the path that led outside went through three large archways. She suspected that each had rooms at either side. She thought she heard some sheep bleating. The sound seemed to come not only from the entrance well beyond the third archway from where she was, but also from behind. She suspected the house had a backyard where animals were reared. Then she thought she heard a muezzin calling for prayers. What prayer was being called, she wondered. Certainly not the first prayer at dawn. So, this must be either the *'dhuhr'*, the midday prayer or the *'Asr'*, the late afternoon prayer. She looked upward into the sky to see where the sun was. It was well past midday. So, she assumed that the time should be around four p.m. or thereabout. How long had she been with the *maigida*? She felt her shoulders burning but could do nothing about it. They went through the second courtyard in which many *Almajiris* were sitting, silently reciting the Quran, and moving the upper parts of their bodies and their heads mechanically forward and backward. All were engrossed and absorbed by their learning, and none appeared to show interest in the veiled woman that was being guided across the compound.

When Mary was led back to be reunited with her girls, they were all relieved to see her. They told her they had all thought she would not come back to join them. She decided not to tell them what she had learnt concerning their being encouraged and convinced to become converted and to accept to get married to their captors. She decided to keep the secret to herself for the meantime. There was no need adding more anxiety to their current predicament. However, she felt obliged to give them an inkling of what lay ahead for all of them and was about to do this when the door to their room was opened and they were asked to go to the adjoining room where they usually ate. One of the girls saw with alarm that Mary had some wet spots on her shoulders. When she touched the spots, she saw that it was blood, some of which had already dried on Mary's shoulder, forming some reddish-brownish clot. She screamed. The other girls surrounded her, and all started weeping, loudly. The men who were supervising them shouted at them and ordered them to be quiet. They both brought out their *bulalas* which they used to flog the group indiscriminately. This led to more weeping. The pandemonium in the room did not seem to have been heard by the *Almajiris* who continued reciting the Quran loudly nearby. It was when one of the men took out a long knife that the girls, petrified, stopped weeping. A few of them continued sobbing quietly. They were all ordered back into their room and were told they would go hungry and not eat until they stopped crying.

Once the door was closed, Mary told them that she had been flogged because she had asked lots of questions which the *maigida*, whom she believed must be someone quite educated, had thought were rude and disrespectful. She told the girls she had asked why they were being detained. The *maigida* had told her he had plans for all of them and that he had contacted the government and was waiting for an appropriate response. He had not told her which government he had contacted, nor why he had contacted such government nor what response he was expecting. She refused to tell them she had been given a new name. She refused to tell them she had learnt they might be convinced or rather forced to marry their captors. She asked them all to stop crying. They needed to remain as healthy as possible, and this meant eating. One of them knocked at the door and asked that she be allowed to go to the toilet. On her way there, she informed the guards that they were ready to eat.

Mary counted the number of pieces of hair she had. She had twenty-one pieces the day one of the girls was told not to go back to the room after they had all had their evening meal. It was the girl who had been explaining all the meals to Mary. Mary panicked, a knot in her stomach tightened and her heartbeat ran faster. Was this the beginning of the end? She had a sense of foreboding that she would not see her student again. She felt guilty at not having warned the girls that they would be forced to marry some of the men that were holding them captive. Maybe she should have prepared them mentally for this eventuality. The girl did not complain at all. She informed the others that she had known all along that things would end up this way for her. If it was Allah's wish, so be it. She said she had been given to one of the men as an *"Amariya"* or new wife. She did not know who the man was but had been promised that she would be well taken care of and that the children she would bear would all be brought up according to what the Prophet Mohammed, peace be upon his name, had taught. If this was her destiny, there was no use fighting against it. Anyway, how could she fight? What power did she have? What tools were available to her except the belief that things would end up fine? Mary hugged her for a long moment and then the four other girls joined them in a tight embrace before they were disbanded. The girl was escorted out of the compound by a third turbaned man who had come into the dining room and whom none of the girls had ever seen before. The remaining four and Mary were ordered back into their room and the door locked.

She counted twenty-six pieces of hair when a grave incident occurred. The Ibo student had told Mary a few days earlier that she did not like the way one of the guards had peeped into the bathroom the last time she went for a shower. Mary asked her why she did not lock the bathroom from inside, as each one of them had agreed to do during the early days of their captivity. The girl said this was what she had always done but that she noticed that the guard had removed the key from the door and put it in one of his kaftan's pockets the last time she had gone for a wash and had stood at the half-open door staring at her all the while. Mary had advised her to be prudent.

Now Mary felt a new sense of foreboding. The Ibo girl had gone to the bathroom and was taking an unusually long time to get back to the room. She knocked on the door to request going to the toilet. There was only one of the habitually two guards behind the door, who informed her to control her bladder or her bowels for some time. She knew then that something was amiss. She invited the other girls and all four of them started banging on the door. They continued banging for several long minutes before the door to their room was finally open. The second guard had his white kaftan all stained with blood. Mary and the girls rushed to the bathroom. There, they saw the Ibo student lying on the wet floor, her legs widely spread, her throat slain, blood oozing slowly from it. They all screamed and attempted to run out through the small courtyard now empty of *Almajiris* but were restrained by three other guards that appeared out of nowhere. They were forced back into their room and could only hear the five guards take the Ibo girl's corpse out of the bathroom and out of the small courtyard.

Mary counted twenty-nine pieces of hair when she was invited once again by *maigida* for a chat. She was heartbroken and felt she had failed in her duty to protect her students. She had accepted to be the principal of a school and had accepted the responsibility that parents and the federal government had delegated to her, not only to ensure that children would acquire the knowledge and skills that would help them better in their future lives, but also that such pursuit of knowledge would be done under safe and secure conditions. She had failed in both missions. She had lost many of her students, but the loss of the two with whom she had shared her captivity was more than traumatic. Who knew in which family the first to depart was going to get married to? How dearly had the second suffered? She imagined her father, the military officer, leaving no stone unturned to try to claim back his daughter. How would he feel if and when he learnt she had been raped and murdered? Could she dare raise the question of the girl's brutal death with the *maigida*? Would she not be whipped again and maybe more violently than the last time, for showing disrespect? She would take the risk.

"Good afternoon, Aisha. I can see you have stopped losing weight. What happened to one of your students is quite unfortunate. She spent her time trying to seduce one of my men. I am told she was not only behaving like a *karuwa*, showing shamelessly her body to the guards each time she went to take a bath, but also sang Christian songs to the hearing of my men. What happened to her was thus a logical result of her immoral and very non-Islamic code of conduct in my house. This should be a warning to you all. I hope you have learnt your lesson, Aisha," the man began.

"My name is not Aisha," Mary dared respond, expecting a whip to fly towards her at any moment.

"You appear not to have learnt your lesson. You are showing me disrespect once more. I have asked my men to be indulgent with you. I have told them that the loss of your student and the tears you have shed will blind you and make you say things you don't mean or lead you to behave childishly. Anyway, I wanted to tell you that I have made contact with the Federal and State governments. They now know what to do if they place high value on your lives," the man continued.

"I am not showing you disrespect. Access to speech and the right to say what one feels is respected everywhere I can think of. When children ask questions, this does not mean they are being disrespectful. A child who keeps quiet when he or she wants to know what is happening around him or her will grow up not being able to understand himself or herself. It is the father and mother who name the child. My name is not Aisha. I am who I am and not who you want me to be. Whipping me to death will not change who I know I am. You seem to have plans for us and for our future. Those plans I do not know. I do not know what you have asked the governments to do for you, but I am prepared to face what will become of me and of us. This I will do as myself, as who I am and as who I will always be, even if today I'm in captivity," Mary responded.

"*Dogon turanchi*! I have begun to know you a little. You are Aisha and Aisha you will remain as long as you are in my compound. I'm very benevolent because if I had listened to some of my men, you would have been given away as a slave a long time ago. You are not as young as the others whom my men can accept as wives. So, the only option is for you to work. Try not to make me run out of patience," the man warned.

"If I become a slave, I will remain who I am. It is the one who enslaves another who does not know who he is. It is not by subjecting another to your whims that you are a man. As a slave, my life remains mine, even if I'm forced to do things that I do not choose to do. The life of a slave master must be very terrible to live. It is not a life I would like to live. You are speaking to me as if you had the power of life and death over me. You are asking me to thank you for your benevolence because you have very generously asked your men not to inflict any more physical harm on me. What you have not understood is that my mind cannot be so easily destroyed and that it thinks. My thinking will always be my thinking. My beliefs will always be my beliefs. Your life, which apparently is based on your belief in your power to enslave or not to enslave another, in your power to inflict bodily harm or not on another, in your power to obtain obedience through threats to another, is not a life I would want to live. Your life is not mine and I'm glad about that. The name you have given me is not mine, and I'm glad about that," Mary explained.

The man was speechless for some time. Mary expected him at any moment to give a signal to his men for the whipping to begin. This did not happen. The man was lost in deep thoughts. Then he spoke in a very cold voice.

"You will no longer stay with your girls. You will be transferred to another room. I do not want you to pollute the minds of the three other girls with you with such childishness."

Mary woke up with a start. It was dark in the room in which she now slept. It was still and quiet, but Mary sensed she was not alone. Then she smelt the perfume. Her stomach twinged and her heartbeat ran very fast. Before she could utter a word, she was violently held to the floor on which she slept and quickly gagged. She tried to struggle but to no avail. She thought of Owobi and Clement and bit her lips strongly behind the gag. She tasted blood, swallowed it and began crying quietly.

3

It was a Saturday night and Clement was in a very discreet social club in Ojuelegba, a very busy and popular neighbourhood in Surulere in Lagos, the bustling economic capital city of Nigeria. The club was discreet and known only to a very limited circle of people. There was a stage in which a man, dressed in tight-fitting blue dress and a white wig, was singing joyfully. About fifty other men, some dressed in drag outfits, were listening, nodding their heads, and cheering. Some were standing but most of them were seated around medium-sized rectangular tables covered in rainbow-coloured pieces of cloth. Clement was among those seating. He was at a table with four others. There was a glass in front of each one of them. Everyone at the table had his glass filled with red wine, except Clement, whose glass contained still water. They were all excitedly expressing their agreement with the singer who was chanting a song entitled 'Wayo man'. The song was well-known, and everyone tried to sing along with the singer. The lyrics went like this:

Wayo man think say he sabi
Pass every naija man or woman
Wayo man think say
Na only him get brain

Wetin wayo man no sabi
Na say all his wayo

Everyone dey yab about
And dey laugh am
Because na him no get brain at all at all

Wayo university don
Wan trade marks for sex
Wetin wayo don no sabi
Na say all them girls dey laugh am
Because he no get shame and brain at all at all

Wayo policeman
Wey dey ask you for dash
Because you no get vehicle particulars
Wetin he no sabi na say
Na him be original sufferhead
You wey he wan arrest
Better pass am well well
Because you dey mind you own business
And no bring palava to another man pickin at all at all

Wayo husband
Wey no give money to Mama Bomboy
To go buy crayfish put inside soup
But wey dey go eat ogbono soup
And drink champagne for another house
Wey dey play rich sugar Daddy for young Baby
Wetin wayo husband no sabi
Na say the day of judgement go soon come
And his punishment
Go bring am original wahala

Wayo pastor
Wey de preach make we all respect
The ten commandments
But wey don commit plenty adultery
With pickins left, right and centre
Wey don buy plenty Mercedes S.E.L
With church money
Wetin wayo pastor no sabi na say
God dey see am and dey vex well well
When pastor go receive fire and brimstone
Na then he go sabi
Say he no get brain at all at all

Wayo Governor
See as he don bellyful
Teacher salary he no wan pay
Medicine for government hospital he no wan buy
But plenty buildings for Victoria Island he don build
Plenty bank accounts for Oyibo land he don open
Wayo Governor don chop all the money
And he don leave common man suffer austerity
Wetin wayo Governor no sabi na say
Na him be jaguda
Na him be sufferhead
Because the person wey decide to steal
No get brain at all at all

Wayo man think say he sabi
Pass every naija man or woman
Wayo man think say
Na only him get brain

Wetin wayo man no sabi
Na say all him wayo
Every one dey yab about
And dey laugh am
Because na him no get brain at all at all

Clement sang with the others around his table. Among these was Tijjani, his flatmate. Tijjani was from Bauchi in the northern part of the country and had chosen to settle in Lagos, where he could live his life without the stress of being stoned to death in his home State. Bauchi, like most States in the north, sentenced those found guilty of same-sex offences to the death penalty. The usual means chosen to apply such a sentence was public lapidation and stoning. Most other States in Nigeria were not any better in terms of openness to same-sex communities. In reality, given the strong evangelical movements in the southern part of Nigeria and support for Islamic law in the northern part of the country, same-sex and gay couples and organisations are criminalised almost everywhere in the country.

Clement had met Tijjani at the workplace, at the restaurant in the five-star Plush Hotel in Ikoyi where they were both employed. They had both been on the afternoon shift and had finished for the day. They were preparing to go to their respective flats. They had started chatting and had hit it off immediately. A few weeks later, they had both discovered that they had chosen to come to Lagos for almost the same reasons: live freely without the finger-pointing under which they were sure to suffocate if they remained in their respective regions. Tijjani had told him that he was considered a Yan Daudu in Bauchi, someone effeminate, someone who is neither a man nor a woman, and that

89

this was frowned upon not only by his immediate family, but also by the society at large. Clement learnt that the Yan Daudu were associated with the Bori cult in Hausaland, a cult that tried to preach some form of resistance and women empowerment. Tijjani told him he had decided to leave Bauchi because he knew that there, he was not protected by the law. He could not, for example, go for HIV counselling. Any public display of same-sex relationship was met by public stoning and lapidation. He felt Lagos would provide him with the right environment to be who he was and not always look behind him to see if a Hisbah policeman was not tailing him. There would be no mob justice in Lagos, he believed.

Clement had listened very attentively to him as he had told his story. Tijjani's story resembled his. Sitting now in the club listening to the cheering crowd, his thoughts flew back to his own story.

His decision to leave the village had been spontaneously and warmly accepted only by his sister, Mary Oyije. He had wanted to have his father's approval, but when he had announced his intention to depart for Lagos where he would look for admission into a Catering Institute in order to be trained in cooking, his father had remained very silent. He had not known how to read the silence. He had asked Mary what she had thought of their father's silence and Mary had told him that such silence did not mean Papa was not happy that his son was going to look for work in Lagos. Clement had had a different reading and feeling. He had imagined that his father was ashamed of him, ashamed of the choice made by his son to devote his working life to a job he personally qualified as unmanly, cooking.

Clement liked cooking. As a child, he was always trying to

help his mother, who spent the whole day trying to prepare what the older men, his father and some of his uncles who were always around, would eat in the evening. The evening meal was the most important. It was the only period the family was reunited, when the men had come from the farms and the women from the market. Preparations for the evening meals began quite early. This was because there were many tasks to perform depending on what was to be prepared. If rice was on the menu, it was imperative to spread the rice on a large tray as early as possible so as to spend hours and hours removing small pebbles and grains of sand from it to avoid damages to the teeth when chewing. It was imperative to go to the bush to collect the wood that would be needed to prepare the fire for the cooking. The dry melon seeds needed to be ground well ahead using the traditional stone grinder, the crayfish ground using the wooden mortar and water obtained well ahead from the Igbilede stream. Several trips to the stream were usually necessary.

Clement liked watching his mother tend to the family. He felt that the mother was the central actor in the running of the family, because she gave and spent her time giving. It was to her that the responsibility of feeding and nourishing fell. When the older men congratulated his mother for how delicious the dry okra soup was, Clement somehow felt that such congratulations extended to him because he had had a share in its preparation. When he got older, he volunteered to pound the yam in the mortar each time there was a meal of pounded yam to be served. He always felt proud when the older men announced that the yam was well pounded and that there were no lumps of boiled yam hiding in the dough that was served. He became a pounded yam specialist and was happy when his mother asked for his advice on what type of yam to boil depending on whether the yam would be served pounded, fried, or just boiled. His choices were always accepted by his mother.

Clement adored his mother. He felt sorry for her. He saw that she was always working round the clock preparing meals, while the menfolk, who of course went to the farm, waited to be served with hardly a word of thanks. He adored his mother but feared his father. He would have liked to tell his father to be gentler with his mother, but he never dared to. What argument would he give? Then, Mary was born. Though she was three years younger than he was, she very quickly became someone who spoke her mind when she was displeased. Their mother sometimes joked that Mary should have been the first child, the boy, and Clement, the second child, the girl. Clement admired his sister, her drive, her strength and her fearlessness. He saw that his father also admired her. Did he wish she was him and he her?

The first night it happened to him, he thought it was an accident. When he had woken up in the morning, he saw that the wrapper he had worn to go to sleep with was very wet and exuded a strong urine odour. It was his sister who took out the mat on which they both slept, washed it and hung it out to dry in the sun. She told him not to worry. When the accident repeated itself over the following days, she had advised him to force himself to urinate before going to bed and afterwards to use a string to tie his penis once lying down. The pressure on his bladder would force him to wake up from his deep slumber and to go out to ease himself at night. He was happy his sister was a strong ally. He was happy that the womenfolk understood him.

His choice to go into the catering profession was not without difficulties. He would have to look for a catering school in Lagos and would have to find a way to pay the tuition fees. He would have to look for an appropriate accommodation. He would have to find a way to feed himself.

He had got a job as a houseboy in the home of a rich man from his village who was living in Adeniran Ogunsanya Street in Surulere. He had been given accommodation in a big container that had been transformed into the boys' quarter, close to the main three-bedroom house. He recollected having surprised the housemaster when he had informed the man that in addition to cleaning the house, doing the laundry, and doing the washing up in the kitchen, he could also cook for the family if Madame was tired or busy. The first meal he had prepared for the family was a plate of jollof rice. He had used Uncle Ben's long parboiled rice which he had seasoned with curry powder and dried thyme and served with *dodo,* fried ripe plantain, and fried chicken. The housemaster had been very impressed and had told Clement that he was gifted in cooking. Clement had then informed him of his ambition, and his need to consolidate his culinary skills in a catering institute. The housemaster had said he was prepared to give Clement some hours off every day if he obtained admission into one of the many culinary institutes available in Surulere. He had recommended the Three-Course-Meal Culinary Academy close to the national stadium. This was where Clement's culinary grooming had taken place.

The first question he had been asked when he met the Director of the Three-Course-Meal Academy was if he was someone patient. He had been taken aback by such a direct question. When he had responded that he was very patient, the Director had broken into a smile and had told him, "You are in the right place and neighbourhood because Surulere in Yoruba means 'Patience is rewarding'."

Clement had chosen a six-month program. He had opted for the formula without accommodation because he had decided to

93

attend classes in the afternoon, from twelve noon to seven p.m., while doing his houseboy job in the morning and in the evening until nine p.m. He therefore only had to pay for tuition. The first month had been very tiring but Clement had weathered the storm and gotten used to the rhythm. The course outline was vast. First, he learnt about kitchen fundamentals or how to behave in a kitchen. Focus was placed on health, hygiene, and safety issues. Then there were lots of lessons on cooking skills with different questions such as pan searing, glazing, sauteing, poaching, boiling, simmering, braising and many others dissected. A third part of the course concerned how to manage food stocks. A fourth related to plating and presentations.

Clement was like a sponge. He absorbed all he learnt. He learnt how to prepare continental cuisine, especially Italian, French, Caribbean, Indian and Chinese cuisine. He learnt different African culinary traditions, learnt how to prepare a large variety of African dishes and how to blend different ingredients to produce mouth-watering meals. He took courses in making dessert as well as in boulangerie and bread-making techniques.

Three months after he had started his program, he offered to prepare a three-meal course for his housemaster one Saturday. He asked the housemaster what type of meal he and his family wished to have. They said they wanted something exclusively continental but from different parts of the world. Clement had offered them a starter from Indian cuisine, the chicken pakora, golden chicken nuggets. He was happy to see how what he placed on the dining table was gobbled in the twinkle of an eye. Everyone around the table said this was a delicious six-star starter. For the main dish, Clement had offered them a Jamaican delicacy, curry goat served with rice, beans, and plantain. What impressed those around the dining table was the big mouth-watering flavours and the succulent texture of the goat meat which Clement had slow-cooked with turmeric, thyme, and curry powder. For dessert, Clement announced that the family was going to land now in Italy. He offered them some Tiramisu, which he had made with some biscuits and rich cream made with mascarpone, cheese, eggs, and sugar. He avoided adding any liquor, though he had been told at the Academy that this gave added flavour to the preparation. The housemaster congratulated Clement and asked him not to hesitate to come to him for any help or assistance he might need when he completed his course.

Clement was not as happy as he wanted to be because he would have wished his father was there with him to witness how his cooking was making others happy. He would have liked his father to have made the statement his housemaster had just made.

During his fourth month in the Academy, Clement decided to take part in a culinary competition. The students were required to prepare one of three dishes, either a starter, a main course, or a dessert. Three prizes would be given, one for each of the meals being prepared. Each winner would be offered an internship with the Academy, in addition to a monetary prize of two hundred thousand nairas. The jury would be composed of professionals from some of the best hotels and restaurants in Lagos and especially the luxury hotels and restaurants in Ikoyi and Victoria Island. The key yardsticks that members of the jury would use to judge included the presentation, the form, the flavour, and the taste.

Clement did not have a lot of money. So, he had decided to make a dessert but to keep it very simple. He decided that he would make a cake using local Nigerian fruit: some bananas, a pineapple, some mangos, and a pawpaw. He first made the dough with some flour, butter, sugar, vanilla sugar, and eggs. Then he added some yeast, and afterwards, some bananas which had been crushed and blended into a creamy liquid paste. Next, he added small rectangular pieces of peeled ripe mangos and pineapples and a tablespoonful of amber-coloured Negrita rum to give the whole dessert a particularly mouth-watering flavour. He cooked the cake in the oven for about an hour, which he allowed to cool before cutting it into slices which he served on a large white and blue plate. The slices, arranged in the middle of the large plate, were all surrounded by medium-sized portions of peeled fresh ripe yellow pawpaw covered with grated coconut. Two tablespoons of cold mango jam were put next to one of the portions of peeled pawpaw.

Clement was very surprised that his cake was an immense success. He was offered two internships, one in the Academy and the other in the luxury five-star Plush Hotel in Ikoyi, whose chef had been part of the jury and who had been very impressed by how Clement had been able to marry simplicity and exquisiteness in his cooking. It was the Director of the Academy who advised him to take on the offer made by the luxury Hotel. Clement had accepted.

His housemaster had been very pleased. He had said he was sorry to see Clement leave his service but that he was proud and happy Clement had been able to achieve what he had come to Lagos for. Clement had thought of his father. He would have wanted his father to see how far he had come in Lagos. He would have wanted a word or two of pride and encouragement from him.

Clement had been well accepted during his internship at the Plush Hotel. He had hundreds of recipes to learn and memorise and he wasted no time trying to have all the most frequently ordered recipes at his fingertips. He had no social life, so most of his time was devoted to his job in the kitchen. Occasionally, he would go walking around Bar Beach. This was where armed robbers sentenced to the death penalty were killed by firing squad several years ago. The dates for the killings used to be announced long beforehand and Bar Beach was usually overcrowded when the date arrived. There was the story told of a famous armed robber, a man called Oyenusi, who had armed himself with many amulets that were supposed to prevent any of the bullets fired from attaining him. The story was told that on the day he was to face the firing squad, he had smiled and laughed when he was being tied to the pole to face death. He had requested the officer in charge of the firing squad to give him a few minutes to light a cigarette and finish it. The crowd had applauded when they saw the military officer putting a stick of cigarette in the condemned man's mouth, lighting it, and standing stoically in front of him as he puffed smoke into his face provocatively. Apparently, Oyenusi's amulets had worked, at least for some minutes, because he had been the last to die, needing several rounds of bullets before he finally took his last breath and slumped. Each time Clement walked on the beach and saw children playing excitedly and running helter-skelter, he could not stop thinking that this was where many bullet-ridden bodies had been untied from poles.

Apart from going to Bar Beach occasionally, Clement was all-work-and-no-play. He refused to go out, especially at night because he was afraid of Lagos. He did not have any knowledge of where to safely go to without facing the risk of being violently accosted, of being aggressed, of being the victim of pickpockets. Anyway, he had not come to Lagos for the morning, afternoon, or nightlife. So, he invested himself in his job in the kitchen and minded his business. After his internship, he was offered a permanent job in the hotel. He continued his workaholic life. Since he did not spend money on his social life, he was able to save considerably. He was thus able to send some money occasionally to his father and mother in the village. It wasn't that his father needed what he was sending to survive. His palm wine trade was highly profitable. However, it was normal and customary for children who were working outside the village to send money to their parents who remained in the village. It was a way of expressing their gratitude to parents who had taken care of them before they could fend for themselves. Clement had arranged with his sister to build a house with a corrugated iron sheet roof for their father in the village. It was unheard of for someone whose daughter was a principal in a federal college in a big city somewhere in the north to live and die in a hut with thatched roofs, like other parents who did not have educated children. Such a father would be the laughingstock of everyone in the village. People would say the father had raised very ungrateful children. Mary had consented to Clement's idea, and the house was almost completed.

Clement softened at the thought of his sister. He was glad he had her. He was glad of her strength and intelligence. He had told her to come and see him at his hotel in Lagos and she had promised that she would as soon as she could. She had told him that managing a school in the north by a woman was not always smooth sailing, but that she was capable of handling things. He had confidence in her. His social life changed when he met Tijjani.

It was Tijjani who opened Lagos for him. Tijjani guided him to know Lagos better. He started by showing Clement parts of

Ikoyi where the hotel in which they were working was located. Clement learnt that Ikoyi was, generally speaking, a high-rise neighbourhood with a high concentration of foreign expatriates working in Nigeria for multinationals and oil companies. Clement observed that most of the streets in Ikoyi were relatively clean, except in the Obalende quarter, which he observed was quite rowdy, noisy, and dirty.

Then Tijjani took him to visit Victoria Island, which he said was the entertainment centre of Lagos. Victoria Island was also home to many luxury hotels, including Eko Hotel, one of the most prestigious hotels in Lagos. Clement observed that there were many foreign Embassies and Consulates in Victoria Island. Tijjani also took Clement to visit Yaba, home to the Yabacon Valley, which like Silicon Valley in the USA, was home to a bevy of tech-centred ventures. They also visited the famous Yaba market in Tejuosho, which is directly opposite the Federal Psychiatric Hospital. Ikeja was also visited. Clement saw the Murtala Mohammed Domestic and International Airports. Tijjani took him to the Ikeja GRA, where Clement was impressed by the quiet and cleanliness of the streets. Tijjani told him they could not leave Ikeja without visiting two very important joints, like he called them. The first joint was the Kalakuta Museum on Allen Street, built in the home of and in honour of the famous afrobeat king, Fela Anikulapo Kuti. The second joint was the New Afrika Shrine, a nightclub opened by one of Fela Kuti's sons, where afrobeat lovers could converge to enjoy this brand of music. Clement told Tijjani he had never been to a nightclub before and wondered how he would feel if he ever went inside one. He said he would not feel safe and secure. It was then that Tijjani had informed him of the joint in Ojuelegba in Surulere, which was safe with a wonderful atmosphere.

Clement saw that all those sitting around the table were singing joyfully along with the man on stage. Some of those standing had started to dance. After the wayo-man song, a discussion ensued on the table about many topics. The problem of insecurity in the country and the increasing number of attacks by armed bandits was raised and discussed. Then someone said he had watched a very colourful gay pride in Berlin, Germany two days before and that he was still wondering about why same-sex couples were criminalised in Nigeria.

"It is only over there in Oyiboland that you can have gay prides. There, people are proud to be who and what they are, and they express such pride openly and no one throws stones at them or brings out the koboko to show them pepper. There, the dominant rule on how people live is: You do you, you are yourself, I do me, I am myself. Did you see the slogans they wrote in very colourful letters on wide and long white pieces of cloth? One of the slogans was 'Liberty, Freedom and The Right to Love'. It is not in this country that such an event can happen," he declared.

"We have not reached the level of tolerance and acceptance that they have reached, you know. Look at how someone from one tribe views another person from another tribe. Look at how a Muslim views a non-Muslim. Look at how men treat women. So how can you expect people in this country to accept two men wishing and willing to live together," one of them opined.

"Not all Oyibo countries are as free as we see on television. I know that in many of them, people like us have to be very quiet and discreet," a third person added.

"We have learnt to be quiet and discreet here too. But unlike in Oyiboland, we face the risk of being sent to prison for fourteen

100

years or stoned to death when we make the error of showing our true selves to others. Have you heard of someone like us being stoned to death in New York?" another questioned.

"As a matter of fact, not only are people like us accepted in Oyiboland, but they can even sue employers to court if they believe they have been discriminated against in their professional careers," someone else added.

"Are you serious," two of them wondered.

"Of course, I am," replied the person being questioned. "In many Oyibo countries, the State is required to protect the rights of everyone irrespective of their age, race, sex or sexual orientation. Our sexual orientation is something private and should not be judged publicly. The day the Nigerian State will accept to protect the rights of all its citizens, that day will never come, I can bet my life," he continued.

"You know, we are not the only people suffering. Our women sisters are in fact in deeper trouble than we are," one of them mentioned.

"Yes, I agree with you," another added. "Look at the more than three hundred girls abducted by Boko Haram in Borno State. Many of the top government officials who are rushing to NTA to express their sadness and their anger are only shedding crocodile tears. They are original wayo-men. It is not their daughters that have been kidnapped. None of them has any guilty conscience at not being able to protect the lives of citizens, even if these are girls. It is a real shame, I tell you."

"It is not only in Borno where Boko Haram has declared war on people, including girls, that women have a hard life. In many of our villages, in all the families, the man is always right, even when he is wrong when decisions are made and taken," someone else said.

"Yes, I agree. It is not easy being a girl or woman in Nigeria. And it is not easy for us to be ourselves in our country. Do we have to migrate to Oyiboland to be ourselves? Do we have to pretend we are not ourselves for others in our society to accept us? A zebra can never erase the stripes it has on its body, neither can a bat be taught to sit upright on a chair," someone concluded.

Clement's heart missed a beat and his stomach suddenly tightened. He felt as if someone had just poured very cold water on his body. He had seen the headlines in bold print on the front page of The Guardian newspaper in his chef's office. His chef had convened him to his office for an urgent matter and was sitting behind his table, staring intently at Clement. Clement's legs started trembling and some cold sweat started to form on his forehead. His chef was silent and had a sympathetic understanding look on his face. Clement was told to sit down in one of the chairs in front of the chef's table. He read what was written on the front page under the headline: School Principal and fifty students abducted at a Federal Girls' Unity College in Sokoto.

"Police have announced that about fifty students and the School Principal have been abducted from an all-girls Unity College in Sokoto in North-West Nigeria, the fourth mass kidnapping of students in the region in the last three months. According to the Police spokesperson, Inspector Abdullahi Adamu, police and army officers have launched a joint search-and-rescue operation around many of the dense forests in the region with a view to rescuing the kidnapped students. It is believed that the bandits came with pick-up vehicles and moved the students and their Principal to an unknown destination. Reliable police sources say the groups operate from forest hideouts and usually demand ransom. The kidnappings targeting schools have been on the rise recently and this has heightened fears for the security and welfare of students. The State government, through its Ministry of Internal Security and Home Affairs, not only denies having paid such ransoms before, but announces that this will never happen. However, very reliable intelligence sources tell us that governments usually pay such ransoms, something that incites armed bandits to continue the kidnapping business, which is becoming very lucrative. The Nigerian President has come under fire for the rising wave of insecurity in rural and urban areas in the country. He is yet to make any statement on the recent kidnappings."

Clement felt as if the floor under him had given way and he imagined himself sinking into a dark hot abyss. His chef handed him a second newspaper in which the father of one of the abducted girls, a Major in the army, was expressing himself.

"Yes, my daughter Ngozi is part of those missing from the school. I do not want to make any statement that will endanger her life and the life of her mates and her principal. I am appealing to those who have kidnapped them for clemency and humanity, in the name of God, the omnipotent and the omniscient. Please do not harm our daughters. I am appealing to the State Government and the Federal Government to do all they can and must do in order to rescue our children and to allow them to continue their learning under better and safer conditions."

The Chef handed Clement a third newspaper that carried the headline "Fifty girls and their Principal missing." Clement was able to read only the first paragraph: "About fifty girls and the School Principal in an all-Girls Unity college in Sokoto are unaccounted for after bandits raided their college last night. Security authorities are maintaining close contact with the staff and student population of the school and efforts are in top gear to track and find the missing girls and their principal. No one knows who the kidnappers are, but sources close to police investigators and military intelligence believe the kidnappers are probably a faction of the local branch of the Islamic Renaissance Movement, which wishes to purify Nigeria, dip the Quran in the Atlantic Ocean, and establish a Caliphate in Nigeria. The same intelligence sources indicate that this movement has very unlimited financial resources, most coming from undeclared donations from many wealthy businessmen and industrialists who agree with its agenda. Fears are being entertained that the spate of kidnappings will rise until the country's internal security apparatus is overhauled and closer cooperation between the various intelligence and security agencies permanently established."

Clement inhaled deeply and held his breath for many seconds. He was at a loss. A succession of several scenarios quickly appeared in his mind. In one of them, which made him shudder with fear, he imagined his sister tied to a pole, with several long-bearded bandits wearing long kaftans with their heads turbaned, gleefully shooting at her. In another, it was the blood curdling face of Mohammed Shekau, the infamous and blood-thirsty Boko Haram leader, which appeared. Apparently, he was pointing a finger at his sister, giving his men unimaginable orders. He could not help controlling his fright and he began to shiver and tremble.

"I knew immediately I read this that I should let you know," the chef said in a low voice.

"Thank you very much, sir. I do not know what to say or what to do," Clement answered, in a trembling voice.

"You have always spoken about your sister in the most laudatory terms that I understand how you feel at present. I'm not sure there's anything we can do at our individual level. We have to trust the government and its security agencies and hope that they deliver what they have promised, rescue your sister and her students," the chef advised.

"I have to go and speak to my father in the village. He will be very worried, as a matter of fact, much more worried than I am. My father and sister are like an inseparable pair, always on the same wavelength, with a bond that none other than them understand. I do not want him to learn about her disappearance from someone else but me," Clement announced.

"I'll speak to the hotel management. I'll convince them to give you a few days off," the chef announced. "You may take the day off today because I'm sure you have other things on your mind than preparing the orders of our hotel clients."

"Thank you, sir. I'll try to switch on the TV set at home and try to hear the latest news, if there is any. Thank you once again, sir," Clement responded.

When Tijjani arrived from the hotel, Clement was sitting with his face not far away from the television screen. He was watching and listening to the program "National Questions" on the Channel 5 network. The invited guest was Dr Ocheme. The anchor was introducing his guest:

"It is my pleasure to have with us today, Dr Ocheme, who is a political science professor at Ahmadu Bello University in Zaria. Prof, welcome to the studio. You were a top professor in an

105

American university before you decided to come back home. This is something very unusual because most Nigerian professors prefer to go abroad, where they think the grass is greener. Why did you leave the green grass to come to brown grass?"

"Thank you Chukwu for inviting me to your very popular and well-conceived program. I am happy to be with you and to be able to speak to the millions of viewers who I'm sure are in front of their screens. Well, in reality, I have not thought of my teaching profession in terms of green grass or brown grass. I have always wanted to be in a system where I am myself in front of my students and where I can say what is on my mind, teach the way I want to teach and try as much as possible to take part in changing mentalities. Where else but at home can one be oneself and say what is on one's mind?" Dr Ocheme replied.

"So, why haven't you chosen to remain in the academia? Why have you chosen to become a Senator, and to make matters difficult, to contest the same senate seat as the current Senate President, Chief Aje? Do you think you can beat an incumbent Senate President? Are you not somehow a kamikaze?" the anchor questioned.

"So many questions in one. I will try to answer them one after the other. Why have I not chosen to remain in the academia? When we academics say things and give advice, we are laughed at as being egg-headed, as living outside reality, as being too theoretical, as living in an ivory tower. When we decide to move out of the academia to try to apply what we teach, we are asked why we have abandoned our territory. Well, let me ask you and our viewers a simple question. Are you, are we all happy with what is happening at the moment in the country? We are an oil producing country, are we not? Where have all the billions and billions of naira that we hear of regularly in the news, gone? Let me tell you where: in the pockets of those who are governing us today and who in reality have been governing us for a long time. I am talking of the governing class, professional politicians, top military brass, key industrialists, who have been able to confiscate the State apparatus for their own selfish interests and who do not give a hook for the life of the common man, the toiling masses."

"So, you think you are strong enough to face who you call the governing class in an electoral battle?" the anchor continued.

"The battle one is sure of not winning is the one that one is afraid of waging," Dr Ocheme responded.

"Can you really see yourself, a novice in politics, beating Chief Aje, the Senate President, decorated a few years ago with the honour of Commander of the Federal Republic, CFR?" the anchor questioned.

"No one thought I would obtain a professorship in the reputed American university where I was for more than five years. It is not because a mountain is high that one should be afraid of climbing it. My people in the village say that if you are cold, you should try to light a fire or get closer to one that is already lit. So, I think that a number of things need to change in Nigeria, which is why I am trying to become a Senator," Dr Ocheme replied.

"Could you give us some examples of the things that need to change or be changed," the anchor continued.

"Well, the list is very long, because the governing class, represented by people like Chief Aje, has left our country in total ruins. Look for example at the question of basic safety and security. The right to life, the right to public safety and security, the right to live and walk freely anywhere and anytime without fear and apprehension is fundamental and inalienable. Has this

107

right been given to all Nigerians irrespective of their stations, sex, religion, and social and economic resources? The answer is a clear and unequivocal 'No'. The rich live in barricaded homes and have police escorts when they wish to go to play golf in members-only clubs. The common man, who is called the talakawa among the Hausa, does not have the luxury of having police protection. On the contrary, when he has to deal with the police, he knows he is in trouble. Our country is rich with tapped and untapped resources. But how many of us can comfortably eat three square meals a day? Very few, I must confess. I know that many of my students skip breakfast because they can't afford to buy cereals or milk. How do you want them to be able to learn correctly on empty stomachs? No, something has to change, and such a change means a change of guards because we cannot ask those who have put our country into trouble to be the people we should expect to lead us out of the same trouble," Dr Ocheme argued.

"I'll ask you the question once more. Can you see yourself, a novice in politics, beating an incumbent, Chief Aje?" the anchor wondered.

"Well, why can't I beat him? What does he have that I don't?" Dr Ocheme asked.

"What does he have that you don't? Many things. First, he has a long experience in matters of public management. Secondly, he is in the ruling political party. Thirdly, he is immensely rich, and we all know that Nigerian politics costs lots of money. Fourthly, he is a Chief, which means that he is well appreciated by your community. Do you want me to go on?" the anchor responded.

"He started his political career one day like me. Yes, he has money, lots of money. But are you not surprised that he is still actively engaged in the management of his oil company while being paid his huge monthly salary by taxpayers? This state of affairs does not happen in any developed democracy, you know. It is a question of ethics. You work either in the private sector or in the public sector. You do not use your position in the public sector to facilitate your accumulation of monetary gains in the private sector. The developed world calls us a banana republic because of this and other issues with the way we organise our democracy," Dr Ocheme continued.

"When you speak about ethics, what do you mean exactly?" the anchor enquired.

"Well, in my opinion, ethics and politics must go together. When you decide to contest an election, what should govern you should not be what you can gain from your elected mandate, but what you can give to those who elected you. I think it was John F Kennedy, a famous American President, who said we should not think of what our country can do for us but rather what we can do for our country. So, I think honesty should be a key element in how publicly elected officials should go about their business. This does not seem to be the case with our current government. May I remind you that Chief Aje was in another political party for several years without succeeding in getting elected. He decided to change from that party to the governing party whose main ideology was the exact opposite of the party he had vigorously defended and for which he was a staunch spokesman before. So, how can you explain this about-turn? The only explanation is that Chief Aje is running for office not to defend his ideas, but to use this office to further his accumulation of wealth. This is clear for everyone to see. My students have no difficulty at all in seeing this," Dr Ocheme explained.

"You spoke about security, safety, insecurity and absence of police protection. What solutions do you suggest, or can you offer to contain the increasing spate of kidnappings in the country?" the anchor asked.

"The problem of insecurity is there because government has failed. Why do you think there has been an increase in the number and frequency of such kidnappings? It is because those who kidnap know that government is weak and unable to protect the common man. Look at the schools that are being targeted. Whose children attend them, in your opinion? I'll answer that question. It is not the children of top government officials, who are at school abroad or in private well-secured institutions here in the country. It is not Chief Aje's children who are there. It is rather the children of ordinary Nigerians, whose lives do not have any value, neither for the kidnappers nor for the government. This is something I'd like to change. I will place high value on the lives of all Nigerians," Dr Ocheme continued.

"How will you make Nigerians better trust the Police? How will you make the Police and other security forces more efficient and better prepared to contain the increasing rate of crimes, kidnappings and killings?" the anchor enquired.

"Well, the only solution is to have a cultural revolution, a revolution by the common man, by the Nigerian lumpen proletariat," Dr Ocheme opined.

"A cultural revolution? Are you serious, Prof? Can you please explain yourself in plain ordinary English so that our viewers can understand you more easily?" the anchor requested.

"My thinking is very simple. We need to reverse the power relations that exist currently in our country. Today, the Police is powerful compared to the ordinary man because the Police thinks it can arrest the common man anytime it wishes to. The Police can stop you on the road for no other reason than the fact that they are wearing a uniform and that this gives them a right to harass the common man anytime and anywhere. We should reverse the situation so that it is the Police who fear the common man. What this means is that the Police Commissioner in every State, and the Chief Police Officer in every Local Government Headquarter should become answerable to the common man, in other words become directly elected by the people, as Sheriffs are in the United States of America. The people should have the power to dismiss these key Police officers if they are not satisfied with the way their men and women are behaving towards the public. The people should thus be empowered to report the slightest occurrence of Police harassment to these key officers, so that the black sheep in the Police force can be rooted out before they do further harm. The relation of power between the governing class and the ordinary man should also be reversed. The governing class should be made aware of the fact that sovereignty belongs to those who have elected them and that these are the ones who can decide their fate. The wanton display of ill-acquired wealth by the governing class should be prohibited and a no-nonsense anti-corruption tribunal set up to try and sanction any public official proven to be living well above his or her official salary. The anti-corruption tribunal should include a jury of common men, chosen randomly from the voting list in different States. Members of the governing class will then know that they may face being sanctioned by the common man if the latter believes they have misused public trust for their personal and private gains. The relations of power will thus be reversed to the advantage of the common man," Dr Ocheme digressed.

"Very interesting. Very interesting indeed. Can you give us an example of a country where such a system works?" the anchor demanded.

111

"Do we have to copy from somewhere else? Are we not mature enough to be innovative?" Dr Ocheme asked.

"So, you want us to construct something that has never been tried elsewhere before. How do you know if the common men, as you call them, are prepared in Nigeria to be leaders rather than followers?" the anchor questioned.

"Do not underestimate the intelligence of the common man. Have you listened to market women engage in discussions on why government is doing nothing to prohibit the hoarding of basic foodstuff by distributors, most of who are members of the ruling political party? Very intelligent discussions, I must tell you. Have you listened to how car mechanics, who we think are uncouth and illiterate, wonder how we have frequent scarcity of oil in an oil producing country like Nigeria, in addition to why the price of petrol is very high? Very intelligent thinking, there too, I tell you. So, do not think that only those who have gone to school and are in top positions in government are the most intelligent," Dr Ocheme explained.

"Talking about the Police. So, you think we should have the equivalent of elected Sheriffs in Nigeria. How do you ensure that it is not people who are rich and are able to buy votes that will either become top-ranking Police officers or put their stooges in such positions?" the anchor wanted to know.

"A lot of safeguards need to be established to ensure the probity of those who wish to become local and State Police Chiefs. Such safeguards need to be examined in detail using a cost-benefit framework, but I'm sure giving power to the people will go a very long way to solving the ills of our society today," Dr Ocheme continued.

"There are so many other questions I'd like to discuss with you, but unfortunately, we have come to the end of our program.

Maybe the next time we see each other, the revolution you have talked about will have happened, the Police will be better equipped to protect common men and the frequency of crimes and high insecurity minimised. It has been interesting talking to you, Prof. Good luck in your contest against Chief Aje," the anchor concluded.

"Thank you. Long live the common man!" Dr Ocheme ended.

"I heard about your sister, Clement. Would you like me to go with you to see your father in the village?" Tijjani asked.

"It is not advisable. He would not understand things and the news I'm going to give him is already bad enough for him to digest. In addition, when I left the village, we were not really on good terms or on the same wavelength. I'd like to face him alone and see if we can iron out our differences without someone outside the family being a witness. I'm sorry, but I have to go and face my father alone," Clement explained.

"That's okay with me. However, there is good hope that your sister will be rescued. I think those who kidnapped her and her students are doing this for money. I'm sure they know that the government will pay any ransom they demand. This has happened in the very recent past. I'm also told that there are a few Islamic humanitarian organisations in the north that are waging a war against movements that engage in kidnappings and who at the same time argue that they are Islamic movements. These organisations have been very helpful in the past in the rescue of abducted people. I trust they will be helpful this time around," Tijjani added.

"My father does not have the money to pay any ransom. Neither do I. Suppose the government does not respond favourably to the demands made by the kidnappers. Who knows what such kidnappers may do, in retaliation?" Clement wondered.

"What we can do at the moment is hope for the better. I'm not sure the government would want the general public to think it does not value the lives of its citizens. Dr Ocheme is a politician, and he is trying to oppose a top-ranking member of the government. So, it is normal for him to paint a very bad picture of the government he is trying to unseat. I'm very sure that at this moment that we are speaking, the government is trying all within its powers to get into contact with the abductors. Things will work out, I think. Or at least I hope, but I'm sure the government is not sitting idle, arms akimbo, doing nothing," Tijjani said.

"So, we'll have to wait for government to raise its fingers to help. I think I will have to go and ask for help somewhere. The Senate President comes from my place. Though Dr Ocheme, who also comes from my place, is insulting him and asking questions about his probity, I will have to find a way to contact him to see if he can help," Clement remarked.

"Let's hope he will agree it is his business to help. You know how these big *ogas* behave. Unless they think or know they can derive some benefit from helping you, most remain inaccessible to those of us they do not know, to those of us who are part of the common men, as Dr Ocheme has rightly mentioned," Tijjani continued.

"I think Chief Aje knows me, or at least my family. I know he has been trying to buy my father's palm tree plantation for some time," Clement added.

"Maybe your father should sell the plantation so that he can have the money to pay the ransom, don't you think so?" Tijjani advised.

"My father's plantation is sacred, and he has said it would be obtained only over his dead body. This is what I learnt from my sister. My sister is on very good terms with one of Chief Aje's sons who works in an oil company with its main office in the Local Government Headquarters which is not far from my village. I will have to go and see him after I have met my father in the village and beg him to ask his father in Abuja to come to our aid," Clement announced.

"Is Chief Aje's son trustworthy?" Tijjani asked.

"What do you mean, trustworthy?" Clement wondered.

"I mean, are you sure if he tells you he will contact his father on your behalf that he will do so? He might tell you he'll help just to get you off his neck, you know," Tijjani explained.

"Well, it's a risk I have to take. I do not have any other option. If I remember correctly, there is a saying in my village that the wind helps those who do not have a cutlass to find and obtain dry branches of wood needed for the fire. My people in the village also say that the antelope does not hesitate to swim across the river to the other bank to search for fodder, the risk of crocodiles lurking around notwithstanding. I will try to contact Chief Aje's son. If I don't, I will not know if they can help or not. If they can't help, at least I will have tried to ask them to do this. If they can, which I earnestly wish, my effort will not have been fruitless. My people say that the person who wishes to produce some charcoal should not be afraid of smoke getting into his eyes. You cannot be able to do something unless you try first to do it," Clement responded.

"Yes, I understand, but it is better to cultivate what you eat, if you can, rather than always depend on buying them. In other words, it is better not to depend on others, if you can avoid this," Tijjani continued.

"If you can avoid it, as you have just said. I'm in a position where I need the help of someone who knows my family and who occupies a very high-ranking position in Abuja. So, I can't avoid going to him for help. If the tree shade does not get to the goat, it is the goat that advances towards it for solace," Clement opined.

"Okay, I agree with you. The hen that is afraid to go out during a drizzle will not have big insects to eat," Tijjani concluded.

The journey home was long. It lasted more than eighteen hours. Clement had to wake up quite early in the morning to take a bus at Okota Road close to the Cele flyover bridge to Enugu. The bus was part of a fleet of luxury buses that linked Lagos to many other Nigerian cities including Enugu. Clement had bought five large loaves of bread and five packets of roll bread the evening before to give to some of his relatives in the village. It was unthinkable for him to arrive at the village empty-handed, even if the circumstances of his trip to the village were tragical. He would not wait for people to ask him if he had brought any Lagos bread before he distributed his present to members of his family. The brand he had brought was called King's Bake, a household name in Lagos in the sector of bread making and confectionary. Clement would have liked to go to the village with a sample of his cakes, but he was in no mood to do any cooking. In addition, he wondered if those in the village would appreciate fine cuisine. So, he opted for what he knew would be appreciated by those in the village, Lagos bread. He would tell those in the village that the loaves of King's Bread he was offering them could only be found in supermarkets, in other words, that they were not accessible to everyone.

Two things worried Clement. One of them was what the

villagers would think of him, coming home without a car, and preferably an air-conditioned car, even if this was a Tokumbo, an imported used car. Ownership of a car was judged as a mark of success in the village. Someone who was working in Lagos was supposed to be successful in life. Someone successful in life was supposed to own a car. So, arriving in the village in a bush taxi bus or taxi motorbike would be laughed at, especially by the many who had doubted right from the beginning his choice to go and do a woman's job, cook for others. He decided not to pay attention to any backbiting that may occur. He was not living his life to please others. He would not try to live above his means only to be appreciated by others. His choice to leave the village and go to Lagos had been made precisely because he wanted to be himself and be his own master as much as possible.

The second thing that worried Clement was how the contact with his father was going to work out. He was apprehensive, very apprehensive. He was anxious, first because he did not know how his father was going to react to seeing him and how he was going to react to his father's reaction. If his father gave him a warm reception, he would certainly be surprised but would be extremely happy. If his father gave him a rather cold welcome, something he feared was the most likely scenario, he was trying to prepare himself mentally to face such a prospect. He would try to avoid getting into any debate or argument with him and would inform him that he was there in the village because he felt he had to inform his father about the abduction of his daughter, which brought Clement to the second reason why he was worried. How would his father take the news about the disappearance of his daughter? Would he cry, as he himself had done after leaving his chef's office, before going to the flat he shared with Tijjani? Would he show any emotion? If so, what type of emotion would he show? Anger? Sadness? Hatred? His earnest wish was that his father would receive the news calmly and agree with him that they should contact Chief Aje and ask for his help. This might be an uphill task because Mary had told him that the rapport between Chief Aje and his father was anything but warm and cordial. Papa will have to learn to put his pride aside, he told himself. He hoped all would be fine when he met his father. A song he had been mumbling to himself for a long time surfaced on his mind. He tried to mumble it quietly as the bus was speeding along the A121 Expressway to Benin City, from where it would pass through Asaba before finally reaching Enugu.

I'm not a nobody
I'm not just anybody
I am somebody
I have a name, your name, Papa
I am made of flesh and blood
Your blood, Papa
So, why can't you see me, Papa?

I am not a nobody
I'm not just anybody
I am somebody
Your direct descendant, Papa
Your life will continue through me
This I accept and like
So, why can't you hear me, Papa?

I'm not you
And you are not me
I look like you, Papa

But do not resemble you, Papa
In how I have chosen to live
And what type of man I am
Or wish to be

Listen to what I say, Papa
See what I do, Papa
See who I am, Papa
A small nod from you
A slight smile on your face
A single word of encouragement
And my joy will be without bounds

Have I brought shame on you, Papa?
No, not at all, because no crime have I committed
Have I any disrespect shown to you, Papa?
No, not at all, because that is not how you brought me up
Have I failed my life in your mind, Papa?
Have others, strangers, not my success cheered?
So, why can't you see and hear me, Papa?

Where do you want me to be
But where I'm fine, Papa?
What do you want me to do
But what I'm good at, Papa?
Who do you want me to become
But who I must be, Papa?
So, why can't you see and hear me, Papa?

I'm not a nobody
I'm not just anybody

I am somebody
I have a name, your name, Papa
I am made of flesh and blood
Your blood, Papa
So, why can't you see me, Papa?
So, why can't you hear me, Papa?

Clement dozed off in the luxury bus which was quite hot and humid. The driver had announced earlier on that the air conditioner had broken down, but he warned that the side windows should not be opened fully, so as to avoid the permanent rush of wind that would penetrate the bus from the outside and send many light objects in the bus flying dangerously and eventually, hurting some passengers. Most of the passengers had dozed off like him. He was sitting next to a man who was far younger than him. They had chatted for a while. The man was an Ibo trader who said he commuted regularly between a city called Nnewi and Lagos. He told Clement he had to pass through Enugu each time, because he had some suppliers in that city, with whom he was in regular contact. Clement learnt that the man traded in an assortment of goods, but principally in the sale of spare parts of a large variety of cars imported to Nigeria, including Toyota, Renault, Mercedes Benz, Peugeot, Datsun, Volkswagen, and Honda. He made fortnightly trips to and from Enugu because he said the demand for motor spare parts was insatiable in Lagos. When he learnt that Clement was working in the restaurant of a top-ranking hotel in Ikoyi, he was very impressed. He jokingly said that the only meal he knew how to prepare was to soak some *garri* in cold water, add some sugar and the meal was ready. Clement told him that he had had to attend a culinary establishment in order to learn what he knew.

His bus mate asked him where he was going. When he learnt that he was going to go beyond Enugu to Otukpo, he told Clement that he needed to be patient in any vehicle he would take from Enugu to Otukpo. Clement was warned that he might be stuck in the traffic for hours on end if the vehicle chose to go through the Ninth Mile, rather than avoid this very busy part of the road linking Enugu and Otukpo. The Ninth Mile was where all the traffic between the northern and south-eastern parts of Nigeria passed through. Several bypasses existed to avoid the gridlock in the Ninth Mile, but many commercial vehicles still chose to pass through it because it had lots of shops and bukaterias where affordable meals were available for passengers. Clement thanked him for the information but added that he did not think he could decide on which itinerary the conductor of the vehicle that he would board to go to Otukpo from Enugu should take.

Clement slept in a hotel close to where the terminal station of the luxury bus was located, along Market Road in Enugu. He decided not to travel by night between Enugu and Otukpo, because there had been many incidents of vehicles being attacked by armed bandits after sunset along many Nigerian roads, and Clement chose not to take the risk of being a victim during such a crucial trip. The next morning, he took a Peugeot 504 Station Wagon taxi to go to Otukpo. The driver avoided the Ninth Mile gridlock.

The journey to Otukpo was however not as smooth as that from Lagos to Enugu had been. First, the road here was badly maintained, with potholes rendering the badly tarred road almost unmotorable. And then, there was the weather. The sky was dark with rain sodden clouds, and it opened for long hours to release very heavy droplets of rain to the ground. Clement was angry at no one in particular, concerning the state of the road. Why was such a very busy road left unmaintained by the authorities, he wondered. Did the big men with their pot bellies and riding in their imported Mercedes Benz cars ever ply this road? If they did, they would surely know that the road was in dire need of repairs. Maybe Dr Ocheme was right after all. If the ruling class, as he called them, valued the life of those they governed, this road would be as well maintained and tarred as the expressway from Lagos to Benin City, he thought.

It was however the state of the road from Otukpo, the District Headquarters, to Agila, his village, that really angered and saddened him. Part of this road, from Otukpo to Igumale was tarred, but the section between Igumale and Agila was a nightmare. He had boarded a Toyota HiAce minibus that was packed full of passengers, goods that had been bought by many of them in Otukpo and two cages that each had seven hens in them. They had left Otukpo a little after noon and he had thought the journey would last the usual three hours it took, even though Otukpo was less than a hundred kilometres far away from Agila. The sky was dark, and the heavy rainfall remained unabated. The untarred twenty-something kilometres between Igumale and Agila were the most nightmarish of all. All the passengers had to go out of the mini-bus twice and the male passengers requested to push the vehicle out of a mud-filled pothole into which it had glided and stuck. The bus had very worn-out tyres. Clement was part of the group of men who pushed the vehicle. The result was that his clothes and shoes became mud-stained. When the bus arrived at the village, the raining had increased and this time it was accompanied by thunder and lightning.

The village was dark. Though there was electricity supply in the village, power had been cut off just a few hours earlier and would remain cut off until the following morning. It was thus in the dark that Clement walked from the village market square, where the bus had offloaded its passengers, to the compound where his father's house was. He saw, from afar, the roof of the house that he and Mary were building for their father. The light from the lightning gave him an inkling of the progress that had been made in the construction. The house was almost completed, and for the first time in two days, he felt a sense of pride. His mother welcomed him profusely

"Adole, the owner of the house. Adole, the one who will never allow his parents to die of hunger. Adole, the protector of his mother. Welcome home. I'm sure you're very tired and thirsty and hungry as well. Let me call one of the young girls to go and bring you some water to drink. I will try to warm some soup and make very quick *eba* for you to eat. Try to change your clothes. I hope all is fine with you and your work in Lagos. You will tell me about this later."

"Thank you very much, Mama. I have brought you all some Lagos Bread. You know how to distribute this to the family and neighbours. But where is Papa?"

"Adole, Papa is having problems with Chief Aje who wants to take over his palm forest. Papa has said that it is only over his dead body that Chief Aje can occupy the forest. Papa has thus gone to live in the forest. He believes that Chief Aje might send policemen to put him in prison so that he may have an easier access to his property, which for him would become desecrated if an oil mill was established in it. I have not heard from him since he went there, but I know he is all right. I would know if something had gone wrong," his mother responded.

"Well, I need to see him and speak to him urgently. I will have to go to the forest to see him now," Clement announced.

"Adole, what is the matter?" the mother asked with a note of worry.

"Mama, do not be afraid. It is nothing Papa and I cannot handle together. I must go and see him now. Though there is thunder and lightning, the lightning will enable me to see where I'm going to and to see the path I'll use to reach him. I know I will have to cross the Igbilede stream before turning left into the forest. I remember that when I was younger and followed him once to the farm, he told me to go walking on straight ahead to the farm while he turned left to see the hut he had built in the forest. So, I won't lose my way. I have to see Papa tonight. I did not come all the way from Lagos to the village to eat and sleep without having met my father. Do not be afraid, Mama. Papa and I will be back in the compound tomorrow morning without failure," Clement declared.

"It is not that I'm afraid. It is that it is now nighttime. Our people say that even dogs are afraid to go hunting in the night," his mother replied.

"I agree with you, Mama. But it is not the night in itself that is dangerous. It is who one meets in the night that is dangerous. I'm going to meet my father, so why should you or I be afraid?" Clement asked.

"You're right but don't forget that the night has no master. We should all be wary of leaving our homes at night," the mother continued.

"Yes, Mama. It is a rule I have always followed in Lagos. But today is different. I have come all the way from Lagos to talk to Papa. So, though I'm a bit tired, seeing him and talking to him will make my tiredness disappear," Clement announced.

The moment Clement left his father's compound, the rainfall

became heavier. He wondered if he should not have heeded his mother's advice and rested until the following morning, but he felt he needed to see his father this night. He knew he would not be able to sleep and felt it would be a waste of time lying down open-eyed all through the night, wondering about his father and his sister. Agila village was not like Lagos, where there were lots of marauders at night. Apart from an accidental meeting with a wild animal, something that had never happened before in the village, what risk was he taking in his search for his father, at night. None, he told himself.

The path he took was not as slippery as he had been afraid of. Though he trod on some wet patches now and then, he was sure he would not slip and fall down. When the sound of the thunderstorm abated, Clement could hear the continuous chirping vuvuzela-like noise made by crickets. Were these crickets trying to attract mates, or were they trying to ward off predators? He tried to listen more attentively to the insects because he felt they kept him company. He felt he was not alone in his trip to his father's plantation. He wondered how big or small the crickets were. How could such small beings not only withstand the rain and thunder, but also be strong enough to announce their presence and to force those around them, friends, or foes, to listen to them, to respect them and their territory, he thought. Then he wondered about how they tasted once roasted. He had never eaten a cricket before. When he was younger, some of his agemates used to go cricket hunting. They would walk stealthily close to a branch of tree where a cricket was seen resting, would pounce on it and catch it with open hands before roasting it and eating it happily. For most of them, this was the only source of meat they tasted since meat was reserved for the elders. The elders thought that if one allowed children to enjoy the taste of meat once, that would make them become gluttons, greedy and lazy, thinking that life was easy. He had never wanted to taste cricket meat when he was young.

A lightning illuminated the sky, and he could see the wooden bridge on the Igbilede stream not far away. After the bridge, he continued walking for some time and then he stopped walking. It was stark dark, and all was suddenly quiet. The heavy rainfall had subsided, the thunder had abated, and no more lightning illuminated the sky. Clement knew he had to turn left soon and take the path he had seen his father taking many years ago to go to his palm forest. He waited patiently for the lightning to resume so that he would see where to turn. There was no way he would know this without some guidance from the sky. He thought once more of the advice his mother had given him earlier but decided not to allow himself to panic. Then he thought he heard some other noise coming from afar. He listened intently. Was it the noise of the Igbilede stream which was flowing more rapidly than usual? Strange. He thought he had crossed the bridge long ago and that the Igbilede stream was very far away from where he was standing. He listened again intently to make sure he was hearing things correctly. There was no longer any noise apart from a few crickets chirping and conversing.

He waited.

After what seemed a very long moment in the dark, he saw a streak of lightning across the sky, followed by some thunder. Then the sky opened again, and the heavy rainfall resumed. Clement continued until he reached the spot where he had to turn left. The path he took this time was much narrower. It had tall bamboo trees on either side and Clement had to sometimes walk with his arms stretched in front of him to prevent having his face and eyes scratched by bamboo branches which appeared to block his movement forward.

He could now hear the Igbilede stream once again. The heavy rainfall had increased its current and one could hear the noise it made as it went through the large roots of many trees along its banks. Strange, he thought once more. He had never been told that his father's forest was this close to the Igbilede stream. He continued moving slowly but steadily along the path. Then he saw a few palm trees ahead of him. He went past them and penetrated the forest which was stark dark. There was a quick succession of lightnings and thunder, and the rain continued to fall very heavily.

Clement was tired.

Where was his father's hut? How far was it? How would he know where to find it? Should he, with the benefit of hindsight, accept that his mother was right and that he should go back to the village and come to look for his father in the morning? He told himself immediately that he had not come this far not to go the whole hog or the extra mile to see his father. He would not be able to accept himself if he now admitted defeat. He had come to the dark forest to see his father. He would see his father this night, come what may.

He therefore continued walking, this time more slowly. Then he thought he smelled some smoke as if someone close by was burning some wood in a fire. The wood must be a bit wet to release such smoke, Clement thought. He decided to follow the smoke scent and saw that the scent was coming from a path that went right from the path he was on. So, he turned right, and became excited because he knew he was getting closer to the source of the smoke. A streak of lightning on the sky confirmed his intuition. He saw some smoke rising into the sky from a hut that was in a clearing in the dense forest, and he was so excited that he slipped and fell to the ground. His father greeted him very loudly from inside the hut.

"Adole, did you fall down? It is raining outside. Come in quickly."

Clement rushed into the hut which was dimly lit by the yellow flames of a small bonfire that was burning in the middle of the hut, close to a large mat on the soil. There was a strong odour of alcohol in the air. Clement saw that these came from about ten kegs of palm wine that had been left to ferment, apparently for quite some time in the hut which had no furniture. He also saw two cutlasses arranged near the mat, two hoes and a medium-sized rectangular log of wood that he assumed his father used as a seat. Next to the log of wood was a large basket made of branches of palm trees in which some wrappers were stored, a medium-sized clay pot that contained some water, and several tubers of yam and cassava.

"Good evening, Papa. How did you know it was me?" Clement asked in wonder.

"The lion recognises the cub even at night. You have a way of walking and dragging your feet that I recognise from afar," the father replied.

"It is the first time you have used my traditional name to call me," Clement said.

"Is it? Well, as you know, Adole is the addition of two words, Ada, which means father, and Ole, which means home. So, you were named as the father of the home and this you have tried to assume in your own manner. It is only normal that I should call you by your name when I see you after not having seen you for a long time. Thanks for the house you and Oyije are building for us. You have not brought shame to us," his father continued.

"I would have liked to speak to you more often, you know.

Your refusal to have a cell phone makes this impossible," Clement said.

"I do not know what you young people do with phones. I do not have the knowledge to use it. And I do not see the use. If I want to speak to someone, I go to the person's house. I do not speak to a machine. How do I know that the person I am speaking to is paying attention, or that other people are not listening to what I say?" his father replied.

"Papa, you may not have the time to travel physically to see someone in order to speak to him or her. What if the person lives very far away from you? Using a cell phone makes it easier to speak to people who live and work in places that are far from the village," Clement explained.

"Well, all the people I speak to are in the village and it is important when speaking to someone to be near the person. Normally, you speak not only with your mouth but also with your eyes, body, and hands. Face to face communication is better. Even those who live in the district headquarters and who wish to speak to me, like Owobi Aje, come to the village to see me. Anyway, you must be cold. I'm going to give you a wrapper which you should put on your body. But first, you should remove your wet clothes. Put them close to the fire so that they can start to get dry. Then stay close to the fire to have some warmth, before you start to tell me why you have braved the thunder to come to my forest, our forest. This is the first time you have come here and I'm happy you have come to reconnect with your ancestors, though I know you bring me bad news," the father added.

"How do you know I bring you bad news?" Clement wondered.

"Adole, there are things we should pay particular attention to. There are events that happen around us that tell us many things, that inform us, that warn us of the consequences of some decisions we might be constrained to take. So, we should always pay attention to things, see things, hear things, even when others do not pay attention to them. An owl has been hooting close to my hut consistently for the last seven days. Then it goes quiet tonight. And then you come for the first time to my hut in the forest where I'm surrounded by the spirit of my ancestors, and you fall down just in front of it. There is no doubt that it is bad news that brings you," the father continued.

Clement listened with awe and respect. If Papa saw things and heard things, why did he not see his son, listen to his son, he wondered.

"Papa, I would like to know you better. I would like to learn from you. I would like to be able to see things better, to listen to things better. But as you have rightly guessed, the news I am bringing is not good news at all," Clement confessed.

"Is it Chief Aje, through his son Owobi, that has asked you to come to tell me when I will be driven from the land that has been in my family since the period when our village was first established? Have they now resorted to using my children to weaken my resolve? When will the wonders I'm seeing with my proper eyes end?" the father asked.

"No, it is not Chief Aje that has sent me. But I think they may be concerned," Clement responded.

His father was suddenly very still. He looked intently at Clement's face close to the fire.

"Something is wrong with Oyije, is it?" his father asked in a low strained and trembling voice.

"Yes, Papa," Clement responded.

He saw the strained look on his father's eyes. He saw the deep pain that suddenly clouded the face. Then he thought he saw

130

his father become older in the twinkling of an eye. The wrinkles on the face were now very prominent. When his father resumed his speech, Clement was taken aback because his father started to stammer.

"Hhhhas sshhe hhad an accccidddent?" his father asked.

"Not an ordinary accident, not a motor-car accident," Clement replied.

"Wwhhat dddo you mmmean nnnot an ordinary accccident?" his father enquired.

"A more serious accident, Papa. Oyije has disappeared," Clement responded.

"Dddisappeared? Are yyyou tttelling mme to ppprepare to bbury mmmy ddddaughter?" his father questioned in a trembling voice.

"Oyije is not dead. She has been kidnapped by unknown people where she works. She was kidnapped with about fifty of her students and the government is doing all it can to rescue her," Clement announced.

His father kept quiet for a long moment. He now had a far-away look on his face. Clement watched him intently. At one point, he thought he saw his father's eyes become slightly humid. He had never seen his father cry before. Would his father let go and let the tears drop from his eyes? Or would he rather remain stoic, control his emotions, as a man ought to in his eyes? Clement suddenly felt an urge to hug his father, but he did not want to take the risk of being rebuffed.

"Papa, can I hold your hands, please?" Clement requested.

He was surprised that his father gave him his two hands which he cupped and held in his own two hands. He was surprised to notice that all four hands were shivering in unison.

"Papa, take a deep breath each time before you speak. I know that my sister is someone very strong. She will be found. But we need to have all the help we can to ensure that she be found as soon as possible. Which is why I think we should try to go and see Chief Aje and ask for his help," Clement explained.

His father's hands were now shaking more forcefully and uncontrollably in Clement's. After a few minutes, his father wanted to know more about the circumstances surrounding his daughter's disappearance.

"Where is my daughter? Does the government know who has kidnapped my daughter and her students?" He had stopped stammering.

"No, not yet," Clement responded.

"If the government does not know who has kidnapped my daughter and where she is, how can they save her from harm," his father questioned.

"If the government doesn't know today, it will surely know tomorrow. There is absolutely nothing that the government doesn't end up knowing. Which is why I think we will need to get closer to Chief Aje, who as Senate President, can better put pressure on the relevant authorities to ensure the rescue of Oyije and her students," Clement answered.

"So, you want me to go begging in front of someone who does not wish me well. I will be like the grain of corn that is put in front of a cock. The grain of maize is always wrong in front of a cock, you know," his father opined.

"Papa, the earth does not refuse a dead body that we must bury in it. A dead elephant cannot ward off flies from its body. There are things that are crystal clear and one of these is to ask for help when we are unable to do things. The person who wants to make charcoal must accept smoke to enter into his eyes. We must sometimes accept to make sacrifices in order to obtain what we want," Clement declared.

"There are some sacrifices I can make and others I can't. I accept to lose face and go to beg Aje for his aid, but I will in no way trade my forest for his support," his father announced.

"What must be will be. No one can avoid the inevitable. The bird's feather floats in the air but always ends on the ground. If your ancestors have protected you all along, they will continue to do this, and it is not Chief Aje who will overcome them. You will not have to lose face, as you fear. What we need to do is to go and ask Ogaba-Idu, the Village Head, to speak to Chief Aje on our behalf and on behalf of our village. Afterall, it is the life of an illustrious daughter of the village that is at stake," Clement added.

"How are you sure Chief Aje would not laugh at us? How are you sure that he should be trusted even if he says yes to Ogaba-Idu? The words spoken by an enemy do not come from the heart but from the stomach," his father continued.

"Papa, anybody who has a benefactor will not lack the legs to walk a very long and difficult distance. We need outside help, and we have someone from the village who can make us walk the long distance in front of us," Clement argued.

"Adole, what you are saying is true. But don't forget that it is impossible to ask the salt to be sugary. You cannot ask someone who is selfish and self-centred to do good for others," his father said.

"Yes, Father. What you are saying is true. But like you elders in the village say, a bird never lands on a tree that it does not know. We know Chief Aje. So, we are better placed to hear and eventually scrutinise the messages he will give us. We will know if he is sincere or not," Clement responded.

"The rat does not go to play with the cat's whiskers. I only hope Aje and his family do not use this occasion to try to force me to do what I am not willing to and will never do. You do not give the dog a piece of meat for safe-keeping," his father ended up saying.

"We'll have to go and see Ogaba-Idu in the morning. Fortunately, I bought some bottles of South African wine which we can take to him as presents from Lagos," Clement continued.

"I thought I had lost a child. And now you have come back to prove me wrong. I thought I had not lost a child. And now you come to tell me she has disappeared," his father resumed speaking after a few minutes.

"Why did you think you had lost a child, lost me, Papa?" Clement asked with anxiety and apprehension.

"Well, I thought you would take over from me. I thought you would remain in the village, found a big family to keep our name running, and be the guardian of our forest. I tried all I could to groom you in this direction. Your mother and sister told me I should not force myself on you, that I should not force you to be who you are not. It is the first time in the village that a first son has not been brought up to take over from his father and continue the family history. Oyije and her mother advised me to let you be who and what you wish to be, to let you do what you have chosen to do and to let you decide what your life and future should be. It was not a very easy decision for me to make," his father further stated.

"I have succeeded in what I went to Lagos for, you know Papa," Clement

"I know you have succeeded. Your mother and sister always tell me how right I was not to stop you from taking the path you have chosen to take. I would have wanted your success to be in the village, to be with people you know and who know you. Here, they can see your success. What you do in Lagos, only strangers know. So, your success is only in the eyes of strangers," the father went on to say.

"No, Papa, my success is not in the eyes of strangers, but in my eyes. I am proud of what I have done, what I have been able to achieve. I am proud of who I am. I am proud to have been able to prove myself in the land of strangers, as you have said. I strongly believe that in order to be yourself, to construct yourself, your identity, and your position in the society and in life, you need to go outside your family, outside known faces, outside known territory. You need to mix with strangers and to be considered the other, to be treated first like the other. It is this that makes you really know who you are, how prepared you are to defend who you are. An elephant knows it is really an elephant only when it is in the midst of other animals. The elephant continues to behave like an elephant and is accepted as such by the others. When others, strangers as you call them, accept you for who you are and are happy at what you do, you have succeeded, because you have made a name. I have defended your name in Lagos, Papa. I have brought no shame to your name in Lagos, Papa. What I want is for you to be proud of me, of what I have done, of who I know I am, your son," Clement voiced.

"Who told you I am not proud of you? I am proud of my children," his father responded.

"Well, why don't you say things? You tell me you see and hear things. You should also say things. Is it not you elders who say that when the heart is full, the mouth must tell the story?" Clement enquired.

"You think fathers must tell their children that they are proud of them? Are some things not as clear as the sun that rises every day? Do you need to tell someone that the sun does not shine in the night? As the left leg always walks on the left and the right leg on the right, it goes without saying that fathers are proud of their children. Your grandfather, may his spirit be in peace, never told me he was proud of me. He did not need to because I knew it," his father tried to explain.

"Some things are worth saying and hearing," Clement went on to say.

"I never had this type of discussion with your grandfather. I do not know of any man in the village that had such a discussion with his father for that matter. Your grandfather brought me up to be like him, a farmer and palm wine tapper. I followed him when I was young, and I learnt from him how to identify and choose the palm tree that would provide the biggest volume of and the best taste of palm wine. At times, he allowed me to choose which palm tree to climb. Then he taught me how to climb palm trees without falling down and how not to feel dizzy when at the top of a tall palm tree. He taught me how to make the woven raffia belt that is used to climb and how to tie the buckle in a solid way. When I made my first belt, he tested it and saw that it was solid and very secure. He did not voice his pride to me, but I knew he was proud of me because he used the belt for a long time and when he wanted to change it, he asked me to fabricate another one. When he decided to put me in charge of his palm forest, where we are at the moment, he did not have to tell me he was proud of me, because I knew it. I knew it because he was trusting me to take care of the family heritage, of the family history. Which is why I will never allow anyone to try to drive me out of where I am, where your grandfather trusted me to defend, because he was proud of me, without announcing it to anyone's ears," the father argued.

"So, are you sad that I won't be here to take over from you?"

Clement demanded.

"I can't be sad. I won't be sad. Why should I be sad that things are as they are? I cannot change what exists. My great grandfather was a successful farmer and palm wine tapper. So were my grandfather and my father. Who knows, maybe Chief Aje will succeed in sending me to my grave and occupy the forest. Then the question of who succeeds me will no longer be asked. If Chief Aje succeeds, I will show you in the morning where I'd like to be put to rest. It's on the way out of the forest, close to the bridge on Igbilede, where my father, grandfather, great grandfather and others before him were left to go and join the village of our ancestors. I have accepted the fact that I will be the last to join them here in the forest," his father commented.

"So, you are worried and afraid because you think I won't have children to ensure the continuation of the family name and its history," Clement wanted to know.

"It is not in my power to determine if you'll have children or if one of them will have the passion to maintain our family history in the village and protect the family property. You know, there are so many men in the village who have wives but who have not been able to have children. Many have gone to see the village seer for consultation and the village herbalist for solutions that will make them and their wives not sterile. All their attempts have failed. It is not in my power to ask you to have children. Parents do not have the power to order their sons to have children," the father responded.

"Why won't you sell part of the forest to Chief Aje, Papa? It is highly likely that those who kidnapped Oyije will ask for a huge sum of money before they accept to release her. The proceeds from the sale would help you pay such a sum without difficulty," Clement suggested.

137

"What you have not understood is that this is not just a forest. It is my source of livelihood. It is my root. It is my family name. A man who loses his family name or sells it because he is offered a huge sum of money dies in shame. I do not want to bring shame neither on you nor on Oyije," the father explained.

"OK, Papa. In the morning, you will show me what you want to show me and then we will go back to our compound in the village before going to pay a visit to Ogaba-Idu. Oyije will be found safe and sound, I promise," Clement declared.

"Adole, thanks for coming to see me here. It takes a lot of courage to take a path you have never taken, in the night, and under very heavy rainfall and to be able to find your way and reach your destination. Though the destination you wanted to reach and which you have succeeded in reaching is important, what is more important in my eyes is your journey, your decision to make the journey and your refusal to allow difficulties to defeat your resolve. I know I can trust you to bring Oyije back home safely," the father concluded.

4

Mary ached all over her body. She was at a loss at what to do. She felt shame, guilt, and self-loathing. Did what happen to her really happen? How could she have allowed it to happen? Did Owobi not refer to her as a Commanding Officer? So, how could she have allowed somebody to assault her, to invade her body, to soil her identity and self-esteem and now to be on the verge of destroying her sense of self and self-worth?

Did what happen really happen or was it rather only a bad dream she had had, a nightmare that would disappear when she would open her eyes?

She tried to move her body a little and stopped immediately because she had bruises over almost all her body, though she was still fully dressed in her black dress. The pain around her waist was unbearable and nerve-racking. She wanted to yell but could not bring herself to start this. Then, she started shivering uncontrollably and began crying quietly.

She told herself she had to be strong and to stop crying. Her students would not want to see her crying because they trusted her resolve to take them out of their present predicament safely. They depended on her. If they saw her crying, they would panic and lose hope. So, she tried to stop crying and to think about the trap she was in, in a more clear-minded manner. She was surprised at the violence of her captor. How could someone who was visibly cultivated and educated allow his primary animal instincts to get the better of him? Was she responsible for what had befallen her? Was this the punishment that she had been warned of earlier on? If so, was this the beginning of a cycle of punishments? Was it because she refused to be dompted by him that he had decided to show her he was the stronger of the two? Would she have to be more obedient, ask less questions, show more respect if she did not want to be sexually aggressed anymore?

She felt shameful. She felt dirty. She had been unable to defend herself, her honour, her body. It was her private space that had been trespassed with impunity. Her captor felt he was empowered to change her name. Now he equally felt he owned her, possessed her body and could pounce on her to use her body without her consent.

Then she felt anxious, first about her safety and the safety of her girls who were at this moment somewhere else in this compound. She was anxious about not having been able to decode the secrets hidden by the compound where she and her girls were being held captives. How far was their captor going to go in how he treated them? Given the brutal physical violence she had been subjected to, she knew that there was no limit to what her captor would do, if his will was not satisfied. If she knew what this will was, maybe she would be better able to plot a course of action that would make him less violent than he had been.

Then she felt depressive. Here she was, alone, with no prospect of succour and help. Who knew where she and her students were being held? How long would it take for her captor's will to be satisfied? What was her father doing precisely at this moment? Was he aware of her predicament? Where was Clement now? Surely, he must have heard the news about the kidnapping.

Warm tears began to flow down from her eyes. She could not control this, so she let go. She cried and cried softly, shivering uncontrollably.

Then she thought she saw herself moving out of her body, flying over, and gazing at the crying woman. She suddenly got angry, very angry. Angry at the crying woman. Was crying not a sign of helplessness? Was she helpless? Was this not a situation where she needed to test her mettle, to overcome her fears, to try to analyse her immediate environment, determine the constraints and threats in order to better plot how to reduce or contain such threats? Had she succeeded all her life in all she had endeavoured to do, only to crash now in the face of an unknown man in an unknown compound in an unknown town or village? She decided she had to stop writhing in self-pity. This was unbecoming of someone who had been entrusted with the management of a school, with handling how young girls could be groomed to become better and succeed in their chosen fields. If she stopped believing in herself, how could she lead her girls out of the quandary in which they now found themselves?

She remembered something Clement had said to her once when they were both discussing how the village would react to his choice to specialise in cooking. Clement had told her this: "No one can bring you down without your consent". She was not going to consent to her destruction by someone she had come into contact with only recently.

Then her anger became directed at her captor. Who did he think he was, organising her capture, organising the capture of many of her students and apparently making plans for their future for which she was not aware? Did he think he could invade her school and now invade her physical integrity as he wished? Her anger emboldened her. She decided to sit upright with her back against the wall to think more fruitfully. Her movement unleashed a fresh current of pain on her thighs, waist, stomach, and shoulders. She closed her eyes for a few seconds and waited for the pain to subside. She needed to attain at least three objectives, she thought. First, ensure that the physical assault would not be repeated. Second, try to establish a relationship with her captor founded less on the use of force, and more on communication. In order words, she needed to maybe bring her captor not to distrust her anymore, to be as open as possible with her, to answer the many questions she had and to tell her what his ultimate objectives in keeping them prisoners in his home were. She was apprehensive because the man remained a total mystery to her and she did not know how he would react at the many questions she knew she was going to have to ask him. For example, she decided that she had to know if he was a married man. She suspected he was and felt she could eventually appeal to his sense of being a family man in order to establish some other form of rapport with her, rather than one based on the use of violence. She would have to take the risk of asking him if he was married and if he had children. Thirdly, she needed to be reunited once more with her girls and so had to devise a plan that would allow her to get back to them. She would try to convince her captor that she was in no way going to foment any trouble nor instil any idea of rebellion into the heads of her girls. She would have to convince him that keeping all his captives together was better than keeping them apart. She would try to convince him that she was in a better position to maintain discipline among the girls than the men who were charged with supervising and looking after them. She thought of the many occasions she had gone on field trips with some of her students and how the simple fact of her mere physical presence was enough to calm down even the most unruly among her students.

She heard some feet shuffling in front of the door to the room she was in. She suddenly became jittery and started trembling uncontrollably. She thought she heard the voices of some men, speaking in low tones. She did not recognise any of the voices. Her stomach tightened. Was she going to be gang-raped? Had the *maigida* told his men to take over from him in punishing her? Would she be able to survive any additional assault on her body? Was her spirit strong enough to resist? Her heartbeat ran faster when she heard some footsteps approaching the door to the room and heard the door being opened. Then the smell of fried food hit her nostrils. Someone placed a tray containing a plate of *akara* and fried plantain on the floor and immediately left and closed the door. Mary was not hungry. She ate nothing.

She dozed off. She dreamt she was a small bird flying above a dense forest. She was happily singing when she suddenly saw a flock of bigger birds that looked like vultures, circling right above and casting an ominous shadow on her. She was frightened because she knew that vultures were attracted by dead animals. She tried to dodge the army of vultures but was unable to. She saw that she was cornered. One of the vultures held her with a large claw and started removing her feathers one after the other. She awoke suddenly. The door to the room was half open and she smelled the perfume. Her stomach lurched and suddenly a wave of nausea swept over her. The fragrance of the perfume now disgusted her, and she felt like throwing up. She bit her lips so hard that she tasted some blood. She was tense and still.

"Aisha, you should eat what is given to you."

"I'm not hungry," Mary replied.

"You have not eaten for over twenty-four hours. You should eat what is given to you," the man insisted.

143

"I cannot force myself to eat when I'm not hungry," Mary maintained.

"Aisha, you should not be afraid of me. I do not wish you any harm personally. I have come to inform you that my contact with the relevant authorities is going extremely well. You may not have to spend more time in my home and enjoy my hospitality for long," he said.

"There is no other harm you can wish me than the harm you have already subjected me to. I am a prisoner in your home. How can you keep me and my girls prisoners and then tell me you do not wish me harm personally?" Mary enquired.

"I can see you're very strong-headed and stubborn. Always contesting what I say. You don't seem to have learnt your lesson. When I tell you I do not wish you any harm personally, you should believe what I say," he responded.

"What will you decide if I do not believe you? Will you ask your men to whip me as they have been doing? Is this what you do to your wives when they ask you questions? I'm sure you're married," Mary ventured to add.

"Yes, I have two wives but how I live with them is none of your business," he declared coolly.

"Please, I have not said how you live with your wives is any of my business. I was just wondering how you would feel if as the husband and the father that you are, you learn that members of your family have been abducted and you have no news concerning their whereabout, which is something the fathers of my students are experiencing at the moment. I'm sure you have children yourself," Mary added.

"Yes, I do," he replied calmly. "What are you driving at exactly," he added.

Mary told herself to tread carefully. She was afraid the man would get angry at the questions she was bent on asking him, maybe allow his animal instincts to get the better of him and subject her to a new round of physical violence.

"You tell me you do not wish me harm. How do I know your men are not waiting in the next room for you to give them the signal to whip me because you think I am asking you questions that to your mind show disrespect?" Mary said.

"My men are not around," he replied calmly.

"Are you saying I can go ahead and ask you some questions? I assure you the questions do not and will not show any mark of disrespect for you," Mary requested.

"Yes, go ahead," the man replied, full of assurance. "I will answer them if I think they are reasonable. Make this quick because I have other more important things to do and iron out."

"Please, do not get angry. You have given me a name, but I do not know yours," Mary ventured to ask, waiting for the man to explode in anger any time.

"You don't need to know my name. Just call me Alhaji or Mallam, though I prefer you call me Mallam," he said.

"Okay. So, it means you have done the hajj, one of the five pillars of Islam from what I know. So, you must have gone to Mecca, walked round the cube-shaped Kaaba in order to wipe off past sins. Is it not true that during your trip to Mecca, during the hajj, you enter into a state of spiritual rebirth, called ihram?" Mary questioned.

"Your knowledge on Islam is interesting. Go on," Mallam instructed.

"No, I don't know anything about Islam, your religion. But I heard long ago that normally pilgrims in Mecca try to give up worldly pleasures, learn patience and tolerance, and shave their head at the end as a form of renewal. Was it there that you shaved the hair on your head?" Mary enquired.

"Where are your questions leading to?" Mallam wondered, in a hard tone.

"I just wanted to know better the man in whose compound I have been housed for quite some time now. I have no intention at all of disrespecting you, if that is what you're thinking," Mary answered.

"Be informed that I live according to what has been handed down to us by the Prophet Mohammed, peace be upon his name. I have peace of mind because I try to give as much as I can to those in need, like the *Almajiris* that I feed, clothe and educate, as you must have noticed, since I know you are very observant," Mallam went on to explain.

Mary thought for some minutes before resuming her speaking. The man must thus be financially well-off because only Muslims who were financially able could go all the way from Nigeria to Mecca for their hajj. He was financially well-off to be able to handle the dozens of children that were learning the Quran every day of the week from morning until evening in one part of his compound. She now learnt that the children were fed and clothed. This discovery only deepened the mystery surrounding her captor, Mallam. What was the motivation behind a visibly educated man, with enough money to cater for the education of children who were not his, becoming the leader of a group of violent Islamists, kidnapping innocent girls, killing some of them, forcing some others into unplanned marital relations and sexually assaulting others? Was it due to an insatiable desire to control others, to express dominance, to show his power? Or maybe he was planning to trade them for a ransom. This did not seem right. He did not look like someone in need of money. He was always dressed immaculately and wore a perfume that was without doubt expensive and imported from Europe, a fact Mary felt was quite ironical, given Mallam's earlier diatribe against Nigeria's ex-colonial masters. There was a question about the *Almajiris* she had always wanted to ask.

"Do your *Almajiris* go begging as most do? Do they bring back the proceeds to you? Don't you think they are being used and exploited?" Mary asked. She was no longer afraid he might get angry.

"*Almajiris* have a very negative reputation. They are seen roaming about and loitering around all the streets in town. My *Almajiris* are an exception. I have chosen to bring them up and to educate them on Islam and its values for them to become Mallams when they become older. They will then be able to teach others how to be good or better Muslims. I am thus trying to change the common view people, especially non-Muslims, have of *Almajiris,* using my own personal resources since the government appears to have abandoned them and us to our fate," Mallam went on to say.

"Please believe me when I say I am impressed to learn what you are doing. As a matter of fact, you and I are in the same boat, so to speak. You and I have chosen to devote our attention, will and energy to educating others," Mary commented.

"No, you and I are not in the same boat. There are two major differences between you and I. The first is that you are trying to educate the wrong population, girls, who should stay at home to help their mothers whose role is to prepare them to be perfect wives. My *Almajiris* are all boys, as you may have observed. I know you have a good power of observation. The second difference, which to my mind is more important, is the content of what the children are taught. What I teach my *Almajiris* will enable them to have spiritual and moral cleanliness whereas what

147

you teach your students will lead to their spiritual and moral decadence," he responded in a proud and condescending voice.

"We are both teachers and educators. We have both devoted our time to trying to improve others. The value we may give to our respective paths may differ but that does not refute the fact that we are both not selfish, not unaffected by the difficulties the younger generation might face in how they live later. This is what I'm driving at when I say we are in the same boat. Why did you choose to educate *Almajiris*?" Mary enquired.

"I wanted to do my best to stop children abandoned by their parents roaming the streets all day, begging for money and food, and doing menial jobs. I wanted to give them a stable environment in which to learn to become good Muslims and good Islamic teachers, Mallams," he answered, his face showing an expression of superiority.

"Don't you think it is the job of the government to do this? The government has better resources to invest in programmes that will remove the abandoned children from the streets and put them in schools where their teachers are qualified and where their progress can be better monitored," Mary questioned.

"The government, your government, is haram. Its values are not Islamic values. So, good Muslims should not hesitate to fill in the void left by the incapacity of the government of infidels, by infidels and for infidels to cater for the future generations of good Muslims," Mallam countered disdainfully.

"Are you sure all your *Almajiris* will become educators, like you, in future. The view most people have of *Almajiris* is that they become recruited into terrorist organisations," Mary asked. She immediately regretted having asked the question, because she was afraid the question might be considered impertinent by her captor. She heaved a sigh of relief when he responded immediately, without taking offence.

"*Almajiris* who are brought up under the care, guidance and love of a foster parent do not turn out to become terrorists," he replied, proudly.

Mary was at a loss. How could someone who accepted to educate abandoned children and give them the care, guidance and love to be better adults at the same time abduct others, and be violent with them? She decided not to ask him the question because she did not want the dialogue she had been able to establish with him to be broken. She was afraid of the safety and security of her students and wanted to ask that she be reunited with them in the other part of the compound.

"Mallam, I am the foster parent of my students who I'm sure are frightened to death at this moment due to my absence. I need to be with them to better guide them and I'm sure you understand my position, which is similar to your position in front of your *Almajiris*," Mary ventured to say, full of apprehension.

"You will be reunited with them. But then, no one should know what happened in this room, yesterday. As a matter of fact, nothing happened. You do agree, don't you?" he asked, staring at her face with a glacial look.

"Nothing happened if you say so and no one will know if anything happened, I promise," Mary said, confused but relieved to hear she would be reunited with her girls. "Could I ask you for a small favour, please? I would like you to give me an exercise book and something to write with."

"Why do you need an exercise book?" Mallam asked, visibly very surprised.

"I am a teacher and I'm used to writing every day. I have the habit of writing down things I want to do or have to do. So, as I do things, I write. When I'm thinking of doing things, I write. At the moment, I'm doing nothing, so writing is about the only thing I think I can do, to while away the long time spent in your compound. I think writing will make me become more calm and less stressed. This might also be useful for my girls. I would like them to be able to write down their thoughts. I think it is necessary for them to be able to voice out what they feel, rather than keep all their anxiety and frustrations pent up. I do not want any of them to get crazy and I believe that voicing out fears makes accepting them easier, which I think will make the girls become less troubled physically and psychologically," Mary explained.

"Your request is very strange indeed. And my men would find it very strange if they learnt I had given you something to write your feelings and thoughts on. But then, what harm would it do to allow you and your girls to express your fears in writing? It would be easier for my men to keep an eye on you all that way than if you chose to express yourselves in a different manner. Yes, I do not see the danger in giving you something to write with. But I will need to think about this. What will you personally be writing about?"

"Nothing in particular. Everything in reality. Thoughts, fears, dreams, wishes, recollections, failures, successes, the list is long," Mary answered.

"Okay, I will think about your strange request. You see that you must believe me when I tell you that I do not wish you harm. However, no matter what you write, do not refer to anything that happened yesterday, because nothing happened, as you yourself have rightly acknowledged. I may ask to see what you write or have written to verify this the day you leave my compound. So, if I end up accepting your request, I will only give you a pencil and not a biro to write with. Then, I will be able to erase things written on the exercise book that I do not agree with, and they will no longer exist as reality," Mallam announced matter-of-factly.

"Mallam, erasing what is written or trying to forget what has been said does not make what is written or said to disappear. There is always a trace somewhere of what one says or writes, even if this no longer exists in physical readable or hearable form," Mary opined.

"I will control the physical trace of what you say or write in my house. If you want to write as a form of therapy, I will give you the means to do this. But not everything you write will remain the way you want it to. And I do not really see the point in your girls writing about their dreams, wishes and what they would like to have as personal successes. This is haram. You are lucky I'm generous. Others in my shoes will not give you something to express your thoughts and feelings in and with. So, nothing you write will leave here the way you want it to. I hope what I'm saying is very clear, Aisha," he said in a harsh voice.

Mary thought very rapidly. If she did not agree with the conditions being imposed by Mallam, she felt she would not have the possibility, even if this was limited, of self-expression. Anyhow, she mused, where were women allowed to freely express themselves, their desires, their hopes, their wishes? She would accept Mallam's conditions and hope for the better.

"Very clear," Mary answered.

"Okay. I will ask one of my men to escort you back to reunite with your girls when I have made up my mind," Mallam announced haughtily.

"Thank you very much," Mary responded, relieved, but still unhappy and apprehensive about what lay in store for them. Why was the government waiting that long to come to their aid?

***

Clement was sitting in the office of the Managing Director of Nakowa Oils in Otukpo, the district headquarters. He had been ushered into the waiting room by a young beautiful lady who presented herself as Imelda, the secretary to the MD. She asked him to be patient because the MD was discussing some important matters with two officials from the State Ministry of Agriculture who had come to see him after having been given some instructions from the State Governor's office. She offered him a bottle of soft drink, either a Fanta or a Coca Cola, which he declined. She offered him three of the daily newspapers the company received and asked him to read them while waiting for the MD to invite him into his office.

He did not feel as tired as he had feared he would be. The last few days had been very hectic and busy. He had not had a single minute of respite. And he was grateful for that because he did not want to fall into the trap of conceiving very negative catastrophic scenarios about his sister. He was grateful his mind was occupied in organising rescue operations rather than wandering into the abyss, seeing his sister chained somewhere with several murderous-looking beginner jihadists surrounding her.

He had been able to sleep in his father's hut in the forest. They had visited a shrine that was about a thirty-minute walking distance from the hut, a shrine that was close to a second bridge on the Igbilede stream that his father had built himself. Apparently, nobody else knew about the existence of the bridge. It allowed his father to be able to visit parts of his forest that were on the other bank of the stream.

152

The shrine was a large open hut that had no walls. It had a thatched roof constructed on a frame of more than ten long round dry branches of trees. The roof was fixed and tied solidly to six trunks of wood solidly embedded in the soil. The wood was special because it never got rotten even when it stayed wet for several months. The roof was however very low, so that Clement and his father had to almost crawl to enter it. Inside the hut, there were five round dry wooden poles protruding about fifty centimetres above the soil. In front of each pole were a few leftover offerings, including roast yams, the dried body of birds and some smoked fish. Clement's father said his ancestors had eaten well and were satiated. He then poured some palm wine he had brought with him on the soil in front of each of the five wooden poles on the ground and asked his ancestors to guide one of their offspring in continuing the journey he had had the courage to make, and to ensure that he brought back his sister safely back home. They had then gone to the compound where his mother had prepared some fried plantain and eggs for them. They had afterwards gone to see the Ogaba-Idu, who had been very surprised to see father and son together and so early in his palace.

"I saw the bad omen long ago. I knew something was wrong with you, our worthy provider of the white liquid of life, the one who makes our festivals joyful, the one who makes our women sing better and our young men dance without being tired. I never knew it concerned your son in Lagos," the District Head had said in a low voice.

"Ogaba-Idu, may your reign be long. Nothing is wrong with me personally. A man's character cannot be washed off by rain. However, your perspicacity is legendary because you have seen rightly. We have come to see you for your advice and help. My

153

son Adole travelled all the way from Lagos to inform me that Oyije, my daughter is in grave danger," Clement's father had announced, while looking at the floor rather than at the District Head's face. It was considered rude and disrespectful to speak to the Chief and establish eye contact with him. This was a protocol that existed since the village had come into being and which no one dared disrespect.

"Oyije, who is the head of a school somewhere in the north?" Ogaba-Idu had asked.

"Yes," his father had replied. "I will allow Adole to tell you more."

He had answered all the questions Ogaba-Idu had asked. He had told him no one knew who had abducted Oyije, nor where she was. His father had allowed him to tell Ogaba-Idu that Oyije was an illustrious daughter of the village, and that the village needed the help, of another illustrious ambassador of the village, the honourable Speaker of the Senate, Chief Aje, to obtain a quicker search and rescue response from the government, for which he was one of its principal leaders.

"The tail of the cow wags from the left to the right and then from the right to the left. A Chief has to look after all who come to seek his help and guidance. I know that Chief Aje is not very happy at your refusal to sell him your forest. It is a refusal that I perfectly understand. I will tell the Chief that goodness enables one, even the weak, to climb and attain the summit of the highest mountain. I will tell him that if you do good for someone, it is actually to yourself that you're doing good. I will ask him to give his time to try to rescue our daughter because giving is a very simple way of saving because the more you give, the more you receive. I will tell him that no one in the village is an enemy of the other and that we are all part of the same family. A bee does not sting another bee. As one hand is needed to wash the other, so must Chief Aje do all he can to rescue our daughter," Ogaba-Idu had concluded.

Sitting here now in Owobi's office, Clement was absorbed by his thoughts, though he had flipped open one of the newspapers, which he wasn't reading. Things had gone extremely well with his father, who had entrusted him with the mission of finding his sister and of bringing her back to her father. He felt a sort of communion with his father. His father had thought him lost and found, but he had never thought he had run away from home. He had only sought a better environment where he could live without pretending to be what he knew he was not. The only person who had understood this had been his sister, who was the one who was now lost. Where was she? Who was she with? How was she being treated? Was she still alive? He shuddered at the thought that she might not be alive. Such an eventuality would damage many people, including his father, his mother and himself. She had to be saved and Chief Aje's aid would be capital in this regard.

The door to Owobi's office opened and Owobi came out with two other men dressed in suits. Owobi and the men were laughing boisterously at a joke one of them had cracked. Owobi was holding one of the men by the arms. They both seemed to be on the same wavelength. Owobi informed Clement that he was going to escort the men to their cars in the parking lot and would be back a few seconds afterwards.

Clement waited for about fifteen minutes before Owobi came back from the car park. He now looked serious. He invited Clement to his office. Clement was surprised at the size of the office. It was very big, more than fifty square metres. There was a large mahogany table with an in-tray and an out-tray behind which was a very large comfortable-looking swivel chair in white leather. On one side of the office was a wide and long sideboard cabinet also in mahogany. Close to it was a meeting table for six, with six office chairs, three at each side. On the other side of the office, a large television-set was placed, next to four armchairs and a round coffee table. The floor of the office was covered in a bright red oriental carpet and the air-conditioner was on.

Owobi directed Clement towards the armchairs and invited him to sit down. He informed Clement that the armchairs were imported directly from Italy. As he sat down next to Clement, he brought out three cell phones, all iPhones, which he placed ostensibly in front of himself on the coffee table. Clement had the feeling that Owobi was trying to impress him. He saw how Owobi was visibly trying to show off the Rolex wristwatch with bright golden bracelets he was wearing. He had other things on his mind and so did not try to beat about the bush.

"Good afternoon, Owobi. You know why I am here. We need your help and the help of your father in Abuja," he greeted.

"Good afternoon, Clement. Yes, I am aware of the reason behind your visit. Your father did not need to have gone to ask Ogaba-Idu to seek our help. You may not believe what I'm about to say, but I have been extremely worried over the past two weeks about Oyije, about her safety, about her health, about the trauma she's currently going through. I did not wait for Ogaba-Idu's instructions before asking my father to do all in his power immediately after I heard news about her abduction. My father has not gotten back to me yet. I'm sure this is not because he feels unconcerned. He has a very tight and busy schedule every day. He came back to Nigeria from Italy only a few days ago. I have left him alone to iron out serious matters pending in the Senate and his political party before reminding him of my earlier

156

request. Hopefully, he should now be in a position to tell me, to tell us how far he has been able to go in his promise to do what he can to ensure Oyije's release. Oyije is your sister, but I consider her my sister as well. I know she's a very strong and determined woman. I know she is going through a hellish predicament at the moment, but I trust her capacity to weather the storm and come out unhurt. What I'm trying to tell you is that you can be assured that I will personally do all in my power to find out where she is and ensure her rescue, no matter what it takes. I hope you believe me," Owobi responded.

"I know how close you are to her. Which is why I suggested to my father that we should come to you and your father for anything you can do to help us. One is rich when one is not alone," Clement added.

"We will have to go to Abuja to see my father. I think it will be much better and easier to iron things out there with him and speak face to face. I hope you have enough time and that you are not required to go back to Lagos, soon. By the way, how is Lagos?" Owobi enquired.

"Lagos will always be Lagos. Lots of go-slows, lots of crowds here and there, a very busy and bustling city. But since I'm all work and play little, I cannot tell you about what sorts of entertainment are available. I know that there is a large variety of social events, but I cannot give you any details since I hardly leave my home when I come back from the hotel where I work," Clement answered.

"The last time I was in Lagos, a friend took me to visit one of the social clubs in Victoria Island. It is said to be Nigeria's first five-star private business and social club with an exclusive membership. All the members are top executives in finance and business as well as top government officials. The club is affiliated to over two hundred private clubs in many cities worldwide. It organises concerts, parties, and tennis tournaments regularly for its members. I liked the atmosphere there. And of course, the meal served was first class. If you have any plans to change your place of work, I would be willing to recommend you to one of the managers of the club who happens to be a cousin to my friend," Owobi offered.

"Thanks for your offer. I'm very happy where I am for the meantime," Clement responded.

"We'll leave for Abuja tomorrow. What car are you driving?" Owobi asked.

"I don't have a car. I do not need a car in Lagos," Clement responded.

"That's okay. We'll leave with one of my cars tomorrow. The Mercedes-Benz has not been serviced for a while, neither has the Volvo, so, we'll take the Range Rover. I will ask Imelda to arrange for your accommodation at one of the hotels in the GRA and I will come to pick you up tomorrow morning before nine o'clock. The road from Otukpo to Makurdi is very bad. Normally, we should be in Abuja before five p.m. Try not to worry too much. Oyije will be found and rescued," Owobi declared.

***

Three turbaned men came to escort Mary back to where her students were. She counted the number of pieces of hair she had. She had thirty-one pieces. She was relieved she was going back to be with her students. It seemed to her she had been separated from them for ages. She still felt some pain and so decided not to walk too fast lest she collapsed and fell down on the floor. She tried to see if she could read the thoughts of the men escorting her, but she could not. They all had their faces covered and all were wearing dark glasses. Yellow men, she thought to herself. Not even courageous enough to show their faces, she continued thinking. She held the exercise book and the pencil Mallam had given her close to her heart as if her life depended on it. She feared that one of the men might want to snatch it away from her. What would she do if such an event happened? Would she shout? Shouting would only make Mallam furious, and who knew what he would do afterwards? He had offered her an exercise book and something to write with as promised. She was sure none of the men escorting her would dare try to snatch away what their master had accepted to give her.

The meeting with her students was full of tears. All the girls surrounded her, weeping, touching her face, holding her hands, and asking her a volley of questions that she could not answer because she was weeping herself. The effusions lasted more than thirty minutes.

For a few minutes, Mary forgot what had happened to her in another part of the compound. Did what happened to her really happen to her? Was she not making a big deal out of nothing? Was the strong bond that now seemed confirmed between her and her girls not what mattered the most? The fact that she was now reunited with her girls expelled some of the thoughts she had had a few hours before the men came to escort her back to her girls. Her mind and body had tried with difficulty to piece together what had happened to her. She no longer felt safe alone. She no longer felt clean. At one point in time, she no longer wanted to live. She had lost hope, lost self-confidence, lost belief in humanity. For how could someone who painstakingly took care of abandoned children, wilfully imprison other children just because these were girls who were not supposed to enjoy the benefits of Western education? One of the girls inadvertently touched her waist and she gasped with a pang of pain. There was suddenly a very worried look on the face of all the girls. She told them everything was all right. She said she needed to go to the bathroom to take a shower. She told the men standing guard in front of the room where they were kept that she was going to spend quite some time in the bathroom and that they should not worry if she did not come out as quickly as she had the habit of doing before. She opened the shower and allowed the cold water to run down her body, imagining that this was some kind of purifying fluid. Then she scrubbed and scrubbed her body, sometimes gasping in pain, but she continued scrubbing. She imagined that it was the impurities on her physical body that were being rinsed off when she stood under the shower for an additional long moment.

When she came back from the bathroom, the girls, who were now quieter, asked her where she had been. She told them she had been kept in another part of the compound because the leader of the group, who preferred to be called Mallam, thought she was a bad influence on them. They told her they had all feared they would never see her again. They wanted to know if she had any information about their future prospects.

She responded first by dissipating their fears and giving them hope. Mallam had contacted some authorities and apparently, was happy about the outcome of such contacts. He had told her that maybe their days of being under his custody might soon come to an end. She told them she was not willing to give them high hopes of liberty regained but that she had the feeling that their days under captivity would soon come to an end. One of the girls asked her in which part of the compound she had been. Was it in a room as big as the one they were in? Were there

Almajiris there too? Was the room guarded by the same number of men as in front of where they were staying? Was there any way they could escape without been seen? Mary asked them not to think of escaping nor ever openly mention such a prospect. She told them Mallam was not one who allowed people to escape from his grip. Trying to escape would be the equivalent of jumping from the frying pan to the fire, she warned them. What they had to do was to wait patiently and hope for the better. She showed the exercise book she had been given to them. She told them they could write their feelings, hopes, and dreams on it if they so wished. She however warned them about writing anything disparaging and insulting about the owner of the house or about hopes of escaping. She informed them that what they wrote may be examined closely by the owner of the house. "So big brother is watching us and will read us to see how we feel under his umbrella?" one of the girls asked.

"We don't have any choice. We can write but must be careful about what we write. Mallam made it clear that he will edit what we write and erase things he does not agree with. He does not look like someone who is afraid, so I don't really know why he wants to see what we write. Maybe he does not want to know how others, girls, see him and the way he behaves. Anyway, if you wish to write anything, be careful what you write and which words you use," Mary said.

"If we have to be careful about which words we use so as not to anger the owner of the house, what is the use of writing to express our feelings?" another girl wondered.

"Writing will allow you express yourself, for yourself, by yourself. It will be an exhaust pipe that will allow all the dirty smoke that has been piling up in your mind to be released. Writing will ventilate your minds, make you name what you think is wrong, so that you can better tame the monster that is trying to engulf you. Writing is an escape route that has no foreseeable dangers," Mary insisted.

"My mind is so confused at the moment that I do not know if anything I write will make any meaning to me or to anyone else who reads it. I will first have to collect my thoughts before being able to put them on paper," a third girl added.

"It is the confused mind that you need to write down. We are all confused at the moment. What we write does not have to make any meaning to us. What we write is what we feel or think now or later. It might be a word, an image, a picture, a hope, a dream, a nightmare. The only rule we have to try to obey is to avoid writing things that might be insulting to and so infuriate the owner of the house, even though this might be difficult especially for me," Mary said.

"Madame, as you have rightly said, it would be difficult for us not to wish to insult the man who has abducted us from our school for no apparent reason. If we choose to write, nothing should reduce the scope of what we wish to say or express," one of the girls said.

"Okay, I think we should go on to say what we each feel. At least, we will have expressed our feelings, even if afterwards, Mallam decides to erase such expressions. But maybe one way out of the difficulty is not to write our names when we make a comment or express ourselves. Then, the owner of the house cannot take anyone of us individually to task. So, anything anyone writes will be our collective responsibility. We are here as a collective of captives and so assume collective responsibility for the feelings expressed by each of us. This is logical since we are suffering together under the same housemaster," Mary added.

"I'm not sure I will be able to write anything. But the fact that I can when I feel like it is about the only good news I have had for quite some time," one of the girls said.

"I do not think I will write anything. I do not have the strength to marshal my thoughts and put them in a readable form," a second girl added.

"Madame, you should go ahead and write what you feel. I am sure what you feel perfectly mirrors what we all feel here at the moment. When the housemaster reads it, he will know it is a collective message, even if he decides afterwards to prevent what is written from being diffused outside his compound in its entirety. If nobody else knows the wholeness of our story under captivity, he, our captor, will," the third girl stated.

***

Mary felt an urgent need to open the exercise book and put down some of her thoughts without any filter.

Day? 31st (Maybe)

I can read the anxiety on their faces. Some of them cry silently when going to sleep. When we eat, their movements are mechanical. Why have I failed to protect them?

The walls in the room are multicoloured. The mattresses are not very hard, so I don't have any back pain each time I get up from it. I sometimes hear the men outside our door conversing and laughing. A very stark difference from what is happening inside the room where we're being kept. When shall we be able to laugh again?

Where are Mallam's family? Are his two wives (should I believe him?) and his children aware that we are living in the

163

same compound and that we have been abducted by their husband? How does he treat his wives?

My students are afraid to write. I however feel the urge to start filling in the blank sheets on this exercise book. I have been quite uncomfortable seeing the white pure blank sheets with all the pages full of clear pink horizontal lines on which things should be written, calculations made, drawings pencilled across many lines, and ideas expressed. Are the blank sheets as blank as what my future, our future will be?

The blank sheets do not reflect what is happening to us, to me at the moment.

My life is not blank, our lives are not blank.

I am not an empty being; we are not empty beings.

So, I need to fill in the pages with my thoughts, my hopes, our thoughts, our hopes, without being afraid to say how I feel. What worse thing can happen to me after what I have been through? No, nothing will be held back even though I'm not sure what will become of my writing. I do not know if the things I write will be modified or censored by Mallam, the "power" that is.

I do not want to express my fears because no one apart from me should have access to them. My father would say that to stare wide-eyed does not make one escape from danger. So, my fears are my fears and only I am and should be aware of them.

Of course, I know that I'm in a dangerous situation. I have been hallucinating over the past two days (I counted two additional pieces of hair since then, so, I'm sure something happened two days ago).

Where am I? Honestly, I don't know. Who has put me where I am? I think I know. It is not a who but a what. It is toxic and bullish masculinity. My present situation and predicament come from this: toxic masculinity that is part and parcel of how so

164

many in my country view a sizeable proportion of its inhabitants. Toxic masculinity is the thinking by men, bullies, that they can suffocate the existence, intellectual growth and personal development of fellow human beings who are collectively considered as being the wrong gender, as being wrong the moment they have a male being in front of them.

So, how am I wrong as a woman, as an active woman, as a daughter, as a sister? Am I undisciplined because I am a woman who asks questions? Am I disrespectful because I dare ask questions to a man? No, I do not think so. But how can I prove that I'm not the wrong person, that I'm not perpetually in the wrong because of my natural condition and that I have to accept the law of the stronger, the strongest, the man?

My voice is being stifled because what I'm writing now will be edited by another, a man. I am losing my sense of self because I'm under the bondage of a man I have never met before and who decides one day, for reasons that are personal to him, that I am the enemy or the enemy's agent. The society wants to shut me up.

What the man who thinks he's a hospitable host to us does not understand is that you don't become stronger and more powerful by excluding others. You don't show your power by subjugating the other.

You don't impose a name on me. I am not Aisha and will never be.

Why are some people unprepared to accept that a woman can be active, can be herself? Where is it written that a woman can be nothing else than a mother, a housewife, someone who has to groom her daughters to become housewives?

I am angry. I am angry that I am not considered socially visible. I am angry that I live in an environment where I can be *trodden upon just because I am a woman. I have committed no crime. I have killed no one. I have stolen from no one. So, why should my name be changed, my identity stolen, my self unrecognised, my credentials unacknowledged, my function disrespected, my calling doubted? Yes, why? Why?*

5

Clement and Owobi had sleepless nights before their joint departure for Abuja, but for totally different reasons. Clement did not sleep well because he was worried about his sister, where she was, who she was with and how she was doing. He tried to put himself in his sister's shoes and felt very uncomfortable. One needed a lot of willpower to withstand losing one's freedom of movement, maybe one's freedom of speech and probably one's freedom of choice of how to dress, of what to eat, and of when to do things one loves doing. He had enormous trust in his sister's capacity to weather storms, but would she have the mettle and strength to withstand the possible violence to which she might be a victim in the midst of her abductors, who were most likely Islamist militants? Would erratic Islamic visionaries capable of sending young under-aged girls clad with time bombs to crowded markets blink an eye for a second at the prospect of liquidating a woman and her students? The thought that he may never see his sister again kept him awake. He would lose her. He would miss her. He would have failed to keep his promise to his father to bring his daughter back from wherever she was. He would have failed to correspond to what his name denoted and connoted.

Owobi also had a sleepless night. He was quite apprehensive about how the meeting, or rather the confrontation with his father in Abuja would go. What he had not told Clement the day before was that his father had told him that investing his time (wasting his time was what he really said) in trying to find out who had kidnapped the daughter to the only village man that had said 'No' to him was not part of his agenda. What would be the possible return on investment, he had wondered aloud. If Oyije's father was strong enough to act like an independent man in the village, he should go ahead to show such independence elsewhere. It was not Ogaba-Idu who was going to dictate his conduct. Did Ogaba-Idu know he was talking to the Senate President? Did Ogaba-Idu not know that the Senate President could have him dethroned from his stool in the blink of an eye? Bloody civilian, his father had bellowed over the phone. Owobi had not wanted to tell Clement all this the day before. Neither did he tell Clement that the two men he had escorted to the car park had come to see him to ask for details about the palm forest that his father wanted to dispossess Clement's father of. They were top-ranking Ministry of Agriculture officials who had been ordered by someone high-ranking in the Governor's Office to ensure that the Senate President obtained possession of the forest. They had asked Owobi questions concerning the said plantation.

"So, where is the forest?" the more senior officer had enquired.

"It's in Agila, in Ado Local Government Area," Owobi had replied.

"Do you know its size?" the man had continued.

"Not its real size but it's quite vast. It's not less than thirty hectares and there's a stream that runs through it," Owobi had responded.

"So, who is preventing you from having access to it? Who is the current proprietor?"

"It's a man called Obande Ofu. He is the village palm wine tapper, and the forest has been in his family for many

168

generations," Owobi had replied.

"Does he have a duly signed certificate of occupancy, what we call a C of O, to attest to his proprietary rights?" the man questioned.

"I do not think so. Most of the land in the village is either communal land, owned by the community and administered by the Ogaba-Idu, the Village Head, or family land, owned by families and held in trust for all family members. Obande Ofu's forest is family land and normally such land cannot be sold or alienated. It is customary land tenancy," Owobi had answered.

"So, what you are saying is that the man giving you and your father all this *wahala* has no official land title, is that so?" the man insisted.

"No, I don't think he has an official land title or deed," Owobi replied.

"Aha, that solves our problem, your problem. According to the Land Use Act, all land in the State is vested in the Governor of the State. Such land is held in trust and administered for the use and common benefit of all Nigerians. The Governor has the power to grant a statutory right of occupancy to any person. Such a statutory right of occupancy extinguishes all existing rights to the use and occupation of the land in question. The Governor can thus authorise the assignment, mortgage and transfer of the possession of land under customary right of occupancy to someone else for an overriding public interest," the man had triumphantly concluded.

"But what would happen to the current owner. He does not need to have an officially signed certificate to claim ownership because the whole village and the district know the palm forest is his family's. There's even a song which is sung by everyone about the Igbilede stream which provides drinking water to the entire village being filtered by the roots of Obande Ofu's palm trees. So, what will happen to the Obande Ofu family?" Owobi had enquired.

"Well, their occupation of the land ceases, and the man who is preventing you from having access to the land and forest can be expelled using the force of the law," the man had responded.

"This will be the first time in the history of the village that such an event occurs. Nobody in the village has a statutory document indicating his proprietary rights to the land on which they have built their homes, or on which they farm and the song about the Ofu palm trees and water purity will continue to be sung. We cannot change the lyrics of a song that even I myself sang happily for several years with my schoolmates," Owobi had wondered aloud.

"What I'm telling you is the law. So, you tell us when we can go together to the village in question to see the plantation and we'll make all the necessary arrangements before we depart," the man had said.

Owobi had felt ill at ease at what he was about to unleash. He felt what his father was asking him to do was wrong. He felt they were about to destroy another family and to generate some unknown crises in the village. Now, he also felt the timing was wrong. Here was a family that was already facing a terrible crisis with the disappearance of their daughter. Here was a family that looked very united. He somehow had lots of respect for the Ofu family and especially for Obande himself who was unimpressed by his father's wealth, power, and influence. Whereas others in the village were cowed by his father, Obande remained defiant and was prepared to face the consequences of his defiance. He now had explanations about where Oyije's strong will, and character came from. He had tried before to advise his father to let the Ofu family and its plantation be. His father had been furious. He had called him weak. He had told him to grow up or else he would be trodden upon by others, bloody civilians, all his life, for having such a soft heart. The priority for the Aje family was not to spend its time and energy to try to save an Ofu girl. The priority was to acquire the Ofu plantation. If Owobi did not feel up to the task, he was ordered to say so, because other willing and able hands could be approached at very short notice to handle the matter, his father had warned. Owobi had told his father that they would have to discuss matters face to face rather than over the phone, because he was not sure if someone was not eavesdropping in the office. He was however apprehensive about the forthcoming confrontation with his father. It was the first time in his life that he was going to question what his father had ordered him to do. He was going to tell his father that the priority was to save the Ofu girl. He was going to tell his father that he had not given the green light to the officials from the State Ministry of Agriculture to start making the arrangements for the transfer of possession of Ofu's forest. He was going to, for the first time in his life, dare to say 'No' to his father. He was going to be a bloody civilian, without shame.

***

On the road to Abuja, Owobi tried to marshal his thoughts. He compared himself very quickly to Clement who was on the passenger seat beside him and asked himself who between both of them had succeeded in his life, who between both of them was proud of what he had been able to achieve personally and who between both of them served others, the community, better. He acknowledged that he was materially better off than his passenger

171

but then, what else? he asked himself. Here was Clement being trusted by his father to rescue a sister. When had his own father trusted him with a mission without coming to check how the mission was being done at all the stages? Here was Clement leaving his job in Lagos, sacrificing his personal comfort, and going on a mission the outcome of which he did not know, but armed with a strong belief that he could and would succeed in doing what he had set out to do. Was he, Owobi, ready to make such a sacrifice? Here was Clement, never showing off, humble, ordinary-looking. Was this not how people should be? Did the education he received from his father in which success was success only if others saw its manifestations really make any sense? Did conspicuous consumption, the ownership of a fleet of expensive cars, the membership of select private clubs, summer vacations every year in the French Riviera, make one live more peacefully?

Owobi had always wondered why he was an only child. He had not had the opportunity as a child to play with siblings. He did not have the joy of measuring his strength against the strength of older or younger siblings, of competing with them, of fighting with them. It was not normal for a man in the village to be contented with having just one child, even if the child was a son, a God-given blessing because this meant the family name would be preserved for yet another generation. There were rumours that Aje, when he got married as a soldier, was sterile and that it was by mere luck that he had been able to procreate, once. Being an only child had many disadvantages for Owobi. First, it meant that all attention was focused on him, especially when he did not do things right. He could not depend on his brothers and sisters making mistakes that would draw the attention of his parents, especially his father, away from him. Second, it meant there was no other person he could discuss with to complain about how his parents, especially his father, were unjustly treating him. And third, all the menial jobs in the house fell on him. There was no one else that could be called upon to clear the table, to water the flowers, to clean the car or to be presented proudly to visitors and to remain smiling stupidly even when one did not at all feel happy about one's privacy being invaded by adults with their traditional advice that one should be a good boy, a good student and never fight at school.

Owobi was bored at home but could not complain because his father was always watching him. His father wanted him to be strong. His father wanted him to be his ambassador, to show to others how the Aje family had succeeded. So, when he went to primary school, he was always impeccably dressed, with a spotless backpack. It was at the primary school that he had met Mary Oyije Ofu. They sat on the same bench. What attracted him to her was her very carefree attitude, and the fact that she spoke her mind without mincing words. When some of the boys would start fighting during recreation, she would admonish them in such a low and quiet voice that the boys would stop fighting immediately. While Owobi refused to play because he was afraid he might soil his clothes, Mary let herself go, would fall down, get up, run around, without thinking of herself as someone delicate or fragile. And to cap things, Mary was the most brilliant in the class.

Owobi and Mary stayed in the same class all through primary and secondary school and they always arranged to sit beside or next to each other. Mary showed she was very good at mathematics and told Owobi she was going to specialise in a science subject. Owobi had asked her if this was the choice of her father and Mary had said that the choice was hers. She had gone on to explain that the choice was hers because it was her future life she was deciding. Owobi had not dared inform Mary that his father had decided that he was to specialise in Business Administration. He had not been able to argue with his father or dare contest his decision. Mary had been so brilliant that she obtained a first-class bachelor's degree in Botanical Science. During the convocation ceremony, the speaker who announced her name, for her to mount the high wooden platform where many VIPs including the University Vice Chancellor were seated to receive her certificate, told the congregation that she had obtained a first class, upper division degree, a grade that did not exist. He must have willingly made the mistake to draw the attention of everyone present to Mary's excellence. Owobi felt that if Mary had become excellent, it was probably because she was free to be who and what she wanted to be without her father breathing down her neck every time she decided to do something. What Owobi therefore looked forward to the most was to take a break away from his father, to be left alone to make his own mistakes, to breathe. He never told his father this, because the village elders said that it is not the owner of the dog who has to obey the barking of the dog but rather the dog who has to follow what its owner orders.

The opportunity for this break came when his father informed him that he was prepared to finance his postgraduate studies in Business Administration in the USA. He had plans for the future and wanted his one and only son to be a key actor in how such a plan was executed. He wanted Owobi to be better groomed in the art and science of business management and what better place to have such grooming but in the USA? Owobi felt that the thousands of kilometres that would separate him from his father would give him the breathing space he had long craved for but lacking the courage to demand. He also felt that seeing and living in the USA, the Eldorado for many Nigerians, would make him learn new things and open his mind to a better way of thinking, but he was afraid he might not be able to adapt to the American system of education.

The first person he had contacted to give the news about his possible departure to the USA had been Mary. He had wanted to have her spontaneous reaction and her advice. Mary had been very happy for him. She had encouraged him not to be apprehensive about discovering a new and totally different country and educational system. She had told him that many less intellectually endowed Nigerians had gone to the USA and had succeeded with flying colours in their studies. She had ordered him to be positive, to have better self-esteem, to believe in himself. She had jokingly warned that she would personally deal with him the next time he raised questions about his capacity to make it in the USA. This was the kind of language he had heard his father use sometimes when speaking to soldiers under his command. He had thus started to refer to Mary as his Commanding Officer.

His stay in the USA was a mixed bag of stories, full of ups and downs even though he was materially well-catered for by his father. He was surprised at many things he saw. He was first surprised at the layout of his university campus. Unlike the university he had attended for his bachelor's degree in Samaru, Zaria in Nigeria which was cut off from the surrounding world and community, the State University he was admitted into in South Dakota was perfectly integrated into the city. What awed

175

him at first was the mixture of historic buildings, modern facilities and wide green fields with hundreds of squirrels running helter and skelter around the campus. Somehow, he found the environment too relaxing to be 'academic', not at all stressful or intimidating but rather like an attractive tourist campsite. There were lots of sports facilities, lots of athletics rooms, two large swimming pools, and indoor and outdoor sports facilities for sports like basketball, handball, squash, and tennis. Owobi learnt that South Dakota was home to a number of Native Nations collectively referred to as the Sioux.

Owobi was enrolled in the School of Business which was located on the campus green. The School of Business was very close to a Fine Arts Center with three large theatres where concerts were regularly organised. Sometimes, Business School students could be seen lying down on the green, enjoying the sunshine, or playing frisbee. What he found very interesting was the internship program that was part and parcel of his MBA degree. The University had lots of partnerships with a variety of businesses within and outside the State and more than half of the teaching staff were people with industry experience. Owobi was surprised one day when one of the richest businessmen in the State was invited to come and give his class a lecture on human resources management and especially on how to motivate employees. Two things struck him. The first was the very casual and simple way the man dressed: blue jean trousers and a white "I Love Aberdeen" t-shirt. No one who crossed his path on the streets would know he was a billionaire. The second was the simple message the man gave, which was that people skills is the most important skill that successful managers possess and must possess. He stated that his personal wealth came from the wealth of experience of his employees who knew their jobs and who were always depended on to solve problems that came up when they were doing their jobs. For the businessman, empowered employees led to successful businesses. Owobi had then wondered how feasible such an approach would be in Nigeria.

Apart from what he learnt at the Business School, Owobi tried to visit and understand the USA better. Mary advised him to try to visit at least one Native American Reservation and also to pay attention to the living conditions of black Americans. He was very surprised at the level of poverty of one of the Sioux reservations he visited. When he asked for some explanation, he was told by some of his classmates that such poverty was due among many other factors to the fact that only a very small percentage of Native Americans could individually own their land. He learnt that almost three-quarters of land on Native American Reservations are held in trust by the Bureau of Indian Affairs in the US Department of Interior. He learnt that the Native American poverty rate was almost double the rate of the rest of the Unites States. Since Owobi was specialising in Business Administration, he wanted to know the level of entrepreneurship among Native Americans. He learnt that this was very low because very few Native Americans could overcome the many hurdles they faced when trying to establish a business including their limited access to capital, and the very complicated energy-sapping business licensing process. Owobi felt this was wrong. He tried to put himself in the shoes of a Native American. Here was someone who was indigenous in the USA. How did it feel to be dispossessed of one's right to one's land and its resources? How would he feel if he no longer had access to land in his village? How would his father feel? Somehow, he started to feel grateful to his father who had left no stone unturned to provide him with all he needed, with all he wanted, with the comfort of a home and with the promise of a rich and exciting life as a business executive.

His visit to the Native American reservation made him to review his initial admiration of the USA. He saw that all was not as rosy in the Eldorado he had long imagined. He told Mary this and she agreed with him that the USA was a land of opportunities but also a land of misery and poverty for many minority groups. Owobi was particularly affected by the poverty of many black Americans he came across. He saw many doing menial jobs and living in derelict homes. He learnt that African Americans earned about one-tenth of the wealth of white Americans, and he wondered what had happened to the famous 'I have a dream' speech by Dr Martin Luther King Jr. When he visited Washington DC, the capital of the country, he was appalled to see many African Americans living in tents near the Union Station, close to the Federal City Shelter. He was saddened and surprised to learn that while African Americans made up just about thirteen percent of the American population, they accounted for about forty percent of people experiencing homelessness. When he discussed this sometime afterwards with Mary over the phone, she drew attention to how lucky he was to have his father. He would never become homeless, would he, she asked. He did not know if Mary was pulling his legs, if she was only joking, or if she was drawing his attention to the fact that he was always complaining of his father's presence behind all he did.

Something else that struck him about the USA was the layout of many of the cities he visited. He was transfixed by two things. First, the mixture in sub-urban areas of historical and modern districts. In the former, he admired the traditional homes, cozy cottages, and bungalows as well as two or three-storey mansions with front porches on tree-lined streets. He saw that many cars were packed on the street with private driveways between homes. He wondered aloud about the safety of the cars. If the crime rate was that high, as it was reported in the USA, thieves would have a field day breaking into the unprotected cars, wouldn't they? In the latter, there were garage houses or houses with front garages with no sidewalks and he observed that there were many dead-end streets in such districts.

The second thing that struck him was the fact that cars never blew their horns. He was so used to cars and motor vehicles blowing their horns very often in Nigeria that he found the relative silence on American streets strange and unnatural. He shared his thoughts with Mary, who at one point asked him if he was sure he was not going to choose to remain in the USA after his MBA. No way, he remembered having told her. He would miss the Lagos go-slow and many other exciting things in Nigeria, he had gone on to explain.

His stay in the USA had taught him to better appreciate all his father was doing to ensure that he did not fall into want. He began to see himself as somebody very lucky. How many Nigerians could afford to send their children to study in the USA? How many Nigerian students in the USA were like him, not being constrained to do many menial jobs in addition to attending classes, in order to have the means to live and study in the country? Here he was in the USA, not homeless, never short of money, able to attend concerts in the campus whenever he felt the urge. He felt grateful to his father. But his father still remained a mystery to him. Why had he stopped at having just a single child? And why was he so hell-bent on controlling the education

179

of this single child? Why was he someone who liked giving orders and having his orders obeyed? He hoped that one day, he would get to know his father better. Maybe the forthcoming confrontation was not negative after all. He would ask his father some of the questions that had been tormenting him for so long.

He looked aside to speak to Clement and saw that he was asleep, his eyes closed, breathing very deeply. He redirected his attention to the road but could not help thinking about how calm Clement was. He must surely know that his own father in the village was facing the risk of being dispossessed of his plantation by the father of the person driving him to Abuja, and yet he still had the peace of mind not to be wary, not to panic, not to entertain fears. Here he was sleeping peacefully, entrusting the achievement of a very dangerous mission to the family that did not wish his father well. He started to admire such a character, such quietness, such tranquillity of spirits. How come a very active dynamic energetic sister, Mary, came from the same blood as the calm, resigned and undemonstrative fellow seated on the passenger seat here with him?

"Do you want to tell me something?" Clement asked.

Owobi was surprised. "I thought you were sleeping," he responded.

"Not a deep sleep. I was thinking of Oyije. But I'm sure there's something you want to tell me before we get to Abuja, isn't it?" Clement went on to ask.

"How do you know I have something to tell you?" Owobi said, all the more surprised.

"My father told me there are things we should see that others don't see or pay attention to. He told me there are things we should hear that others do not pay attention to. I see that you are a bit apprehensive about taking me with you to see your father. I know your father and mine are not on very good terms at the moment. Something tells me that your father has other things on his mind today than focusing his attention on the rescue of a girl he does not know and who happens to be the daughter of someone giving him some headache in the village. Is that what you wanted to tell me?" Clement enquired.

Owobi was silent for some time. Then Clement continued.

"You know, I understand your father very much, after what I've learnt about him from my father," Clement went on to say. Owobi suddenly stiffened in the car.

"What did you learn about my father, and from whom?" Owobi asked.

"We spent the entire night with my father discussing about lots of things. I came to understand him better and to know why he would never allow anyone take over his plantation, which means more than mere palm trees to him. For him, the plantation is proof that his father believed in him and trusted him to take care of something that had been in the family for ages. Your father believes in you, which is why he has entrusted his business to you. So, for my father, the plantation is where the soul of the family is, where the heart of the family beats. The plantation is his roots but also his means of livelihood which he loves dearly because it is this that has enabled him to feed his family without difficulty. You do not give up something you have eaten or something that will enable you to eat better if you are in good health, and if there is no war that is ravaging your village," Clement explained.

"I think I'm aware of the fact that the plantation is his means of livelihood. There's nothing that stops my father from allowing him to retain a small part of the forest to continue doing what he's very good at doing," Owobi said.

"You do not give one part of your body and self for sale, thinking you can live satisfactorily with the other parts. You do not sell your family history and heritage and name, no matter the high price someone else is willing to pay. But that is not all. My father also told me that when they were younger, your father and he were very close," Clement advanced.

Owobi's heart started to beat faster. He decided to slow down his driving because he believed he was about to hear some things he had never heard before concerning his father.

"Yes, your father was a loner when he was younger. Apparently, your paternal grandfather did not forgive him because his birth led to the death of your paternal grandmother. It was not your grandfather that brought your father up but rather a sister to your grandfather," Clement continued.

"A sister to my grandfather? I have never been told this," Owobi voiced.

"Well, even in the foster family he was brought up in, your father was ostracised. The only friend he had in the village was my father. They were so close that they sometimes confided in one another. Your father told my father when they were young that he would have only one child, especially if the child was a boy. He would try to take care of his son in a different way from the way his own father had taken care of him. In other words, he would lavish all his attention, love, and effort on his one and only son, and bring him up so that he could face the vicissitudes of life without want or deprivation. He would not abandon his son as his own father had abandoned him," Clement continued to explain.

"I now understand a number of things better. But then if they were close friends when they were younger, why are they now on the war path," Owobi wondered.

"Very interesting, in reality. Because they were friends, but also rivals. When they engaged in wrestling tournaments, it was my father who usually beat yours. When there was a sprinting contest, my father always came first, and your father second. And then came their marriage. They both wanted to marry the same girl, my mother. It was my father who was chosen by my mother's family. Can you imagine? If your father had married my mother, you could have been me, and Oyije could have been your sister," Clement went on to say.

"I could have been you? Oyije could have been my sister? Very surprising news," Owobi mused.

"I do not know what really happened afterwards for the relations between both of them to grow sour. When I asked my father questions, he refused to answer. He told me that if I don't want to be stung by bees, I should avoid trying to put my hands into a beehive to gather honey. In order words, he was advising me not to try to get involved in the dispute between others. His refusal to dwell on what really made things to fall apart between them leads me to think with certitude that something else must have happened, apart from the marriage question, for them to stop talking to one another. They speak once in a while to one another but are they really saying things to one another? You know, there's a difference between speaking and saying. Saying things means asking questions and responding to questions. Saying things means listening to the other but also hearing what the other is expressing. It is when we say things with others that we grow wiser and become more mature. I spent the whole night saying things with my father, listening to him and hearing him while he was also listening to me and hearing me. The lesson he taught me in such a short space of time is that we should not only look at people but also pay attention to see them. We should not

183

only listen to people but also pay attention to hear them. We should know how to say things but also learn how to respond to questions or search for responses to our questions. We should not be afraid to ask when there are things we do not understand. So, how come your father is unwilling to help mine, someone he was very close to when they were younger?" Clement asked.

"That is not a question I can answer. And it is not a question I am willing to ask my father. What I know is that he has a very tight schedule, especially now that we are in a period of political campaigns. Though he's not afraid of Dr Ocheme's candidacy in our constituency, he has lots of things to iron out before the forthcoming elections. As a matter of fact, there is a rally this evening that is being organised by his political party, the party in power at the federal level and in twenty of the thirty-six States, to welcome three State governors and several State legislators who have recently defected from the opposition party and chosen to join the ruling party. My father, as incumbent Senate President, has been made the chairman of the caretaker committee whose responsibility is to organise the open and joyful ceremony to welcome the new converts from the opposition party. We'll go and attend the rally before going to see him this night," Owobi explained.

"Okay, as far as I'm concerned," Clement responded.

"Clement, can I ask you one question? How come you are so calm, whereas you must be suffering like hell not knowing where your sister is at the moment?" Owobi enquired.

"Well, Owobi, when the river is full, it flows silently. Thus, the greatest pains are numb and dumb. Anyhow, my getting restless will not change things. It is not the amount of tears I shed or how long and loud I scream that will change things, make the government launch a rescue operation faster or incite the kidnappers to see reason and release my sister. Grief or sorrow do not mean always crying. Grief and sorrow are not supposed to be displayed openly. I know for example that you're afraid too that something dangerous might happen to my sister, though you're not saying so openly. It is nice to see things and to hear things and to know that I'm not the only one who wishes to have my sister rescued. Thanks a lot, Owobi," Clement responded.

The journey to Abuja was finished in total silence. Owobi switched on the radio set and found a radio station that was playing naija music. There was a song by a famous Nigerian singer called Wizboyy entitled "Woman go dey" which was being aired. Clement and Owobi listened attentively. Clement was able to capture some of the lyrics including phrases and sentences like "Anything wey you dey do, my brother, woman go dey for sure" and "Na woman dey do if small pickin go cry, Na woman go dey if hunger dey for town, Na woman go be say man go succeed or fail, don't underestimate her power". If only all men could think like the singer, Clement thought. He was sure Owobi was having the same thoughts. When they arrived in Abuja, Owobi said they had to go directly to the MKO Abiola National Stadium which was the venue chosen for the rally because it had a capacity to accommodate more than sixty thousand people. In addition, there was a Presidential Lounge where the many dignitaries that were sure to attend the ceremony could be comfortably taken care of. Owobi had to park his vehicle along Independence Avenue quite far away from the stadium. The parking lot inside the stadium was full of fleets of sparkling four-wheel drive vehicles with dark tinted glasses used by the various State governors who had come to grace the occasion. An uncountable number of Police Land Rovers filled the car park. Chief Aje arrived on a helicopter which landed on the helipad in the stadium. There was a very loud ovation from the large crowd gathered there. He was the keynote speaker, and he was surrounded on the big wooden dais that had been constructed, by those who had defected from the opposition party to the ruling party at the federal level. These included three governors, three senators, ten members of the Federal House of Representatives and many members of three State Houses of Assembly. Ten governors from the ruling party at the federal level as well as many ministers were also attending.

Chief Aje was visibly very happy. He began his speech by saying, "I am happy to welcome our new brothers and sisters into our fold. I am very happy to announce that the governing party will count among it three governors who have seen the light and have decided that unnecessary opposition is a crime against the growth and development of our great nation. I am happy to welcome senators who are no longer willing to engage in sterile debates on the Senate floor or to wish to block projects that our great party painstakingly conceives to enable Nigeria to become a beacon of development in Africa. I am happy that several members of three State Houses of Assembly have chosen the path of wisdom and national pride. You will not regret your choice to join our family. Like you, I was in the opposition too for several years but was fed up with the small-mindedness of the leadership. I was fed up with the tendency to always criticise what government does. I was fed up with being asked and sometimes pressured to refuse to vote budgets for no other reason than that the budgets were conceived by people who were not members of the opposition party and did not think like us. So, I understand why you have taken the decision to change camp. This shows that you are men and women of principle. This shows you are governed by the will to serve the nation, rather than attempt to paralyse the activities of government. This shows your preparedness to join hands with the ruling party to move our country forward. Your decision to change camp is a welcome development for our country because it shows that not all our people are blind to what the ruling party has been able to do for the country and is willing to continue doing to make our great country better for all its children, irrespective of their tribes, gender, and religion. In the name of our great party, I say welcome to our new members."

There was a loud ovation and all the people in the stadium stood up and started clapping their hands. They clapped for about ten minutes nonstop before they were informed to proceed to an area next to the dais to receive some presents, including a cap with the insignia of the ruling party, and some soft drink and biscuits.

***

"Papa, your rally was a huge success. Congratulations," Owobi said to his father. Clement sensed that Chief Aje was not very happy to see him, though he tried to be outwardly affable.

"It will be a success when all the new members pay their membership fees," Chief Aje replied.

"Well, that should be a foregone conclusion, shouldn't it? The amount is not that high as to frighten governors, senators, and top elected officials," Owobi added.

"Well, you never know people. You should always be on your guard because some people say things they do not mean and present themselves in very good light when they interact with others. I'm sure you must have learnt that in your marketing lessons at the university," Chief Aje opined.

187

"You mean that those you have openly congratulated this evening, and who occupy very important decision-making roles at both federal and State levels are not reliable in what they say?" Owobi wondered.

"You still have lots of things about life to learn, my son. Go to the Senate Guest House, where you usually stay when you come here to Abuja. Ask for a second room for your friend and come back to see me in my office tomorrow morning. I will make some phone calls this evening. I'm sure your friend must be extremely tired. He's been travelling for the past few days. Allow him to sleep very well, so, don't wake him up tomorrow morning. Come alone to see me in the office. The security guards will be informed of your arrival," Chief Aje concluded before dialling a number on one of his multiple cell phones. He looked at both Clement and his son Owobi and gave them a nod to indicate they had been dismissed. He pressed the intercom in his office and asked his secretary to usher in the first batch of visitors who had booked an appointment to see him.

***

"You are going very soft-hearted. This is not the way I brought you up," Chief Aje said to his son, sternly. He was visibly angry.

"This is not how you are going to succeed in your life." He continued, "The world is full of hyenas and crocodiles who will tear you apart and eat you up without the slightest hesitation if you go on this way. We cannot solve the problems of all the people in the village who come to us for help. What we need at the moment is to give priority to where it belongs, which is how to ensure the continuous growth of our venture. I am told you are yet to give the greenlight to those my friend the State Governor sent to help us."

Owobi kept quiet for a few seconds and took a deep breath before responding.

"Yes, Papa, I have not given them the green light and I do not think I will. But then, I'd like to ask you a question. Why the bad blood between you and Obande Ofu? You were very close friends when you were younger," Owobi dared to say.

His father was slightly taken aback and stared at him for a few seconds.

"How do you know we were close friends when we were younger?" he asked.

"Papa, as you like to say, there are things I like to know that I know. What went wrong such that your initial friendship and connivence has now turned very sour? Is it because he took the woman you wanted to marry?" Owobi continued with his questions.

"I can see you have been doing some homework. I hope Obande is not trying to turn you against me," the Chief said.

"No, he isn't trying to and even if he was, he wouldn't succeed. What I'd like to know is why you are so hell-bent on dispossessing someone you used to be very close to of his source of livelihood and his family heritage. There are other plantations that can be acquired. So, why the obsession with Obande's? Why not live and let live? Why the compulsion to erase the Obande Ofu family from the village? And why has such obsession now been translated into your unwillingness to try to rescue his daughter? Do you know what Clement told me? He said if you had married his mother, as you had earnestly wanted to, you might have had him and his sister as offspring," Owobi responded.

"No, I wouldn't have had more than one child, so I wouldn't

have had a daughter," the Chief explained.

"I am aware of that too. I now understand better why you think I'm a soft heart because I did not go into the troubles and challenges you faced when you were my age. But, Papa, no matter what went wrong between you and Oyije's father, you cannot refuse to help them when you know your aid can be very precious. It is traditional in our village for us to help each other. You have been doing this for long, so, why aren't you prepared to do it much longer? What value do you give to someone's life? What will the possession or not of Obande's plantation add or subtract from what you have been able to achieve, for yourself, for me, for the village, for the country? What use is power if it only benefits the powerful? Do not forget that hot water always remembers that it was first cold. We cannot forget where we come from because if we do, we will have great difficulty reaching the destination we have given ourselves, or that you have instructed me to reach. When an animal itches, it scratches its body against a tree. A man asks a relative to scratch his body. It is to the neighbour that one goes to look for fire, Papa. One should always give when one can. All the teeth in the mouth are friends," Owobi added.

"Well, Obande has always wanted to show me he can do things without me. Now you want me to give him my time and energy? Everyone should be required to scratch the part of his body that has been stung by a bee," the Chief opined.

"Papa, you're a constructor, as you showed amply yesterday. A constructor is not a destroyer. Anyway, I will not be your agent of destruction because I do not think what we are doing is right. If this was right, Ogaba-Idu would have come out openly to support us long ago. I do not intend to give the Ministry of Agriculture officials the green light to establish a C.O in your

190

name. I think we will lose our honour if we tell Ogaba-Idu we won't raise any finger to save a daughter of the village. We will surely win the elections but what is the point in winning an election but losing your honour, Papa?" Owobi pursued.

"We'll talk about the Ministry of Agriculture officials at a later date. I have some news to share with you concerning the daughter of the village you're so concerned about that you have chosen a path of confrontation with your father. An obedient child never dies of hunger, but that is another matter entirely. I have tried to make you a man. You seem to want to choose a different path. Maybe when the daughter of the village is finally released, which I think will happen sooner than later, you will come back to your senses and see what I am doing and have been doing for you. And by the way, the time and effort I'm spending calling friends here and there is an investment which I hope will yield appropriate returns in the near future," the Chief concluded.

***

Owobi was very calm when he got back to the Guest House where he had left Clement who now looked less tired. Clement knew something was in the offing.

"What did your father tell you? That we should go back to Otukpo and stop disturbing him?" Clement asked fearfully. Owobi asked Clement to wait for a minute for him to order some drinks from the bar. He asked Clement what he wanted, and Clement replied that he was not thirsty. Owobi ordered for a bottle of ice-cold Star beer. He waited for the drink to be delivered before he responded to Clement.

"No, my father did not ask us to go back to Otukpo. He told me the kidnappers have asked for a huge sum of ransom.

191

Apparently, they have calculated the price for each girl and multiplied this by the total number of girls, to which they added the price of the School Principal, Oyije. He says the payment of the ransom should not be a problem or a big deal. There is a special contingency fund in the Governor's Office that can be used to meet such unbudgeted expenses. What government is thinking of doing is to try to identify those who have done the kidnapping and eventually bring them to face the strong arm of the law. There is an army officer, a Major, who is leaving no stone unturned to try to get at the kidnappers. Apparently, his daughter is one of those in captivity. It would appear that the girls are probably not in a forest, as we are being led to think. Another girl, someone called Zainab, who was also captured long before her other mates were, was released a few weeks ago when her prospective husband, a very rich businessman, agreed to pay a huge amount of money demanded by the kidnappers. According to intelligence reports, Zainab is said to have told the police that she was not housed in the forest but in a compound in a big village or a small town. She was not able to give any clear indications of the location of the village or town, but she stated clearly that she was housed in a compound belonging to a Muslim. There is a Muslim humanitarian organisation, a kind of foundation, which wishes to rehabilitate the image of Muslims and to show that the Muslim way of life abhors violence and such ungodly acts as kidnapping children, which is helping security forces in their attempts to discover the hideouts of Islamic militants in some towns and villages which have been identified by intelligence agencies. So, the good news is that Oyije is safe at least for the meantime. The good news is that the kidnappers have made contact with government. The good news is that government is acting and not standing passively with its arms akimbo," Owobi said, after having gulped some beer from his glass.

"That is very good news. Thanks, Owobi. I know how your father feels and I'm grateful you have chosen the path you have chosen."

"We are human beings. We should not be like the elephant which steps on the baby elephants it has given birth to and kills them. The elephant mistakenly kills its babies and it griefs for a long time because it never forgets what it has done. I do not want my father to knowingly kill someone he is capable of saving," Owobi explained.

"Thank you for convincing him," Clement added.

"Now, we have to wait a couple of days and hope that the outcome will be positive. If that is the case, we might have to go to Sokoto or thereabout. When people kidnapped are released, somehow for some strange reasons, the press and key government dignitaries are there to welcome them back to their normal lives. If Oyije and her girls are released, do not be surprised to see the wives of the President and the State governor being there to warmly welcome them and to draw the attention of the public to the good things their respective husbands are doing and have done for the common man and woman," Owobi declared.

"News media attention and laudatory speeches by the wives of key political figures during the current period of political campaigns is not what is bothering me. I am worried about Oyije's health, mental and physical. I can guess how much she must have suffered under captivity. I hope the press and all the dignitaries who may go to see her, if and when she is released, will not suffocate her with questions. I'll make sure she's left in peace and allowed to get back her bearings," Clement announced.

***

Clement decided to phone Tijjani in Lagos to keep him abreast of things and to dissipate his worries. He waited until he knew Tijjani had finished working at the hotel.

"I was getting worried," Tijjani said.

"I'm sorry I did not call you earlier than now. I have not really had the time," Clement explained.

"You don't need to apologise. I was getting worried that your meeting with your father did not pass well and that things are unnecessarily being complicated by those you have gone to for help. So, what is the news?" Tijjani enquired.

"Well, I'm in Abuja with Owobi, Chief Aje's son," Clement announced.

"Ah, so his father is prepared to help you and your father after all. It is not very easy to know people. Man is a mystery," Tijjani exclaimed.

"I'm not sure it is the father who is willing to help. I believe it is Owobi, the son, who has been able to convince his father that his help is needed. This is even more so since it is our Village Head who asked Chief Aje to help save a daughter of the village," Clement explained.

"How do you know it is the son and not the father who is willing to help," Tijjani wondered.

"Well, there are things that can be seen and heard when one pays attention. This is what my father told me before we went to see the Village Head," Clement replied.

"So, your meeting with your father went on very well, then," Tijjani commented.

"Oh yes, more than well. It was excellent. I have never felt as close to him as I do today," Clement declared.

"I'm very glad for you, and for him, though the circumstances are not conducive to any effusion of joy," Tijjani said.

"My father has a form of intelligence that is rare. He has more intelligence than most of those who are invited to speak to us common men on television or the radio," Clement declared.

"You know, the Fulani say that gifted ears only grow on gifted heads. The intelligent man is intelligent because he learns from all he listens to and hears and makes use of this in his daily life," Tijjani added.

"He thought he had lost me because of who I am and what I have chosen to do. He was happy that I have succeeded in being who I want to be. He has confidence in me. He believes me and in me. It is great to know that one's worth, one's self, and one's words are recognised and acknowledged by those whose name we bear," Clement stated.

"I'm very happy for you. Any news about your sister?" Tijjani asked.

"Yes. Chief Aje asked his son, Owobi, to go and see him alone this morning. Apparently, he has been making telephone calls here and there since yesterday. It appears that the kidnappers have contacted the government and have asked for a huge sum of money in exchange for the release of those kidnapped," Clement responded.

"Which government? The Federal government or the State government?" Tijjani wanted to know.

"Owobi did not tell me. If I had been with him, I would surely have asked the question," Clement replied.

"Are you saying you have not met his father since you were

195

there in Abuja?" Tijjani enquired.

"Just for a few minutes yesterday at the Mashood Abiola National Stadium when he welcomed some new converts from the national opposition party to the governing party," Clement replied.

"Ah, yes, governors and senators who would like to be able to chop and continue chopping as they see their colleagues in the governing party doing. When will this country have men of principles to govern us, men who do not engage in cross-carpeting as a favourite pastime? I do not know your father, but I think the country would be better if it was governed by people like him. You do not need to have gone to school and obtained different degrees to be able to understand that you govern to make people's lives better and not to fatten yourself and your bank account using the public coffer while those you're leading are dying of hunger," Tijjani commented.

"I never knew you were a fan of Dr Ocheme. Anyway, what is important for me is Chief Aje's willingness to help. It appears there's an army officer, a Major, who is spearheading the government response to the kidnappers' demands. What I hope is that Oyije and her girls will be found safe and sound. If that happens, I might have to go to Sokoto to be with her. Owobi has kindly accepted to take me there in his vehicle," Clement revealed.

"You're lucky to have someone who is willing to go the whole hog with you," Tijjani said.

"I think Oyije and Owobi are very close. They were in the same class at school and have always remained in contact, even when Owobi went to the USA for his postgraduate studies. I know I can trust him with my sister. This is not what I would say concerning his father, though it is the father who is telephoning

196

here and there on our behalf," Clement remarked.

6

Mary felt very tired. She told herself she needed to regain a sense of control over her emotions and her pain, but she was aware that this would be a very difficult process, especially given the risk that what happened to her might repeat itself. She felt scared, though she did not show this. This place was not safe anymore. Her school was not safe anymore. The world was not safe anymore. But what she felt the most was the shame of having been soiled. She could not avoid being haunted by unpleasant memories. She hoped she was not going mad, remembering very vividly what she had been forced to endure. She felt helpless and defective. She should have known and anticipated what Mallam (what was his real name? she wondered) had been up to right from the beginning. Why hadn't she fought back more vigorously? Did she not really ask for what happened to her, given her penchant to ask him questions he considered rude and disrespectful? She felt dirty and weak. Who could she talk to and share her pain with in order to lighten the burden? She could not confide in her students. It would make them even more frightened. Clement? Well, he was not there, and he could not have been there because no one knew she would be where she was at the moment. So, she decided to fight against her feeling of helplessness and powerlessness. She had to be able to manage the tough times she was being subjected to. There was only one way out for her, she thought, which was to name what she was undergoing, to write it down. She was going to write what she felt, even if Mallam or whatever his name was had warned her he would scrutinise her writing. What she would write would not only be her own personal feelings but an expression of what she thought was the position of women in Nigeria in general. She would start first by naming what happened to her and then try to indicate the conditions in the Nigerian society that allowed this to happen. She opened the exercise book and started writing. She wrote down thoughts as they came to her.

33rd day (I have counted 33 strands of hair)

I have lost appetite
The aroma of what is served to us now makes me want to throw up
I know I have to eat in order not to fall ill
But I just can't force myself to eat

What is happening at my school at the moment?
Are classes still being held?
Is there a general assembly every morning in the main hall
Preceded by students and staff singing the national anthem?
Is the school library functioning as it should?
And what about the weekly inspection of the girls' dormitories?
Has the Vice-Principal stepped into my shoes
To ensure that all academic and non-academic activities
Are not at a standstill?
What about the netball and basketball competitions
That we have spent long months preparing?
Have the competitions been held as scheduled?
Have the trophies been bought and distributed?
Is the school functioning as usual?

199

I am a sad woman, a helpless woman, an abandoned woman
I do not know what the future holds for me
If my future will change for the better
If the pains will finally vanish
Or at least subside
The pain is not self-inflicted
It is caused by someone
I have never met before
Someone aided and abetted
By the society that has groomed him
To be what he is today
My body had been trampled upon
And my soul aggressed
Today, I am anguished
Will tomorrow be better?
I used to be joyful, active, full of life and enterprising
Now I see myself from afar and do not recognise
Who is sitting or standing in my place
I see a woman, frail and despondent
In a cage, in a man's cage
When will you men let us be?
When will you stop taking us for granted?

What you have done, Mallam, is called rape
It is called rape because I did not give you my consent to touch
my body
I know that in your world
The man's world (some men are exceptions, fortunately)
The word 'consent' spoken by a woman has no meaning
Or you must think that the word 'consent'

Is again something left behind by our ex-colonial masters
To miseducate our girls and women
And teach them values that are 'haram' to you and your male
associates
If you allow me to borrow a word you are fond of using.

You say you are married
Somehow, I believe that you are
I am sure that in your household
Are the following twenty commandments for your wives
Which they are required to obey
So that their husband, you, can live a quiet life
And do what you want, when and where
Rule number one
Never raise your voice for any imaginable reason
Against your husband
Who is always right
In what he says and does
Rule number two
Don't expose your husband's weaknesses
To your family
His strength and fortitude
Should be defended at all times
And at all cost
Rule number three
Never compare your husband to other men
Especially those who seem more successful
In what they do
And who sound more reasonable
In what they say and how they say it
Rule number four

Don't dare attack his ego
His worth should never be questioned
And his belief in his superiority
Never debunked
Rule number five
Don't question his love for you
Believe him when he tells you face to face
That you're the only woman he loves
And that the other women he marries
Are there to help lighten your burden
As mistress of the house
Rule number six
Which is linked to rule number five
Don't threaten to leave his home
If he wants to marry other women
And show to his fellow men
That he has, like them, made it
That he's able to head a big family
And maintain peace
Among womenfolk
Naturally inclined to quarrel and fight
Rule number seven
Do your duties
Take care of the children
Prepare all the meals
Ensure that the house is always clean
Don't wait for your husband to tell you what to do
He has other more pressing matters
To attend to
Rule number eight
Never blame your husband

For doing something wrong
Husbands are never wrong
Though they may sometimes
Not do some things the way we women feel they should
It is we who have not properly understood things
Which are far too complicated
For our simple minds to comprehend
Rule number nine
Never waste the money he gives you
On such unnecessary things as make-up or perfume
Though he may invite his friends for drinks
Which he pays for with the money
Meant for the school fees of the children
Believe in him and his friends
For a husband without friends
Is haram, Mallam, to borrow your favourite word once again
Rule number ten
Never answer questions in public in your husband's name
You are not his spokesperson
Though he can answer in public in your name
It is you that bear his name
And not he that bears yours
Rule number eleven
Never challenge your husband openly in front of children
Never question his authority
Before those who think he is God
He will not take this kindly
And he will be right in showing his displeasure
Even by violent and manly means
Rule number twelve
Do not ask your parents to talk to him on your behalf

When things start to go wrong
Know that when things go wrong
The fault is always yours
So, you should apologise
And seek his mercy and forgiveness
Rule number thirteen
Don't be a nagging wife
Always complaining
Be happy that you are a wife
To such a strong courageous manly husband
Many would like to be in your shoes
To taste the joy of being catered for
By someone so perfect
Rule number fourteen
Avoid being too demanding on your husband
Take what he gives you with joy and happiness
Do not forget that what he needs
Is peace of mind
For how can he face all the tasks involved in being a husband
If he has a wife
Always asking for more?
Rule number fifteen
Be a good listener
Always listen to your husband quietly
And don't ask too many questions
For he might think you're trying to catch him out
To corner him
His reaction might be violent
But the fault will surely be yours
Rule number sixteen
Don't starve your husband of sex

Your body belongs to him
He can want it anytime he feels like it
Your role is to satisfy his desire
Rule number seventeen
Avoid saying bad things about your husband to your friends
His reputation should never be soiled
Among your circle of friends
Who should always see him as the magnificent
The good husband that every sane woman
Is dying to have
Rule number eighteen
Love your mother-in-law
Thank her for having nurtured
Such a wonder
For having groomed
Such a man
Treat her as a queen
When she comes visiting
And forgive her
If she treats you as a mere housemaid
Rule number nineteen
Don't tell your husband
How many children you would like to have
It is not the woman who decides
The size of the family
The man is the housemaster
The size of his household
Only he has the authority to decide
Rule number twenty
A husband lost can never be regained
A wife lost can always be replaced

So, do not forget your position
You are a mere woman
A mere wife
A mere mother
Under the guidance and protection
Of a man, a strong man
Of a husband, a powerful husband
Of a father, with his natural authority
To groom, to educate, to steer, to govern
In his name, and his name alone

(Sometime later: I don't know how many hours later)

The words I'm writing, Mallam (I wish I could know your real name)
Are first addressed to you but equally to other Mallams, other men
I am where I am today
Because of who I am
Because of what I am
A woman, an active woman
I am an active woman who is being deactivated
I am being punished for who and what I am
A woman, an active woman
I have been kidnapped, isolated and raped
My girls and I
Are in solitary confinement
But then
Have we ever been free
Before we came here
To this man's land

This no-man's land?
Is our country
Not in reality, a man's land by design?
Were we as girls, as young girls,
Allowed to have dreams of our own?
No, we were brought up
In preparation for being obedient wives
And good mothers
The daily chores at home
Were to us given, naturally
Sweeping the compound
Going to the stream to fetch water
Going to the bush to fetch firewood
While the boys, future husbands
Played football
And engaged in wrestling contests
In preparation for their difficult lives
As housemasters
None of our anguish
Of our fears and apprehensions
Of our doubts
Did anyone, any man care to hear and listen to
None of our rage to be
Of our desire to be seen
Of our wish to be recognised
Of our yearning to do things other than housekeeping and
house cleaning
Was attended to
By a society which prides itself in being patriarchal
So, a woman can be humiliated
No one raises a finger

Nor thinks this inappropriate
Violence is used to suppress legitimate questions asked
Which the man equates with impertinence and dissent
Who can listen to our voice?
Who is willing to see us for what we can be and can do?
Who can we go to so as to complain about our plight?
Can we go to the policeman
And tell him we have been raped?
He will tell us we are not dead
And that we should be happy to be alive
Can we go to the judge and ask him for compensation?
He will laugh at us
And read to us a piece of legislation
Made by an all-male legislature
That one cannot accuse another without tangible proof
Or the confession made by the person accused
We thus live in a country
In a world
Where our humanity is wilfully negated
Our identity openly despised
Our selves blatantly intimidated and degraded
We hear of human rights everyday
Women's rights never seem to be highlighted
It's a man's world
But we shouldn't make the mistake of losing hope
Because we are strong
Not everyone, not every man can handle
What we have gone through since childhood
What we are going through now
How we have found some hidden strength
Not to despair but remain optimistic

How though vulnerable and socially marginalised
We remain active and awake
Never allowing our minds to be polluted
By negative man-imposed images of our nothingness
Of our uselessness
Of the right of property that the man has over us
Over our bodies, names, and psyche
We are not ordinary subjects
But strong and resilient beings
Capable of withstanding a few accidents that come our way
To test our resolve
To be who and what we are
Women, Active women
Alhaji, this is my message to you
Maybe when you read this
I will be no more
But what I have said
You will have read.

(Some time afterwards, after a short rest)

The calm and resolve on Papa's face
As he prepares to go to his forest
I recollect how he examines various empty calabash kegs
Sizing each up
Until he finally chooses three, four or five
Before he announces to Mama
That he is off
Mama tells him to be careful, as usual
An advice he accepts sometimes with a laugh
Before he tells her that an egg

Knows when and where it can dance

I remember the many lessons
Papa taught me when I was young
Like how he would tell me
That the upper teeth
Would inevitably grow in the mouth
When he thought I was afraid of my capacity to do something
He always taught me to be courageous
Telling me that a small axe
Ends up felling even the largest of trees in the forest
Telling me never to lose hope
By saying that the day breaks
Even when the cock is not there to crow
Teaching me the virtues of generosity
Reminding me that what you give to others
You give in reality to yourself
Giving to others being in reality a form of savings
That yield untold benefits in the long run
How he told me to be always proud of who I am
Never to think I was small and unimportant
Telling me that even the tiniest bird
Has feathers with which to fly, like bigger and stronger birds
Advising me never to hate my neighbours
Because he or she who hates others
In reality hates himself or herself
Inculcating in me the virtues of hospitality
By telling me that it is the domestic hen
That shows the way to the newly arrived
Warning me to always be careful where I walk and what I do
Not to be like the rat

That knowingly
Pulls the cat's whiskers
Advising me not to be afraid of hard work
Reminding me that it is the water that comes out of our bodies
That enables us to fetch drinking water from the well or stream
And that it is the person who wakes up early
Who chooses the best fruit that have fallen from the tree at night
And also that
It is because the legs have moved
That the stomach is full
I also remember him telling me
To learn well at school
Even if the conditions were difficult
He used to say
That the hen which does not go out during rainfall
Will not have good insects to peck and swallow
Words of wisdom which I have never forgotten
In the way I have lived
My personal and professional lives
Always ready to work without counting the hours spent
So that others may become better fulfilled and happier

I can see and hear Mama and her neighbours
Chatting while preparing the rice that would be cooked later in
the day
Painstakingly removing the stones and pebbles together
A very deep sense of community among the village womenfolk
I long for such sense of community
And the possibility of listening to small talk

I hope I will be able

To see Mama and Papa again
To see the sometimes quizzical look on Papa's face
When I said or did something that surprised him
To witness Mama's intelligence
As she gave good advice to her mates with marital problems
Will I see Papa and Mama again?

Dear mother
Mama
You are unsung
Your presence taken for granted
Your readiness to sacrifice your comfort
So that your family does not suffer want admirable
Your goodness taken as given
As come rain come sunshine
You patiently prepare the broth for others
Even as smoke gets into your eyes
And your fingers are burnt by the fire
That you try to keep alive with a raffia fan
Sometimes in the dark
I perceive a face which I recognise as yours
I see the worry and anxiety
In the thin lines that stretch from the left to the right
On a once smooth face now wrinkled with pain
I see cheeks once chubby
Now reflecting the passage of time
And not knowing what has become of a daughter
Dear mother
If a perfect woman ever existed
That would be you without question
Teaching us values of respect and responsibility

You are always giving and never asking for anything in return
Though you are unsung, mother
You are more than a chapter
In my book of life
A book I will hold on dearly to
As I try to charter my path
While following your footsteps.

Dear Father
Papa
I do not know
If I will ever see you again
But this conversation with myself
I must have now
Because rather than wait
Until I no longer exist
Or am able to write, or speak or sing
Must I now express my gratitude to you
For being who and what you are
The lizard no matter how big
Will never become a crocodile
Some men no matter how strong they wish to appear
Can and will never become masters of themselves
Let alone masters of others
I thank you Father
For being modest but incomparable
For being simple but extraordinary
For your lessons in humility
For your openness, tolerance, and generosity
Though I sometimes broke boundaries
You let me be

Though I usually wanted to do things my way
You let me do
And defended me when other men
Raised eyebrows
Wanting me to be where they assigned me to be
Wanting me to correspond to what a daughter should look like
You have shown that you are not blind
And that you see and know others for what they are worth
You are the tree
And we are all your branches
Thank you for showing us the right path
And for giving us the freedom to make mistakes
Which for you is the right way
Of knowing which wrong paths not to take
Thank you, Father
I wish all men could be like you.
So that every one of us is allowed to live his or her life
Peacefully without intimidation
So that men become men
Not when women are silenced
But when women are allowed to blossom
And become totally fulfilled
In their chosen routes to personal success
So that women can become good mothers
But also, good engineers, teachers, astronauts, and governors
Active agents in their communities
Which need them as much as the men
To contribute their might, rightfully
To the achievement of the public good.

Sometime afterwards

214

I must be courageous
And I must accept to learn new things
About myself
And also about others
Life is a lesson of courage
A lesson of pain
For everyone and not just a few
To be courageous
We need to believe in ourselves
Even when circumstances are dire
We need to avoid
Casting doubts on who we are
Even when we are forced to question
Our integrity
Our humanity
Our identity
Our name
Life is like a big hospital
Where we are required to heal ourselves
From the ugliness thrown to us by others
From the pains inflicted to us by others
We have the right to be sad
We have the right to be happy
We have the right to go wrong
We have the right to be who we want to be

Sometime afterwards

My students want to know when this nightmare will end
When I tell them it will soon end

I do not know if I am right
But what else can I tell them?
Will they believe that the man
Who has kept them in bondage for a while
Is now suddenly turned a friend?
A well-wisher...?

7

Dr Ocheme had been advised that he needed to go and visit the Village Head and ask for his support if he wanted to have any chance of success in the forthcoming election. Unlike his opponent, he was relatively unknown in the village, so he needed people who could influence villagers to convince them that he was someone solid who had the satisfaction of their interest as his guiding compass and primary goal. Who better to woo than the Village Head, he had been lectured. He was given a crash course on decorum and protocol. It was indispensable he went to see Ogaba-Idu, as someone who had succeeded in his life, as someone who had made it so that the villagers could believe his promises and words. Do not forget that the footprint of the elephant wipes off the footprint of the antelope that had trodden on the same path, he was reminded. So, his counsellors had concluded, the most effective way of showing he was a serious contender rather than a mere bird of passage was to impress the Village Head with a very large variety of presents. His arrival in the village and his visit to the Village Head's compound should be full of noise, he was advised. He was equally advised to ask one of the members of the Council of Chiefs to escort him to the Village Head's compound. This would show Ogaba-Idu that he was not alone in the village or district. That would give him better credibility.

Dr Ocheme did not want to engage in such ostentatious display of success or wealth. He felt this was an old way of political campaigning which he knew was antithetical to how he viewed things and the changes he wished to bring to the contest for political power in Nigeria. He could not discredit the money-centred nature of Nigerian political contests before his students during his lessons at the university only to become its willing disciple, he argued. He told his advisors that it was improper for him to show the Village Head who and what he was not. If his opponent, Chief Aje, engaged in such display, he, Professor Ocheme, was different. The change he was preaching had to start from somewhere. It would start by showing everyone in the village that he was different from Chief Aje, and that he had a different agenda from that announced by his opponent, a member of the old guard. Unlike his opponent, he, Professor Ocheme, wanted power to be given to the people. He wanted the people to know he was one of them. Giving expensive presents to the Village Head would only mean that he had lots of money to throw around. The people would not believe his message and would think he was part of the ruling capitalist parasitic elite, that he was a member of the club of vampires, sucking all the blood from the body of the country, and leaving it barren and unable to cater for the welfare of the common man. His counsellors told him this would be suicidal, but he remained adamant. He however accepted to ask one member of the Council of Elders, Chief Ebenezer, to go along with him to Ogaba-Idu's compound.

He was surprised to see the whole Council of Chiefs assembled in Ogaba-Idu's compound waiting for him. When Ogaba-Idu had accepted to receive him, nothing had been said about his being required to expose his ideas to the entire Council. Chief Ebenezer did not seem to have been put in the know either. Or maybe he was pretending to show surprise while in reality he had known what was being staged. The Chiefs were sitting in a row of chairs with Ogaba-Idu sitting in an armchair placed in the middle of the row. There were two empty chairs. One was in the row on which the Chiefs were sitting. Chief Ebenezer went to sit on it. A second was placed about three metres away in front of this row, facing it. Dr Ocheme was directed to sit on it. Before sitting on it, he bowed down to greet the Village and District Head.

"May your reign be long, peaceful and prosperous, Ogaba-Idu," he greeted.

"Welcome to my abode. We are happy to welcome an illustrious son of the soil back to the soil where he grew up," Ogaba-Idu responded.

"We always find the way back to our homes, even in the middle of the dark night with no moonlight. We cannot go to unknown destinations if we forget where we come from," Dr Ocheme responded, obsequious.

"Wisdom does not live in a single house or in a single village, you know," the Village and District Head declared.

"Yes, but it is advisable to go to where you know that there is no scarcity of wisdom. Where else can one go except where one was first educated and taught the basics of life by elders?" Ocheme responded.

"That is quite true. A child who has been taught by elders to wash his hands can eat with elders anywhere else he goes. So, what brings you home from up north. We are told you want to change the world," the Village and District Head asked.

"No, Ogaba-Idu. Not change the world. I do not have such a pretension and I'm not presumptuous. I do not want to change the world. I only want to change how our country is governed and to give the common man the power that is rightfully his," Ocheme explained.

219

"Do you know what the common man wants? Does he want power or food to eat and water to drink for himself and his family?" the Village and District Head enquired.

"The two are not opposed, and as a matter of fact, go together. The more power the common man has, the more access to basic necessities such as food, water, hospitals, good roads, uninterrupted electricity and others he will have," Ocheme indicated.

"So, you think you are better placed than our son-of-the-soil, Chief Aje, with all his experience and network, to make our lives better?" Ogaba-Idu wondered. The other Council members were looking at Dr Ocheme without showing any visible signs that expressed what they were thinking. Dr Ocheme did not know if they were interested in what he was saying or not. Only Chief Ebenezer Akpoge appeared to show some sign of interest. He was listening to him more attentively than the others.

"I am not saying I am better placed than Chief Aje, who like you know has been in the governing circle for decades and decades, to make your lives better. I do not have that pretension. What I'm saying is that I will do things differently. I will put myself in the shoes of those in the village and try to use this as my guiding principle in preparing government programs. I will visit the village very regularly to see how projects we have started are being implemented. I will not think that the way I live in a posh quarter in Abuja is the way other Nigerians live. I will view life and living conditions from the point of view of villagers who do not have regular electricity supply, who do not have potable water, who do not have good roads and who barely manage to survive in a country blessed with numerous resources which are unfortunately being stolen by those in power for their sole benefit," Ocheme explained.

One of the members of the Council of Chiefs, Ella Ohe, who had escorted Chief Aje to Ogaba-Idu's compound the last time Aje had come to campaign in the village, coughed and shuffled his feet on the floor. He asked for the floor.

"Professor, are you serious when you say you want to put yourself in our shoes?" he asked.

"Very serious, Chief. If I wasn't serious, I would not say it. Others say things they don't mean. I say things I mean, which is why I am teaching at the university, where I mean to change the mentalities of those we are grooming to become leaders tomorrow for them to think first of the nation and its millions of marginalised and secluded inhabitants before thinking of themselves and their bank accounts. Yes, Chief, I mean what I say and say what I mean," Ocheme responded.

"I am surprised. It is not the person who talks better who is better. It is not the one who has a long beard who has a longer and better experience at doing things. The inexperienced fisherman who owns a very small boat cannot honestly promise the village that he will catch enough fish to feed the entire village for four years. No, this just can't be possible. You say you'd like to put yourself in our shoes. Can I ask you a few questions?" Chief Aje's man went on to request.

"Yes, please go ahead, honourable Chief," Ocheme responded.

"You live in the senior staff quarters in your university, don't you? So, your housing is provided by the government. You have tap water, good toilets, continuous electricity supply just to mention a few things that common men like us here in the village don't. You have a comfortable air-conditioned office with all the furniture provided by government, haven't you? Are you telling us that you are really willing and prepared to change from such government paid comfort and come to live like us here in the village, Professor?" the Council member enquired.

"When I say I'd like to put myself in your shoes, I did not mean leaving where I work and live in Zaria to come and live like you in the village. There are things you are very good at doing in the village that I am not and will never be able to. I did not mean that I was willing to change my lifestyle. What I mean is to change how government goes about its business. To see things from the point of view of the village. To see where problems are in the village and to solve such problems. This for me is the essence of government, solving problems. Government is not about receiving foreign visitors with all the pomp and pageantry in Abuja. Government is about making better the lives of those that are governed, especially those who live very far away from Abuja and other big cities like Lagos, Kano, Enugu and Port Harcourt. I'm sure you'll agree with this, Chief," Ocheme argued.

"Making better the lives of those governed, of course I agree with you. Can our lives be better if we don't eat more than once a day? Chief Aje provides us with the palm oil we need regularly to make our stew. Can our lives be better if we don't drink? Chief Aje gives us the money to buy things to quench our thirst. What do you bring to us to make our lives better?" the Council member enquired.

Chief Ebenezer coughed and asked for the floor.

"My brother Elder Ella has said things right. Like we elders say, the man who knows how to speak will never become poor. But then, let us not expel the second child from home because only the first brings us water to drink and food to eat. Let us listen to his project and see how we can make it work. We should avoid putting all our feet in a single hole. The hunter who is sure of

222

catching the antelope is not the one who puts his trap in one place alone but one who puts traps in different places," Chief Ebenezer said.

"Yes, Elder Ebenezer. Except that a good hunter knows exactly where to lay his trap. A good hunter does not forego the big game that he's sure of catching for a smaller one he is not sure of catching," Chief Ella replied.

"I agree with you, Elder Ella. But you know, sometimes it is necessary to change the place you go to catch games. If you remain in one place, the game you catch will become rarer and rarer," Chief Ebenezer opined.

"Yes, Elder Ebenezer. But don't forget that what belongs to you is what you have swallowed. What you own is what you can see and touch and smell. What you can't catch with your hands does not belong to you, no matter the good words spoken by our son- of-the-soil here, our distinguished professor. Waiting for a better tomorrow that may never come is not what will make me feed my family. With Chief Aje, I can feed my family today. Chief Aje does not talk but does. The last time he came, everyone in the market became richer. The last time he came, we did not go thirsty for several weeks after he left. When your eyes itch, you scratch them very gently because it is with them that you see. You do not rub them violently thinking that another person is there to lend you his eyes," Chief Ella declared.

Ogaba-Idu made a slight movement with his hands and the debate between his two Chiefs ended. He did not want the honourable professor to be humiliated. He was young and had not understood the code when coming to the village to ask for support. The professor was a good speaker. He was a teacher after all, wasn't he? But then, making good speeches did not mean one was strong enough to lead and to govern. What his people in the village needed was not good speakers but those capable of giving them things, those who showed they had succeeded and wanted to share the proceeds of their success with their village men and women. What had the honourable professor brought with him to share with the village? Nothing, absolutely nothing. Did someone who had taught in a university in Oyiboland for several years have nothing to show to the village that he had made it? Why all this talk and palava about change and change if such change did not have a visible physical expression? Of course, the professor was still young and inexperienced. He was still a green banana. Was it not one of his ancestors who had said long ago that a green raw banana becomes yellow and ripe with time? He would have to advise the professor to be patient. When you rush your eating, you face the risk of burning your mouth. It is the rain which falls little by little that ends up filling the river. He would advise the professor to retire from the race and join the village in supporting Chief Aje's candidacy. The professor might not like his message, but he was sure of what the village would obtain from Chief Aje if he became successfully re-elected. The worm prefers to go into a humid section of the soil and the elephant has confidence only in its own tusks, he mused.

"Thank you very much, professor, for coming to see us in the village. We are all very happy to see that our successful sons have not forgotten where they come from. If you forget where you come from, you will be unable to know where you are going to. We are happy that we have two illustrious sons who are capable of being our eyes, ears, and voice in Abuja. Not many of our neighbouring villages and districts can boast of who and what we possess. I know that you are a man of quality and that you will do great things for our village and for the country as a whole. The chick that will become a strong cock in future is identifiable right from the start. You will become a strong cock that will till the soil for the village to eat better. But, you see, another illustrious son of the soil has already come to seek our support. I do not want to have two sons of the village quarrelling about who is better at being our face in Abuja. I do not want any enmity between both of you. I do not want any hatred to grow between both of you. I would like both of you to get to know yourselves better because I think your differences come from the fact that you have not been able to understand yourselves better. The village is going to stand for Chief Aje for the simple reason that you give gold only to the person who knows about gold. Otherwise, the person will think it is valueless and will make an axe from it. You do not show to the old gorilla the way to the stream. You wait for the tree to grow and become big before tying your cow to its trunk. Chief Aje is a man of experience. Try to get in touch with him. Try to be together with him, because together, you will be stronger, professor," Ogaba-Idu concluded.

Dr Ocheme was discussing with Chief Ebenezer.

"What Ogaba-Idu wants me to do is to retire from the contest and endorse Chief Aje who is the incarnation of all I have been fighting against. My students will take me for a joker. They will say I have become a turncoat, that I have sold my soul for a few dollars, that all I have been trying to do all along has been to make noise so that I can be picked out and bought by the grande bourgeoisie that is in control of the affairs of the State. All those who listened to and watched me the last time I was invited as a guest to the national television network, many of whom sent me congratulatory messages for my courage at calling a spade a spade, will now laugh at me and despise my name. I can't bring myself to do that, Chief," Dr Ocheme complained.

"You know I warned you beforehand. Chief Aje is so entrenched here that any attempt to contest his power and influence is suicidal. Only one man, Obande Ofu, the owner of the large palm tree forest close to the Igbilede river, has so far resisted his power," Chief Ebenezer responded.

"Are you talking of the palm wine tapper, the one whose daughter, the principal of a girls' unity college in Sokoto, was abducted a couple of weeks ago?" Ocheme enquired.

"That is the man. Chief Aje has been wanting to drive him out of his forest for quite some time but he has refused to cave in. All the threats and intimidations coming from Chief Aje have not weakened his resolve in any manner. What is strange is that Chief Aje and he were very close friends when they were younger. No one knows when things went sour in their relationship and what generated this sourness," Ebenezer said.

"Do you think I should go and see him and solicit his support?" Ocheme demanded.

"It is not advisable. He has other things on his mind at the moment, given the abduction and disappearance of his daughter. And Ogaba-Idu told us recently that he has asked Chief Aje to do all that is necessary and in his power in Abuja to get the daughter found and rescued. It appears Chief Aje has accepted this mission. You cannot therefore go to someone and ask him to support you in your fight against the person who has accepted to rescue his daughter. No, it is not advisable to go to him. You should maybe think more seriously about Ogaba-Idu's advice. The possibility of having the village and district behind you does not appear very high as things stand," Chief Ebenezer advised.

Owobi had just received a phone call from his father. He rushed excitedly to Clement's room in the guest house to inform him of what his father had just told him.

"Prepare your suitcase. We have to leave for Sokoto immediately. My father tells me that he has been informed by very reliable sources that some kidnapped girls would be released within the next two or three days in Sokoto. This means that they might be released as soon as tomorrow morning. No one knows where they will be found, but apparently, the conditions demanded by the kidnappers have been met. My father did not tell me what these conditions were. No one in government wishes to admit that ransoms are being paid by government through circuits no one knows about. Papa will telephone me tomorrow morning in Sokoto to give me further details, but we have to be off immediately for Sokoto," Owobi announced.

Clement's heartbeat went faster than normal. He had been standing in his room, pacing up and down in deep thoughts. He sat down and took a deep breath for a few seconds.

"Are we sure it is the kidnappers holding my sister and her girls captive who have made contact with government? How come government is in contact with them but is unable to locate and neutralise them?" Clement wondered.

"You want the government to try to locate and neutralise them and in so doing endanger the lives of those kidnapped?" Owobi asked.

"Don't tell me that with all the billions that are spent every year on Nigeria's defence budget, we do not have the necessary equipment to trace where kidnappers are contacting government officials from in order to locate and root them out. Do we not have several squads of elite soldiers?" Clement said.

"We should be happy that those kidnapped are going to be released. My father is sure Oyije and her girls are part of those who will be released as soon as tomorrow. I'm sure the government will try to find out from the girls as much information as possible in order to get to know the hideout of the kidnappers and eventually organise a military expedition. That, I'm sure of, one hundred percent," Owobi maintained.

"I hope the government officials who will debrief Oyije and the girls will speak to them with tact. They have gone through a very traumatic experience and what they need when they are released is to be left alone to slowly and steadily recover their senses and rediscover the lives they used to live before their abduction," Clement wished loudly.

"I'm sure the intelligence officials are well trained. They have the experience of negotiating with kidnappers and of supporting victims of abduction. You needn't worry about that. But first things first. Let us go to Sokoto, bid welcome to Oyije when she's released before we worry about the qualification of those who will simply be doing their job by asking Oyije some crucial questions."

They had eaten their supper long ago. Mary and the girls heard many voices speaking in the room where they had eaten. They fell silent and were petrified. There seemed to be more voices than the voices of the two men who usually stood guard there. There were a few new voices that they had never heard before. Mary and the girls knew that something was in the offing. Two of the girls started to cry silently. The voices continued to chatter. Then, the men chatting started laughing apparently at a statement or joke one of them had shared. The chatting went on excitedly for some time and then all became quiet. A voice, Mallam's, told one of them to open the room where the girls were preparing to go to sleep. Mary smelt the perfume and almost threw up. She exhaled slowly, held her breath for a few long seconds and then inhaled very quickly. Mallam was dressed impeccably with a long sky-blue kaftan. He wasn't wearing any cap on his head. He asked Mary to show him the exercise book he had given her. She picked it up from under her mattress and gave it to him. When Mallam opened the first page, he saw that there were many strands of hair hidden in it.

"What are these," he asked.

"They are pieces of my hair which I have cut and which I count to know the number of days we have been held in your compound. We don't have any idea of time, so this is my only way of knowing the number of days and how time is flying," Mary replied.

"So, how many pieces of hair have you got here with you, now?" Mallam enquired.

"There should be thirty-three or thirty-four," Mary answered.

"That can't be true. You have not spent thirty-three or thirty-four days in my compound. You have spent far less," Mallam declared.

Mary kept quiet for a few seconds. Was she going insane? Had she lost all sense of reality? Each time she had slept after supper and woken up, she had diligently cut a strand of hair from her head and had used the stock of strands as a form of clock.

"Well, take back your hair. I don't want to have any trace of your passage in my compound. Secondly, I have changed my mind. I will keep your exercise book because I don't want you to leave with any trace of how you and your students feel, of what you saw or heard. I can see that the exercise book is quite full. I can see some words crossed out and replaced by others. I did not want to give you an eraser with the pencil because I wanted to know all your thoughts," Mallam continued.

"There are some thoughts that are not expressed, you know. So, it is impossible to know all the thoughts of someone else," Mary responded.

"I can see you have not learnt your lesson. You are always either asking questions or speaking when you are not supposed to," Mallam said, coolly.

"I'm sorry, Mallam. I did not wish to be disrespectful," Mary acquiesced.

"You are all leaving this compound now. You will be blindfolded and gagged. Do not resist because this will anger my men, who as you can see are in a very good mood at the moment. So, don't resist and don't ask questions. Have I made myself clear enough?" he asked, looking intently at Mary.

"Yes, you have. Nobody will resist and nobody will ask you questions. We surrender ourselves to your goodwill," Mary responded.

Then he addressed his men in the Hausa language.

"Kun san abin da ya kamata ku yi," he addressed them.

"Mun ji ka, yallabai," they all responded in unison.

"Bai kamata kowa ya gan ku ba," he warned them.

"Za mu yi da hankali," they all responded.

The girls, blindfolded and gagged, were led outside the room. Mary had the feeling they had crossed the courtyard that led to the part of the house where she thought they had stayed for more than thirty days. She then imagined they were walking out of the house altogether. Everything was quiet. She started to panic inwardly. Where were they being taken to? Were they being transferred to another house owned by Mallam? Or a house owned by one of his lieutenants? Then she thought she heard the sound of a motor engine running. Yes, it was the sound of a motor engine that had been left running. She listened attentively and she was sure it was not one engine running but several. She was shoved in brutally into one of the vehicles. It was a car, a station wagon, because she heard two men sitting in front of her, most probably the driver and a colleague, two girls crying beside her and three or four girls equally crying behind her. She had a tight knot in her heart. She did not know who was sitting with her in the car and she could not tell them to stop crying. Then the car suddenly shot forward, turned left after a few minutes, drove on for three to five minutes and negotiated a roundabout three times before taking a road and picking up speed. The road they were on appeared to be tarred because the drive was not bumpy. All the glasses in the car had been wound up but Mary tried to listen as attentively as possible to capture any strange noise that might come to her from outside the speeding car. She heard nothing apart from the girls crying beside and behind her in the car. Sometimes the two men in front spoke quietly to one another in Hausa. They spoke in a confident manner, Mary thought. Where were they being taken to, she wondered again? Was Mallam going to be there to meet them? How was he going to act and react after having read what she had written in the exercise book? She had written what and how she felt because she had thought she would eventually one day leave her captivity with her exercise book. There again, she had been misled by Mallam, she acknowledged. What other surprises had Mallam prepared for them? She reflected on his wish to be called Mallam instead of Alhaji. Was he trying to show himself as a simple man, a 'Mister' as the word 'Mallam' can signify or did he wish to show her that he was himself an educator, a teacher, someone learnt in koranic studies, as the title 'Mallam' can also signify? He had shown himself to be someone well educated. If he preferred to be called Mallam, it was certainly a way of drawing attention to the fact that he was a learned person. Was this a way of trying to impress her?

With hindsight, she thought this might be the only logical explanation. If he had been trying all along to impress her and to show that he was more learned than she was, she thought she now better understood some of the things he had said to her. For example, his anger when she had drawn his attention to the fact that they were both in the same boat as teachers. He had tried to diminish her role as a teacher, had tried to show she was being pretentious in thinking that she, as a woman, could ever imagine she was exercising the same profession as him, a man. Was it this uncontrollable desire to show his superiority to her that had led him to brutally assault her sexually? How could her mere presence as a woman ignite such uncontrollable violence?

She hoped that he would not be infuriated by the things she had written and that if they came into contact once again, she would not be subjected again to his violence and brutality. She would prefer to die rather than face the same ordeal. Yes, maybe that was the way out. Just disappear. Wipe herself out of the face of the earth. Then, no one would be able to hurt her anymore. She would rest in peace and have eternal peace of mind.

She felt the car slow down and heard a few other cars behind theirs blowing their horns. Their car seemed to turn left and drove on for what seemed an eternity. Then it slowed down. The girls had all stopped crying. The car seemed to take a road that was a bit bumpy. There was a sudden sharp rise and fall on the surface of the road, or maybe it was a street, that caught the girls in the car unaware. They all grunted and kept quiet immediately afterwards. They had promised not to complain. The car ground to a stop. Mary heard other cars stopping behind theirs. She heard one of the two men in front of the car leave the car. She listened attentively and thought she heard other car doors behind her being shut one after the other. She thought she heard the men discussing. Then she thought she heard some of them walk away to somewhere.

They came back after what seemed to be an eternity and spoke to the others who were waiting for them around the parked cars. The driver to her car came back and gave instructions to his colleague. His colleague went out of the car and opened the door for all the girls in their car to come out. He told them to hold each other's hands because they were going to be led into a big room where they would each be led to a spot where they would be required to sit down. They were not to try to engage in any physical contact with one another. They were to remain silent and wait in the room. Mary thought she heard other girls being led into the room in front of her before her turn came. She held the hand of the girl in front of her with her left hand and that of the girl following her with her right hand. She sensed passing through an open door, of being led forward for a few seconds before someone violently seized her two hands and directed her to a spot where she was ordered to sit down on the floor. She sensed the other girls sitting not too close to her. The room was dark, but it smelt somehow familiar. Or maybe she was getting delusional. What were they waiting for? Who were they waiting for? She had lots of things she would have liked to put into print. She had no other choice but wait.

Waiting and waiting. This is what she had been doing for more than thirty days, in her mind, though Mallam had announced she hadn't been in captivity for that long. Who was right? The captor or the captive? When was this captivity going to end? She wished it would end, even if it meant dying. She was tired. She was fed up. She could no longer stand being gagged, blindfolded, and being transported to an unknown destination by unknown people acting on behalf of an unknown master for an unknown project. Her energy was depleted. She felt the warm tears running down her face and allowed them to run, quietly. She heard footsteps dragging on the floor around her. Then the dragging and noise of footsteps abated. Then the noise disappeared altogether. Only the sound of girls crying softly, or sniffing could be heard.

Mary panicked but sat still. They were surely in a big spacious room. She thought she heard the noise of some far away vehicles, but she was not sure if it was not her mind making things up once more, as it had calculated thirty-three days for a duration that was far less. Her life history unfolded in her mind very rapidly. Was this not what usually happened when one's hour to depart was imminent? She was now willing. She was extremely tired of struggling against forces she could not master, could never master.

8

The girls could hear lots of voices. Someone with authority was shouting orders. Someone else violently kicked the door to the room slightly open and two men penetrated the room cautiously. One of them shouted to those who were outside, all of them with their hands on the trigger of the heavy assault weapon each was carrying. He told them, "Roger! They are here!"

The man barking orders outside instructed both men to check the room to ensure there were no bombs hidden and to be very careful. The men were visibly part of an efficient trained elite corps. The checking was done very quickly before the other members of the rescue team penetrated the room. They removed the gags and blindfolds from each of the captives in the room and opened the door and the windows widely.

They were in a large room at the Giginya Memorial Stadium, not far from the Usman dan Fodio University Teaching Hospital in Sokoto. The girls were asked to slowly try to get their eyes used to the light. Small bottles of mineral water were distributed, and the girls were told that their captivity was over. There was a large crowd including members of their families, the press, and top government officials, including the wife of the Governor of the State, who were waiting to welcome them back to their normal life. They were told not to answer questions from the press. Some military intelligence officers would chat with them, and they were advised to answer questions as honestly as possible. They should not be afraid to give any information they might think useful or important. They were now safe, thanks to the effort of the government and nothing would happen to them again. Then they were told that an experienced medical practitioner working with the search and rescue team of the joint military and police squad was going to talk to them before they were allowed to go out of the room and meet their waiting families.

A man wearing a white blouse with a stethoscope around his neck was ushered into the room. He made a rapid examination of all the girls and spent a few minutes longer with Mary. He then informed Mary and her girls that the following days might be very difficult for many of them. Some of them might face what he called posttraumatic stress disorder. They might have sentiments of intense fear, helplessness and even horror. This was normal, he told them. Some might feel very depressive, perhaps not immediately, but long afterwards. This was also equally normal. Some might have nightmares for several days, weeks, months and even years. This was also quite normal. They should not panic and should know that there were very qualified medical doctors and psychologists working at the University Teaching Hospital who had been contacted and were at their disposal to help them face these challenges. Their school had been closed indefinitely since their abduction, so they should take the time to reconstruct themselves. There was no hurry in this reconstruction which was going to take a long time before yielding the desired results.

This was the first time Mary heard her school had been closed. She became distressed. She had thought that plunging herself back into her tight daily routine would help her to gradually forget the experience she had undergone. She had imagined in some far-fetched dreams she had had what she would do in her school to try to make up for lost time if she were released one day from her captivity. There would be mountains of files in the in-tray to attend to, undone tasks to start and finish rapidly and new projects conceived and put into gear. Now, she was being told she would remain idle, while trying to reconstruct herself. She could not think of how she could possibly bring herself to doing nothing, of having an empty agenda and re-establishing her identity at the same time. What would she be doing twenty-four hours a day and seven days a week? Then she looked at her girls. Something was wrong. There were far fewer girls than when they had been captured and taken by several vans to the forest. Where were the others? Had they been released earlier on?

She saw the head policeman (or was he an army officer?) look at her intently. She told him there were other girls missing. The officer nodded his head in agreement and responded that the authorities were aware of this, which was why any information given by the released girls and herself would be of immense importance to intelligence agencies. The officer then addressed the girls in a very soft but grave voice. They were reminded that their aid was capital in the fight against insecurity and were told once more that they should say anything that they could remember about where they stayed during their capture and who their captors were. They should not think any information as minor. If they remembered anything about the men they were with, their height, their number, anything about where they were kept, noises, smells and any other thing that struck them during their captivity, they should not be afraid to talk about these.

Mary listened silently. She tried to remember things about Mallam and his compound but was alarmed at her sudden amnesia. Her memory was completely lost. The more she tried to remember things, the more she was unable to recollect anything. She started to sweat. The medical practitioner was looking at her. He advised her not to try to force her mind and to try to take things easy. She was however warned to be prepared mentally to face the outside world they were about to be connected with. They should not be caught unawares by the loud clapping that would surely greet their appearance by those gathered outside the room and waiting for them. The crowd had been waiting since eight in the morning. Now, it was almost ten, they were informed.

There was a loud roar as the girls were led outside into the open field of the stadium. Then there was a brief silence as the crowd suddenly realised that all the girls were dressed in black chadors with a veil covering their heads but leaving their faces free. Then the crowd started clapping. This went on for more than five minutes. Mary saw an elegantly dressed woman wearing a dress in mermaid style and surrounded by a few policemen, come towards her. This was the wife of the State Governor. She had come on behalf of her husband and his government, to welcome them back to the real world. She hugged Mary and each of the girls to the accompaniment of incessant flashes of photographs that were being taken by many journalists who had been convened to the event. Then she held her breath. Was it Chief Aje she was seeing? This could not be. She pinched herself to see if she was not dreaming. Chief Aje was beaming with joy. No, this could not be. How come he was there as part of the welcoming delegation? He came towards her, hugged her, and waited until all the photographs had been taken before releasing her. He told her there were two other people who were dying to meet her. Mary started sweating and almost fainted. Two journalists held her until she came to and could walk without help. Then she heard a very loud and excited "My CO! Welcome back to us, my

CO!" She turned towards the direction the shout had come from and saw Owobi and Clement rushing towards her. She stopped dead in her tracks. This was impossible. She now knew she was seeing and hearing things. Clement was supposed to be in Lagos. Owobi was supposed to be in Otukpo. Chief Aje was supposed to be in Abuja. Had the elections been held already? She did not think she had been away for that long. Why were the three of them here in Sokoto? she wondered. How did they know she would be out today and how had they arranged to be in Sokoto at the same time? Owobi hugged her. She retreated quickly and stared at him. She wanted to ask him a question, but her mouth went dry. Then Clement held her very tightly for an interminable period. Both of them started trembling and sobbing. Owobi and his father stood back and waited for them to calm down. Mary pinched Clement on the face. She explained she was trying to make sure she was not dreaming. Then she looked at Chief Aje and at Owobi. She thanked them for coming to Sokoto to see her. She asked Owobi if he had used some perfume or after-shave. Owobi was surprised. He responded that he had put on a very mild after-shave and was surprised at her question because he had long been using the same after-shave and that she had never asked him the same question before. She did not explain why she was suddenly interested in knowing if he had used an after-shave.

Chief Aje told them he had to leave for the airport. He had to go back to Abuja where serious matters were waiting for him to attend to. He said he was glad the rescue operation had gone well, even if not all the girls had been released. He was sure the three of them had lots of things to discuss among themselves. Clement informed his sister that they had reserved a suite for her at the hotel they were staying in. It was advisable she did not go back to her residence at the school which had been closed

239

indefinitely. Mary wanted to know how long the school had been closed. She was told the school had been closed almost three weeks earlier so less than twenty-one days. Mallam was therefore right when he told her she had spent less than thirty-three or thirty-four days in his compound. Her sense of time during captivity had thus been seriously impaired, even though she had prided herself in having thought of an ingenious way of counting the days and nights. She accepted Clement's plan. As they were about to depart from the stadium, Mary saw an army officer walking briskly towards them.

"Good morning, Ma. I am happy to see you. My daughter, Ngozi, used to speak about you. I am happy to see you after all I have heard about how you manage your school. What has happened to your school can happen anywhere. My daughter, Ngozi, was among those kidnapped but I have not seen her today. I do not know where she is. Do you know where she is? Was she with you? Were you all together in one place or were you in different places? Sorry for asking you all these questions but I'm very worried," the man said. Mary looked at the man and suddenly tears started running down her cheeks. Clement and the army officer were alarmed. Mary started to shiver uncontrollably, and Clement had to wrap his arms around her. Mary stopped shivering and she apologised to the army officer for allowing her emotions to take the better of her. She did not know how to answer him. Was she bound to tell him the truth or was it more humane to allow him to entertain the hope of seeing his daughter one day? She was facing a cruel dilemma. To be honest with him and herself and tell him the truth that his daughter had been raped and killed or to understand the pain he was going through and not give him an additional burden, the bad news that he would never see his daughter again? She told him that the girls were secluded

240

in different places and that she had no news about his daughter. The army officer thanked her profusely and wished her all the best in her subsequent struggle to overcome the traumatic experience she had gone through.

"Why did you not tell the Major the truth, dear sister?" Clement asked.

"How do you know I did not tell him the truth, Clem," Mary responded.

"My dear sister, I know you need to have some rest, so I won't bother you with unnecessary questions. But there are things that can be known if one sees and listens carefully. I know for example that there are lots of things that are bothering you, but I won't ask you any questions. I will be here to listen to you any day and any time you decide to unburden your heart. Don't forget that, sis," Clement responded.

"I have the feeling I am hearing my father speak. It is a very curious feeling. Any news about him, by the way?" Mary wondered.

"He's very worried about you. I had to go and drag him out of the forest for us to go together to see Ogaba-Idu and ask for his help," Clement answered.

"Are you telling me you went to the forest to see Papa? Wonderful! You had vowed never to set foot in the forest, remember, because you thought Papa was not proud of you. So, you finally decided to breach your vow. That is the best news I have heard for a very long time. I have always hoped that the relationship between both of you would improve for the better. That this has happened while my back was turned is one of the mysteries of life I won't be able to understand. For the first time in a long time, I can say that I'm happy, Clem," she went on to say.

"I'm very happy too. I have not been as close to Papa as I am now. Papa is a fountain of knowledge. A minute spent with him makes me ten years more mature and twenty years wiser," Clement added.

"So, you travelled all the way from Lagos to the village? Thanks for the trouble. But how did Chief Aje and Owobi get involved? I do not see Papa crawling to Chief Aje with whom he is in conflict to ask for his help. Papa is too proud to do that. Papa has always said that Chief Aje's wealth is stolen money and that Aje should be ashamed of himself when he comes parading in the village before people who know the meaning of making a real effort every day to feed their families," Mary wondered.

"It was not Papa who asked Chief Aje to help. It was Ogaba-Idu," Clement responded.

"Ogaba-Idu? How did Ogaba-Idu get involved?" Mary enquired.

"It was my idea and Papa allowed me to explain things to Ogaba-Idu when we went to see him. Ogaba-Idu was quite cooperative. So was Owobi. Owobi's father took some convincing from his son before he finally accepted to lift his finger and make the phone calls that brought us to Sokoto to wait for you. Owobi and I have been in Sokoto for three days. Chief Aje came here last night. We were surprised when he called us last night and told us where we should meet this morning. We never expected his presence here in Sokoto. He never told us he would be coming to be part of the welcoming party. I saw how surprised you were at seeing him. You seemed to cringe away from him when he hugged you," Clement observed.

"Did I? If I did, it was not something calculated. I was just surprised that someone who has always been at loggerheads with

242

Papa should be here in Sokoto and try to hug me warmly as if my safety and security were the most important things that mattered to him. By the way, have the elections been held?" Mary asked.

"No, not yet. Why are you asking?" Clement questioned.

"I think I understand his presence better and how eager he was to have all the journalists snap as many pictures as they could," Mary opined.

"That was what crossed my mind too. And you would not believe it, Owobi has the same impression. His father is visibly pursuing his political campaign. Owobi said it was very unethical for his father to want to reap some immediate political benefits from your ordeal. I am beginning to like him, you know. Behind all his attempts to show off, he is a kind and humane person," Clement commented.

"He must be waiting for us to have dinner at the restaurant. I am not hungry at all. Lots of things have happened in such a short space of time. Go and eat with him. We will see ourselves tomorrow. I hope I will be able to sleep. I have not slept on such a large comfortable bed as I have in the suite here for quite some time. I have slept on a mattress on the floor with five, then four, then three of my girls. I hope I'll get used to sleeping alone," Mary declared.

"Don't panic anymore. I am here. I promised Papa I would bring you back home," Clement said.

"It is not easy to stop panicking. It is not easy to stop thinking of what we have been through. It is not easy to feel safe, even in such a secure hotel as this. I thought my school was safe and secure. Look at what happened. My trust in those around me has evaporated. It is nice you're here with me because I don't know if I would have believed anyone who told me I was now safe and sound. I am afraid of having nightmares. I will be afraid if someone knocks at my door. But then, I know I will have to learn to forget what happened to my girls and I. I know this, but can I really bring myself to do this, to forget? I don't know if I can, to tell you the truth," Mary stated.

"I know there are some things bothering you. If you want to share them with me, I will be there for you. Don't forget that extreme suffering does not mean one is dead. Joy does not mean one should always be laughing. Real joy does not need to be shown, it is something discreet. When my eyes see you, I do not laugh but I'm joyful. When you are alive, you should be joyful because you can feel things, you can say things to people who appreciate you, you can show your different emotions, you can live. So, don't let what is bothering you destroy your life. You do not allow the beans you have cooked to get cold before you put some oil in it to eat. You should not wait to be dead before you appreciate the life you have, even if some things go wrong," Clement affirmed.

"I have the strange feeling I'm hearing Papa speak," Mary commented.

All the major Nigerian newspapers ran sensational headlines. There were pro-government headlines such as 'Government Saves Our daughters' or 'Government Shows Its Power and Compassion' or 'Fortunately, Government has Won a Battle Against Insecurity'. There were also highly critical anti-government headlines including such statements as 'Many Other Girls Missing: What is Government Waiting For?', or 'Three weeks of Procrastination: Inefficiency at the Highest Level' or 'Nobody is Safe Anymore Anywhere'. For each headline, there was a corresponding article that was either for or against government response to the problem of abductions. Below the headline 'Government Saves Our Daughters', under which there were two large pictures, one showing the wife of the State Governor in an elegant dress hugging one of the released girls in a black chador, and the other showing a joyful and smiling Senate President, Chief Aje, hugging the principal of the school from which the girls had been abducted, readers read the following article: 'Today is a day of joy. Today is a day of rebirth and renaissance. Rebirth and renaissance for dozens and dozens of fellow citizens who have had their personal freedom and liberty curtailed for three weeks in the hands of what and who we can call ruthless and brainless brigands. The dastardly act committed by the group of terrorists hiding under the cloak of Islam could have been left unattended to if our government had not decided very courageously to take the bull by the horns and leave no stone unturned to get in touch with the abductors and arrange the peaceful release of the girls and their principal. The message our government has sent to those who wish to disrespect our laws and our individual liberties and freedom to live without fear for our lives anywhere and anytime is that they will be chased to their hiding places and their capacity for nuisance reduced by the might of government. Our daughters are back with us, and we should rejoice that they are back because of the concerted effort of all the intelligence agencies that government ordered to work together to achieve a single objective: ensure that the search and rescue operation be done without any abducted person dying.'

Below the headline 'Nobody is Safe Anymore Anywhere', which was accompanied by the picture of many of the released girls all dressed in black, one could read the following text: 'What a circus we have been invited to watch! What absence of dignity and self-control! Whereas only a few of the abducted girls were released (for a sum of money that no one wants to talk about

245

because no one wants to spoil the sport), there we were watching top government officials shedding crocodile tears and trying to show an empathy that they don't have for the released girls and their families. How can the same government that negotiates with kidnappers tell Nigerians they are not aiding and abetting their trade? How can a government that preaches that it is engaged in a do-or-die battle against terrorists, discuss with their representatives and satisfy conditions demanded by such terrorists? Where can we be safe in a country now governed by people who are afraid to use the heavy arms of the law to flush out terrorist groups that are now multiplying by hundreds because they know they have the understanding ears of government? Nowhere, is the answer. We are not safe anymore in Sokoto. We are not safe anymore in Kaduna. We are not safe anymore in Ilorin. We are not safe anymore in Enugu. We are not safe anymore in Port Harcourt. We are not safe anymore in Benin City. We are not safe anymore in Lagos. We are left anywhere we choose to live in to the mercy of groups of individuals who can decide, when their bank accounts are in the red, to kidnap us and obtain huge sums of money for our release. Rather than contain the multiplication of such terrorist groups, we are given the spectacle of people who live in plush residences and who have their rich and extravagant lives paid for by public money coming to show their sympathy to people they hardly care about in reality. Yes, a circus indeed.'

Many of the newspapers equally published a communique. It was from a leading Islamic Literacy Foundation which wanted to draw attention to the fact that Islam was against violence, especially towards women. The communique was brief and read 'The Abdullahi Garba Islamic Literacy Foundation, which has branch offices all over the nation, wishes to draw the attention of

246

the Nigerian public to the fact that Islam is a non-violent non-discriminatory religion. Islam states that in the eyes of Allah, men and women are equal and have the same obligations. There is thus spiritual equality between men and women, who are complementary. In Islam, there is no distinction made between the acquisition of knowledge between men and women. Each woman can engage in the pursuit of knowledge and the development of her intellect so as to better herself and help her community better. The Quran and the Sunnah make it a duty for every man and woman to seek education and to try to better himself or herself. Abducting girls who wish to fulfil this obligation is thus not the work of people wishing to promote the Islamic faith. These people forget that Aisha, Prophet Mohammed's third wife, was herself a teacher and that she taught both men and women. Those who are choosing to abduct our daughters and who present themselves as Islamic groups are infidels who have wrongfully appropriated our religion in order to portray it in a very bad light, worlds apart from our essence and the teachings of our Prophet Mohammed, peace be upon his name.'

Mary received a call from the hotel receptionist. There were three men, from Military Intelligence, who wanted to speak to her. They were waiting at the lobby. The receptionist informed her that the visit would not last long and that the officers just wanted her to fill in a few loopholes in the information they had been able to obtain using other means. Mary panicked. She knew she could not refuse to go down to see the officers at the hotel lobby, but she was afraid to be alone with them. Had some intelligence officers not visited her school after Zainab's disappearance a few days before the school was invaded by Mallam's men? She told

247

the receptionist she would be down but asked him to tell the officers that she would be coming with her brother, whose room was beside hers in the hotel. She knocked on the door to Clement's room, told him three people who introduced themselves as Military Intelligence officers were down in the lobby to speak to her and that she wanted him to be with her during the conversation.

"Good afternoon, Ma. Sorry to disturb you. We know you have been through a very traumatic experience, and we are aware of the fact that you need to be left in peace. We only wish to speak to you for a few minutes to see if we may learn something from you that will enable us to better know which groups of bandits we are dealing with. Please, do not hold back on anything you know, you saw or you heard. Everything you tell us will be of extreme importance and we hope it will lead us to get closer to the organisation or the organisations that have decided to wage a war on innocent citizens. So, what can you tell us about where you were, who you saw, what you did and what you heard?" one of the men said.

Mary was not at ease. All five of them had been led to an office behind the reception counter where five chairs had been arranged in a circle. It was when they were all seated that she registered a very strong body odour which made her stomach churn. She wanted to throw up but controlled herself by biting her lips. She requested that the door to the office and one of the windows be left open so that some fresh air from outside could enter and circulate in the room. She had the impression of having some difficulty in breathing. Clement asked her if she was all right. She asked him in a low voice if he did not smell something abnormal in the room and he said he didn't. She said she would like to sit near the open window. Clement took a chair next to hers. The man who had just spoken was pot-bellied. He had a short black goatee and he seemed to be the leader of the three. He was in a chair that was facing Mary's. Mary thought he spoke with a heavy Hausa accent.

"What information would you like to have from me? I hope I will be able to provide them because there are lots of questions I have been asking myself for which I have not been able to find answers," Mary responded.

"We already know that you and your girls were not held in a forest. By the way, do you think you know which forest you were taken to in the first place?" the man continued.

"No, I don't. We were all blindfolded and, in any case, all forests look the same at night," Mary replied.

"That's okay. So, can you tell us anything about where you have been over the last three weeks? Anything and everything that come to your mind. For example, where you slept, how you ate, who you saw, what you did, anything and everything you remember, Ma," the man said. His two other colleagues each brought out a small pocket-sized notebook and prepared to jot down things Mary was going to say.

"I think you should ask me questions and if I can answer them, I will. It would be better that way," Mary suggested. She asked Clement for his opinion, and he agreed with what she had suggested.

"That's okay, Ma. We will do as you have suggested. So, first, do you know how long the drive was between the forest where you and your students were first assembled and where you slept on the first night?" the man asked.

"No, I don't for the simple reason that all our watches were seized," Mary replied.

"Oh. So, you can't tell us how long you were driven from where you slept the first night to where you were held the days afterwards, neither," the man continued.

"We were not transferred elsewhere, at least not me and the girls that were with me. We spent the whole period in the same compound," Mary announced.

"This is very essential information," the man said excitedly. "So, you were all put in the same place, all of you?" he pursued.

"No, not all of us. Five or six of us were together. The others were assigned to other members of the group. We were, I think, in the compound of the leader, because it was he who ordered that my students and I be divided into many small groups and it was he who assigned each small group of students to a guardian, as he called them," Mary said.

"How do you know you were with the leader of the group?" the man enquired.

"It was easy to see. There was deference from the others each time he spoke. Anything he said was an order that was carried out without question from those around him," Mary explained.

"So, you were in his compound, were you? Was the neighbourhood in which you stayed quiet or noisy? Did you hear the sound of cars, motorbikes and other sounds that you hear in a city?" the man demanded.

"We spent most of the time indoors, locked in a room. So, it is difficult to answer this question," Mary responded.

"All the time indoors? Are you sure? Did you never leave the room you slept in?" the man insisted.

"I was personally taken once or twice to go and see the leader in another part of his compound," Mary replied.

"Was it a big compound?"

"Yes, a very big compound. I remember asking myself why

a man who was visibly rich, because the internal walls of his house were all beautifully decorated, why such a man should engage in kidnapping others to be paid a ransom. A ransom was paid for our release, wasn't it?" Mary enquired.

"I do not know. Let me do the questioning, Ma. So, when you were taken to go and see the boss, did you notice anything, hear any sound that might direct us to where we should be focusing our attention on?" the man continued.

"No, the only sound I can remember hearing was that of some sheep bleating. Ah, yes, I also remember hearing the call of the muezzin. So, the house we stayed in was close to a mosque," Mary said.

"Close to a mosque? There are many mosques in all the cities around us. It is impossible to start searching using this criterion. Were there any vehicles in the compound? If yes, can you recollect what types of vehicles?" the man went on to ask.

"No, no vehicle was parked inside the compound. When we were being driven out of the compound blindfolded, we had to go out of the compound to board the vehicles that were used to transport us to the stadium," Mary answered.

"What else can you tell us about the compound?" the man added.

"There was a koranic school inside. The leader has a group of *Almajiris* who he says he's bringing up to become future Islamic teachers," Mary declared.

"How do you know this?" the man enquired.

"He told me," Mary responded.

"What else did he tell you?" the man asked, with an excited tone.

"That my school should not exist. That girls should stay at home to be brought up by their mothers to become good wives rather than go to schools such as mine to have Western education that is a colonial legacy," Mary replied.

"What was your response to him?"

"Well, I tried to tell him we were both teachers and that girls as much as boys should have the right to pursue knowledge in order to better themselves," Mary answered.

"What was his reaction?" the man continued.

Mary suddenly went quiet. All became silent in the room. The voices of some people speaking at the receptionist's could be heard vaguely. Mary tried to speak but was unable to. It was as if her mouth had suddenly become paralysed, her jaws stuck and her lips unable to move. Clement saw her trying to open her mouth with difficulty. Then the tears started dropping from her eyes, first lightly and then profusely afterwards. Mary began to shiver, first slightly, and then violently with convulsion. Clement rushed to her and held her in a very tight embrace, asking her not to worry anymore, not to be afraid to speak, because he was there with her. Mary was left to cry on Clement's shoulder for quite some time. Her shivering subsided and Clement asked her to dry her tears. This was the first time he had seen his sister so vulnerable. He held her in the tight embrace until she stopped shivering and asked her if she wanted to continue answering questions from the three men. She responded that she was willing to go on with the debriefing exercise.

"Were you well fed?" The man resumed his questioning.

"Yes," Mary responded.

"Were you forced to do things, to sweep rooms, to prepare meals for example?"

"No. The girls only had to sweep the room we were sleeping in every morning."

"Did you have easy access to toilets and bathrooms?"

"Yes."

"You say the leader had a koranic school inside his compound. Did he try to convert you to become a Muslim?"

"No, he didn't. But he gave me a new name," Mary said.

"What name was it?"

"Aisha."

"Aisha? How did you react?"

"I told him I would remain the person I am."

"How did he react?"

"He said I would be Aisha as long as I was under his care."

"So, he said that, did he? Did he give the others new names?"

"No, none that I am aware of."

"The leader and his men, do you know how many they were?"

"No, not at all."

"Did they talk in your presence?"

"No, not at all. I think they must have received orders not to talk to our hearing."

"Were they violent with you and the girls?"

Mary went silent again. Clement jumped from his chair and held his sister in a tight embrace for the second time. He told her not to struggle to control or stop her tears. Mary sobbed on his shoulders for minutes and minutes without end. When she stopped sobbing, Clement asked the leader of the three men if the debriefing could be concluded rapidly. Did they not see that his sister was psychologically damaged? What was the use asking her to go, for a second time, through the traumatic experience she thought she had escaped from?

"Sorry, Ma. We'll end very soon and will stop disturbing you. When you were being driven from the leader's compound on the night of your release, can you say approximately how long it took the vehicles you were in to travel from the city you were held to the stadium in Sokoto?" the man went on to say.

"As I told you, none of us had a watch and even if we did, we were all blindfolded," Mary responded.

"Okay, Ma. We won't disturb you any longer. Thanks for having answered our questions and sorry for what you have been through," the man concluded.

"Can I ask you a question?" Mary requested.

"Please, go ahead," the man replied.

"How come the government is in contact with people who abduct girls with impunity, accepts to negotiate with them and yet is unable to identify them, locate where they live and neutralise them?" Mary wondered.

"Can you please explain yourself more clearly?" the man asked, taken aback.

"My question is, how can the government negotiate with someone, agree to pay him a ransom and yet pretend it does not know who it is dealing with?" Mary insisted.

"Personally, I do not know what you're talking about. I am only trying to do my job, which is to find out who is behind your abduction and to make sure he doesn't, or they don't repeat their dastardly act. I have never been involved in negotiating with any group of bandits, because that is what they are. We are going to leave you for you to try to forget your terrible experience. I'd like to tell you that we are all very sorry about what you and your students have gone through. I am giving you my business card. If you remember something you think will be important in helping us to locate the compound of the leader of the group which kidnapped you and your students, please do not hesitate to get in touch with me. All the best, Ma."

Chief Aje was very happy. Things had turned out better than he had expected. His smiling face was on the first page of many of the major newspapers which had a very wide circulation nationwide. His decision to travel to Sokoto had been taken at the last minute. When he had learnt from his very reliable sources that the school principal and some of her girls would be released the following day, he had decided less than five minutes afterwards that Sokoto was where he needed to be the following day. He had made a few calls and the journey was finalised. He asked his source if the relevant military and police intelligence agencies knew when and where the released girls would be left by the kidnappers. He was informed that this information had not been divulged by the kidnappers for fear that security forces might lay a trap for them there. The source had however told him that the girls would be released in an open rather than closed space, most probably at the Race Course or in one of the city stadiums. It was late at night after he had arrived in Sokoto and had booked into a hotel that he was informed that the girls would be found at the Giginya Stadium the following morning. This information would be confirmed very early the next morning so that the families of the captives and the press could be asked to come to the stadium. All the families had been informed that their worries might soon be a thing of the past though they had been warned that not all the kidnapped girls would be released and be among the batch that would be welcomed imminently.

Chief Aje had taken his son Owobi by surprise. Owobi was speechless for some time when he had called him to tell him he would inform him very early the following morning about the time and venue of the meeting with the released captives and that they would meet there. Owobi had asked where he was calling from and was left open-mouthed when he had learnt this. The

255

person who was taken aback even more was Mary, the released captive. Chief Aje knew he had to have pictures of him hugging her taken by the many members of the press that would be around. So, he had gone straight ahead to hug her before she was able to get her bearing, and who knows, rebuff him. This would be disastrous for him, for his image and reputation. So, he had to do this rapidly, in a split second, in a military-style hit-and-run raid.

Things had gone according to his plan. He was happy to see his face on the front-page of many newspapers, though the comments in some were cynical if not openly hostile.

He thought he had been able to kill three birds with one stone. First, he had been able to show Ogaba-Idu that he was a man of his words. He had promised he would push all the right buttons in Abuja to get the government acting more efficiently in its drive to rescue Mary, a daughter of the village, from the hands of those who wished her harm or ill. Secondly, he had shown that there were no daggers drawn between himself and Obande Ofu. He had shown the entire village, including Obande himself, that he was prepared to do things for the man who refused to do things for him. Thirdly, he knew he had nailed the coffin of his challenger, Dr Ocheme. Like the villagers had rightly said, this was a johnny-just-come, someone who believed that possessing a Doctorate degree in political science gave him the necessary qualifications to contest let alone win elections. How can somebody who does not possess any teeth ask for a piece of meat with bones? Who but an inexperienced child picks up hot charcoal with his bare hands? A very turbulent and undisciplined goat should not be surprised when its horns get broken one day. In which society does a young chicken engage in a fight with a cock and wins? Not in my village, Chief Aje thought.

He imagined Dr Ocheme buying a newspaper and seeing the face of the man he was daring to challenge on the front page, accompanied by the good news that several members of the population Dr Ocheme qualified as the common man had been rescued by someone he had presented all along as part of a selfish, corrupt, and parasitic governing class. If Dr Ocheme was as intelligent as he tried to show, surely, he would withdraw from the race. This would ensure that Chief Aje, as the sole candidate in his constituency, would have a resounding victory, an argument he might need to use in his bid to become re-elected as Senate President by his colleagues in the Senate.

Chief Aje thought that this was the first part of the plan: show his influence at the federal level, show his willingness and readiness to do something to save lives, including the life of someone from the village, and neutralise possible opposition to his political ambitions. The second part of the plan now had to be put into gear. This involved neutralising opposition to his economic plans. He needed to acquire Obande Ofu's forest. He thought that he now had a few ace cards up his sleeve. Surely Obande would like to show him his gratitude for having done all that was necessary to rescue his daughter, by accepting to sell his forest, after so many years of resistance, wouldn't he? Surely, Ogaba-Idu, who had personally asked him to act on his behalf to come to the aid of the Ofu family, would not understand Obande's continued resistance to his offer, after the success of the rescue operation he had promised to encourage, would he? This second part of the plan was for Chief Aje the most important. It was to his economic business that he would turn towards if things went wrong in his political life. Though the possibility of a military coup d'état happening was quite dim, he did not want to keep all his eggs in one basket. He needed to anticipate risks, and this meant diversifying his activities. The links between himself and his Italian associates were strong and the trust between both parties high and reciprocal.

The one worry he had concerning how the second part of his plan would be successfully executed concerned his son, Owobi. He had watched the way Owobi had hugged Mary in Sokoto. He had seen the tears in his eyes. He had seen his huge relief. And of course, he could not forget what Owobi, his only son, had told him a few days before: that he was not prepared to be his father's agent of destruction.

What does he know about destruction anyway, given the extremely comfortable life he has had up to this moment? Chief Aje mused. One could not construct, without destroying something, could one? he wondered in his mind. As you needed to break eggs before being able to make a plate of omelette, so you needed to cut down trees to make firewood and to kill an antelope in order to eat a piece of meat. If he wanted to continue to have pieces of meat in his soup, he needed to have a constant supply of antelopes. He needed to have a constant supply of palm nuts and palm kernels. He needed to expand his sources of supply. Obande Ofu's forest had to be had. He was apprehensive about going on the warpath with his son, but his decision was taken: he was going to contact the Ministry of Agriculture officials in the State himself and give them the greenlight to finalise the writing of the certificate of occupancy in his name. He had wasted enough time, and time-wasting was not what he had learnt long ago at the Armed Forces Command and Staff College in Jaji. What must be done must be done.

He was sure he would convince his son that he was working to protect the family interest, his family's interest. Did the village elders not say the hind legs of an animal follow the forelegs and not the contrary? Children therefore have to follow the footsteps of their parents, he concluded. But he would wait until his re-election first as Senator and then as Senate President was in the bag, something he knew was a foregone conclusion, before trying to tame his son. He needed his son's assistance in the first and did not want to jeopardise this by getting into an open antagonism with him. He was sure he would make Owobi see eye to eye with him in the long run. He needed to be patient. Did the elders not rightly say that it is one drop of wine after the other that fills the calabash?

For the meantime, he needed to calm his nerves and better manage the stress and strain of the moment. He dialled a number, heard a young, excited girl call him 'Daddy', and told her they would meet at the usual place two hours from then. He had a few outstanding matters to handle at the Senate before joining her.

Owobi had offered to drive Clement and Mary to the village directly from Sokoto. He told them he was aware that many villagers would not understand why he was driving them himself to the village, given the bad blood that existed between their parents. He said his response to anyone who asked him why he was doing what he was doing would be that the elders themselves wisely said that a foetus does not know its age, in other words, that a child is not answerable for his parents' acts. Clement and Mary thanked him for his offer but said they would use Mary's car, parked in her residence at her school and that they could go from Sokoto to Otukpo in a convoy before both of them went ahead to the village alone. Owobi had insisted that he would like to follow them to the village, just in case something happened to their vehicle before they reached the village. Mary and Clement knew there was no use arguing with Owobi, so they had reluctantly accepted. Owobi then advised Mary to try to see a medical doctor as soon as she could. He knew of a very fine doctor in Otukpo who had a cabinet with two or three other specialists, including a physiotherapist. The physiotherapist might be able to suggest some useful exercises that would help drain the enormous tension and anxiety generated by three weeks of being held in captivity. Mary thanked him for the suggestion but said what was on her mind then was to see her father and try to relax as much as possible in the village. She said she needed the quiet of the village to try to start her gradual rebirth. If she felt she needed any medical attention, she would not hesitate to get in touch with him.

Owobi was driving behind Mary's white Peugeot 504 car. It was Clement who was driving his sister's car. Owobi knew that what he was doing and planning to do would not please his father at all. He had seen the way his father disapproved of the long and warm hug he had given to Mary at the stadium in Sokoto. But what surprised him the most was the fact that his father had himself hugged Mary. He did not know at first why he had come to Sokoto, but when he saw his father hugging Mary but looking squarely into the TV camera and at the various reporters who were taking pictures rapidly, the mystery was uncovered. He remembered having mumbled a statement to the hearing of Clement that the spectacle they were watching was very unethical and unpardonable. Once a politician, was one bound to always be a politician? he questioned. Was it not part of good breeding to show restraint and be less self-centred when others were in pain?

Owobi thought of the two people in the car in front of him. He imagined them chatting and discussing. He would have liked to be discussing with them. Here he was in a very luxurious Range Rover, alone, with no one to talk to, with no one to share his dreams, fears, hopes and projects with. He had never had anyone to really share his thoughts with. He somehow felt a sense of loss. Being an only child was not easy. He would avoid making this mistake when he would be ready to found a family.

Owobi thought about what the future held for him. He would never abandon his father and his father's business, but he was equally never going to bully the Ofu family anymore. The Ofus had enough troubles already and he did not want the Ajes adding a supplementary trouble. He would tell the Ministry of Agriculture officials that the acquisition of the Obande Ofu forest was not a priority anymore. His father would be furious, but he was prepared to maintain his decision.

"Are you feeling better or are you still as tired as you were a few days ago, sis?" Clement asked.

"I do not really know how I feel. Sometimes, I feel what I'm going through is not real. I feel that what I went through never happened. But then, I also sometimes feel that it is real, because I can remember some conversations very vividly, I can remember very vividly things I smelled. I seem thus to be going to and fro between dreamland, nightmare land and reality. It is very strange," Mary responded.

"It is normal for you to feel that way. Anybody who has gone through what you have will feel the same way. I even think that your reaction so far is exemplary, sis," Clement continued.

"My mood changes from relief to anger, from belief to distrust, from self-confidence to self-loathing. I'm happy to be out and to be alive but I'm sad that there are other girls missing. For some, I know why but for the many others, I don't know

261

anything. Not knowing is not a feeling I'm used to having. When I don't know things, I usually ask people I know can help for advice and guidance. Who can I ask here to find out where some of my girls are still being held captive? I cannot go back to Mallam to ask? I don't even know where he lives, or where we were kept," Mary complained.

"Who is Mallam?" enquired Clement.

"He is the man who held us captive, at least the man who was visibly the head of the compound where we were secluded in a dark room," Mary explained.

"Mallam is a title, not a name. You mean you were secluded in a dark room for three weeks? Why did you not say this to the intelligence officer who debriefed you a few days ago?" Clement asked, surprised.

"What tangible result would that have generated? The military intelligence is supposed to know things that for one reason or the other it doesn't. Yes, all six of us at first. Then the number decreased to five, then to four."

Mary kept quiet for many long minutes. Clement continued driving and made no comments. "From six of us, we became four and I could do nothing to stop that. Sometimes, I wonder if what happened to us was not my fault. I failed to protect myself and my students. My school is closed, and my girls can no longer acquire the knowledge they are so eager to acquire. I must have gone wrong somewhere. I must have…" Mary went quiet again. Tears started to stream down her cheeks. Clement still made no comments. This time, his sister was not shivering as she had been a few days earlier. He could imagine the pain and trauma that went with the experience that was being recollected by his sister. He did not think it was wise to try to interfere with this recollection and how his sister interpreted her experience. The elders said that the wise listener opens his eyes and ears but not his mouth. One never spits out all the saliva in one's mouth, one is constrained to swallow parts of it, he reasoned. There were thus moments where silence was the best response when listening to someone in pain. He waited patiently for Mary to resume her remarks. After about ten minutes of silence during which Clement concentrated on his driving, while making sure that Owobi's car was not far away behind him, Mary resumed her comments.

"I must have angered someone somewhere for my school to be targeted," she declared.

"When terrorists strike, anyone can be a target. You are in no way responsible for what happened to you. Are you saying the principal of the school from which the Chibok girls were kidnapped by the Boko Haram group had done something wrong and was being punished? No, this is not and cannot be a justification for someone deciding to invade a school at night, abduct innocent students and then negotiate their release, most probably for money," Clement explained.

"So, you are sure money was paid to Mallam for our release? Why did the intelligence officer not acknowledge this?" Mary enquired.

"Who is this Mallam who does not have a name? Of course, money must have been paid to him. I don't see how he or the group he's working for would have accepted to release some of you. Of course, the government will never openly announce that it accepted to pay money in exchange for the lives of hostages. This would be a greenlight given to criminally oriented groups to see hostage taking as a very lucrative business. Everyone knows that money must have changed hands for you and some of your girls to have been released," Clement added.

"So, when Mallam was telling me he had made useful contact with the government and that we might not enjoy his hospitality for much longer, he was in reality telling me that the government had agreed to pay some money for our release. Are you saying I should thank the government for accepting to pay for our release?" Mary demanded.

"No, not at all. What you need to do is to try to forget your experience as a hostage. I know it won't be easy. Maybe you should take up Owobi's suggestion about seeing a medical doctor and a physiotherapist in Otukpo, after having spent some days in the village with Papa. I will remain in the village with you for just a couple of days. I will have to go back to Lagos and resume duties at the hotel. Please call me the moment you start not feeling well in the village. I will arrange to come to the village to see you and help you out. What are brothers there for if not to support their sisters, strong sisters who in reality do not need their help?" Clement said.

"In order to start not feeling well, either in the village or outside the village, I need first to start feeling well. I am not feeling well at the moment because I do not know why what has happened to me did happen to me. While I was in Mallam's compound, I tried to reflect on things, tried to explain things by writing them in an exercise book that I requested from Mallam," Mary announced.

"You wrote things in an exercise book given to you by the person holding you hostage?" Clement asked with stupefaction.

"Yes, I did. I felt it was a useful exhaust pipe for me and my girls. I felt it was better we vented our feelings rather than allowed them to be pent up in our minds and gradually destroy us from within. None of the girls had the courage to write but I wrote extensively and that enabled me to better come to terms with my captivity," Mary answered.

"The man who captured you and put you in a dark room gave you something to write with in order to express your fears, sentiments, and frustration at having your fundamental liberties curtailed, is that what you're trying to tell me, sis?" Clement asked with incredulity.

"Yes, that is exactly what I'm telling you," Mary responded.

"We have a strange specimen there," Clement commented.

"Do you know that he takes care of the *Almajiris* that learn under his roof as if they were his own children? He has a dozen of them whom he feeds, clothes and educates for them to become Islamic teachers, Mallams, when they become older," Mary informed her brother.

"Yes, a very strange specimen. Must be someone mentally deranged, certainly," Clement concluded.

"It is not the impression I have or had. I had the impression of listening to someone who knows what he is doing even though he has a very high temper. I thought the main reason we were being held in captivity was because he was against girls being educated in Western-style institutions," Mary answered.

"Where is the exercise book now?" Clement enquired.

"In Mallam's possession. He seized it from me the night we were transported from his compound to the stadium. I was quite surprised because he did not tell me he would keep the exercise book the day we would leave his compound. He had only told me he would read what I had written to erase things he did not agree with. However, I am not sad that I don't have the book with me anymore. At least I know that what I wrote has been read by the eyes that are the source of my traumatic experience," Mary remarked. She went silent again and Clement again decided to let her choose to continue speaking or not. He tried to establish a mental profile of the Mallam in question but was incapable of deciding if the man was tall or short, old, or young, bearded or not bearded, with a heavy baritone voice or a normal voice. He tried to imagine the way the man dressed but was unable to come up with a lasting image. What he knew was that the man must be at least educated and fluent in English to be able to engage in talks with his sister. He waited for her to resume her remarks and waited and waited. He felt the intense sadness that was being exuded by his sister and felt very sorry for her. Her captivity must have been living hell for her. He felt she was a broken woman. The Mary he had known before was someone very jovial and lively, someone very positive-minded, someone always a step ahead of him in terms of projects and ambitions. The Mary he was now driving to the village was different. She was withdrawn, quiet, and her eyes had a sad far-away look as if she was living in another world, a very inhospitable one. Clement felt sorry for his sister. Something told him she had not spoken about all the things she did or that happened to her as a hostage. He would be there to listen to her attentively and with all the warmth that went with his brotherly love for her the day she would decide to share her trauma with him.

Dr Ocheme was at the Senior Staff Clubhouse at the university in Zaria. He was sitting at a table with a number of other colleagues who taught in different faculty departments from his. The group was composed of the President of the Zaria chapter of ASUU, the Academic Staff Union of Universities, a history professor who, because he wished to contain his stammering, spoke slowly and emphatically. The history professor was pro-communist and pro-Russia and pro-China and he was always drawing attention to the fact that millions of Nigerians lived below the poverty line in a country blessed with oil wealth. Such a situation would never obtain in a communist country where means of production were collectively held, private property ownership curtailed, and revenue generated by the State shared in such a way as to benefit first and foremost the have-nots.

Dr Ocheme tended to agree with this analysis. Among the group were others who had a diametrically opposed view of communism, of Russia, of China and of the reasons behind the presence of extreme inequality in Nigeria. There was thus an animated discussion, especially about the state of insecurity in the country and what the outcome of the forthcoming federal legislative elections would be. A few members of the group refused to join in what had become the tradition of government bashing when discussions were held at the Staff Club by the academic staff. Many were afraid that the walls of the large sitting room where the tables were arranged for club members to sit and relax had ears. Many club members suspected that somehow national intelligence agencies had access to discussions held within the premises of the club, and that people who spoke too radically against the State, after having drunk a few bottles of beer, were often targeted with different sorts of reprisal afterwards. Many drew attention to the disappearance into thin air of a Jamaican sociology teacher, a certain Patrick Wilmart, after he had spent a whole evening vilifying the government of the day at the federal level. Nobody knew where he had gone to. Some people said he had been reported seen in London, while others said he was a spy who had been uncovered by the Nigerian intelligence network.

The group around Dr Ocheme was discussing boisterously, while waiting for the plates of goat meat pepper soup that had been ordered by almost everyone to be served. Outside the sitting room, several other club members could be seen either playing lawn tennis or sitting around tables that had been arranged outside, enjoying a quiet drink while looking at those who were chatting noisily in the swimming pool nearby. One of those sitting with Dr Ocheme decided to comment on events that had occupied the attention of the national media in recent times.

"Did you see how the press reported the recent release of the school principal and some of her students in Sokoto the other day? What is your feeling?"

"Mere window dressing and a very obnoxious attempt by an indecent government to divert public attention from its incapacity to provide basic services and basic security for all," the ASUU President opined.

"A tragi-comedy, if you want my opinion," Dr Ocheme added. "Everyone knows that government paid a huge ransom to obtain their release. It is only in Nigeria that the people supposed to protect the common man openly accept to pay those who threaten the safety and security of the common man. This is preposterous, to say the least. Yes, an indecent government, no doubt about that at all."

"Is it that preposterous? The payment of ransom fees to hostage takers by governments is something current even in Europe, you know. Many European countries, like France for example, have had to quote negotiate unquote with terrorist groups that have abducted their nationals in the Middle East and in Africa. Everyone knows what such negotiation entails, you know," someone else objected.

"Okay, so even European countries negotiate. But they negotiate with terrorist groups in foreign countries. They wish to show that their nationals are not forgotten when their rights are abridged when they work and live several thousands of kilometres away from their countries. What is happening here in Nigeria is quite different. Unlike the European countries you are talking about where the safety and security of citizens are guaranteed, with a very effective system of the maintenance of law and order by the police, here in Nigeria, with a corrupt police force, there is no safety anywhere for the common man. A Nigerian does not need to go abroad before he or she is taken hostage. You are working quietly in your office one minute; you are taken hostage the next. A government that is unable to protect the rights and safety of its citizens and that then organises a widely covered welcome-home spectacle in the presence of anxious families and parents to obtain public approval for its inefficiency, can exist only in Nigeria. This is a shame and I think all well-thinking Nigerians should agree with my observation," another colleague said.

"Doc, you are going to face an uphill task, trying to unseat the Senate President. Did you see the way he was smiling happily in the midst of the released girls? That was the most effective publicity he could ever get, now that we are just a few weeks to election day. He has shown even the most reticent voter that he is there when and where problems are solved," the ASUU President commented.

"I knew I would face an uphill task the moment I decided to be a candidate in my constituency, which also happens to be the Senate President's. I knew I would face even a more difficult uphill task when I went to my district recently to solicit for the support of our District Head who told me, in very diplomatic terms, to withdraw from the race, and announce my decision to join Chief Aje's camp," Dr Ocheme replied.

"Why did you go to see your District Head? He must surely have been bought over by the Senate President," the ASUU

President remarked angrily.

"I knew he had been bought over. I just wanted him to know that I was suggesting a different path towards bringing government closer to our people. I was suggesting a path where it is the ideas that you have, rather than the amount of money you can throw around, that should determine who governs for the people," Dr Ocheme revealed.

"Tell me where in the world money does not govern who gets elected. Even in the USA, God's own country, where banknotes have the inscription 'In God We Trust', all elections are preceded by heavy fund-raising. Presidential elections cost billions and billions of dollars and candidates rush to have as many rich donors as possible. Politics and elections without money do not exist and have never existed anywhere in the world, not even in communist countries," one of those who had spoken earlier observed.

"So, Doc, what is your decision. To withdraw or not to withdraw, that is the question, to borrow a famous phrase," someone else who had equally spoken earlier on asked.

"In my opinion, Doc, you should not withdraw. There should be a different message given to the people apart from the quote I-will-be-at-your-service unquote rubbish and jazz that those who have been long in power and wish to continue to reap bountiful rents from their positions of power are going to inundate the people with," the ASUU President maintained.

"Then you should be ready for a heavy and resounding defeat. And you should also pay attention to your safety. One never knows what political heavyweights are prepared to do in order to frighten their opponents," someone advised Dr Ocheme. The plates of pepper soup were brought, and a second round of drinks ordered by Dr Ocheme who offered to foot the bill.

270

Dr Ocheme was driving home from the Staff Club. He had remained there chatting and answering questions from several other colleagues who passed by his table inside the clubhouse and stopped to wish him the best of luck in his campaign effort. It was dark and he had switched on the headlamps of his deluxe saloon Volvo car. He had bought the car while in the USA and had thus brought it along with all his other belongings to Nigeria. He was listening to Queen's song, "We are the Champions" on his CD player.

He suddenly sensed that he was being followed. A car had been tailing him since he had exited the Staff Club. The car now flashed its headlights continuously behind him for a few seconds. Dr Ocheme had slowed down thinking the car behind wanted to overtake him. This was not the case. Then the car flashed its headlights once again. Dr Ocheme started to panic. The car behind him was apparently asking him to stop. Who could this be?

He remembered Dr Patrick Wilmart's story and accelerated in order to pick up speed. He negotiated a roundabout and turned right to go to his residence which was in the Area E Zone, reserved for senior staff members. He saw that the vehicle behind him equally picked up speed and began to come closer and closer to his car. He observed that it was not a car but a Land Rover. Suddenly, he was jerked forward. The Land Rover had intentionally run into his car using its bumper. He picked up speed once again, this time panic-stricken. The vehicle behind him picked up speed equally and ran into him more forcefully this time. Then it overtook him quickly and immediately screeched to a stop in front of Dr Ocheme, who was now petrified. Three heavily-built men wearing berets rushed out of the Land Rover and approached Dr Ocheme, who panic-stricken,

271

had wound up his car glasses. Two of the men were each holding a hammer. One of them smashed Dr Ocheme's side window with his hammer. Broken glass flew everywhere, and some fell on Dr Ocheme's laps. The second man smashed the windscreen, broke the windscreen wiper and smashed the rear window glass as well as the taillights. The first man then smashed the sunroof glass. The third man, whose face could not be clearly seen in the dark, spoke menacingly to Dr Ocheme.

"So, na you be the Mister or Doctor Common Man wey de yab all the time, abi? Mr. Common Man wey get Oyibo wife, wey don spend all his life for Oyiboland and wey think say Naija land na Oyiboland? We go show you say na we sabi pass you, johnny-just-come. We go show you original naija pepper if you no comot from our road quick quick, you understand, you ignoramus? Mr. Common Man wey no sabi waka but wey wan join running competition! Dis na your first and last warning, you dey hear? If you continue to dey yab as you dey do now, we go first show your Oyibo woman naija pepper before we send you to Armageddon. Bloody nincompoop! When trouble sleep and Oyiboman with his iyanga go wake am, make Oyiboman no complain afterwards say he don lose all his teeth, you dey hear?"

The men left Dr Ocheme on the road, trembling with fright. He would have to drive carefully to his residence and wait for tomorrow before deciding on what to do. Go to the Police to file a complaint? Would the police believe him? Would the police not think he had drunk too much at the Staff Club and had had an accident? He remained still and trembling for several minutes. All was quiet around him. He decided it was better he drove to his residence immediately. What if the three men came back to finish the business they had started? He switched on the ignition, was relieved to hear the engine running smoothly and drove back carefully to his house.

9

Chief Aje was in very high spirits. He had won a landslide victory. He was the only candidate in his constituency, and he was proud to tell his Senate colleagues that all the registered voters in his constituency had cast their votes and that he was the recipient of all the votes cast. Who else among them could boast of having a hundred percent of voter confidence and trust? Which made him the natural candidate to be Senate President, given the fact that he already had the experience of managing the Senate, would not waste time trying to understand the intricacies of managing such an august assembly but would get down to business from day one. A number of Senators, who said they were speaking on behalf of Ndigbo, argued that important federal positions needed to be filled on a rotational basis and that they felt it was the turn of the south-east zone and particularly someone of Igbo extraction to produce the next Senate President. Their argument was that the Igbos had been side-stepped for many ages in the distribution of federal positions of power and that now was the time to really lay the ghost of Biafra to rest. This suggestion had been greeted with hostility from another group of senators who said they were representing the Arewa zone and felt that experience should not be sacrificed on the altar of zoning. An experienced Senate President had been crowned by his constituency and they saw no use in the sterile debate concerning his legitimacy to continue his good work as Senate President. Chief Aje was elected as Senate President during the first round of elections. He had been opposed to three other candidates, but he was sure he was going to win since many of the Senators who had decamped from the opposition party and who he had welcomed personally into the fold of his party not long ago, were eager to cast their votes in his favour.

He was happy as well as relieved. He had thought his son lost. He had thought Owobi, given his sudden transformation into a rebel (or rather an ungrateful son if one was honest) would refuse to do what he needed to do to mobilise the necessary support of voters in his district. This he had done perfectly. He had been told Owobi had followed Clement and his sister to the village to meet the man who was refusing to go along with him. He felt there was no need asking Owobi what had gotten into his head, or if he knew what he was doing. That would only lead to unnecessary tension between father and son. He needed his son and was sure his son needed him too. He had been informed of how his son had managed an incident that would have complicated his landslide victory. Apparently, a Youth Corper who prided himself in having had Dr Ocheme as teacher in Zaria, and who had been posted to work in the State Electoral Commission, had wondered why all the registered voters had actually voted. He had admitted not seeing many people come to vote and was thus surprised at the number of ballots in the ballot box when the counting had started. Owobi had been able to convince the Youth Corper to sign and validate the results. Chief Aje therefore felt that his son continued to be a reliable ally. He would wait until the new Senate session was cruising along well before he resumed his project to buy Obande Ofu's forest. He hoped that his son would be less willing to question this project and that Obande himself would be more reasonable and show his gratitude to one who had contributed to saving his daughter from

275

inevitable death. He would have to go to the village one of these days and thank Ogaba-Idu for his support during the elections. He would also need to better know who he could count on when he would do all that he planned to do to acquire the forest he was bent on acquiring.

Mary was in low spirits. She had been in the village for almost three weeks, but she still felt at a loss. Clement had gone back to Lagos, and they talked on the telephone almost every day. Owobi called regularly from Otukpo to find out how she was doing. Clement advised her not to spend too much time indoors, listening to the radio. The more she listened to the radio, the more she would hear bad news about the growing insecurity in the country and the higher the risk that she would recollect her own experience. She was advised to take advantage of the quiet of the village to regain her strength. She chose to follow her father once in a while to his forest. He had resumed his palm wine tapping. What Mary liked was to remain quiet in the forest and try to hear as many of the surrounding noises as she could. She would try to listen to the soft music generated by the water running in the Igbilede stream, and this would fill her with a sensation of freedom and gentleness. She would listen to the orchestra of so many birds communicating with one another, mates and families separated by several palm trees but engaged in very civilised conversations. Sometimes, she would admire the families of squirrels she bumped into and who would scuttle rapidly up the nearest palm trees. She would watch them climb up to a safe distance and admire their climbing skills. She thought such expeditions into her father's forest would make her feel better, but she felt better only for a very short period of time. She started to get sullen.

The pains were at first mild, accompanied by cramp. The pains were first located on her neck and shoulder and afterwards on her abdomen and pelvis. She thought this was a carryover from her aggression several weeks earlier. Then she began to feel dizzy once in a while and to crave for food while at the same time showing high intolerance towards the food she ate. She became slightly worried when she noticed she was suffering from vaginal bleeding, but she did not immediately think this was something serious. Maybe it was her menstrual cycle that was playing pranks with her. She started to get worried when her abdominal pains, on one side of her lower abdomen, became more severe.

"Oyije, my mother, you are in pain. Would you like to go to the village herbalist for treatment?" her father asked, looking at her intently.

"The pain will go away, Papa, don't worry," Mary replied.

"You repair the bridge before someone falls into the river and not afterwards. It is always advisable to anticipate and solve those problems we know might appear rather than wait for them to appear in a more complicated form," her father maintained.

"Don't worry, Papa. I'm sure the pain will go away," Mary insisted.

"You know I'm very proud of you, don't you?" he went on to say. Mary became alarmed. She had never heard her father speak like this before.

"Don't be surprised. Adole told me there are things that need to be said even if we feel them," he went on to say.

"Papa, I have always known that you are very proud of me. You don't have to say it for me to know," Mary responded, still alarmed. Did her father suspect or know about the terrible things that had happened to her during her captivity? Had he read through her, decoded her occasional mutism, how often her mood changed, how she was wont to cry easily, though she never cried when others were around or watching her, and how she was very tired without having done anything physically exhausting?

"It is good that you know. It's all I wanted to know," her father concluded, before going about his business.

Mary reflected deeply. What had her father seen or perceived for him to be so anxious, though he did not want to show this? She believed what she had told him; the pains would disappear with time, so there was no need getting alarmed.

She became really alarmed when she saw that her vaginal bleeding had gotten worse and the pains on the left side of her lower abdomen and pelvis more acute and severe. She did not want to go to the village herbalist because she did not trust his capacity to diagnose what was wrong with her, if anything was wrong with her in the first place. And she did not want her medical condition being public knowledge in the village and becoming the subject of gossip here and there. Many people had come to greet her when Clement and Owobi had brought her home, but she did not believe that all the people that came were well-wishers. This was one of the reasons why she had kept mostly to herself and only engaging in social chit-chat with close relatives and friends of the family. She remembered Owobi's suggestion that she see a medical doctor and telephoned him to ask for additional details. She informed Owobi she would be in Otukpo the following day.

Obande Ofu was very worried. He had never seen his daughter taciturn and depressed since her birth. She must have gone through hell to be so despondent. The Oyije he used to know was fiery, pugnacious, alert, and full of life and energy. The Oyije that now occasionally went with him to the palm forest was quiet, withdrawn, with dull far-away eyes. Maybe she was feeling too bored in the village, where there was nothing special to do for someone used to interacting with the young, to holding regular meetings and to preparing short-, medium- and long-term projects for her school. It was not the fact that this was possibly the reason behind his daughter's uncharacteristically long silence when people came to greet her that worried him the most. What made him anxious was his daughter's melancholy, as if she was perpetually grief-stricken. He had also observed that she was spitting more regularly than he felt was normal. There was something wrong with his daughter and she was not telling him, she was not confiding in him, something he thought was abnormal given the tradition they both had of sharing their joys and pains. If his daughter was not willing to tell him things, what was troubling her must be grave. He would go to see the village medicine-man-cum-seer and find out what was troubling his daughter.

He took along with him two kegs of fresh palm wine and three yam tubers. The medicine man lived in a compound a bit far away from his. Many villagers were afraid to go to see him because they feared he might be either good and protective or malevolent and thus curse them forever. One could never know how the medicine man was going to receive the person who dared go to his compound for advice and guidance. The story that was told was that his malevolence was generated by his stomach. The only way of neutralising such malevolence and avoid the prospect of being cursed was to go to see the man with foodstuff and drinks. This would erase the perpetual frown that the man had on his face and would make him more willing to guide the visitor out of his or her woes. Obande believed in the existence of some form of continuity between the physical world and the world beyond, the spiritual world. He believed that those who departed the physical world were assembled above in the spiritual world and that they were omnipotent and omniscient. There was therefore a fountain of knowledge in the spiritual world that was inaccessible to all except the initiated. Obande believed the medicine man could explain misfortunes of humans because he had direct contact with inhabitants of the spiritual world. He could see them, he could talk to them, he could understand their language. It was to him that many villagers, even those who went to the church regularly, went to obtain amulets that were supposed to reduce illnesses. He wanted the medicine man to be able to see his own future and especially his daughter's. What was his daughter hiding from him? He waited until his daughter had left for Otukpo before going to see the medicine man. She had told him she was going to see a medical doctor to have some drugs prescribed for her headache. She told him she preferred such drugs to the concoction prepared by the village herbalist for whom she had lots of respect.

When he arrived at the home of the medicine man, the gate of the fence made with bamboo poles was open, so he walked in, while loudly asking if anyone was at home.

"The eyes, ears and mouth of our foregone ancestors on earth, are you there? The only one who sees beyond and whose perspicacity is unequalled, are you there? The son of his father, the father of his son, are you there? Greetings to the one who protects us from sickness and death," he announced.

"Our respected and respectable elder, the one whose medicine brings us joy and happiness, welcome to my compound. How is your body? And the school principal?" he enquired.

"My body is still with me, as you can see. It has not started to give me troubles yet. It has not let me down. I am thus lucky. Like our forefathers used to say, we should not compete among ourselves to have luck. It is not we that choose luck but luck that chooses us," Obande responded.

"What you say is very true. You do not hail loudly on luck to come and visit you. The louder your call, the more you will frighten it away from you," the man stated.

"Yes, you have spoken well. I have brought you a few things to drink and eat, because I want to benefit from your intelligence and the intelligence of our ancestors. The school principal has gone to Otukpo to see a medical doctor. She is not feeling very well," Obande added.

"It is good to ask when one does not know, but it is better to ask the right person. A blind man does not ask another blind man to indicate the path that leads out of the forest. Our ancestors see things before they happen. We need to always ask them questions for, like they used to say before departing from us, the child who knows how to ask will not eat the forbidden chicken," the man replied.

"Yes, we need to listen to the words of wisdom of our ancestors. We need to go to them to acquire and consolidate our intelligence. No one becomes intelligent alone. If the small stream meanders rather than flows in a straight line, this is because it is alone. I have tried to read the messages sent to me by my forefathers in the forest, but they are unusually quiet. I find this very strange. It is either they are silent because there is nothing to worry about or that they are silent because there is something grave to worry about. I decided that you would know, so I decided to leave the palm trees to dance with the winds and to come to benefit from your eyes and ears," Obande commented.

The man brought out a bag made from dried goat skin. The

bag contained an assortment of beads of three different colours, red, black, and white. He put his hands inside the bag and mixed the beads very randomly, with a serious look on his face. He then told Obande to take out one bead after the other from the bag until he was told to stop, and to throw the beads when told to do so gently on a small brown square mat that he had equally brought out. Obande was told to stop after the first two beads. There were two red beads which Obande threw on the mat. The beads rolled on the mat for a few seconds before they ground to a halt. The man read their message and shoved them to one of the angles of the mat. Then he told Obande to go on to pick another set of beads. Obande was told to stop after he had taken out seven beads. There were four red beads, two big white beads, and a big black bead. Obande threw all seven on the mat. After they had rolled for a few seconds, they ground to a halt in three separate sets. The first set consisted of three red beads and one white bead, which halted near the angle where the first two red beads had been arranged by the man. The second set consisted of one red bead and one white bead, which both halted at the opposite angle to that where the first two beads had been arranged. The third set, the single black bead was at the centre of the mat. The three sets of beads could be easily connected by a straight line that went diagonally from one angle to the other. The man nodded his head in appreciation, while mumbling some words that Obande could not decipher, before spending a minute or two reading attentively the message that was displayed in front of him, without making any comment. He then told Obande to pick up a third and final set of beads. Obande was told to stop after he had picked twelve beads. There were six red beads, four white beads and two black ones. When Obande threw the twelve beads on the mat, these fell again in three sets. The first consisted of five red beads close to the first set of two red beads, the second consisted of two black beads at the centre and the third consisted of one red bead and four white beads near the angle where one white and one red bead had been previously arranged by the man. Thus, there were finally three sets of beads on the mat, ten red beads and a single white bead at one angle, five white beads and a single red bead at the opposite angle and three black beads at the centre in between the two extremities. The man took several long minutes reading the messages in front of him. He had an anxious faraway expression on his face.

"The brave fear neither dawn nor twilight to go on their journey but you cannot walk a long distance when you have a huge wound on your feet," the man said with a low soft voice.

"Is it that bad?" Obande asked.

"No one can stop the child who goes to his house or to his grave from advancing but we can slow down the rapid walk of life in many cases, if we ask for the light to shine on our minds and make us wiser and stronger," the man continued.

"Calamity never books an appointment before it knocks on your door. That much I know. I also know that the upper row of teeth always ends up being complete. What is inevitable is inevitable. No matter how big a boat is, it can capsize as easily as a small boat. What do you see? Do not hesitate to tell me. I can take even the worst piece of news. A dead body is not afraid of getting rotten," Obande stated.

"I know your name and your character, my good friend. Someone who walks through a forest he does not know will not know which tree to cut down in order to have firewood. This is not your case. You know life with all its ups and down. There is harmony in your home. There is good understanding. However, some trees will fall down although the forest is growing. The

283

trees which fall down will make more noise than the other trees that are growing in the forest," the man advanced.

"I understand. What is sweet and what is bitter never travel together. What is your advice?" Obande asked.

"Well, if you have just one spear, you should not think this is enough to protect you against the leopard that is willing to extend its hunting space to your territory," the man said. He stared at Obande for a few minutes. "Every wound leaves a scar. The scar might appear very quickly or slowly, but it takes a very long time to disappear," the man said, still looking directly into Obande's eyes.

Obande left the seer's home confused. He had the impression that the seer was trying to tell him something but did not have the courage to do directly in plain language. What could this be? he wondered. What he had seen and read must be grave for him to have chosen to keep the information only to himself, Obande thought. Did it concern his family as a whole? His palm forest? Adole, who had gone back to Lagos? Or Oyije, who was now in Otukpo to see a medical doctor about her pain?

Mary felt the pain on the left-hand side of the abdomen. It was not acute, but it was getting more and more unbearable. She was in the waiting room with other patients, many of whom had been there before her. These were surprised when the medical doctor came out of his consultation chamber to greet her personally and to invite her into the chamber immediately.

"Owobi phoned me yesterday to expect your visit this morning. Sorry for all you have been through. I'm really sorry," the doctor said.

"Thanks, doctor," Mary responded.

"I'm told you are having pains in your abdomen, shoulder

and neck?" the doctor enquired.

"Yes, mild and sometimes quite acute pains. Sometimes also on my pelvis," Mary replied.

"I am going to examine you very rapidly. I'm going to palpate parts of your body. Tell me if you feel any pain," the doctor explained. He then went on to do his palpation. He asked Mary a question which took her by surprise:

"When did you have your last menstrual cycle?"

"I have had some vaginal bleeding now and then," Mary answered, panic-stricken for the first time in many weeks.

"Well, I have observed that your breasts are quite tender. There is no doubt that you are pregnant. With the vaginal bleeding and the abdominal pains, your pregnancy is a complicated one. It is called in medical language, ectopic pregnancy. Do you smoke?" he asked.

"No, I have never smoked in my life," Mary replied.

"Well, what is sure is that you're pregnant. Might be around ten weeks, from what I can guess. Your fallopian tube is certainly inflamed. If you say you don't smoke, then this must most probably be caused by some sexually transmitted disease. The fertilised egg has not attached to the uterus but to the inflamed fallopian tube. This needs to be quickly treated because your health is in extreme danger. The fallopian tube can be ruptured, and this may lead to internal bleeding. So, emergency surgery is needed. The embryo has to be quickly removed for your health. There is no time to waste," the doctor warned, in a grave voice.

Mary was aghast. So, there was no way she could forget the three weeks she had spent in bondage, she mused. Here she was hundreds of kilometres away from him and now she learnt that part of him lived inside her, painfully reminding her that she would always remain a captive, his captive. Was she prepared to

285

accept that her body be invaded this time by a medical expert to expunge the results of an earlier invasion from it? she wondered silently. Would her captivity never end? she questioned. What would happen if she refused the surgery? she debated with herself. She would die, most certainly, but wasn't this in the final analysis the best option, since she would no longer have to struggle with the image and scent of her erstwhile abductor? she concluded.

She would have to tell Owobi that she was pregnant, and she did not look forward to this. It was none of his business. She would have to tell Clement she was pregnant and maybe even have to explain to him that she had been raped. She did not know if she would have the courage to do this. And then she thought of her father in the village. He had bid her safe journey to Otukpo for the treatment of mild pains she was having on some parts of her body. She felt she would rather die than have to announce to him that she was pregnant. She was unmarried and it would bring shame to the Obande Ofu family for a daughter to give birth to a bastard. It is the fingers that adorn the hand, that embellish the hand. In other words, it is children who make their parents proud. Announcing to the entire village that the Obande Ofu family has given birth to a fatherless child would destroy the family's reputation. No, she could not do this to her father, one who had always believed in her, always let her be and let her do things the way she felt. As a bee avoids stinging another bee, so would she avoid destroying her father's reputation.

Owobi tried to make her see reason. She had ended up telling him that she had been raped while in captivity, that she had failed her students, her school, and that she was not willing to bring shame to her father, who had always supported her and forgiven her when she had made mistakes. She believed she had two impossible options. One was to hope for the better and carry on her pregnancy until when the baby would be viable enough for he or she to be prematurely given birth to by medical assistance. This option was impossible for so many reasons. First, she did not want the child. Secondly, she did not want to have to endure the pain she was experiencing for someone she had never desired to have. Thirdly, the child would be fatherless. A premature baby, with no father, would start his or her life on a very wrong footing, and she was not prepared to take that path. On the other hand, and this was the second option, if the surgical operation meant aborting the unwanted child, who according to the doctor was already at least ten weeks old, she did not think it was right to end a life that had hardly begun. She did not think she had the power of life or death over anyone. She would be like her erstwhile captor if she arrogated to herself that power. No, she would do nothing at all. She would go back to the village and await her fate. Owobi had disagreed vehemently with her.

"One should not jump into a river without first determining how deep the river is. My CO, I have never known you not to think seriously of all possible consequences before acting. I know you are tired of fighting, but this fight is a fight for your life. You should agree to have the operation. The doctor has told you he is not equipped to do it here in Otukpo. There are many well-equipped clinics in Abuja. Let me contact one of them and book a room. We can leave in an hour and be in Abuja before six in the evening, while driving gently. Please, my CO. Let me call Clement in Lagos. I'm sure he will agree with me," Owobi implored.

Clement was afraid. He and his friend Tijjani had both managed to escape being captured by policemen who had raided the discreet social club in Ojuelegba, where the gay community met on Saturdays to socialise. He was now in his flat with Tijjani and they were watching the television where the Lagos State Police Commissioner was speaking to a group of journalists.

"Good evening, ladies and gentlemen of the press. I am happy to announce the arrest of many young able-bodied men who rather than do things that are productive for our country have chosen to engage in very immoral and shameful animal behaviour. I personally ordered the raid that swept up more than forty men after we received a tip-off that young men were being initiated into a 'homosexual club'. As you know, homosexuality runs contrary to the Same Sex Marriage Prohibition Act. It is the duty of everybody, not only the police, to ensure that such antisocial behaviour, such vices, such crimes, are checked so that we can create communities that protect our children from such deviant behaviour," he said.

The television cameras swept over the faces of the forty men held, capturing expressions of guilt, shame, fear, shyness, and anger. Clement and Tijjani did not know all of them. Most of those being shown remained quiet. Some of them had bruises on their heads and faces, results of beatings they had received from the police who had succeeded in arresting them while they were trying to run away from the club. It was reported that the arrested men would spend a few weeks in police detention before being arraigned in front of a court. They faced the possibility of being sent to prison for fourteen years.

Clement thanked his stars for having been able to escape with Tijjani. He did not know how they had managed not to be caught by the many policemen that were milling around. He was sure the police raid was going to hit the headlines soon and if he had been caught and news about his capture and imprisonment read by people who knew his sister and father, he would not have been able to withstand the shame and additional problems he would have inflicted on his father and sister. He knew his sister was undergoing a long and painful journey back to normal life, but he was apprehensive about her capacity to forget the trauma she certainly underwent during the three weeks she had been taken hostage. There was no need adding more distress to her. He thus decided, with Tijjani, to avoid going to places where gays congregated discreetly, or attending parties organised by them. One never knew if the neighbour who greeted you very warmly in the morning was not the person giving the police some tip-off about 'strange people' he or she had seen partying in his or her neighbourhood. He also decided not to engage in social interaction on the social media with people who pretended to be part of the gay community. He and Tijjani did not want to take the risk of attacks called 'Kito', where supposedly gay men asked to meet other gay men but turned out to be bandits who either kidnapped their victims or attacked and robbed them. They also decided to be on the lookout for 'area boys', groups of young thugs who tried to uncover those who display same-sex affection so as to extort money from them or to threaten them with calling the police.

His telephone buzzed. It was not a number he was used to seeing on the screen to his cell phone. He accepted the call and was surprised to hear Owobi's voice. His heartbeat quickened rapidly, and he had a sense of foreboding. Owobi told him very calmly that he was in Abuja with Oyije, at a private clinic which had the latest state-of-the-art medical equipment. His sister had asked him to call her brother as soon as they had safely arrived at the clinic from Otukpo. She would like him to come to Abuja as soon as possible to see her. She would then personally tell him what was wrong with her. He was not authorised to say anything except to ask him to hurry to Abuja. Clement called his chef and asked for the authorisation to be absent for at least a week. His sister was gravely ill in an Abuja clinic and had requested his presence there with her. Tijjani was very helpful. He volunteered to do extra hours at the restaurant in order to compensate for Clement's absence and this was accepted by the chef. Clement prepared his suitcase and departed for Ikeja to take a flight to Abuja. Several thoughts crossed his mind during his flight. He hoped Oyije's illness was not serious, though something told him it was. Why else would she have been advised to go to Abuja? He had suspected all along that she was not as fine as she was trying to show after her rescue, but he never thought what was wrong with her needed the attention of medical specialists in a modern clinic. He felt sorry for his sister. He tried to put himself in her shoes. No, it was not easy to be a woman. No, it was not easy at all.

When he got to the clinic, he was met by an Owobi that he did not recognise at first. Gone was the Owobi who was fond of showing off, with spick and span dresses, sparkling jewellery and walking as if he owned the world. The Owobi who met him at the main hall was dishevelled, anxious, nervous, and humble. He greeted Clement and warned him he would be shocked at the sight of his sister. He was advised to prepare himself mentally. No preparation could have been enough to enable Clement to accept the view before him. He saw a woman in front of him with a swollen face and swollen feet. He saw a woman who had aged very rapidly. Gone was the impetuous challenging look on the face that used to be Oyije's. Now was a very sad, despondent look. The medical doctor who was handling her case joined them

290

in the ward. He beckoned Owobi and Clement to come closer to him and spoke in a very low voice so that Mary could not hear what he was saying.

"You must be Clement. Welcome. The first thing your sister said when she was brought here by her friend was to call you and ask you to come here to see her. I do not want to beat around the bush. Your sister was brought to us a little bit too late. What she has is a very complicated pregnancy, her fallopian tube being blocked. Let's hope the tube does not end up bursting because the chances of saving her life would be dim if not non-existent. Your sister seems to have given up already. I can see this very clearly. We cannot save someone who has decided not to be saved. You need to tell her to fight and to keep on fighting. Apparently, she believes in you and will do what you advise her to do," the doctor explained.

Clement went to his sister lying on the bed and cupped her hands in his. All four hands were trembling. He looked deeply into her eyes and saw a form of sadness and hopelessness he had never imagined his sister would display. Tears started to flow down her face. He restrained himself from crying.

"Dear sis, why didn't you tell me? I suspected that there was something you were not sharing with me, but I never knew it was this grave," Clement stated.

"I could not bring myself to tell you I had been sexually assaulted. I felt filthy and soiled and did not want to share such filth with you, seeing how happy you were to see me," Mary responded.

"You should have. If you had, we could have come to this clinic a long time ago and the complications we have now would have been certainly avoided," Clement added.

"My life is complicated already, as you know. I tell myself

that I am important. I tell myself that I matter. I tell myself that I am me and that I exist as someone whose being doesn't have to be validated by anyone else. You know as much as I do that this is nothing but a pipe dream. I do not matter because a man one day decides it is his right to take me hostage and to abuse my physical, psychological, moral, and social integrity. I do not matter because the government negotiates my release with him, for a large sum of money and organises a well-publicised welcome party, without trying to sanction him for what he has done. I am not important because someone else has been named to replace me at the head of my school, a man. Having complications has been part and parcel of my life. Why continue to face such complications? I am tired and fed up. I am tired of having to do more than others in order to be recognised. I am tired of having to accept crumbs that are left on the table as my rightful due. I am tired of developing a tough skin in a very aggressive male-dominated society. I am tired of not being taken seriously. I am tired of being always asked to justify my right to be in the room. Why do I have to continue to prove my worth, to prove my abilities, to prove my excellence everywhere I go, everything I do, every time I act? Would you not be tired yourselves if this was the life given to you by others? I have run out of ammunition, and I don't want to go on this way any longer," Mary complained.

"Dear sis, I understand your complaint. Yes, I understand it very well. It is a complaint that I could formulate myself, but that has not led me to accept that I am vanquished. I have always known you to be on the driver's seat, to be the one who takes the bull by the horns. Life is full of complications. We all cry at birth. This indicates that we are conscious that it is a hostile world that awaits us, both as men and as women," Clement replied.

"I agree but you should also agree with me that women have more complicated lives than men, than some men. The irony is that, in reality, women matter more than men. I can even say that women are superior to men, given their innate force. It is women that give life, that nurture life in their wombs for ninth months. It is women who hold the hands of their children until these can walk alone. It is women who manage the household. Women are the spinal column of homes, heroines of everyday life, creative magicians who intelligently resolve a multitude of problems unknown by men or unattended to by them. Women have such a heavy mental burden that I am surprised we are called the weak sex. Homes would collapse, the world would collapse without women. When shall we stop being taken for granted? When can I walk safely on the street without the fear of being aggressed by a man, not for any offence I may have committed, but simply because I am a woman? Is being a woman now an offence? I am tired of fighting against a society which believes that except I am a First Lady, in other words, wife to the man governing the State or country, I am an offence," Mary argued.

The medical doctor noticed that Mary's voice had started to falter, so he advised Clement and Owobi to vacate the ward so that she may rest for a while and regain her strength. While Clement and Owobi were out, Mary asked the medical doctor to give her a sheet of paper and something to write with. She assured him she was strong enough to write. She told him to give what she was writing to her brother, Clement, should anything grave happen to her.

Mary passed away that night. She passed away peacefully in her sleep. Clement and Owobi were informed the following morning when they came to visit her at the clinic. Apparently, there was a rupture of her fallopian tube which had caused profuse internal bleeding. The doctor informed both men, standing still and shocked, that she had died without pain. She had written something she had requested to give to her brother. Clement took the sheets of paper given to him and read the following:

Forgive me, dear Father
You have always taught me to be strong
To keep on fighting
Even when by another
Sure of his might and wealth
I am engaged in a battle I think lost
From the beginning

Forgive me, dear brother
No other man would I ever wish
To have grown up with and beside
You have always believed in my strength
Showing pride in what I accomplished
Boasting to others about who I am
Right from our childhood

Forgive me, Papa and Clement
I do not want to bring shame on you
To give birth to an unknown child
From an unknown father
Who believing himself to be a strong man
Decided to inflict raw violence on me
Right from the forest

Forgive me, dear Owobi

Your Commanding Officer
Is tired of giving orders and instructions
Her position and office disrespected
By those higher up the ladder
And her troop collectively despised
Right from its creation

Forgive me, dear Father
I am sure I will deceive you enormously
But I must go to the land of silence
Place me somewhere in your forest
Where I can continue admiring the squirrels
My place with your forefathers long ordained
Right from the beginning
Right from my origin

Clement could not hold back his tears, neither could Owobi. Both were saddened by the death of someone they had always seen as a model of fortitude and courage. Clement was saddened by the loss of a sister as well as a protector. What worried him the most afterwards was how he was going to announce this news to his father in the village. His father had no cell phone and so could not be called and told he was going to have to make arrangements to bury his daughter. He reflected briefly on the dramatic irony of his current situation. He had promised many weeks earlier to bring her alive to their father. This he had been able to do. Now, he was going to have to make a second journey back to the village, this time to deliver her dead body, without being able to call him to warn him well ahead. Owobi suggested calling someone in the village and asking the person to go and deliver the bad news. Clement felt he could not allow someone else to be the messenger of death to his father, to his parents, to his family. No, he would have to take Mary's corpse home unannounced, even if this would be a shock to all in the village, but especially to his father. They decided to transport the corpse in Owobi's vehicle to Otukpo, where Mary's car had been left when Owobi had taken her to Abuja. Clement would then transport Mary back to the village in her own car. Owobi asked if he should follow Clement to the village. Clement declined, saying this was family business, but thanking Owobi for all he had done.

Obande Ofu had a strange feeling in the morning. When he left his house on the way to the forest, he thought the birds in the trees were flying away from him more quickly than they used to. Normally, many of them remained in their trees, singing as he walked past under them. Today was different. It was as if the families of birds flying noisily away from the trees he was approaching were sending an open message to other families perched in the trees farther off in front. Those in such trees flew away before Obande reached them, as if they were frightened of seeing him or he seeing them. This was very strange. Obande observed the same reaction with the many families of squirrels he came across. Each family scuttled away at the sound of Obande's footsteps and took cover in the shrubs very far from the path Obande was walking on. This had never been the case. On previous occasions, many squirrels would remain playing with one another on the ground as he walked past them without any of them dashing off at the sound of his footsteps. He had been taught to look for the extraordinary in the ordinary. So, what appeared to him now as the behaviour of ordinary animals seemed to him to signify a message, an extraordinary message he had difficulty in decoding, as he had had difficulty in understanding the seer's lesson a few days earlier. He however decided to go about his business. He had several kegs of fresh palm wine to fill. When he had finished, he walked back pensively. He was quite far away from his compound when he knew. He heard the murmur of women crying. He quickened his pace and saw Oyije's car. The sound of the women crying became louder. He saw Clement, looking frail, walking towards him.

"Adole, the name is the man and the man the name. You have behaved like the father of the house, and I thank you very much," he said

"Papa, I wish I was a different messenger," Clement declared.

"Adole, do not worry. It takes a very long time for us to grow up but a very short time for us to be called to join the beyond. Do not worry because I have known all along that Oyije was a shadow of herself and that there was slow death destroying her from the inside. She was too proud to confide even in me. I always told her to be proud of herself. Anyway, life and death are members of the same family. The very hot flame ends up as cold ash. Life is a village that none of us can leave alive," the father announced.

"She will remain with me for as long as I live. It is the body that has disappeared and not her name and her character," Clement stated.

"Where is my daughter, where is her body?" he enquired.

"Inside the parlour, at the centre, with the womenfolk surrounding her," Clement responded.

"Let's go and ask the women to stop crying. We should try to maintain some dignity even though we are very sad. We will have to start digging a grave behind the house to bury her," he announced.

297

"Oyije specifically requested to be buried in your forest, close to your forefathers," Clement announced.

"This is impossible," his father responded.

"Why?" enquired Clement.

"The forest is reserved for men, for fathers. No woman has ever been buried there. My ancestors will be very angry with me if I do not obey the tradition. Who knows what illnesses and diseases they will send to us to express their anger and disapproval? No, it is impossible," he repeated.

"Papa, nothing is impossible. Oyije is you as you are your forefathers. Oyije bears your name, your forefather's name. I do not see our forefathers getting angry because my sister, their daughter, their descendant, wants to sleep in their company, wants to be protected by them. I am sure they will be happy," Clement explained.

"Oyije has always had her way, right from her childhood. She has always broken barriers and I have always gone along with her. Now, though she is no longer with us, she wants me to break another barrier in her name," he reflected.

"Papa, traditions must be respected, so must the unity of a family. It is you elders who tell us that the river cannot go one way and the fish the opposite way. The river and the fish must go together. It is only normal for Oyije to be placed next to those whose name she bore proudly. I am sure she knew this is what you would do if she made the request," Clement advised.

"Okay. Let us go and tell the women to stop crying. We should all try to hide our sadness and afterwards to control it to avoid this sadness transforming itself into a slow death that will destroy each of us from inside. I am very proud of you, Adole. The man is the name, and the name the man," Obande concluded.

"Papa, you are the name. You are the man. The lion does not

give birth to a sheep. Pure water never thickens and gets dirty. It is you that have brought us up in your image, guided by your values. Thank you, Papa, for allowing us to be, and for defending us when we have broken barriers," Clement responded.

"You need to take better care of yourself. Look at the way you're dressed. My Italian associates would not think us reliable partners if they paid a surprise visit to us here in Otukpo. What has gone wrong with you? Don't you think I have other more important matters to treat in Abuja than coming here to ask you to grow up?" Chief Aje, visibly angry, said to Owobi in the Nakowa Oil office in Otukpo.

"Nothing is wrong with me. Who told you something is wrong with me, Papa?" Owobi enquired.

"You come to the office late, you are absent-minded when you are being spoken to on the telephone, you forget important appointments, you forget to call back people you promise to call back, and you're telling me nothing is wrong with you? Why don't you grow up, young man? You're behaving like a bloody civilian," Chief Aje declared.

"Nothing is wrong with me, Papa. Who told you something is wrong with me?" Owobi repeated.

"You would not look the way you do if nothing was wrong with you. What are you thinking? Are you thinking that you are responsible for the death of Obande's daughter? You left the whole company in Otukpo without any head while you rushed her urgently to Abuja. What if the Ministry of Agriculture officials had come here for you to sign very important documents? Tell me, what would have happened," the chief, adamant, asked.

"Why would they have come to see me with papers to sign?"

Owobi wondered.

"Now I know that something is really wrong with you. We have a company to run. We have our corporate expansion to plan and execute. We have new property to acquire, and I will not allow anybody to stand in my way. Let me repeat myself: I will not allow anybody to stand in my way. Do I make myself clear?" Chief Aje demanded. Owobi did not answer. He looked at his father with a blank face. This angered his father even more.

"Stop behaving like a woman," he ordered.

"What do you know about women behaviour, Papa?" Owobi dared to ask.

"A lot more than you know, young man. I thought I brought you up to be a man. Your association with Obande's son seems to have changed you into a woman. You must come out of it immediately, for your own sake, and for the sake of our company," his father instructed.

"So, you think Clement is a woman, do you, Papa? You judge someone without having socialised with him. I had the same approach as you before I met him. No, Clement is not a woman, if you think being a woman means one is weak. And anyway, what is wrong in being a woman or in behaving like one?" Owobi argued.

"I now know that something is wrong with you. You and I and the whole village know that Clement is not a man, does not behave like a man. What has gone into you, young man? The death of his sister? It's a pity, but we cannot allow the death of someone not close to our family to compromise our preparedness to grow and expand, can we? No, we can't, and we mustn't," his father affirmed.

"Papa, what I learnt recently is that you do not judge someone by his or her appearance. That Clement looks

300

effeminate does not mean he is not a man. It is not the envelope that is important but the letter inside it. Manliness is not a state, but an art. Manliness is not proclaimed but acted. And manliness does not mean we should not express our emotions. Manliness means having the courage to be, to think, to do, to feel, as our minds dictate at particular times without being paralyzed by the fear of being judged negatively by others. And, Papa, I must also add that the same things can be said about womanliness. It takes lots of courage to be a woman and I do not think you or I or anyone who proclaims himself a man is in the right position to say who a woman is let alone judge how a woman is or should be nor judge who another man is or should be," Owobi maintained.

"Well, what I want is a man who is capable of steering the ship of my company in my absence without me being summoned urgently back home to iron things out. I think you should go on vacation until your senses are back. I have a number of people who are willing and capable of replacing you. They are all aware that we are in a very critical phase of our expansion and are prepared to do all that is necessary to ensure the smooth execution of this phase. So, take a vacation. Go on a trip to Europe. Get refreshed and come back to be the young man full of promise that I have always wanted," his father declared.

Ogaba-Idu had convened a special urgent meeting of the Council of Elders in his palace. He had received a message from Chief Aje which he wanted to share with the others so that the village could prepare for what was announced to happen. He felt powerless. He felt that what was about to happen would have dire repercussions on social relations among the village elders and maybe lead to unanticipated crises in the village. This he would like to avoid at all costs, but he knew he was not in a position to go against the will of Chief Aje, who had been elected not long ago as Senate President by a very wide margin. He had been told to be prepared to meet two officials sent by the State government to finalise arrangements for the transfer of the certificate of occupancy of Obande's forest from Obande to the State government. The forest would henceforth be declared government property and no trespassers would be tolerated. The two government officials had been informed that they would be met by the Village and District head who was aware of the move and had approved it. Ogaba-Idu had never approved such a move, but he could not tell Chief Aje that. It would be his word against Chief Aje's, but who would believe a mere and ordinary Village Head, who had not even finished his primary school, who had chosen to be engaged in an argument with a powerful Senate President, an influential member of the governing party at the federal level and in two-thirds of the States? He would be ridiculed and laughed at. Chief Aje would think he was very ungrateful. Had he not run to the Chief to solicit his support when he wished to ascend to the throne some years before? Did Chief Aje hesitate a minute before endorsing Ogaba-Idu's candidacy and assuming the financial costs that went with the lavish coronation ceremony that followed?

The more Ogaba-Idu reflected, the more he knew that he could do nothing against Chief Aje's will. So, he would receive the officials from the State. But then, he could not leave Obande alone. A village king does not have any brother. Like the tail of the cow keeps watch over the left and the right in order to ward off flies, so must the king take care of all his subjects, no matter their stations. This was even more necessary if the subject in question was a respected and respectable elder who had suffered mishap recently, the death of an equally respectable daughter.

The animosity between two people who used to be very close friends when they were young was the subject of conversations between many village elders. What had gone wrong to breed such hostility between them? Why was Chief Aje so hell-bent on destroying a former friend? Apparently, Chief Aje's son, Owobi, had chosen a different path from his father's. There was talk in the village that he would have liked to marry Obande's daughter but that he never dared raise the question before his father because he knew he would be disowned by his father if this was his intention. It must be difficult being the children of either man, Ogaba-Idu mused.

"Honourable elders, welcome to my abode. In order to find the safest route to take, it is advisable to ask those who have taken several routes before you. Wisdom does not live in a single home. Wisdom is not something we can swallow. It comes with experience. You are all very experienced elders and I want us to use your wisdom and experience to prepare two things. Both concern our respected and respectable son-of-the-soil, the Senate President, Chief Aje, whom we elected triumphantly not long ago. He asks me to extend his very warm greetings to the Council of Chiefs and Elders. He asks me to tell you he is very grateful for your support and confidence. He asks me to tell you he will never fail his village and district, and that you can count on him to leave no stone unturned to bring development to the village. He wants to bring government closer to the people, using his past experience as military governor, and his present position and experience as Senate President. He plans to visit our village very soon, in the company of the State Governor, who was one of those who recently left the opposition party to join his party. He wants us to do two things. First, make arrangements for the

303

planned visit by the State Governor. This means contacting the relevant age grades of young men and women and preparing singing and dancing events. He is willing to bear the costs involved. Then, he wants us to prepare to welcome two officials from the State who are coming to see us with official papers ending Obande's ownership of his forest. It is to this second question that I want us to address our reflection and thoughts," he announced. Everyone was quiet and deep in thoughts. Nobody wanted to be the first to speak. Nobody wanted to give his own opinion. All the elders wanted Ogaba-Idu to first give his thoughts on the matter. It was Chief Ebenezer Akpoge who first spoke.

"Ogaba-Idu. Our village does not lack men of wisdom. You are the epitome of our wisdom. What are your thoughts on the matter?" he asked.

"My dear Chief. You know as much as I do that I always listen to your words of wisdom before I share my own point of view. Telling you how I feel from the start will defeat my purpose of assembling all of you, all of us here for us to think together. It is to the neighbour that we go to obtain fire to cook the meal in our homes, just like it is from others that we obtain intelligence," Ogaba-Idu responded.

"As I see things, and I'm sure I am seeing only a very small part of things, we have two illustrious sons of the village who are at the war path. They are like two elephants fighting in the woods. One of them is stronger than the other. Both of them know this. But the weaker elephant is prepared to die in order to defend his territory, his family, his name. The stronger elephant knows this. In such a situation, it is the shrubs and trees around them in the woods that suffer, that are trodden upon, that bleed. We are the shrubs and the trees. How can we protect ourselves? How can we make the two elephants see reason?" Chief Ebenezer asked.

"I have always wondered why our honourable Senate President is so interested in removing Obande from a forest that has been in Obande's family from time immemorial. Is he not rich enough? Why the hunger for another man's property? The man who eats too much ends up vomiting, you know," another member of the Council of Chiefs opined.

"Yes, I agree with you, Elder. When and where will our honourable Senate President's appetite end? Something tells me he is seeking vengeance for something our respectable palm wine tapper did to him in the past. Can the past not be left to the past for us to spend the present peacefully? You should not refuse to share your banana with someone who in the past refused to share his maize with you. You should not use one wrong to respond to another wrong," some other Chief added. Ella Ohe, the member of the Council who was Chief Aje's eyes and ears in the Council and in the village asked to speak. Ogaba-Idu nodded at him.

"Ogaba-Idu, although pepper hurts the eyes it does not make someone blind. We should therefore not be afraid to say the truth. The truth is that the Senate President wishes to ensure the development and modernisation of our village, to make sure we have very steady income from our palm trees without being anxious about whether locusts would destroy our crops or whether the rains will fall in time to make what we have planted to grow. The refinery he plans to build on Obande's property will benefit all the village and not just Obande and his family. What is wrong in that? Why does Obande not want Agila village to become more modern? I am told he even refuses to possess a cell phone. Can you believe that? All of us here have at least one, don't we? So, how can anyone now blame the honourable Senate President for having the interest of the entire village at heart and say he is doing wrong to someone who is visibly ill-advised by people who bear a grudge against the Senate President?" he questioned.

"No one here in this august assembly bears our honourable Senate President a grudge," Chief Ebenezer affirmed. "What bothers me, and what I think should bother all of us is how someone, no matter how powerful, can decide one day to take over the land that has belonged to another family for ages simply by snapping his fingers. What would stop him from wishing to take possession of my farmland? What would stop him from coming here to your palace, Ogaba-Idu, and deciding that he wants it? I would like us to think ahead of the consequences if the honourable Senate President obtains what he wishes. First, I'm not sure Obande would surrender his possession that easily. He has said it is only over his dead body that Chief Aje would take possession of his forest, which like we all know is sacred to him. Are we prepared to accept Obande's death to satisfy Chief Aje? Will Chief Aje accept responsibility should a very important member of our community disappear? The elephant, no matter how big, dies with its tusks. Will Chief Aje be asked to repair damages he is sure to cause if he goes along with his plan? That is the question I think we should ask ourselves," he concluded.

"We all know that Chief Aje is an ex-military officer. Inflicting death on others used to be his profession long ago," a member of the Council commented. Chief Ebenezer asked to speak again.

"The question is not about accepting or refusing to modernise our village. The question is not about anyone of us accepting to possess a cell phone or not. You do not forget your roots, your traditions, your heritage. Hot water never forgets that it was first cold. It was our forefathers who taught us that even if

306

we don't know where we are going to, we should never forget where we come from. Our respected and respectable palm wine tapper is a pride to us because he is fighting not to forget his origin. All of us would do the same thing as him if we had to, I'm sure and certain," he affirmed.

"We are being required to choose between two respected sons of the land, but in reality, between two opposed visions and forms of behaviour, the arrogance of the powerful on the one hand, and the humility and sense of decency of the modest man who minds his own business on the other hand. Are we being told to give our backing to the powerful who wants to shred the life of a very respectable anchor of our community? I think Elder Ebenezer should be heard and listened to," someone who was speaking for the first time added.

"My respected Elder, I do not think the choice is between power and modesty. I think it is between modernity and backwardness. Are we prepared to have industries built in our village or do we wish to remain a backward and forgotten hinterland, where palm trees that can produce wealth for all are left unexploited because we wish to respect the stubborn will by those who believe the spirits of their ancestors should not be disturbed in their deep slumber?" Chief Ella Ohe interjected.

"I do not think the choice is for us to make. I think it has already been made by the Senate President. We will have to think of how to accompany Obande. He has been through many difficulties already but I'm sure he has the force that will enable him overcome the approaching challenge," Ogaba-Idu announced.

"Who will be coming with the officials when they come? Is it Owobi, Chief Aje's son? He followed Obande's daughter to the village after she was rescued. Will he feel at ease to come back now to harass someone who welcomed him and thanked him profusely the last time he came to the village and to chase this same person from his property, where the rescued daughter's body lies? This is plain madness," a different Council member stated.

"No, Owobi is out of the country, and it is someone else, who I'm told is not from our village but an Ibo man, who is now managing Chief Aje's company in Otukpo," Ella informed the others. Chief Ebenezer asked to speak again.

"So, from the look of things, our hands are tied. I would like to know how Chief Aje plans to address the question of water pollution which some of us raised legitimately long ago. The Chief promised then that he was going to build boreholes in the village so that we can have a better and more hygienic source of water than what our women fetch from the Igbilede stream. Where are the boreholes he promised? We continue to have tapeworms now and then. And what about the road to Igumale? He promised long ago that this would be tarred. What is he waiting for? Are we sure his foremost interest is to modernise and develop our village? Are we prepared to destroy the fortunes of a very respectable member of our community because another equally respectable member, who has his stomach full already, wishes to eat what is in another man's plate? The only person with a swollen stomach that we congratulate is a pregnant woman."

"Are we strong enough to stop Chief Aje from doing what he wants to do? Are we ready to be transported by the police in their Black Marias and locked up in their station for disobedience to constituted authority? Don't forget that he is the Senate President and that his powers are extensive. He helped to organise the release of Obande's captured daughter before she

308

unfortunately fell ill and died at the hospital. Do you think we have the power to stop someone who can order police and military men to do things by simply nodding his head from getting what he wants? My respected Elders, let us not overestimate our power. Unfortunately, if Chief Aje has decided that he wants to take over Obande's forest, he will take it over and it is not us, an assembly of wise men, who will tell him "No!". Do not forget that the little rat never dares try to suck milk from the nipples of the porcupine. In other words, we should not try to meddle in affairs that do not concern us, in affairs that concern only Chief Aje and Obande, two former friends now turned foes. Let us be careful about what we say and what we do. We are taught to avoid dancing too energetically when we are carrying a basket full of raw eggs. Let us not invite the wrath of Chief Aje, who will certainly not take it kindly if we give him the impression we are no longer behind him. Don't forget who he is: the President of the Senate, someone who always has police escorts everywhere he goes to. Let us be very careful," a Council member who had been quiet all along advised.

Two Land Rovers arrived in front of Ogaba-Idu's palace. One was full of policemen. The other had four men, a driver and three men wearing brightly coloured *agbadas* with *fulas*. A group of children who had run following them now gathered noisily outside the palace as the three men went inside. The children were pointing excitedly at the policemen, some of whom had come out of their vehicle to stretch their legs. The children had the feeling that something interesting was about to happen in the village. Maybe someone was going to be arrested. Who could that be, they wondered?

Someone came rushing out of the palace. The boys heard

him saying he was going to Elder Ella Ohe's house to ask him to come quickly to Ogaba-Idu's palace. Ella Ohe was Chief Aje's ally in the Council of Chiefs and apparently, the three men who had arrived at the village had been briefed in the State capital that he would be the one to take them to the Ofu forest, where they were supposed to measure the area of the property, take pictures, and eventually draw a map which would be officially recorded with the certificate of occupancy that would be issued. The policemen were to accompany the three men, two officials from the State government and the man who had replaced Owobi at the head of Nakowa Oils, to manage any threat to public order that the current owner of the property might generate. Chief Ohe arrived at the palace about twenty minutes afterwards. He had been waiting at home, had not gone to the farm because he had been informed the day before that the two State Ministry of Agriculture officials and the new Managing Director of Nakowa Oils would be in the village the following morning. However, he had not been told that they would be accompanied by the police. Well, Chief Aje was showing his might, something that would have been avoided had Obande been more reasonable. The sun will always set no matter what humans do. One should never pick a fight with someone stronger than one, he mused.

In Ogaba-Idu's palace, he was told he had to take the group to the Ofu forest. He was told to join the policemen in their Land Rover, which should drive immediately towards the forest followed by the other Land Rover. When the children knew where the convoy was heading to, they ran following them. The two vehicles drove very slowly because the route they were taking was not motorable. The children started singing the following song, which Chief Ohe, visibly furious, asked them to stop singing, but which they sang even more loudly:

310

Where do we go to look for our fish?
Nowhere else but the Igbilede stream
Protected by the Ofu forest
A population of majestic palm trees
Dancing proudly to sweet music played by the winds
A dense canopy that filters the sun
So that no fire can boil
The water in which the fish we eat flourish
Trees that continue to give life to our village
In many ways no one can deny

Where do we go to fetch our water to drink?
Nowhere else but the Igbilede stream
Flowing proudly through the Ofu forest
Tree trunks serving to control the flow
So that even the little child
Can his clay pot fill without any risk
Of drowning when the mother is not looking
Tree trunks that filter the mud in the stream
So that clear and pure water we can happily drink
As we all perform our daily tasks

Where do we go when we want to be clean?
Nowhere else but the Igbilede stream
We all sing joyfully because we are friends to Ofu forest
Which provides us with all the branches
And leaves we need
To scrub our bodies
For us to feel better long afterwards
Happy to be alive

Happy to have such a friend
Who has been with us
For ages and ages and ages without failure

What happens to the Igbilede stream when there is too
much rain?
Ofu forest is there
To prevent our farms from being flooded
What happens to the Igbilede stream when there is no rain
at all?
Ofu forest is there
To retain moisture
To quench our thirst
After a long hard day
Toiling under the hot sun

So, thank you, Ofu forest
So, bless you, Ofu forest
So, live long, Ofu forest
Your friendship we will always venerate
Your name we will never forget
Because it is thanks to you
That we can from the Igbilede stream
Be protected by you come rain come sunshine
Obtain the fish we eat
The water we drink
And what to make our bodies clean and pure
Before we lie down to sleep
In order to begin the next day full of hope

Obande Ofu heard the children singing from afar. He

immediately recognised the song they were singing. Then he heard the sound of an approaching vehicle. Two vehicles, after he listened carefully. He could not make them out from afar initially because there were shrubs and tall grasses that hindered his sight. He had left his hut in the forest, had visited very briefly the other hut where his forefathers were resting in peace, and he had looked intently at the sixth pole that had been added only recently. He told himself he would surely have to come back to this shrine before long.

For the meantime, he had to go and ward off the most serious threat to the quietude of the haven left to him by his father, a haven he had vowed to protect. He had thus crossed the bridge across the Igbilede stream and walked up to the outermost section of his forest to confront the intruders. He saw the first vehicle, a police van. Who was he seeing, sitting in front with the driver? He was not surprised at all. He saw the second vehicle and expected to see Owobi but those he saw were perfect strangers to him. They were all impeccably dressed. Very strange, coming to the bush dressed as if one was going to a government office, he thought. The singing children ran in front of the police van and assembled fearfully in one group, eyes wide open. They were expecting to watch the policemen pounce on Obande and bundle him directly into the back seat of their vehicle. They were disappointed that this did not happen. Rather, Chief Ella Ohe and all the policemen came out of their vehicle, followed by the three others in the second vehicle. They all approached Obande who had not moved an inch from where he was standing. He was holding a cutlass and a big calabash filled with wine.

"Welcome to my forest. May the spirits of my ancestors look kindly on you. I have some palm wine to offer you, because here, we like to share what we own. But I see that our Elder Ella Ohe is here to share with us his wisdom. I am not surprised to see you here, Ella. You are living in accordance with your name. The name is the man and the man the name. Your name is Ella, which means trouble in our language. Your family name is Ohe, which means ill-will. So, you have shown that you are who you are, what you are. You have brought perfect strangers to my land to desecrate the memory of my ancestors, to trample on their honour, to sell your soul for a few coins that are dropped from the table of someone who thinks he is powerful, someone who builds his wealth by destroying the wealth of others. I am sure you know how other Elders call you. They call you 'Commissioner for Long Throat'. You are the first to arrive at the venue where free meals are offered, free drinks served, and the last to leave such venues. So, welcome, Mister Commissioner. Welcome to your delegation. At least you are providing a good lesson to the children here. Where is Owobi?" he enquired.

One of the well-dressed men took a small step forward.

"My name is Uche Chukwu. I am the new Managing Director of Nakowa Oils. We are here to measure the size of the forest, which will henceforth be transformed into government property before it is transferred to Chief Aje after the relevant documents that will lead to the signing of the Certificate of Occupancy in his name are assembled. We are going to place some signboards on a few randomly chosen places indicating that penetrating this forest is strictly prohibited to unauthorised people such as you, mister," he declared.

"Elder Ella, can you see the folly in what you are doing? You bring strangers to my land to insult me in front of very young children and you do not feel that something is wrong? Please tell the young man who has just spoken who I am," Obande said.

"Well, tell him yourself," Ella responded.

314

"Young man, I know that the eyes of the young are condescending towards the old. Many impetuous young men think they know better than the older generation. Old men have not bought the wisdom they possess. Such wisdom is the fruit of their experience. Your father saw ants long before you. Has our respectable elder here given you my name, my family name?" Obande enquired.

"Yes, he has. As a matter of fact, I knew this before we left Otukpo to come to the village."

"That is good, young man. Who am I?"

"What a question. You're Obande Ofu. We all know that already. Why are you trying to delay what we have been instructed to do? We have to be back in Otukpo before dark, you know," Mr. Chukwu responded arrogantly.

"Ofu is my name. In my language, Ofu means force, Ofu means strength. Unlike your guide here, I have the strength of my values. I do not go trying to destroy someone else's home in order to renovate mine. I have the strength of my beliefs. I believe in the dignity of the individual, I believe in the force of the community, the collective will of all, I believe in solidarity, I believe in doing good. I have the strength of my roots. This is where I was born. This is where my father and those before him were born and raised. No one can come and remove me from my roots. Not those who do not have such roots and are thus lost. You cannot find your roots by going to uproot someone else from his. You will remain a stranger, no matter the amount of friends who flock to your compound to eat free food and drink free drinks. Somebody who forgets his roots is in serious trouble," Obande lectured.

"I did not come all this way to listen to a lecture by a palm wine tapper. I have to do what I've been instructed to do by people who are by far better qualified than you and who know what they are doing," Mr. Chukwu affirmed.

"You are a young man, a stranger in our land. Nobody knows if the fish sweats under water. The stranger does not know the secrets and traditions of a village. The stranger is like the white hen. You notice him or her immediately. Go ahead if you want to put signboards. I have brought you a cutlass because you will need it. I will not pick a fight with you because I don't think this is necessary and I do not want to give the children here the very bad education that we are not hospitable in our village, in our forest. I will leave the cutlass and the keg of palm wine behind as I go back to my hut, deep inside the forest. I have to tell some people there how our meeting has gone. I don't want to keep them waiting longer. Elder Ella, the trouble shooter, Mr. Commissioner, do not forget that the person who shakes a basket covered by soot above his head receives the soot on his head and body. The intelligent goat that is very hungry avoids going to cry behind hyenas," Obande said, as he disappeared into the palm forest.

All was quiet. He picked up a big keg of palm wine he had left in his hut. He had done what his ancestors would have expected from him, welcomed those who had come to see him as sworn enemies. He had shown them hospitality, given them something that the forest had produced for them to drink and a cutlass to help them find their way around the shrubs and grasses that acted as a natural barrier to the forest. Did the ancestors not say that the person who does not have an enemy in his home will not have any enemy elsewhere? In other words, that the most dangerous enemy is among people close to you, people you think you know, people you have confided in?

316

Why had Agbo become so selfish, so callous, so bullish, so preoccupied with amassing worldly material acquisitions? What was he bent on proving? He had succeeded in setting up his lucrative business and in being elected as Senate President, hadn't he? So, why the uncontrollable desire to destroy an erstwhile friend and confidant? This could not be because of his having been chosen by the woman both of them were courting, could it? Could the past not be left to the past? This could neither be because he had refused being given a chieftaincy title by the then Ogaba-Idu at the same time as Agbo had been given one, could it?

He had refused to receive a chieftaincy title at the same time as someone who he judged to be unqualified and even disqualified because his wealth was gotten illegally. You become a Chief thanks to what you have been able to construct using your own effort and not thanks to how many members of the Council that nominate candidates you have been able to bribe with government money, with stolen money, he remembered having said openly. Agbo had confronted him then and he had explained himself and stood his ground. He had refused to apologise. Was this what was still burning Agbo's heart, many years afterwards? Did Agbo not know that the angry man has no friends? Did Agbo, now Chief Aje, think he was surrounded by friends? He was certainly intelligent enough to know that the likes of Chief Ella Ohe were not friends that could be relied upon. The friendship between both Chiefs was like the friendship between oil and water in a bottle. This was impossible, thought Obande, since the oil would stay above and the water below.

He took the keg of palm wine and a red mat and decided to go to the shrine close to the bridge. He bent down to go inside the hut. He poured drops of palm wine in front of the five poles denoting the departed fathers. He mumbled humble greetings to all. He then turned towards the sixth pole, the latest addition to the assembly of poles, and told the pole he was very proud of it, of her. Then he gulped down the remaining content of the keg. Though the palm wine was fresh, it had a bitter taste. When he had finished emptying the keg, he placed his mat next to the sixth pole, lay down and closed his eyes. Sleep came gradually. He saw himself walking on the small bridge he had constructed on the Igbilede stream. Then he thought he heard so many squirrels running towards him from afar. As they came nearer, he saw that they were being pursued by a young girl, who was running after them and telling them she only wanted to play with them. He had to step to one side of the bridge for the squirrels and the woman pursuing them to cross over to the other bank of the stream. It was Oyije, and she beckoned to him to join her in the race. Obande recollected how he used to run very rapidly when he was younger and was now excited to move and run rather than remain passively on the bridge doing nothing. He took off after the running squirrels and Oyije, who was visibly happy she was no longer alone pursuing the animals. Then from nowhere, two enormous birds descended from the sky. One picked Oyije up and the second picked Obande up. The birds flew above the palm forest. Obande had the impression the forest was much larger than usual, and that the palm trees were all much taller than usual. After what appeared to be several long minutes, he sensed that the two birds were slowing down, and he saw them approaching a palm tree taller than all the others, with a very big wide nest. Oyije was first put down. He heard masculine voices welcome her back and ask her if she had met anybody during her daily pursuit of squirrels. She pointed above her head to the second bird carrying Obande. Obande was very excited, because he

318

recognised one of the masculine voices. He looked down at the nest and saw five men, each holding a calabash and washing it meticulously with some white liquid. He asked the bird to drop him off gently. He had arrived at his chosen destination.

Chief Ebenezer Akpoge heard the drum beating and he knew that something was amiss in the village and that elders had to converge as quickly as possible to Ogaba-Idu's palace. The drum being beat was the special talking drum, a large drum shaped like an hourglass with many strong dry leather strings stretched from the top to the bottom. The sound that this gave was a low round sound because the drum was being beat at the centre rather than on the edge of the drumhead. The tempo was deliberately very slow, a message immediately decoded by the initiated. Chief Ebenezer left his compound to go to the palace. He saw that other elders, with anxious questioning looks, were going in the same direction. No one spoke. Though many had already gathered in Ogaba-Idu's parlour, no one was speaking and engaging in social chit-chat as they would have under normal circumstances. It was Ogaba-Idu who spoke first:

"My respectable Elders. Disaster has struck our village. A very illustrious member of our community has decided himself to go and join his father and forefathers."

"This is a very serious matter. Many of us knew it would end this way. How did he go?" someone asked.

"He poisoned himself," Ogaba-Idu responded, in a soft low baritone voice.

"This is a very serious matter indeed. We cannot give him a befitting burial. We do not salute someone who has taken his life, even if the man is an elderly man of Obande's worth. It is against our tradition, as you all know. Normally, when an elder goes to

319

join our ancestors after a long illness, it is appropriate to show one's sadness that he has gone on his final journey, but also our joy for all the things he achieved during his lifetime. Which is why visitors never go empty-handed to a burial ceremony of an elderly man without something to eat or to drink, a goat, a cow, a bag of rice, yam tubers, crates of soft drink or cartons of beer just to name a few items. We cannot bury Obande with such things. Our forefathers will not take that kindly because they will think we are encouraging people to take their lives. How can such an illustrious son, father, elder and palm wine tapper be buried quietly like a new-born baby? This is a very serious matter indeed," another Elder added.

"Has his son in Lagos been informed? He is going to cry like a baby rather than behave like a man. Now that his father has gone, Chief Aje's possession of Ofu forest is as good as done," another man commented.

"Clement has been informed. When I told him his father was ill and that he had to come home quickly, he told me to tell him the truth, which I did. He should be here this night or early tomorrow morning. He asked me where his father's body was. I told him the body was in one of the huts in the forest and informed him that we needed to send some young men there to bring the body back to the village to avoid wild animals coming to feast on it. He asked me in which of the two huts the body was. When I told him the body was lying on a mat in the shrine, he told me to leave his father alone there. No animal would come there to disturb him. His father would not have gone to sleep there if he had thought wild animals would come roaming around. Clement is going to surprise many of us, many of you, I think. He has specifically asked me not to do anything concerning his father until he comes to see me," Ogaba-Idu announced.

"So, we have to wait for him," Chief Ebenezer concurred. "While waiting, I'd like us to agree that this is an exceptional matter in exceptional times. This is the result of our unwillingness to tell one of our illustrious sons, the Senate President, to temper his hatred and allow another equally illustrious son to exist. I think we will not be men of honour if we refuse to give elder Obande a befitting exit. We all know that he once refused a chieftaincy title long ago, for reasons many of us judged legitimate. It is not only a man, an elder who has gone. It is part of us, part of our values, part of our beliefs in how we live or should live, part of how we bring up our children, not to forget their roots and families, to be kind and gentle even with people we have never met before. Our ancestors will not be angry that we are celebrating the physical going away of someone who ended his life. I think our ancestors will be angry that we have allowed such a fountain of knowledge and know-how to suffer unnecessarily from one of us, a bully, such that the only way not to generate a wider communal crisis was for him to sacrifice himself. We are talking of someone sacrificing himself for communal entente and harmony. We need to praise him, rather than despise him. I know of someone who will be the first to be there the day we decide to offer food and drinks to village elders to remember Obande Ofu, may he be at peace wherever he is," he concluded.

"Chief Ebenezer has spoken well. Elder Obande decided to sacrifice himself to avoid the personal conflict between Chief Aje and himself degenerating into a crisis in the village, breeding unnecessary animosity between those who support him and those who support Chief Aje, creating needless conflict between those who think the village should modernise rapidly and those who think we should maintain some of our traditions, especially those

321

that pertain to showing respect to our departed ancestors. I am even told that Obande offered a cutlass to the government officials for them to use it to better find their way through the grass. He even offered them a keg of palm wine as a sign not of hostility but of hospitality. Who other than a very wise man behaves like that? No, he deserves our respect. And so, even as we wait for his son to come and tell us how he feels, we should start to show our respect without further delay. Guns should be shot so that the entire village is informed that someone important to us has travelled to the beyond," an eminent member of the Council of Chiefs added.

"This will be done," Ogaba-Idu announced.

"Chief Ella Ohe has not said anything. It would be nice if we heard his opinion, since we all know his close relationship with Chief Aje," Chief Ebenezer remarked.

"Ogaba-Idu, you are the epitome of our wisdom. What you decide is what will happen. I never knew things would end up like this. I will see Obande's son tomorrow and tell him how I feel, Ogaba-Idu," Chief Ella answered in a subdued voice.

"Ogaba-Idu, may your reign be long, and your wisdom continue to guide us all," Clement greeted. He was in Ogaba-Idu's palace in the presence of all the members of the Council of Chiefs. Everyone in the room talked about his father in highly laudatory terms. Clement knew that not all those in the room had defended his father in his long-drawn battle with Chief Aje, but he did not want to go into this. He did not want to have any bitterness in his heart because as his father would say, there was no use allowing slow death to destroy someone from the inside. He remained bowing down respectfully as Ogaba-Idu cupped both of his hands in his, telling him how an accomplished and respected man, elder, model and farmer his father had been. Clement listened quietly, nodding silently as Ogaba-Idu continued to speak, about Obande's palm wine tapping skills, about how he was ready to help others, about how he never wished to enter into any conflict with anybody, about how the entire Council of Chiefs wanted to honour him as was befitting someone of his value. His body would have to be brought from the forest into his compound and the entire village convened to come and honour him.

"Ogaba-Idu, thank you for your words of wisdom. My father told me he wished to be allowed to sleep in the forest with his forefathers, with my forefathers. He showed me exactly where he wished to be placed and I promised him I would place him there. This is what I am going to do, Ogaba-Idu, with all due respect," Clement announced.

"The Council of Chiefs unanimously agreed to give him a befitting exit. We did not want to proceed without your presence," Ogaba-Idu maintained.

"Ogaba-Idu, I thank the Council of Chiefs for its unanimous decision. But my mother does not want any big ceremony. And like my father would say, we should not show our sadness too much and for a long time. We should try to control it to avoid the sadness transforming itself into slow death that will destroy us from the inside. Papa has gone to join my forefathers and my sister. My mother wants us to leave him in peace where he is and that is what I promised her I will do, Ogaba-Idu, with due respect," Clement responded.

"The forest is no longer yours, you know," affirmed Chief Ella Ohe. "There are numerous signboards that announce that the forest is now government property and that no one should trespass it," he added.

"My respected Elder, Chief Ohe. My father was afraid that

323

after him, no one would be here to continue to protect the family forest. I promised him that I would be here to continue what he has been doing in the same way as he was there to continue what my grandfather had been doing. When I make a promise, I always keep it. The forest will be Ofu forest for as long as I live, Chief," Clement declared solemnly. All the Council members watched him intently and it was Chief Ella himself who saw the cold determination in Clement's eyes, which suddenly frightened him. He had been planning initially to speak alone to Clement afterwards, but he thought better about such a plan and abandoned it. The other Council members looked down on the floor, waiting for somebody to resume speaking.

"The forest is no longer Ofu forest and you know it, young man," Chief Ohe reacted. "It is now, I repeat, government property. Chief Aje's tractors will be here quite soon to start preparing the zone where a modern oil refinery will be built," he added.

"If Chief Aje's tractors come to the village, they will go elsewhere other than Ofu forest, where the bodies of my father and sister are lying in peace. That much I can tell you, respected Chief," Clement responded.

"You think you can challenge Chief Aje? Ogaba-Idu and my respected Elders, can someone tell this young man that he is playing with fire? Do we want to weep for another death in the Ofu family?" Chief Ohe implored.

"I can see that you are very confident. I can see that you have a plan. However, do you know that you will be alone in your desire to face Chief Aje? He will trample on you and reduce you to pieces without thinking twice, you know," Chief Ebenezer commented.

"My respected Chief, no, he won't trample on me and he

won't reduce me to pieces. No, not at all. And no, I won't be alone. Owobi, his son, is with me, will be with me," Clement announced. There was contained pandemonium in the parlour as all the Council members started to speak at once, asking questions loudly and not listening to one another anymore. Ogaba-Idu raised his hands for all of them to stop speaking.

"We all thought he was in Oyiboland. How can he be with you in Nigeria while he is there?" Chief Ebenezer asked.

"He has been in Lagos for some time. I'm not sure his father knows this, because Owobi does not want him to know. But his father will surely know he is Lagos very soon. So, I repeat, no, Chief Aje will not trample on me. He has been allowed to trample on my father for too long. He is the Senate President, okay, I agree. He is powerful, okay, I agree. But I'm going to remove his signboards from our forest, from my forest, and that will be the end of the story. I would like to thank you Ogaba-Idu, for your kind words. I will go alone to the forest to bury my father and to clean his two huts. Then I will remove all the signboards as my father would expect me to do. Then I will spend some time with my dear mother before I depart for Lagos, where I have one or two important things to finish. And do not worry about Chief Aje. I am adult enough to take care of myself and to take care of him. The village will not suffer any damage, I promise," Clement announced with assurance.

10

One widely-read national daily, The Nigerian Observer, carried the news on its front page with the headline 'Senate President and State Governor as Land Grabbers?'. Other newspapers reported the news item either on the second page or on the back page. There were different sensational headlines, such as 'Senate President in Land Tussle in his Village', 'Senate President? Or Palm Oil Magnate?', 'Senate President Causes Suicide of Traditional Landowner', and 'Sadness Engulfs an Entire Community'. The content of the news reported in each was similar though how the news was reported differed slightly from one paper to another. On the entire front page of the Nigerian Observer, the following text was printed:

'The entire Agila village and district, home to the current Senate President, Chief Agbo Aje, who was re-elected triumphantly during the last Senate elections for a new mandate, is bereaved following the sudden and untimely death of a respected elder and anchor of the community. The deceased, elder Obande Ofu, took his life not long ago. He was a very renowned palm wine tapper and owned the Ofu forest, a vast orchard of palm trees that his family has owned from time immemorial, and which Chief Aje, proprietor of Nakowa Oils, has been wanting to acquire for a long time for a very paltry sum. The forest is considered very sacred by the Ofu family and lineage, which is why elder Ofu has always declined Chief Aje's offer of purchase. Though Mr Ofu has no formal proof of his proprietary rights either in terms of a deed or a certificate of occupancy, his rights emanate from customary law that should normally protect him from expropriation. The Ofu forest being a family-owned property transmitted from one generation to the other and being the source of livelihood of elder Ofu himself, he felt his right to remain there and to hold the forest in trust for his descendants was guaranteed by the law.

Apparently, this was not Senate President Aje's thinking. Working in conjunction with the State Governor, one of the Governors who cross-carpeted from the opposition party and who he welcomed very recently into his party, Chief Aje has succeeded in declaring the Ofu forest first as government property before a certificate of occupancy is drawn up in his name. Elder Ofu knew he could not face the might of government, so he preferred to take his life.

So many questions need to be asked here. First, has a village notable committed suicide because of the greed of the Senate President? Secondly, has the Senate President decided to eliminate all those who go against his will, his interests and especially his private interests? Thirdly, is the Senate President a full-time public servant or is he spending more time paying attention to his private interests as a palm oil magnate? We have tried to get in touch with Chief Aje but to no avail. So, we don't know what responses he is prepared to give to us and to the nation at large.

Fortunately, we have been able to speak to someone close to him, Mr Owobi Aje, his unique son. Mr. Owobi Aje, who used to be the Managing Director of Nakowa Oils based in Otukpo, is now working as a middle-level human resources manager in a firm in Lagos. One of the questions we asked him was why he had abandoned a top-management position in his father's firm for a more junior post in Lagos. His response is of great significance. He said he wanted to be a better man. When asked what he meant by that, he said he had always been brought up by his father to think he was the best and that this made him blind, because he was groomed not to see the best in others. He said he had always been brought up by his father to be the boss, to act the boss, never to apologise to subordinates, to always give orders, in other words to act like a man, according to his father. He said he now wishes to see how other men are, how those ordered behave, how those who are not bosses manage to remain themselves, to live their lives, to have their dreams, to plan ahead, to do things. He said he needed a lesson in humility, a lesson in being required to follow and obey instructions from others. This, he said, was what he thinks makes a man, makes a better man. He said he disagrees with his father's approach to treating others, whether friends or foes. He said he disagrees with his father's way of achieving success: to vanquish the enemy, to eliminate the opponent, to destroy the person who says "no" to him. He said one should not continue to get fat and be happy, eating lots and lots of imported chocolate bars from the morning to the night when others living in the same house and under the same roof are getting thinner and thinner for lack of enough *garri* to drink. He said he had advised his father to leave the Ofu forest alone, but that his father had called him a bloody civilian who did not know how to fight and win crucial battles. He informed us of his willingness to be interviewed again by our correspondents any time we feel the information he may provide to us will be useful in future news reports. We are going to continue with our investigations and try to speak as soon as possible to Chief Aje to get his side of the story. It is strange that he cannot be reached at this moment, whereas he is someone who has always been a friend of the media, using the slightest opportunity to be in the limelight.

What we can write for the meantime is that the alleged show of power and force by the Senate President, aided by his new friend, the State Governor, has produced the first direct victim. We do not know how many more victims, direct or collateral, will follow. The entire village community is living under the threat that Chief Aje's appetite might now extend to other communally-held lands. The global question we can ask at this stage, as the current drama unfolds in a secluded village somewhere in our country in the twenty-first century, is this: Can an ordinary villager anywhere in this country be in a position to stop any big man in power from arriving in his village and barking the statement, "Your land is mine!"? Are we willing to have more elders take their lives as the only response, as the last resort?'

"Bloody civilians!" Chief Aje muttered.

"Daddy, why you dey vex like this? Wetin don happen?" the young girl asked.

"Bloody civilians. My son has abandoned me after all I have done for him. My father abandoned me when I was young, now my son is abandoning me at my old age," the Chief complained.

"Make you no worry, Daddy. He go come beg you after make you take am back," the girl responded.

"And see all the rubbish in these newspapers. I have to tell my Italian associates not to worry. I have to convince them that things are under control. They should not abandon me too," the Chief reflected loudly, visibly anxious.

"Daddy, make you no knock your brain like that. Wahala come, wahala go. You go catch stomach ulcer and your heart fit jam after, if you no stop. Make you jeje your own, I beg. Make you take your life jejelly, biko," the girl advised.

"My friend Obande Ofu stole my promised long ago. Now, he has stolen my only son," the Chief said, in a furious voice.

"Daddy, wait make I prepare the original drink wey you like well well. Your mind go cool down quick quick and stars go begin to shine for your eyes after, I swear!" the girl announced.

"Bloody civilians!" Chief Aje thundered.

Glossary (Meanings of phrases and sentences in the Hausa language and in Nigerian pidgin English)

A`a	No
Abi?	Is that so?
Agbada	Traditional attire worn by men in formal or ceremonial occasions.
Almajiri	Young children who attend koranic schools in Northern Nigeria. Also used to refer to groups of young children, usually of school age who spend lots of hours begging for alms on city streets and doing petty jobs for a few coins.
Bai kamata kowa ya gan ku ba	You should not be seen by anyone.
Bari mu bar gandun daji de sauri	Let's leave the forest quickly.
Bari mu kai su makarantan koran karatun da aka saba	Let's take them to the usual koranic schools.
Biko	Please
Bulala	A whip
Comot from our road quick quick	Stop rapidly being an obstacle to us. Get off our neck very rapidly.
Dogon turanchi	All words and no substance
Don Allah, a je a	Please go and get the boss quickly

331

kira maigidan de sauri

Eba	A staple food made from *garri*, dried cassava semolina
Everyone dey yab about	Everyone is talking about
Fada masa mun dawo	Tell him we are back
Fula	a woven headgear worn by men
Garri	Dried cassava semolina
Gyara	extra items requested by buyers.
I beg	Please
Ina kwana, Ina gejiya	How are you? How do you do?
Ina shugabban?	Where is the boss?
Ina shugabban mata?	Where is the headmistress?
Iyanga	Arrogance
Johnny-just-come	A novice, a freshman, a beginner.
Karuwa	A prostitute
Koboko	A cane
Kun san abin de ya kamata ku yi	You know what you should do.
Labari mai dadi, kwarai de gaske	Very good news indeed.
fiya. Zan dauki shugabban makarantar zuwa wurina	La OK. I will take the headmistress to my place.
Maigida	The boss, the head of the house.
Maigidan za yi farin ciki	The boss will be happy.
Make you jeje	Be calm and collected; Take things easy, Avoid being stressed, Relax, Do

332

your own, make you take your life jejelly	not panic
Make you ne vex, I beg	Please do not get angry.
Man pickin	The common man
Mama bomboy	The mother of a young boy
Mudu	A bowl in different sizes used to measure the quantity of foodstuff such as rice, cassava flour etc. sold.
Mu tafi de nan de nan	Let's leave immediately.
Mun ji ka, yallabai	We hear you, sir.
My promised	My fiancée
Naija country	Nigeria
Na so be so	This is life, This is how things are
No palava	No major problems, no major worries.
Oga	Sir
Ogaba-Idu	His excellency, Your excellency
Oga patapata	The big boss, the headmaster, the highest authority
Okporoko	Dried stockfish
Okrika	Second-hand or used clothes.
Sabi	To know
Sabi waka	To know how to walk
Shin tana da wahala?	Was she difficult?
Small pickin	A child
Tana cikin dayan motocin	She is in one of the vehicles.
Think say	Thinks that
Think say he sabi	Thinks that he knows
Think say he sabi pass every naija	Thinks that he knows better than every Nigerian.

333

man	
To vex	to get angry.
Wahala	Difficulty, difficult, problem, problematic
Wayo-man	A trickster
Wayo policeman wey dey ask for dash	The corrupt policeman asking to be bribed.
We go show you original naija pepper	We will make your life in Nigeria hellish.
Wetin wayo man no sabi na say	What the trickster does not know is that.
Yalla	Let's go
Yana cikin bukkarsa	He is in his hut
Your heart fit jam after	You may have a heart attack afterwards
Za mu yi de hankali	Za mu yi de hankali: